THE BRIDE FINDER

The Bride Finder

Susan Carroll

Fawcett Columbine
The Ballantine Publishing Group • New York

A Fawcett Columbine Book
Published by The Ballantine Publishing Group

http://www.randomhouse.com

Library of Congress Cataloging-in-Publication Data
Carroll, Susan, 1952–
The bride finder / Susan Carroll. — 1st ed.
p. cm.
ISBN 0-449-14927-7 (alk. paper)
I. Title.
PS3553.A7654B75 1998
813'.54—dc21 97-47289
CIP

Designed by Debbie Glasserman
Manufactured in the United States of America
First Edition: May 1998
10 9 8 7 6 5 4 3 2 1

To the memory of my mother, Sally
A most patient, practical and gentle woman
who encouraged her daughter to dream

PROLOGUE

Few men dared enter the old part of the Castle Leger. The light of a thousand candles would not have been enough to dispel the darkness of the great medieval hall with its lurking shadows and ancient secrets that had gathered for centuries, thick as dust on the rough, uneven floor.

The present master of Castle Leger did not fear the old hall as much as he despised it, the cold stone walls littered with portraits of ancestors that no sane man would ever claim as his own. But it was a good place to come if a man desired to be alone, to conduct business of a most private nature. That is, if one didn't mind the sensation of being watched by a dozen pairs of painted eyes, the feeling that a specter might glide out from a portrait as soon as one's back was turned.

Anatole St. Leger was accustomed to it. Sometimes he felt as though he had been haunted from the hour of his birth. Stripped down to the white linen of his shirt, the leather breeches that clung to his powerful thighs and his heavy country boots, he inched the carved armchair closer to the oak banqueting table.

Beyond the narrow arched windows, the gray evening of another winter's day faded into night. The fire that blazed on the hearth cast an almost demonic glow over Anatole's angular cheekbones and sent the shadow of his muscular frame looming up the vast stone wall.

He appeared like some warrior king as he contemplated the medieval sword placed before him, the weapon that he had sworn never to touch again. His mouth twisted into an expression of self-contempt.

Anatole resisted temptation for a moment more, then drew the sword closer. The wrought gold hilt gleamed even in the soft light, but it was the sparkling stone embedded in the pommel that caught and held the eye. A crystal of remarkable beauty and clarity, it was all that remained of the sorcery of some long-dead ancestor, Lord Prospero. But it was enough, even that small piece of crystal providing a window to the future as much as if all of Castle Leger had been made entirely of glass.

Anatole cradled the pommel in his hands, annoyed by the way his leather-toughened fingers trembled. Staring into the crystal, at first all he could see was his own image reflected back to him, the high forehead, square jaw, and hawklike nose he'd inherited from his English ancestors. His midnight eyes, swarthy skin, and mane of ebony hair that flowed wild to his shoulders came from his Spanish blood, along with stranger, darker gifts.

But the scar that slashed across one temple, that was all his own, Anatole often thought bitterly, a recent legacy of hate and fear.

Gripping the sword in one hand, he pressed the fingertips of the other to his brow, attempting to delve deeper into the crystal, past his own image.

"Concentrate. Damn you, concentrate," he chanted to himself. He felt the familiar tingling sensation begin, painful at first as though a hundred white-hot needles pricked at the back of his eyes. His body seemed to be dwindling, telescoping into the crystal.

The shard of glass clouded. Then through the swirling haze, the vision began to take shape. . . . The shape of a woman. It was her again, the woman with the flowing mass of hair, blown into a witchlike tangle by the wind, hair so red-gold, it appeared to be on fire.

"The woman of flame," Anatole murmured. He strained harder to make out the lines of her face, all but crushing his fingers against his temple, the pain behind his eyes waxing more intense. As in the previous times he'd consulted the glass, her features continued to elude him. And yet he had the inexplicable sensation that she was drawing closer.

The hairs at the nape of his neck prickled, and he was seized with foreboding, a premonition of impending disaster, that whoever and whatever this creature was, she was going to prove the undoing of Anatole St. Leger.

"Beware the woman of flame. She comes. . . ."

Anatole was scarce aware of murmuring the words aloud. The vision began to fade. He was losing it, no matter how he struggled, until he felt as though his skull would split in twain. The fiery-haired woman vanished into mist, and Anatole was left staring at nothing more than an elegant wrought sword.

He exhaled deeply, closing his eyes until the searing pain in his head began to subside. Only then was he able to think, to consider what he'd just seen.

Beware the woman of flame. Exactly what the devil did it mean? Anatole's heavy dark brows knit together in a scowl. It was a fine premonition to keep having when he'd recently made up his mind to take a wife. Visions of some witch-woman, dark, disturbing, promising nothing but trouble. But then, when had his future held promise of anything else?

Replacing the sword back in its scabbard, he rose and returned the weapon to its mounting upon the wall. Of course, there was one simple solution to the whole thing.

Continue to live behind the walls of his fortresslike home, as he'd done these past twenty-nine years, barring entrance to all members of the fair sex. Forget about taking a bride.

Simple, but quite impossible, for the decision to marry was not exactly of his choosing. In fact, he had no real choice in the matter at all. It was but another facet of the family curse. St. Leger men always knew when the time had come to mate.

It was a hunger that went bone deep, far beyond mere lusts of the flesh. An instinct ages old, a longing as wild and powerful as the sea crashing below the cliffs of his castle, a desperate loneliness that made Anatole want to range out onto the moors at night, like some great black wolf, baying out his soul to the moon.

To resist was agony. Anatole had tried hard enough these past months to deny the stirring in his blood, but like all St. Legers before him, he'd been forced to yield. Curse and rail though he might, he'd finally done the unthinkable. He'd sent for the Bride Finder.

The old man was likely on his way to the castle even now. Anatole awaited the Reverend Septimus Fitzleger's arrival with a mixture of sullen resignation and impatience. Impatience that had led him into the mischief of consulting that damned crystal again.

Shoving back from the table, Anatole rose to his feet. He paced to one of the windows as though by staring outward he could hasten Fitzleger, have this unpleasant business over and done with.

The old hall was built away from the seaward side of the castle, the narrow window facing toward the night-darkened hills. A hunter's moon shimmered over the wild and barren landscape, making it a place of legend. Cornwall, the land of King Arthur, of the star-crossed Tristan and Isolde, of ancient priestesses buried beneath mounds of earth, of mysterious rings of stone. A land of magic.

Anatole loved the land, but he could have done without the magic. He had too damned much of that in his life. A weariness stole over him, and he wished he could live out his days as other men did. No crystal-adorned swords, no women of flame, no parts of his ancestral home lost in shadow, and most of all no Bride Finder. He longed for the freedom to choose his own bride as it took his fancy, to breed fine sons noted for their horsemanship not their strangeness, to die a contented old man, not broken and embittered as his own father had done before him.

Futile wishes, indeed, if your name was St. Leger.

He could already feel himself tensing, his senses coming more fully alert. Fitzleger had arrived at the castle. Anatole would have liked to have believed his hearing was just unusually acute, but he knew better.

He was *sensing* Fitzleger shuffling through the cloisters that joined the new part of the castle with the old. Turning from the window, Anatole focused on the heavy connecting door.

He felt a flash of pain, and at that precise moment the door creaked open. It was a power that Anatole was usually careful not to display, but the old man who stood framed in the threshold was too familiar with the secrets of the St. Leger family to be disturbed by anything so trivial as a door apparently opening itself.

Huddled in the depths of a long brown cloak and hood, Reverend Fitzleger shuffled into the great hall. It gave him a sinister monklike appearance until he threw back the hood. There the illusion ended.

Fitzleger's hair was thin in the middle, but flowed back at the sides in two pure white wings, his weathered cheeks reddened by the cold winter air. The lines of his face bespoke a gentle patience, his pale blue eyes bearing the look of one who grieved over the ills he saw in the world, but remained ever hopeful of its improvement.

"Good evening, Reverend," Anatole said.

Fitzleger bowed. "Good evening, my lord." Like many of the people from the village, he still accorded Anatole the courtesy of the old title, even though it had been lost to his family generations ago.

Noting that the old man was shivering, Anatole made haste to invite him closer to the fire. Holding out his delicate blue-veined hands to the blaze, Fitzleger sighed.

"Ah, that is much better. 'Tis a bitter cold night."

He handed off his cloak to Anatole, and Anatole noted the clergyman had dressed almost regally for the occasion, in his best wool coat, waistcoat, and knee breeches, a simple white cravat knotted around his throat.

It made Anatole conscious of his own state of undress. He should likely have demonstrated a little more respect for the man who had once been his tutor, his guardian, who would have been his friend.

But who could be friends with a blasted saint?

Almost in defiance, Anatole shoved back his shirtsleeves as he dragged a chair closer to the fire for Fitzleger. It often amazed him to think that he and the fragile old man were distantly related, like trying to reconcile the spawn of Satan with the herald of the angels. They bore no likeness in common, except for the infamous St. Leger nose. And yet they shared the same ancestor, the wicked Lord Prospero St. Leger, who had merrily scattered his seed about the countryside.

One such had borne fruit, becoming a bastard branch of the St. Leger line, eventually known by the name Fitzleger. No doubt it would have amused that devil Prospero to know that the descendants of his by-blow had evolved into a family of respected clergymen.

But then, everything had apparently amused Prospero. Anatole glanced with disgust toward the portrait that dominated the end of the hall, a knight garbed in tunic and cloak, his black eyes twinkling, the full lips twisted in a mocking smile, half concealed by his beard.

The cursed man always appeared on the verge of laughter. Legend had it that he'd even laughed on his way to the stake to be burned for sorcery. . . .

Wrenching his eyes from the portrait, Anatole became aware that an uncomfortable silence had settled between himself and Fitzleger. Although not close to the old man, he usually never had any difficulty talking to him. Perhaps it was his remembering that Fitzleger did not come here tonight to discuss tithes for the church or to solicit aid for the village poor.

He came in his more ancient role of Bride Finder. That put Anatole at a disadvantage, thrust him into the role of supplicant. He hated it.

While he searched his mind for a way to begin, it was Fitzleger who cleared his throat, breaking the silence.

"I am sorry to be so late in answering your summons, my lord. But I was detained after supper. Young Bess Kennack came to consult me about the baptism of her sister."

Anatole tensed at the name. He did not want to ask but could not seem to help himself.

"And how fare the Kennack children?"

"As well as any young ones can who have so recently lost their mother. Bess takes it the hardest. She is still most embittered."

"Against me? That is . . . understandable."

"Understandable, perhaps, but wrong."

"Why is it?" Anatole stared moodily into the fire. "Marie Kennack braved her terrors to consult the dread lord of Castle Leger because she was worried about the future of the child she carried in her womb. I gave her the bitter comfort that her daughter would be born in safety, but that Marie would not live to see her."

Fitzleger leaned forward in his chair, and Anatole felt the gentle touch of a hand upon his sleeve. "Having visions of a tragedy is not the same as causing it, my lord."

Anatole knew that. It didn't help. He pulled away from the old man's touch with a rough impatience.

"You did all that you could, my lord. Sent your own cousin to attend her. Marius is the most skilled physician in all of Cornwall, perhaps all of England—"

"But it wasn't enough, was it? It never is. What's the cursed good of having these visions if I never can—" Anatole heard the anger rise in his voice and struggled to check it, along with the burning sensations of helplessness and frustration.

Taking a deep breath, he managed to say in milder tones, "But I did not summon you here to discuss the Kennacks."

"I know that, my lord."

"Of course, you would. Sharing the same peculiar heritage as myself." Anatole whipped around to face the old man. "Tell me, Fitzleger. I've often wondered. How do you reconcile our devil's gifts with your more spiritual calling?"

"I believe any gifts a man possesses come from God, my lord. It is only when they are misused, they become the product of the devil."

Anatole gave something approaching a snort. It was easy enough for Fitzleger to talk. He didn't possess the strange powers that were Anatole's torments. Fitzleger's gift consisted of a simple basic one, the unerring ability to select the right bride for a St. Leger male, to find the mate for his soul.

Anatole doubted such a woman existed for him, but he lacked the courage to fly in the face of family tradition. His father had, and Anatole had seen what tragedy that had produced. If he was ever tempted to forget, he had his scar to remind him. He started to trace the age-old wound with his fingertips, but stopped, the gesture alone was enough to release a flood of painful memories. He paced off a few brisk steps in front of the fire.

"Fine. We both know what we are here for. Let us get down to business. My requirements in a wife are simple and few. I will list them off for you.

"I want a sturdy woman with sound limbs. Since I am tall, I would prefer a female that stood this many hands high." Anatole indicated a height just above his shoulder level. "She should be prudent, practical, a good rider, and possess some knowledge of hunting and horses. It will give us something sensible to talk about at dinner."

"My lord confuses me," Fitzleger complained. "What exactly is it you wish for me to find for you: a horse, a bride, or a new groom for your stables?"

Ignoring him, Anatole continued, "She should be a woman of courage, with nerves of iron."

"Why? Besides the hunting and riding, does my lord also plan to have the lady help guard the castle?"

Anatole glared. "I don't require she be a beauty. It would be better if she was plain, not some useless creature forever primping in front of a mirror, providing a temptation to other men to make me a cuckold."

"My lord—" Fitzleger tried to interrupt again, but this time Anatole refused to let him.

"And I don't want any woman with flame-colored hair. It can be black, brown, blond, even gray. Anything but red."

"But, my lord—"

"She shouldn't be delicate. I prefer a full-figured woman, a little plump with wide hips and ample breasts."

"Shall I take a string with me to measure?" Fitzleger managed to break in at last. His soft laughter irritated Anatole. "My lord, this is not how it works."

"Then, would you mind explaining to me just how the devil it does work?"

"I work by an instinct as unexplainable as your own abilities. When I am in the presence of your bride, I will just know her. Like the magic of a divining rod being attracted to a precious metal."

"My own divining rod has attracted me to the beds of some of the wenches in the village. But that doesn't mean any of them would make me a suitable wife."

"That is lust, my lord. We are talking something far different here, and you know that. You must place your trust in me. I will find you your one true bride."

"If she is my true bride, she will be all the things I listed off for you."

"That's as may be, my lord."

"That's as it *will* be, curse it!" Anatole smacked his fist against his palm. "I am free to choose the horse, the gun, even the dog that suits me. Am I to have no say in the selection of my wife? Damnation!"

"I understand how hard this must be," Fitzleger soothed. "To relinquish control of such a personal matter to another man. But I have done well for your family in the past. I found your grandmother for your grandfather when I was scarce more than a lad. And they enjoyed a long, happy union. Likewise your uncles and cousins. The only bride in this family I did not select was—"

Fitzleger broke off. Looking uncomfortable, he cleared his throat.

"You did not select my mother," Anatole finished for him. "I need no reminder of that."

The image of his mother was indelibly burned in his mind even though it had been nineteen years since her death. He could still clearly see her pale face with its fine bone structure, her faery gold hair, but it was her eyes that he thought would haunt him forever.

A boy should see only love in his mother's eyes, not terror.

"I am sorry, my lord." Fitzleger's voice snapped Anatole back to the present. "I did not mean to distress you by raising up ghosts from the past."

"No one has to raise the ghosts around here, Fitzleger. They manage quite well on their own."

Anatole forced his mind back to the subject at hand. "There has to be more than one woman in England that comes close to meeting the requirements I listed for you. I see no reason you can't confine your divining amongst them."

"But, my lord—" Fitzleger shot Anatole a pained glance, though he seemed to realize the futility of further argument. Heaving a long sigh, he said, "Very well, my lord. I shall do the best I can to find you such a woman."

"Good. When will you commence your search? I want this matter settled before next summer is out."

"My lord is that eager?"

"No, my lord merely doesn't want to be plagued with a wedding when the shooting is good."

Fitzleger's mouth quirked in a wry smile. "Of course not. One would not wish your lordship to be inconvenienced. I can see I'd best commence my search immediately. I shall set out for London tomorrow."

"London!" Anatole fairly spat the word. "You'll find no bride for me there! Amongst a parcel of town-bred chits who want to do nothing but shop and gossip the livelong day."

"I am sure there are women of good sense to be found in London as well as anywhere else, and that is where my instinct tells me to go." Setting aside his wineglass, Fitzleger struggled to his feet. "Fortunately my eldest daughter is married to a city merchant. I will stay with her while I seek out your bride. Then when I have found her, I will send for you."

"That you bloody well won't. I've never set foot in London, and I don't intend to. That city has always proved a curse to St. Legers."

"It is true that unfortunate things have happened to some of your ancestors—"

"*Our* ancestors," Anatole reminded him with a certain grim relish.

Fitzleger's gaze shifted involuntarily to the portrait of Lord Prospero, as did Anatole's. The old rogue seemed to smirk at them, and both men were quick to look away.

"But I don't believe in any sort of a London curse," Fitzleger continued. "If you don't come to the city, how will you court your bride?"

"You woo her for me. We can have the wedding by proxy."

"What!" Fitzleger's jaw dropped open in dismay.

"If I don't get to select the blasted chit, I don't see any reason why I should court her."

"My lord, you cannot possibly mean to marry without meeting the lady first."

"Why not? You said I could place all my trust in you, *Bride Finder*."

"Yes, but—but—"

"Besides, I'm not a man formed by nature or temperament for wooing."

"But, my lord, these are not medieval times. No gently bred lady of good family will consent to marry you, sight unseen."

"Why not, if she is already destined to be my bride?"

"Even destiny must be helped along a little, my son."

"That is your task, is it not? I don't doubt you'll wax eloquent enough on my behalf, and I am prepared to offer a very generous settlement."

Fitzleger looked shocked. "You cannot buy a wife, my lord."

"Of course you can. It is done all the time. Just find some female of little fortune, and you can dazzle her with the size of my estates and income. You may even appall her with a description of my appearance and delightful disposition. But there is one thing you will not tell her."

"And what is that, my lord?"

"Anything about my rather unique heritage."

"Do you think such concealment wise, my lord? I mean—" Fitzleger hesitated, then said diffidently, "I fear that is the same mistake your father made."

"No, my father was very frank with my mother before they wed. Since my father possessed so little of the family *gifts,* I believe my mother found the whole St. Leger history rather romantic . . . at least until I was born.

"But we aren't discussing my mother. We are talking about my own wife. Do you think any woman in her right mind would marry me, knowing who and what I am? No! My bride shall remain in ignorance until I determine the best time to enlighten her."

"But how will you keep such a secret? She will be bound to hear some rumors from people in the village or your own servants."

"None will dare if I command otherwise," Anatole said fiercely.

"But there is *one* here that you don't command." Fitzleger gestured uneasily toward the portrait that dominated the hall.

Anatole grimaced. "Yes, well, fortunately that *one* will confine his whispering to this part of the castle. I will simply forbid my bride ever to come here."

"My lord, this is not good. To begin a marriage cloaked in such secrecy."

"Nonetheless it shall be as I say." Anatole folded his arms across his chest. "We do it my way, or we don't do it at all."

Anatole had rarely seen signs of distress in the placid Fitzleger. But now the little clergyman raked his hands back through his snowy tufts of hair. When he tried to don his cloak, he appeared so agitated, Anatole had to move to help him.

"Not good. Not good," Fitzleger murmured over and over again. "These are hard conditions you set, my lord. Very hard. I don't even know how I shall remember all your instructions."

"Ah, that is why I had the forethought to set them down on paper." Bending down, Anatole reached inside his boot and produced the small roll of parchment he had tucked there hours before.

Unfurling it, he checked it himself one last time before handing it over to Fitzleger. Of course, since he had inked out his commands earlier that afternoon, it said nothing about his ban against the chit having red hair. But Fitzleger could surely remember that much.

The rest was all there . . . the sturdy limbs, the ample bosom, the good horsemanship, the plain face, the practical mind, the courage. Yes, most of all the courage.

Lest she be frightened to death.

The thought no sooner entered Anatole's mind than, as if on cue, a chill passed through him, an icy blast of air that caused the candles to flicker.

The parchment flew out of his hand, snatched away by invisible fingers. Anatole heard a soft mocking laugh. He tensed for a moment, then cursed.

Pursuing the fluttering paper, he tromped down upon it with his boot just in time to save it from being whisked into the blazing hearth.

As suddenly as it had come, the wind stopped. The candles resumed their normal, steady glow. Compressing his lips together, Anatole bent down to retrieve the parchment.

He straightened to find Fitzleger staring about him with wide eyes. The old man did not look frightened, only a little unnerved.

"Was that *him*?" he asked in hushed tones.

"That devil Prospero. Who else?" Anatole glared at the rogue's portrait. Prospero's black eyes mocked him back. Anatole let out a mouth-filling oath. "It would be a wonderful thing, Fitzleger. To have ancestors that when one bid them 'rest in peace,' they had the courtesy to do so."

That silky taunting laughter echoed through the hall again.

Fitzleger sighed and laid his hand upon Anatole's sleeve. "My poor boy. You are the one I wish I could offer some peace from all of this."

"Peace?" Anatole gave a bitter laugh. "I don't expect that until I die. And given that I'm a St. Leger, probably not even then."

Taking Fitzleger's hand, he upended the clergyman's palm and slapped the parchment into it. "No, old man. There's only one thing you can do for me."

With a single flash of his eyes, Anatole opened the cloister door.

"Go," he commanded. "Find me a bride."

Chapter One

The cavalcade looked out of place as it rumbled along the narrow country road. Outriders in scarlet livery preceded two carriages pulled by teams of showy bays, the first of these vehicles an awe-inspiring sight. With its sky blue exterior and gilt trim, it was like something spun from legends of the Cornish fisherfolk, tales of the faery coach that overtook unwary travelers across the moors, spiriting them off to the phantom world.

The young woman who peered out the window of the first coach could well have been mistaken for the faery queen. Her face was fine-boned, her complexion so pale as to be almost ethereal. Her slender neck appeared scarce strong enough to support the weight of her headpiece, a powdered wig of thick curls set beneath a large-brimmed black velvet hat adorned with four white plumes.

Yet there was nothing in the least fey about Madeline Elizabeth Breton's green eyes. Set beneath dark, delicate brows, they gleamed with a lively curiosity and intelligence. Bracing herself against the jolts of the carriage, Madeline studied the scenery rolling past.

It was a bleak, rugged land that spring appeared to have forgotten. Not a hint of green to be seen anywhere, only the endless moors with their black heather and shrubs of broom. Here and there a gnarled tree stretched barren branches skyward like the skeletal fingers of some poor damned soul straining toward heaven.

She was traveling on the border of *his* lands now, the very edge of *his* world. Anatole St. Leger. Her husband. The man she'd promised to cherish and obey forever in a proxy ceremony a mere fortnight ago.

Madeline's hand crept involuntarily toward the miniature she wore beneath her gown of embroidered apricot silk. Suspended by a thin blue ribbon, the ivory oval nestled just above her breasts. The small portrait of her bridegroom had been given to her by the Reverend Fitzleger, along with the plain gold ring that now bound her finger as tightly as the promises she'd given to a man she'd never seen, at least not in the flesh.

Madeline felt the shape of the miniature through the layers of her gown and shift, conjuring up the reassuring image of the gentle dark-haired man depicted there. It was a reassurance Madeline found she needed more and more, the closer she approached her destination. For the past few miles, even the carriage wheels had seemed to creak at her.

What have you done? What have you done?

"Good lord, Madeline, this is the end of the world." The grim voice of Madeline's traveling companion drew her attention back to the interior of the coach.

"No, it is only the end of Cornwall, Hetty," Madeline said with determined cheerfulness. Settling back against the velvet squabs, she faced the dour visage of her cousin.

At the age of thirty, Miss Harriet Breton was a tall, commanding female with a formidable pair of shoulders most of the London fops couldn't achieve without padding. Her dark brown hair strained back beneath a plain wide-brimmed hat that only accented the severity of her expression.

"This is the most godforsaken land I've ever seen," Harriet said. "There's nothing out here. Not even a farmhouse. Just where is this Castle Leger?"

"I don't know. It cannot be much farther."

"That's what you said when we stopped at that last wretched little village. But we've seen nothing but this lonely moor. Just the sort of place to be set upon by brigands and left for dead."

"You're always so full of joy, Hetty," Madeline complained.

"I told your papa from the beginning we needed more outriders for our protection. Well! I am sure no one can blame me if we both end up being ravished and all your bride clothes stolen by a band of murderous robbers."

"These desperate cutthroats of yours would look remarkably foolish parading around in my night shifts. You spend so much time imagining being ravished, sometimes I think you secretly wish for us to encounter a handsome brigand or two."

Harriet's only response was a shocked and indignant glare, and Madeline abandoned her teasing smile. She kept hoping that by some miracle her cousin would develop a sense of humor. Five days of being shut up in a coach with the woman and her gloom-ridden predictions had almost been enough to make Madeline defy convention and the elements to ride alongside. She was only restrained by her terror of mounting any beast that moved faster than a jog trot.

Harriet stole one more disapproving glance at the bleak landscape and started in again, "I hope you are quite satisfied, my girl. This is what your rash decision has brought you to, this savage, uncivilized—"

"Oh, Hetty, please!"

"If I have said it once, I've said it a dozen times—"

"A hundred," Madeline put in wearily.

"This is purest folly! Marrying some mysterious gentleman whose family no one in London has ever heard of. What do you even know about this bridegroom of yours?"

"I know . . . enough," Madeline said with more conviction than she felt.

"Humph!" Harriet snorted. "I still cannot imagine how you ever persuaded your parents to consent to this very odd match."

"As soon as I made known the extremely generous settlement Mr. St. Leger offered, the hearts of both Mama and Papa were quite won over."

Madeline didn't mean to sound cynical or bitter, but she knew her charming, and rather feckless parents all too well. There was Mama insisting that the town house needed to be redecorated from top to bottom *again*. There was Papa with his fatal addiction to faro and bestowing expensive trinkets upon opera dancers.

And then there was the rest of the family, her two lovely younger sisters, Juliette and Louisa, with their penchant for fine clothes and jewels, for marrying men of large titles and small purses. And finally her brother Jeremy to whom life was just one long grand tour.

None of them ever appreciated the fact that all these activities cost a great deal of money until the entire Breton family teetered on the brink of ruin. It had always been up to Madeline, the practical, to find a way to save them.

Harriet shook her head darkly. "All I know is, you have not behaved like your usual prudent self, Madeline."

"Yes, I have. What could be more prudent than a marriage of convenience? They are arranged all the time."

"Not like this one, with a bridegroom who doesn't dare show his face, as though he had some dreadful secret to hide. Instead of sending me, your parents should have made this journey with you. One would think that at least they would want to be certain they hadn't married you off to some ogre."

The same thought had crossed Madeline's mind, but being sensible, she had quickly dismissed it. It was, after all, the height of the Season in London. Mama had a dozen balls to attend, Papa at least as many new gaming hells to explore. Now that the family was in funds again.

"I only hope the family is grateful to you, Madeline," Harriet droned on. "For this terrible sacrifice you've made."

"Oh, Hetty! You think it a sacrifice to marry any man. Mr. St. Leger wanted a wife. I needed a husband of substance. It was that simple. I am no martyr. Wedding him was merely the logical thing to do."

"Poor lamb. Poor, poor lamb."

Madeline winced and pressed her fingertips to her temple. Even when Harriet sympathized, she was capable of preying upon one's nerves.

It was a great relief when the older woman lapsed into silence. She knew Harriet meant to be kind, but her cousin only stirred up doubts and fears that Madeline fought to keep at bay. More than once on this journey, she'd been tempted to order the coach around to carry her back to the life she'd known in London, the empty round of parties, balls, and salons, a world where she'd never felt she belonged, but one that was safe, all too familiar.

Only one thing stayed her. Madeline tugged at the ribbon around her neck. Slowly she drew out the ivory miniature, cupping it in her hand like a secret treasure.

She gazed down at the handsome face, the masculine features softened by the fine strokes of watercolor. It was the face of a poet, a lover, a dreamer. Hair of midnight tamed back into a queue, a sensitive generous mouth, a strong, determined jaw. But it was Anatole's eyes that had captivated Madeline from the first. They seemed to stare out of the portrait, lit by a dark inner fire, speaking to her of powerful longings, haunting her with untold sorrows.

When she was certain Harriet wasn't looking, Madeline raised up the miniature. She brushed it lightly against her lips and spared a smile for her own folly.

Settlements, property, convenience. Madeline had made fine speeches on those issues to Hetty, to the rest of her family, even to herself. The truth was that there had been nothing logical at all about her decision to marry Anatole St. Leger. She was far worse than any silly girl who'd ever lost her heart to a suitor she'd just met.

She had lost her heart to a portrait, had allowed herself to be wooed by an odd little man with white wings of hair and an angel's eyes.

Mr. Fitzleger had not been the kind of man to attract much notice in London or to receive invitations to the best houses. Just a modest gentleman, a provincial clergyman. Madeline would not even have been inclined to waste much time upon him herself. She generally found country parsons to be crude, rough-mannered, ignorant.

But Mr. Fitzleger had proved to be soft-spoken and surprisingly well educated. Still, that alone did not seem to be enough to account for why she had felt so drawn to him. Their first meeting had occurred by accident when she had been browsing through one of the bookshops in Oxford Street. He'd dropped his tricorne, and she had picked it up for him.

Madeline was not certain exactly how that had led to an acquaintanceship. Day after day, she had begun to look for the quaint little man to call, almost like waiting for an old friend. He was a learned man, but she had not sought him out to discuss books or philosophy.

No, what had intrigued her most was the strange errand that had brought Mr. Fitzleger to London. She had longed to learn more about this Mr. St. Leger who would trust a humble clergyman with the task of finding him a bride.

"And you say Mr. St. Leger lives alone in this great old castle?" she had asked.

"With a handful of servants. Castle Leger is very isolated. Mr. St. Leger has never stirred more than a few miles from the place in all his life."

"What! Not even to go to university or take the grand tour?"

"No. Mr. St. Leger sets a high value on his privacy and solitude."

That had touched a definite chord with Madeline, but she had continued to press, "And is he so shy, then, that he would not even stir forth to seek his own wife?"

"Mr. St. Leger has good reason to place confidence in my abilities. I was once his tutor."

"Is he a clever man? Accomplished?"

"He possesses many . . . unique talents." Fitzleger had broken off, seized by a sudden coughing spell. Madeline had waited eagerly for him to continue.

"Mr. St. Leger is a good master. A very conscientious man. He takes prodigious care of his tenants, all his people. Castle Leger is a wealthy estate, the house full of—of history."

"What sort of history?"

"Well, it—it has an extensive library, the work of many generations."

"And your Mr. Anatole, he is fond of reading?"

"Oh . . . oh, yes, he makes great use of books."

"Ah!" Madeline had sighed.

Her own fertile mind had filled in the rest of the details about Anatole St. Leger. She could see him so clearly, this gentle scholar who preferred a life of solitary contemplation to the shallow pleasures most men sought. Likely he would be pale and slender from his long nights of study, seeking wisdom from a score of books.

By the time Fitzleger had pressed Anatole's miniature into her hands, Madeline had been completely spellbound.

"My young master gets very lonely there in his castle by the sea," Fitzleger had said.

"It is possible to be lonely even in the midst of a bustling city, sir," Madeline had replied with a sad smile.

"You could relieve that loneliness, my dear Miss Breton. I believe you are destined to become Master Anatole's bride."

"Me?" Madeline had laughed and shook her head. "I fear I have neither the wealth nor the gentle graces that most men seek in a wife."

"Mr. St. Leger is not most men. I cannot explain how, but I know . . ." The old man placed his hand over hers and gave it a squeeze. "I *know* that you are all Anatole St. Leger could ever want. I believe with all my heart that you are the only woman he could love."

Madness. But staring deep into Fitzleger's earnest blue eyes, Madeline had believed it, too. It was most strange because she had long ago surrendered any hopes of marriage.

She knew she was not possessed of the charm that could flatter a man into forgetting she had no dowry. If she had not been aware of her womanly shortcomings, she had Mama and the rest of London Society to point them out to her.

Madeline's intelligence, her logic, her forthright manner had alarmed what few suitors she'd ever had. Poor Mr. Brixstead still hid behind the nearest pillar whenever he saw her enter a ballroom.

At the age of twenty-two, Madeline had resigned herself to ending her days like cousin Harriet. A childless spinster, the poor relation, ever trying to make herself useful to the rest of the family, invited to supper when she was needed to even out the numbers at the table.

Now, all of a sudden, Mr. Fitzleger was holding out to her the prospect of so much more . . . her own home, babes, and a husband to care for her, who would offer her more than mere wealth, but also the rich gifts of his mind, a man who would value hers in return.

I know you are all Anatole St. Leger could ever want. Madeline had hugged those words close to her heart. Gazing at Anatole's portrait, for perhaps the first time in her life, Madeline, the practical, had dared to dream. . . .

Madeline was abruptly jarred out of her dreamings by a sudden lurch of the carriage that nearly tumbled her from the seat. The coach suddenly slowed.

"Now what?" Harriet exclaimed, scowling. "Highwaymen?"

Madeline tucked her miniature out of sight.

"In broad daylight? I doubt that—" she began, then broke off as one of the outriders galloped into view. A young man in powdered wig and scarlet livery, he kept pace with the coach on his chestnut mount, gesturing to Madeline to let down the window.

Over Hetty's protest, she did, bracing herself against the blast of raw spring air.

"What is it, Robert?" Madeline called.

"I see the castle," the youth shouted, his voice cracking with excitement. "Castle Leger."

Madeline's pulse gave a wild flutter. Despite the threatened damage to her powder and plumes, she thrust her head partly out the window, peering into the distance.

The land sloped upward sharply. At the crest of a rocky outcropping, Castle Leger seemed to rise out of the land itself, a granite fortress, its crenellated towers and battlements stark against the lead gray sky.

"It's a gothic nightmare!" Harriet gasped, her face pressed close to Madeline's as she leaned across the seat to peek out.

"Nonsense," Madeline said, although she was a little daunted herself. "It's only an old castle. That must be the abandoned keep Mr. Fitzleger told me is no longer used."

"It looks to me as if the whole place should be abandoned."

Madeline ignored Harriet's remark, her eyes fixed in the distance, no longer conscious of the creakings of the carriage as it strained uphill or her cousin's grumblings. As the castle loomed closer, Madeline stared as if mesmerized by the massive towers and the ancient drawbridge, slammed closed as though to forbid any unwary visitors.

The aspect of Castle Leger was terrifying . . . yet wild and magnificent in its isolation, like some castle that had fallen under an enchantment. A once and forever place that seemed to defy time itself. Kings and kingdoms might rise and fall, but Castle Leger would rest there still.

Madeline pressed trembling fingers over the region of her heart, overwhelmed by a powerful emotion she could scarce put a name to. It was as if all of her life had but been a prelude to this. She had reached her destination at last, a castle by the edge of the sea, the sweet prince trapped within those forbidding walls waiting for her to break the spell of his loneliness.

After years of wandering, Madeline St. Leger had finally come home.

Shrinking back from the window, Madeline shook her head as though to clear it of these strange notions. She struggled to focus on more practical matters, how in a few minutes more, she would be stepping down from the carriage to greet her new husband.

A wave of panic assailed her, but she fought it down, nervously moistening her lips. Never in her life had she taken such pains with her appearance as she had today. It had been her younger sisters with their regal blond beauty who had brought the gentlemen flocking around. In that moment Madeline believed she would have traded all her cleverness and book learning for either Louisa's tall, buxom figure or Juliette's melting blue eyes.

Despising herself for the thought, Madeline reached up to pat one powdered curl and to smooth out the neckline of her gown.

"Hetty. Do I look all right?" she demanded anxiously.

Harriet sniffed. "Well enough to impress some provincial oaf."

"My Anatole is not an oooff—" The last word came out as no more than an indignant gasp as the carriage lurched to a halt.

Madeline's heart lurched along with it. When the coach door was flung open by one of her own bewigged servants, she struggled for composure as she descended the coach steps.

Hitching her fur-trimmed pelisse about her shoulders, she clutched at her hat to protect her hair from the stiff breeze. Even the air seemed rougher here. Heavy with the scent and power of the sea, the wind whistled with a low keening sound around the stonework of the mansion.

The second carriage, weighted down with Madeline's trunks and her elegant French maid, had pulled into line behind Madeline's own coach. Both vehicles had halted on the gravel drive before a wing of Castle Leger that appeared to have been remodeled for a more modern look. The windows were enlarged, and a Palladian-style facade added, complete with Corinthian pillars and a portico. A double set of curving stone stairs swept up to the imposing front door.

The place had a stateliness about it, far more impressive than the snug brick manor on her parent's country estate they so seldom visited. And yet . . .

Madeline frowned. The new part of Castle Leger jarred the senses, oddly mismatched to the medieval aspect of the castle. It was almost as if the present owner had tried to forget the existence of the grim, forbidding towers that hovered in the background.

Released from the carriage, Harriet tramped to Madeline's side. She surveyed the mansion with her usual sour expression.

"So where is he?" she asked. "I see no sign of this eager bridegroom of yours."

"Robert rode ahead to announce our arrival. I hardly expected Anatole to be at one of the windows, watching out for me. We are, after all, several days early."

"One would expect to see at least a groom or some sort of servant stirring. Where *is* everyone? Are they all gone away or merely dead?"

Before Madeline could reply, she caught the faint echo of masculine laughter. But the direction of the sound was difficult to trace. Her gaze was drawn inexplicably back to the distant tower.

Someone had been watching out for her after all. She could just make out the silhouette of a man pacing along the ramparts, a rather odd figure with a pointed beard, wearing a—a tunic and cloak? Madeline's lips parted in surprise as the strange figure paused to sweep her a courtly bow.

She shielded her eyes for a better look, but the man was gone, leaving her to doubt if she had seen anything at all. Perhaps it had been nothing more than a trick played upon her by the sun breaking through the clouds.

She shivered all the same, dragging her pelisse more tightly about her. But she forgot all about the strange vision at the sound of approaching footsteps. Someone was running eagerly down the mansion's stone steps. Pulse racing, Madeline turned, preparing to sink into her most respectful curtsy for her new husband.

But it was Madeline's own outrider, panting to catch his breath.

"Robert! Did you not announce us?" Madeline asked.

"Yes, madam. But they won't let us in."

"What!" Harriet exclaimed.

"A horrible old man answered the door. He said Mr. St. Leger is not at home."

"Not at home?" Madeline repeated weakly.

"He said we should go away and come back later."

"Of all the impertinence." Harriet bristled. "Did you tell him who we were?"

"I'm sorry, Miss Breton. The old fool never gave me a chance. He slammed the door in my face."

Harriet's lips folded with steely purpose. "We'll just see about that."

"No, Harriet," Madeline said. "There is no sense flying into a pelter until we find out what—"

But Madeline's caution was lost on her cousin. Harriet was already charging up the stone stairs like a general setting out to take the castle by storm. Madeline exhaled a deep sigh, and minced after her cousin as well as she could in her uncomfortable heels. By the time she reached the top of the stairs, Harriet was hammering out a tattoo with the brass knocker, calculated to rouse the entire household.

Before Madeline could beg her cousin to proceed more gently, the door cracked open. A grizzled old man with a balding pate peered out. His bright black eyes glistened beneath bushy brows, reminding Madeline of a tale her old nurse had spun about a gnome who had mined for gold in the dark secret places of the earth.

This particular gnome's lower lip jutted out in annoyance. "I told you people to go away," he growled. "Lucius Trigghorne don't let no strangers in when master's away, 'specially not *women*." He spat out the last word as though he were referring to some annoying species of vermin.

"We are not strangers, you impertinent dolt," Harriet said. "Now, where has Mr. St. Leger gone?"

"He's gone out ridin'."

"When is he likely to return?"

"Couldn't say. Maybe within one hour, maybe within ten. The master don't account for hisself to no one."

"That is one thing that is going to have to change," Harriet began haughtily, but Madeline cut her off.

"Harriet, please!" With an experience borne of smoothing over countless contretemps in her parents' household, Madeline stepped in front of Harriet. She faced the old man with her most confident and placating smile. "Of course, you are very right to obey your master's orders, Mr. . . .-er—Trigghorne, was it? But you don't quite understand the situation, sir. I am your master's bride, come all the way from London."

"Aye." Trigghorne did not yield the door an inch, regarding Madeline with even more contempt than before. "I heard tell about the master taking hisself a Lunnon wife."

"And I am she. So if you would just be good enough to allow us inside and perhaps summon the housekeeper—"

"Haven't got none." Trigghorne's thin chest puffed out with obvious pride. "Been no females on these premises for many a year."

He added under his breath. "Leastwise none that stayed sane."

"What!" Harriet gasped, but Madeline strove to ignore the remark, struggling to hold on to her patience as well.

"Then, at least show us into a drawing room to await your master's return."

"Not possible. Not when master's away," Trigghorne repeated stubbornly.

"But she is his wife, you idiot," Harriet snapped.

"No 'ceptions." And with that he slammed the door in Madeline's face. She stood there, stunned until she was roused by the sound of Harriet's indignant voice.

"Of all the outrages! What sort of welcome is this? What kind of place have you brought us to, Madeline, where the mistress of the house is not even allowed to set foot across her own threshold?"

"I don't know, Hetty," Madeline murmured, turning slowly away from the house, feeling daunted herself. First no tender bridegroom, then the way to her enchanted castle barred by a grumpy troll of a man. Nothing was unfolding as she'd expected.

As she retreated from the doorstep, Harriet trailed after her, shrilling, "And what did that Trigghorne person mean when he said there were no women at this place, at least none that stayed sane?"

"I don't know, Harriet. *I don't know.*" Madeline pressed her fingertips to her brow in an effort to think. "Perhaps it was just that odd little man's notion of a jest, or he thought it his duty to drive us away. Obviously there has been some sort of mistake."

"And you made it by coming here." Harriet clutched at Madeline's arm. "I think you should leave here while there is still time. This is a very dark and strange place." Glancing back at the grim aspect of the castle, Harriet gave an eloquent shudder. "I'm sure no one would blame you if you headed back to London at once."

No one? Madeline felt the weight of the miniature between her breasts. The memory of the lonely young man depicted on that smooth oval of ivory helped to fortify her.

She shook free of Harriet's grasp. "I am not about to be chased away by a servant who is simply a little . . . overzealous. I'm sure when Mr. St. Leger returns, he will be appalled at the way I was treated."

"And what do you plan to do in the meantime? Sit down on the front steps and wait for him?"

"Yes, if I have to."

Harriet shot her an exasperated look. They were still debating the matter when a shout arose from the foot of the stone stairs.

Young Robert ran halfway up, his powdered wig going askew as he waved his hat in excitement. "A rider approaching, madam. Perhaps it is your husband."

Madeline tensed, becoming aware of the thunder of approaching hooves herself. From her vantage point on the stairs, she could make out the silhouette of a lone rider galloping down the track leading to Castle Leger.

It must be Anatole. It could be no one else. She looked back at Harriet to give her a triumphant smile.

"Anatole is coming home. Now you will see, Hetty. Everything will be fine."

She didn't wait for her cousin's reply, but turned back to shield her eyes and watch the road with a mingling of excitement and nervous anticipation. But as the horseman loomed closer, Madeline's smile faded.

It was not her Anatole, but a tall and powerful stranger, a man who looked far more like one of Harriet's dreaded brigands than Madeline's gentle bridegroom. Garbed all in black from his riding cape to high-top boots, he rode a large midnight-colored stallion. His shoulder-length dark hair tangled about his face in a mane as wild as that of his horse.

"Merciful heavens!" Madeline heard Harriet breathe. "Never tell me that that great brute is your—"

"No!" Madeline's hand groped toward the miniature of Anatole, clutching it as though it were a talisman to ward off evil. "Certainly not!"

But a foreboding crept over her the closer the rider came. She experienced a strong urge to flee back to the safety of her coach.

It was already too late. The horseman galloped into the courtyard, Madeline's own servants scattering back as though the ground had split asunder spewing forth the lord of Hades.

The stranger drew rein abruptly in the courtyard below. "Where is she?" he roared out in a voice rife with eager impatience.

"Where the devil is my bride?"

Chapter Two

The dark stranger's words seemed to reverberate all around Madeline, echoing off the castle walls with a harsh mockery.

Where the devil is my bride . . . my bride?

Her heart stood still, her fingers clutching the miniature until she all but crushed the delicate ivory.

"No!" she breathed, but the word came out more plea than denial. Through the haze of her shock, Madeline became aware of Harriet eyeing her doubtfully.

"No, it is not him, I tell you!" Madeline blurted out before Harriet could speak. "That is not Anatole. It cannot be." But her voice sounded fierce with desperation even to her own ears.

"This is some sort of mistake. A dreadful mistake," she repeated weakly.

Or a bad dream.

As the stranger dismounted from his horse, Madeline gazed at her portrait, half dreading, half hoping she would find some resemblance between this alarming man and the Anatole she so long had dreamed of. There was none. The man in the courtyard below bore not a trace of dreamy-eyed gentleness about him.

He moved more with the gait of a warrior than a poet, the set of his powerful shoulders carrying an aura of authority, the kind that brooked no disobedience. Stable hands who had been conspicuously absent before when her own carriage arrived, now seemed to scurry out of nowhere. Bowing and scraping, they crept forward to take charge of the spirited stallion.

The dark-haired man tossed off the reins with a careless grace, then strode across the courtyard with a bold assurance. As though he owned the place.

Madeline felt her heart sink. Even Robert appeared deferential as he directed the man's attention toward the top of the stairs.

As he gazed upward, Madeline shrank back, no longer able to fight off the realization. Deny it though she would, the dark-haired man could be no one other than Anatole St. Leger.

Her husband. Madeline's stomach gave a sickened lurch. The miniature slipped from her fingers to dangle at the end of its ribbon. Feelings of complete betrayal warred with heartsick disappointment only to be replaced with a more immediate emotion as Anatole mounted the stairs. A strangling sense of panic.

"Harriet," she said, groping for the support of her cousin's hand.

Harriet also appeared pale with alarm, but not enough to prevent her scolding, "I told you we should have left when we had the chance. If that's not your husband, you'd best get a pistol and shoot him at once. He looks savage enough to ravish you on the spot."

"If he is my husband," Madeline whispered back hoarsely, "he doesn't have to." That thought alone was enough to make her go weak in the knees.

Anatole took the last stair and poised at the top, hesitating. He was an even more alarming sight up close, the wind caught in his wild mass of black hair, heavy brows lowering over eyes fierce enough to have belonged to some ancient Celtic warrior. If the land of Cornwall itself had been able to assume the shape of a man, it would have been him—rugged, dark, and brooding. His face was all stark angles, from the predatory shape of his nose to the high cheekbones, the broad line of his forehead slashed by a pale scar.

His intense gaze skimmed uncertainly over both women. "Madame St. Leger?" he said gruffly.

Madeline started to sink into a trembling curtsy, but Harriet swept forward, challenging. "And who is it that asks for her?"

The man's grim features lightened for a moment.

"*Mister* St. Leger," he said dryly.

He closed in on Harriet, his eyes raking over her with what appeared to be approval.

"So you have come at last, Madeline. Welcome to Castle Leger, lady."

Before Harriet could correct his error, Anatole yanked her into his arms like a man determined to do his duty. His head bent down, claiming Harriet's mouth in a hard kiss.

Madeline watched in horrified astonishment. After a feeble attempt to struggle, poor Harriet went limp in Anatole's arms, no match for the ruthless strength of his embrace. She had never been kissed by a man in her life.

Neither had Madeline. She had never even seen anyone kiss the way Anatole did, with such raw passion, with such unabashed hunger. It was almost as if she could feel the heat of it on her own mouth. Madeline raised her fingers to her tingling lips, a shiver coursing through her.

He released Harriet at last, his mouth quirking in a grimace that could have been a smile. Harriet stared back at him, flushed and wide-eyed.

It was the first time Madeline could ever remember Harriet being stricken to silence. A long moment passed, and then Harriet drew in a shuddering breath. She blinked and found her voice in a series of earsplitting shrieks.

Shoving past a dumbfounded Anatole, Harriet half ran, half stumbled down the stone steps. She made it as far as the bottom, where she collapsed, swooning into Robert's arms, dragging the young outrider to the ground with her.

A slow stain of red crept up Anatole's neck, washing over his proud warrior's cheekbones. An awful silence ensued in which Madeline was aware of nothing but the thudding of her own heart.

Part of her longed to rush to Harriet's aide, but she could not move a muscle. Anatole blocked her way to the stairs, a formidable barrier of wounded male pride and angry humiliation. If he had ever noticed Madeline's existence, he seemed to have completely forgotten about her.

Someone needed to explain, tell him the truth, but as Madeline glanced desperately toward the carriage drive, she knew no help would be coming from there. None of her servants milling about dared to glance up, let alone mount those stairs to inform Anatole St. Leger he'd just made a colossal fool of himself.

Instead all the men gathered about Harriet's recumbent form, offering muttered suggestions. The lady stirred long enough to moan piteously.

Anatole shot one last dark glance in her direction. Then pivoting on his heel, he stormed toward his front door. In another moment he would have barricaded himself within his fortresslike house, still not knowing his true bride hovered but yards away from him, cowering like a timid mouse.

Disgusted by her own cowardice, Madeline charged after him. She managed to catch up to him on the doorstep, reaching out to pluck at his cloak.

"Mr. St. Leger . . . Anatole. Sir?" She felt like an idiot, scarce knowing what to call him.

He spun around, and for the first time Madeline caught the full force of those remarkable dark eyes. They seemed to thrust her back with an impact that was almost physical. She snatched her hand away.

"Yes? What do you want?" he snapped.

"I—I—it's about your bride. I just wanted to tell you—"

"Nothing needs to be said. It's obvious my bride is frightened to death of me." Some emotion flashed in his eyes, something bleak, perhaps even a little despairing. Was it possible this rough-hewn man possessed a more sensitive side after all?

"You made a mistake, sir," Madeline said. "That lady you kissed is not your bride." She took a deep breath. "I am."

"You!" The fierce look he gave her caused her to flinch.

"Yes, I am Madeline Bret— That is, Madeline St. Leger." She forced a smile to her lips that evaporated when he stalked closer.

His eyes narrowed, tracking over the costly elegance of her gown and pelisse, the elaborately powdered headdress, absurdly out of place in this wild country setting. He attempted to circle her, but Madeline couldn't bear the thought of it. It was like letting a large predatory wolf out of one's sight. Her stomach fluttering, she skirted around to prevent him.

The two of them paced like a couple caught up in some mad minuet until Anatole roared out, "Hold still!"

Madeline froze.

As he stalked slowly around her, she could feel the hairs prickling at the back of her neck. Gripping her hands together, she held herself perfectly still, the absurd notion chasing through her brain: If I don't make a move, he won't bite. Will he?

What would he do when his inspection was over? Tender her an apology for his error? Then set upon her as wolfishly as he had Harriet? The thought made her tense, set her pulse to racing.

When he paced back in front of her, she flung up her hands as though to ward him off. But he made no move to kiss her or even touch her. The scorn in his eyes was obvious. But he had approved of Harriet. The thought stung Madeline more than she cared to admit.

Placing his hands on his hips, his face darkened with a mighty scowl. He took one more look at her and let fly an oath that caused Madeline to wince.

"The old man must have run completely mad," he growled.

"What old man?" Madeline asked.

"Fitzleger. Who else? The bloody damned fool."

Madeline did not feel in charity with the earnest little clergyman herself at the moment, but she couldn't resist coming to his defense.

"I am sure Mr. Fitzleger did his best, sir," she said. "I take it you do not approve of his choice of bride?"

"By all the powers of hell, no!"

Her new husband was obviously not one to mince words. He continued, "You don't match even one of the requirements on the list I wrote out for him."

"List?" Madeline gasped. "You wrote him out a list for a bride like—like sending a servant off to market?"

"Aye. Only instead of a sensible order of mutton and vegetables, I ended up with bonbons. I had hoped at the least for something . . ." Anatole's gaze traveled over her again, lingering on the region of her breasts. "A little larger."

Madeline crossed her arms in front of herself, outraged. She had thought to soothe his mortification, but he had little concern for hers. To think for a moment she had imagined that this oaf might possess some sensibilities.

She drew herself up with an air of injured pride. "It so happens you are scarcely what I expected, either, sir."

"No?" Anatole's tone suggested total indifference, although he asked, "What did the fool tell you about me?"

"It wasn't so much what he said as . . ." Madeline drew forth her portrait, her heart breaking anew at the sight of the handsome face that had formed such a large part of her dreams these past weeks.

She heard the sharp intake of Anatole's breath as he wrenched the miniature from her grasp. Since it was still attached to the ribbon around her neck, she was dragged far too close. She became terrifyingly aware of the power that emanated from the man, like the force of a storm barely held in check.

Anger glittered in his eyes. "Where the devil did you get this?"

Her heart raced with fear, but she managed to reply, "From Mr. Fitzleger. He—he said it was your likeness."

"So that's how he lured you here. With this?" Anatole shoved the miniature inches from her nose, forcing her to lean back. "This is what you thought you were getting? Some God-cursed fairy-tale prince?"

"Not a prince. But at least a gentleman."

Anatole yanked on the miniature, the ribbon giving way with a brutal snap. Madeline stifled a soft cry. She pressed her hand to her stinging skin as he flung the portrait away with a savage force.

Bewildered and alarmed by the depth of his anger, she shrank back as he rounded upon her again.

"Let me tell you something, madam—" he began, only to freeze in mid-step. He stared at her as though transfixed.

What was this savage planning to rip off her now? Madeline wrapped her pelisse more tightly about her. She cowered as he reached for her again, but to her astonishment, she thought she noticed his fingers tremble.

The look in his eyes became dark and unreadable as he touched a spot near the base of her throat. He seemed to pale, but beneath his deep layering of tan, it was difficult to tell. Going nearly cross-eyed, Madeline glanced down, straining to discover what drew his attention.

All she saw was that one of her own curls had sprung loose, escaping from beneath the confines of her powdered wig.

"Your hair," he rasped. "It—it's *red*."

"Yes, so it is. I suppose you were hoping for a blonde."

But he didn't seem to hear her. His eyes dilated as though he had lapsed into some sort of trance, staring at some awful sight invisible to her. The expression was in its way more alarming than his anger.

"Sir? Anatole?" she breathed.

"The woman of flame," he muttered, fingering the stray curl.

"I beg your pardon?"

He snatched back his hand as though she'd scorched him. If the notion had not been so absurd, she would have sworn she caught a flash of fear in his eyes. Without another word he retreated and stalked toward the door, which seemed to fling miraculously open at his approach.

As he crossed the threshold, she heard his hoarse bellow. "Fitzleger! Somebody fetch me that son of a parson. Now!" The door slammed behind him with a force calculated to crack the very foundations of Castle Leger.

Madeline stared after him. It took her several moments to realize how badly she was shaking from her encounter with her bridegroom. Then she leaned up against one of the Corinthian pillars for support.

Not only a savage, but mad as any bedlamite, she thought with despair. She had no idea what had set him off. The portrait? Her hair? The mere sight of her?

It scarce mattered. The fact remained that for the second time Madeline found herself locked out of what was to have been her new home. With bitter irony she recalled her blithe remark to Harriet.

"Anatole is coming home," Madeline mimicked herself cruelly. "Everything will be fine."

She hardly knew whether she most wanted to laugh or cry. As though from a great distance, she could hear Robert calling her. The footman crept to the top of the steps. Even though Anatole was gone, he appeared reluctant to approach any closer.

"Madam, you must come at once," he pleaded. "Miss Harriet, she's in a bad way. We managed to get her inside the coach, but she's acting feverish, groaning like she was possessed. I tried to get your maid to come, but she's too scared to leave the other carriage. And the coachmen—they're mighty uneasy. They say this is an evil place. They don't even want to unhitch the horses."

An evil place? Madeline thought. No, only one of desolation, emptiness. A place where she had thought to find everything and had instead found nothing.

"Madam?" Robert prompted when she didn't reply.

"I'll be right there," she said dully.

The stolid Harriet would choose this moment to have hysterics and, of course, Madeline's maid Estelle would be useless. The Frenchwoman was good for nothing but dressing hair. As always it was up to Madeline the practical to locate the smelling salts, give orders to harried servants, soothe ruffled feelings.

But Madeline had never felt less practical in her life. Even when Robert darted off again, she could not bestir herself to follow him.

She was suddenly exhausted, drained, wanting to do nothing more than sag down before Anatole's front door, cover her face with her hands, and weep. It was as if after such a long and wearying journey, so many eager hopes, she had arrived to find that the man she had fallen in love with had died.

Only she couldn't even mourn for him because that Anatole had never really existed. A lopsided smile twisted her lips. Wasn't it just her luck that things would end this way? The handsome prince turning out to be an ogre who spurned her, the princess abandoned on the doorstep, expected to go revive the other maiden who had received the kiss.

At her age she should have known enough to leave fairy tales alone.

Madeline didn't know how long she stood there, dry-eyed, aching as though a stone lodged where her heart used to be. It took her awhile to realize she was no longer alone. A soft cough sounded discreetly behind her. Thinking that Robert had returned, Madeline swung around only to come face-to-face with the Reverend Septimus Fitzleger.

She had not seen him since their parting after her proxy wedding ceremony in London. She had had still much to do to prepare for her journey to

Cornwall, and he had been gone from his parish for too long already. He had been anxious to hurry back to his young master, and assure him that all was well.

All was well. Madeline compressed her lips. It only angered her the more to note that Fitzleger still looked like an absurd little angel of a man. How could anyone be as deceitful as he and not show some sign of it in his face?

His tricorne hat clasped humbly before him, the old man appeared as though he had just arrived from a bout of hard riding, his wings of white hair windblown, his withered cheeks pink from the exercise. His expression was as mournful as that of any man of God arriving to view the aftermath of a terrible battle.

"Madeline," he said. "I heard what— I—I am so sorry."

The sympathy on his face caused Madeline's throat to constrict. She couldn't say anything for a moment. She could only reproach him with her eyes.

"Anatole was with me at the vicarage when word came that your coach had been seen passing through the countryside. He was off before I could stop him, and I had no hope of keeping pace with that mad beast of his. But I did so want to be here when you first met."

"Did you? How odd. I would have thought you would have desired to be elsewhere, at the other end of the earth perhaps."

"It did not go at all well, then? Your introduction to Anatole."

"You are a master of understatement, sir. Except of course when you are extolling the virtues of Mister St. Leger, telling me how wonderful—" Madeline couldn't finish. She winked back the hot sting of tears.

Fitzleger tried to clasp her hand, but she refused to let him.

"No! The—the worst part of all this is that I thought you were my friend. And you betrayed me."

Fitzleger hung his head. "I am more sorry for that than you will ever know, child. It was dreadfully wrong of me. I should have been more forthright."

"Yes, you certainly should have."

"But I was so anxious to win you as Anatole's bride. I knew no other way."

"Than by lies and deceit? Oh, come now, sir. You knew how desperate my family was for money. You only had to mention the settlement, and I would have agreed."

"Ah, Madeline." Fitzleger regarded her with those sad, knowing eyes. "Your family has been just as desperate many times before and survived. You never wed Anatole St. Leger for his money."

That Fitzleger should realize this only added to Madeline's pain. One tear escaped. Turning away from him, she dashed her hand angrily across her eyes. "How could you do such a thing? Encourage me to love a man who wasn't even real? Let me believe that the man in that portrait was Anatole."

"But it is."

"Then, the artist must have been blind! That painting looks nothing like the brute who assaulted my cousin, who all but trampled over me in his haste to get away."

"I fear you have seen the worst of Anatole. The true heart of the man lies buried deep beneath that rough exterior. That portrait is a reflection of his soul."

"How marvelous. It would have helped a great deal if you had mentioned that little fact sooner. Unfortunately it is his body I will have to deal with. That, let me tell you, sir, is rather formidable."

And she shuddered at the notion. Ignorant as she was of connubial matters, she had given little more than a passing thought to the prospect of her wedding night. She had been far too confident that her tender and sensitive bridegroom would soothe her maidenly fears.

But the prospect of being shut up in a bedchamber with that savage, a man who could ravish a woman senseless with just his kiss— It was enough to chill Madeline to the bone.

Fitzleger's hands closed about her shoulders, gently bringing her around to face him again.

"My dear child," he said. "I know Anatole can seem very alarming. But Anatole would never desire to hurt any woman."

Madeline arched one skeptical brow. "That's not something I really have to worry about." She gestured toward the closed door. "Because he won't even let me in."

"He locked you out?"

"Yes, he despises the sight of me." Madeline hated the quiver that crept back into her voice. "You told me that I was all that Anatole St. Leger could want, that I was the woman he would love."

"And so he will, my dear . . . one day."

"Apparently today is not the day. So what am I to do in the meantime, Mr. Fitzleger? Pitch a tent on his front lawn? Or better still, return to London?"

Alarm chased across Fitzleger's face. "Oh, no! You would not do that!"

Madeline regarded him in stony silence, then she relented with a bitter sigh. "No, I would not. Like it or not, my vows have all been made. My family has spent Mr. St. Leger's settlement six times over. You did your job well, Mr. Fitzleger. You have me most finely trapped."

"I did not want you trapped, my dear. Let me go speak to the lad. I will get this matter sorted out, and in the meantime do not give up hope. All the things that I promised you in London will come true if you have patience. You and Anatole will know a love such as—"

"Oh, please, Mr. Fitzleger." Madeline flung up one weary hand. "Spin me no more pretty tales. I may have not acted much like it lately, but I am fundamentally a sensible woman. I am accustomed to making the best of bad situations. I have had so much practice, you see."

She drew herself up proudly. "Now, if you will excuse me, I must go see to my kinswoman. She, too, has been a little overwhelmed by your master's attentions."

Fitzleger looked as though he desired to say so much more, but sketching her a courteous bow, he stepped aside to let Madeline pass.

She got about halfway down the steps when something caught her eye. A thin spiral of blue silk. The miniature. It lay faceup close to the stone balustrade, where Anatole had flung it in his fury.

A thin crack now marred the surface of the delicate ivory, cutting directly across her bridegroom's wistful features.

The portrait of his soul, Madeline thought scornfully. That had to be the greatest piece of nonsense Fitzleger had tried to foist upon her yet. If Anatole even possessed a soul, it was no doubt as black as his temper.

Madeline lifted her skirts, intending to sweep on, leave the miniature lying there. But something held her back. Perhaps she was far too practical to discard what was after all an exquisite piece of artistry.

Or perhaps . . . perhaps she simply couldn't bring herself to abandon what she had held so dear. Rustling over to where the miniature had fallen, she cursed herself for a fool. But she bent down all the same, to pluck what remained of her dreams up off the ground.

CHAPTER THREE

Anatole pulled the brandy decanter closer, dragging it across the dusty surface of the walnut side table. He wanted nothing more than to get roaring drunk. But as he uncorked the decanter, he hesitated, knowing that even that pleasure must be denied. For someone of his peculiar talents, losing control over his mind was not a wise thing. Intoxication could make him a very dangerous man.

And he was already feeling dangerous enough. With a muttered oath he recapped the bottle and shoved it away from him.

At that moment the study door creaked open behind him. He felt Reverend Fitzleger slip quietly into the room. Anatole's pack of hunting dogs, dozing before the hearth, bestirred themselves to give joyous greeting to one they recognized as a friend.

"Down!" Anatole commanded without bothering to look around.

As the hounds subsided, Anatole wrestled with his temper, struggling to remember that he was about to address the rector of his church, his former tutor, and not just the old fool whose mistake threatened to blight the rest of Anatole's life.

Turning to face Fitzleger, Anatole ground out, "Come in and sit down."

"Thank you, my lord." His tricorne held before him like a shield, Fitzleger stepped farther into the room. The study was a thoroughly masculine chamber, the walls paneled of sturdy English oak after the fashion of the last century, the furnishings a hodgepodge, some of which dated back to the Tudors.

It was one of the few chambers that had survived both the depredations of Cromwell's New Model Army and Anatole's late mother.

Cecily St. Leger had gilded, draped, and wallpapered the rest of the house in her efforts to civilize Castle Leger, and turn it into a proper country residence. One might as well have tried to hand around angel's wings in hell, Anatole thought acidly.

He gave Fitzleger enough time to sink into a tapestry-covered armchair before launching into him.

"What have you done to me, old man?" he asked with a deadly calm.

"Done to you, my lord?" Fitzleger did not meet Anatole's eyes, but he replied with dignity, "Why, nothing that I know of. Except find you the perfect bride."

"The perfect bride?" An image of Madeline rose in Anatole's mind, his temper escalating along with it. "That fragile china doll? One good puff of wind would blow her away if she wasn't weighted down by that ridiculous wig."

"Madeline meets all the requirements you set down for your wife."

"The devil she does!" Anatole roared. Several of the dogs raised their heads to stare at him, but the old hound, Ranger, slept on. Either he had become too accustomed to the sound of his master's rages or he was going deaf.

"I told you no fashionable beauty, no flat chests, and most of all no accursed red hair." Anatole ticked off the points on his fingers, only to fling up his arms in disgust. "I might as well not have troubled to even make a list, but you are reputed to be a scholar. I assumed that meant you could read, or do your eyes begin to fail you?"

"There is nothing wrong with my eyesight," Fitzleger said indignantly. Groping in the pocket of his redingote, he produced the tattered remains of Anatole's note. Perching a small pair of wire-rimmed spectacles on his nose, he began to read, "A woman of kind and nurturing disposition. Possessing the gentle breeding of a lady. Clever and fond of learning—"

"What! Let me see that." Anatole wrenched the scrap from Fitzleger's hand. He scanned the inked words in disbelief.

"A complexion like ivory and roses," he muttered. "A light and pleasing figure with trim waist and dainty ankles. Her manner of dress to be wholly feminine. Eyes like emeralds, hair like golden flame. . . ."

Anatole's head snapped up to stare accusingly at Fitzleger.

"What the devil is this? It's my handwriting, but you've changed every word of it."

"I did no such thing, my lord. How could I possibly forge your hand? And why would I wish to?"

"I don't know, but it had to be you. Who else—" Anatole began then broke off, a discomfiting memory surfacing. That night in the old hall, presenting the list to Fitzleger, the chill wind blowing through, snatching the paper from Anatole's hand. The ghostly laughter mocking him.

"Prospero." Anatole stalked the room again, grinding his teeth. His ancestor had once been famous for his tricks of sleight of hand. "May the bastard rot in hell. This is his sorcery at work. As if the infernal man did not make enough mischief in his own lifetime, he needs must linger to plague mine."

He wadded up the note and flung it into the empty hearth, disturbing the dogs again. Even Ranger opened his one good eye.

"So you believe that old devil Prospero switched the list? Those were all his suggestions? Well, well, well!" Fitzleger covered his mouth, but was unable to stifle his amusement. "For a ghost over three hundred years old, he remains remarkably perceptive. The gentleman always was reputed to have an eye for the ladies."

One glowering look from Anatole, and Fitzleger's chuckles ceased.

"Damn Prospero's eyes and his reputation. This disaster is still your doing, old man," Anatole said. "I made my desires plain enough to you with or without that blasted note."

"Alas, I warned you from the beginning, my lord, that it did not work that way. A higher instinct than yours guided me toward Madeline."

"Your instinct was wide of the mark this time, *Bride Finder*. Well, there is only one remedy for it. She will have to be sent back."

"What!" Fitzleger's eyes flew wide. "My lord, this is your bride you are talking about. You cannot just return her like—like an ill-made pair of boots."

"Why not? I haven't bedded the wench yet. The only vows exchanged were by proxy."

"But were just as sacred for all that."

"I still see no reason why an annulment could not be obtained."

"No reason!" Fitzleger leapt agitatedly to his feet. "What of honor? Of simple kindness and decency? That young woman came so far, full of such hopes and dreams."

"I saw her dream, dangling by a ribbon about her fool neck. I thought I had destroyed that cursed portrait long ago." There was as much of anguish as wrath in Anatole's voice. The sight of that miniature after all these years had torn open inside him an old vulnerability, the more painful because he had fancied it healed.

"I know not how you came by the ivory, Fitzleger," he said. "But how dare you give it to her, pretending it was a likeness of me!"

"I am sorry, my lord, but you left me little choice." Fitzleger spread his hands helplessly. "You would allow me to tell her so little. You would not come to woo her yourself. What else was I to do? I had to persuade the girl somehow."

"So you let her fancy I was some handsome young dolt? And you allowed me to believe my wishes were being obeyed. Tell me, sir. What did you imagine would happen when we came together? Were you hoping we'd both suddenly be struck blind?"

"I had hoped I would be present to ease the way."

"I wish to God you had been here. To prevent me making a bloody damn fool of myself. Kissing the wrong woman." Anatole's face burned at the memory.

"That is something I do not understand, my lord. How you of all men could make such an error, with your extraordinary perceptions—"

"It was a natural mistake, curse you! The tall, strapping female appeared to be all that I had asked for in a bride. I barely even noticed your precious Madeline."

"I find that hard to believe. You felt nothing at all when you gazed into Madeline's eyes?"

"Not a bloody damn thing," Anatole said. But he was lying, and they both knew it. From the moment he had first glimpsed the fairylike creature, a towering uneasiness had seized him. In some strange way she was unlike any other person he had ever met. She was outside the range of his senses . . . all of them. He had avoided looking her way, pouncing upon the dark-haired wench instead, with what had amounted to desperation.

Fitzleger regarded him with a troubled frown. "Tell me, my son," he said softly. "What is it about Madeline that frightens you so?"

"Frightens *me*?" Anatole gave a bark of incredulous laughter. "I think you have, in truth, run mad, old man."

"Then, why else did you react to her so strangely? Barring her from the house. Wishing to send her away."

"Because she is not the bride I wanted. A fragile little chit of a thing! Hell and damnation, if I accidentally roll over her in bed, I could crush her to powder."

Anatole turned away from Fitzleger to avoid the old man's eyes. The clergyman had struck, as usual, uncomfortably close to the bone.

He did fear Madeline, with her air of fragility, with her fairy-princess-like beauty. She reminded him of all those delicate figurines that had once graced his mother's china cabinet. An exquisite collection of nymphs, shepherdesses, goddesses, and sprites.

The morning after his mother's death, Anatole had stood staring at those fragile china figures poised behind the cabinet's glass doors. At the age of ten, he had not yet learned to entirely master either his emotions or his powers. Overwhelmed by grief, anger, and guilt, his eyes had blazed through his tears. The figurines had begun to tremble, then shattered one by one. Much later, when his sobs had ceased, he'd been horrified by what he had done. He had sat upon the carpet for hours, the fragments of china spread out before him, concentrating until his head throbbed, trying to will the figurines back together again. A hopeless task.

That had been his first taste of the bitter truth. His was only the power to destroy, never to mend. . . .

"My lord?"

Fitzleger's voice called Anatole back to the present. The memory had taken some of the fire out of him. When he wheeled back to face Fitzleger, his manner was subdued.

"Perhaps you are right, old man. This Madeline of yours does—" Anatole hesitated. He still could not admit to the fear.

"She disquiets me. It was not just for a whim that I asked you to find me a strong, tough woman. I want no more tragedies in this house."

"The only tragedy will be in sending Madeline away."

"Don't be so sure of that." Anatole stalked away to stare out the long windows that graced the back of the study. Resting one hand against the casement, he could see the distant shimmering shape of the inlet spread out below him, the waves lapping at the rock-strewn cliff base. Usually the sight soothed him, but whitecaps churned the waters today, the sea as turbulent as his own dark mood.

After a lengthy pause he confessed, "I have been consulting Prospero's crystal again about my future."

"Oh, my lord!" Anatole did not have to see the old man's rush of alarm. He could feel it.

"You swore never to touch that devilish thing again. You vowed that—"

"So I did," Anatole cut him off. " 'Tis a vow I broke all the same."

He gave an impatient shrug. "I looked in the crystal that night last December when I dispatched you to find my bride. I've consulted it again several times since. The vision is always the same. That of a woman. Her face unclear, but her hair burning bright around her, a tangle of red flame."

"I wish my lord had told me of these visions sooner."

"Why? Would it have made a difference in your choice of bride for me?"

"No." Fitzleger sighed. "What does this woman in your visions do to you?"

"Do to me? Why, nothing exactly. It is more of a feeling she gives me of unease. I have a strong notion should this creature come too close, she will prove my undoing."

"Is that all?"

To Anatole's amazement, a shade of relief crossed Fitzleger's aged features. "It is not always a bad thing for a man to be undone by a woman, my son."

"Seek out my father's grave and tell him that!"

"My poor Anatole. You need to put the tragedy of your parents behind you. And as for these visions of yours, is it not possible that for once they herald the arrival of something good in your life?"

Anatole fixed Fitzleger with a skeptical eye, but the little clergyman rushed on, "You must give Madeline a chance. Beneath that fragility, there is a kind of quiet strength and a courage that even you must admire.

"She is a sweet-tempered lady with a delightful sense of humor. And such learning, such perception in one so young. She possesses a beauty that goes far deeper than her remarkable eyes—"

"You sound as though you fell in love with her yourself," Anatole interrupted. "Could that possibly have clouded your instincts, Bride Finder?"

"No! Of course not."

But Anatole was faintly amused to see a trace of pink steal into Fitzleger's cheeks. He continued to taunt, "You've been a widower too long. You should have married the chit yourself instead of bringing her here to plague me."

"If I were forty years younger, I would have done so." A wistful light shone in the old man's eyes, only to be quickly extinguished. "Alas, it would have been impossible even then. She belongs to you, Anatole."

"What am I supposed to do with her? With her frills and powdered hair. She appears something too grand for the wilds of Cornwall."

"You could start by apologizing to her for such a boorish welcome. You did not even alert your servants to prepare for the coming of your bride."

"My marriage is no one's business but my own. Besides she arrived earlier than I had expected."

"Does this mean you have not told any of your relatives about Madeline, either? Your cousin Roman?"

"No, why the deuce should I?"

"You carry your passion for privacy too far, my lord. Roman should have been told of your plans to wed. He considers himself your heir."

"Then, he is a damned idiot." Anatole felt the familiar prickle of irritation that Roman St. Leger's name always aroused. "There is no way I would ever permit Castle Leger to fall into the hands of that—"

He broke off, sensing footsteps in the hallway beyond moving purposefully toward the drawing room door. He called out, "Come in."

There was a pause, and then Lucius Trigghorne stepped inside, grumbling, "It would be nice, just once, if a body had the chance to knock first."

"I told you I did not want to be disturbed," Anatole said.

The grizzled old man did not even flinch. Wiping his hands on his apron, he sauntered farther into the room. " 'Tisn't me doing the disturbing, yer worship," he said. "That powdered-up woman is hammering at the door again, demanding to be let in."

Fitzleger gasped. "Madeline is still waiting on the doorstep? You fool. I told you to escort the lady into the front parlor while I spoke with Mr. St. Leger."

"No disrespect to you, Reverend," Trigg said. "But I take orders from none but the master."

"And what does the master say?" Fitzleger asked, his steadfast blue eyes offering Anatole no quarter. "Is the lady to be admitted or no?"

Anatole squirmed, knowing Fitzleger referred to far more than Madeline's entrance into the house. Was she to be admitted to his bed, his board . . . his life? His spirit rebelled, then gave way at the sheer futility of it. If he had intended to defy the authority of the Bride Finder, he should have done so months ago.

Anatole made a gesture of defeat to his servant. "She is my bride, Trigghorne," he said wearily. "Go let the infernal woman in."

Chapter Four

Madeline followed Trigghorne across the entrance hall, lifting up her skirts to avoid brushing them against the black marble floor badly in need of sweeping and polishing. The walls of Castle Leger towered over her, magnificent but barren of any warmth such as might have been provided by a few family portraits or some idyllic landscape scene. A perpendicular stair swept up to the next floor, cobwebs clinging between the supporting posts of finely carved mahogany banisters.

As Trigg led her deeper into the silent house, Madeline felt as though she had breached the defenses of some long barricaded castle, but there was no feeling of enchantment here, only sorrow.

Or perhaps the sorrow was all hers.

Stiffening her shoulders, Madeline refused to allow any more pity for the foolish young woman who had seen her romantic dreams so cruelly dashed on the steps outside.

For the past half hour she had tended to her distraught cousin, soothed her agitated maid, calmed her nervous servants, and done her best to transform herself back into plain, practical Madeline again.

She believed she had regained some measure of composure until Trigg halted before a formidable oak door.

"Master's in the study there." Trigg nodded with a jerk of one dirty thumb and prepared to shuffle on his way.

"Wait!" Madeline cried. "Aren't you going to announce me?"

To her astonishment the sour old man's face split into a stump-toothed grin. "Announce you? Lord help you, mistress. There's never any announcing necessary with master. You needn't bother knockin', either."

And he went off, chuckling over some jest Madeline failed to see. Puzzling over it, she supposed it could be thought amusing, a bride asking to be announced to her own husband. But she had not been treated much like a bride so far.

For all she knew, Anatole could have summoned her to his study just to tell her to go to the devil. And from what she had already seen of her husband and his temper, she would almost be glad to go.

But she had resolved that whatever the outcome of all this, whether she was bidden to go or stay, she was not going to be intimidated by Anatole St. Leger again. Abandoning her pelisse and velvet hat upon a table in the dusty hall, she smoothed out her skirts and started to give a timid knock, then stopped, remembering that Trigghorne had told her not to bother.

Bracing herself, she turned the knob. As the door inched open, she peered inside the study, gloom-ridden with dark paneling and that faint layering of dust that seemed to coat everything at Castle Leger. Most of the light spilled through the tall windows at the far end of the chamber.

And that was where *he* stood, staring at her. All her newly formed resolve threatened to desert her. During the past half hour, she had tried to soften the image of her husband in her mind. She had almost managed to forget what a daunting sight he was with his thick mane of wild black hair and hard, unsmiling eyes.

If Mr. Fitzleger had not also been present, Madeline feared she would have turned and fled. It was the clergyman who stepped forward, saying warmly, "Do come in, child."

Madeline crept across the threshold, never taking her eyes off Anatole. A low rumbling sounded. Dear heaven, she thought in dismay. The man was actually growling at her.

Then she realized the sound emanated from the area before the hearth. A trio of large hounds stretched to their feet, the growling escalating to a series of sharp barks.

"Quiet!" Anatole commanded.

But Madeline had no fear of dogs. She approached the largest hound, holding out her hand to be sniffed. He was a disreputable-looking old beast, his ears tattered, one eye scarred closed. He remained wary as his cold black nose snuffled over the back of her hand. Madeline cooed some soothing nonsense words, and the dog's tail began to wag.

As he permitted her to stroke the shaggy dome of his head, the other two dogs seemed to take their cue from him. Madeline laughed as her hands were assaulted by several warm, wet tongues, and then Anatole's shadow fell across them.

"Ranger. Brutus. Pendragon. Down!"

The hounds cowered back immediately. Anatole stalked to the parlor door and swung it open. "Out!"

For a startled moment Madeline was unsure if he meant her or the dogs. But as three hounds slunk past him, she protested, "Oh, no. You don't need to put them out on my account."

She reflected that it was the warmest welcome she had received so far. But glaring at the dogs as if they were a pack of traitors, Anatole chased them from the study and slammed the door.

He turned back toward Madeline, and the two of them regarded each other in awkward silence. Mr. Fitzleger cleared his throat and rubbed his hands nervously together.

"I should probably be going as well," he said.

"Oh, no," Madeline cried, unable to conceal her alarm at the prospect of being left alone with Anatole. "I—I mean. Must you go so soon?"

Fitzleger gave her a melancholy smile. "You have no more need of me, my dear."

"Aye, the damage has been done," Anatole muttered.

"And Mr. St. Leger has much he wishes to say to you," Fitzleger continued with a stern look in Anatole's direction. Taking one of Madeline's hands, the clergyman pressed it between the warmth of both of his.

"I shall see you again soon. Mr. St. Leger and I have arranged that your final vows will be taken tomorrow in my very own church."

"Oh." Madeline said with a wan smile. "That sounds very . . . final."

Until that moment she did not realize how much she had been hoping for some reprieve, that perhaps Mr. Fitzleger would not have been able to persuade Anatole to accept Madeline as his bride. It would have been humiliating to have returned home to her family, rejected, but—

Be sensible, Madeline, she adjured herself. Vows have been taken, promises exchanged. The man's money has been spent.

"If you think tomorrow is too soon for the wedding—" Anatole began.

"Oh, no. Tomorrow will be fine," Madeline said, hanging her head.

"Good. Then, I shall leave the two of you to become acquainted." Fitzleger carried Madeline's hand to his lips in a courtly gesture.

He added in a whisper for her ears alone. "Courage, child. All will be well."

Would it? Madeline wondered bleakly. Heaven knows, she still felt as though the clergyman had betrayed her trust completely. But as Fitzleger made his bow to Anatole and prepared to leave, it was all she could do not to cling to his coattails.

When the door closed behind him, it was as if she had been deserted by her dearest friend. The heavy silence settled again. Then Anatole made a brusque motion with his hand.

"Well, would you like to sit down?"

It sounded more like a command than an invitation. Madeline glanced about her for a seat. Behind her was a tapestry-covered chair, but one of the claw feet had broken off. Anatole had propped the chair leg up with a volume of John Milton's poetry.

Mr. Fitzleger's words echoed in her head. *He makes great use of books.*

Madeline sighed. "No, thank you," she said. "I think I prefer to stand."

"Please yourself." Anatole strode past her and took to pacing in front of the hearth, a moody expression clouding his eyes.

Madeline shrank back against the sideboard, making sure she stayed out of his way. It was like being closed in a small place with something dark and dangerous. As spacious as the study was, it didn't seem large enough to contain Anatole with his powerful frame. He should have been out tearing across the countryside on that devil-spawned stallion of his. A wild spirit of a man who belonged to the black moors, the rugged cliff side, the sea-lashed shore . . . not the sort of gentle soul who could ever belong to Madeline Breton.

"I regret that I had to interrupt your conversation with Mr. Fitzleger," she said. "I tried to be patient. But my poor cousin and my maid are still huddled in the carriage, and my coachmen wanted to know if they should unhitch the horses."

"What!" This at least had the effect of bringing him to a halt. His brow furrowed. "I'm sorry. I shall give Trigghorne orders to see to their comfort at once."

"Thank you," Madeline started to say when he continued, "The horses must be taken care of. It is not good to keep them standing about."

"The horses? What about my cousin?"

"What's the matter with her?"

"She is still overcome from your greeting."

"Damnation! I only kissed the woman. I didn't rape her."

His crudity caused Madeline to blush. He waved his hand impatiently. "Have the wench carted up to one of the bedchambers."

"I don't think I could persuade Harriet to set foot in this house, let alone a bedchamber. She is terrified of you, sir. She keeps begging to go back to London."

"Then, let her" was Anatole's callous response.

Madeline stiffened. "And perhaps you think I should go with her."

"If that's what you want," he said coldly. "Return my marriage settlement, and we shall find some way to call it quits."

Madeline would have liked nothing better than to fling every penny back into his hard, arrogant face. Her pride rose like a lump in her throat. But she had to swallow it and confess, "I—I cannot return your money, my lord. It's been spent."

"What!" His fierce look of incredulity made her flinch. "How could you possibly have gone through such a sum already and—never mind. Don't trouble yourself to answer." He shook his head in disgust. "I should have guessed as soon as I saw you needed a second carriage. I suppose it is stuffed with more expensive silk nonsense like you've got on your back."

Actually the second coach was crammed with a treasure far more precious to Madeline, her collection of books. Anatole's settlement had been merrily dispersed by her mother and father. But she made no effort to correct Anatole, though she scarce knew what kept her silent. Shame for her family or her own stubborn pride.

What did it matter? Anatole had held her in contempt from the beginning. Nothing was going to change that.

"I shall see that your money is returned, sir," Madeline said. "Even if I have to hire out for a chambermaid and scrub floors to do it."

"Hang the money and hang this talk of your leaving," he snarled. "You know as well as I do that you are not going anywhere."

Madeline stared into his eyes, and for a flickering second it was like looking into a dark mirror of her own despair.

She tussled with her pride a moment more, then conceded, "I suppose you are right, sir. We must go through with this marriage. Honor constrains us both."

"Honor?" A grim smile touched his lips. "There are far more powerful forces in a man's life than honor."

"Such as?"

"Fate."

Madeline blinked at this cryptic remark, but before she could question it, he went on, "We simply will have to learn to make the best of a bad bargain."

"What a charming way of putting it."

His dark brows snapped together. "We will get on much better, madam, if you do not expect pretty speeches. I am no good at them. Or at tendering my apologies."

"Neither am I. But then, I have had little practice," Madeline said wryly. "I am so used to being right."

"Wonderful. I can see we are going to deal extremely well."

But for the first time, Madeline caught a glimmer of humor in his eyes. It heartened her as nothing had done thus far.

"For some reason," she said, "Mr. Fitzleger believes we are well suited."

She was afraid Anatole might sneer at the notion, but he nodded solemnly. "Aye. The Bride Finder is noted for his wisdom in these matters."

"The *Bride Finder*?"

"Fitzleger."

"That is what you call him?"

"That is what he is. I sent him to London to find me a bride, didn't I?"

"But . . . Bride Finder? You speak like it is a title or some sort of position."

"Yes, well . . ." Anatole rubbed the line of his jaw. "There are a few things you should know about Fitzleger. And myself."

"Yes?" Madeline prompted when he hesitated.

Anatole cast an uncertain look at her. His hand seemed to stray involuntarily up to touch the pale crease of his scar.

"Never mind," he murmured. "That can keep until another time."

He straightened, saying in a brisker tone, "Are you fond of horses?"

The abrupt change of conversation disconcerted Madeline, but not so much as the question itself. She was tempted to lie. But there had already been enough misunderstanding between them.

"No, actually I'm rather afraid of them."

"Then, you don't ride at all?"

"Not if I can avoid it."

He scowled.

"Do you like books?" she ventured.

"Books? What kind of books?"

"Like the one you used to prop up your chair. Do you read?"

"Not if I can help it."

She sighed.

Anatole was the first to recover from his disappointment.

"It scarcely matters," he said. "It is not as though we are going to become boon companions after all. Only husband and wife."

"Yes, only husband and wife," Madeline echoed sadly. A marriage of convenience. That could have been enough if only she had not allowed herself to dream of so much more.

Anatole held out his hands to her. "Come here, then," he said, like a man resolved to do his duty. "Let's have another look at you."

Not another inspection, Madeline thought with alarm. But she obeyed, coming closer, slipping her fingers warily into his. His hand engulfed hers, large, rough, infusing her cold fingertips with heat.

A shiver coursed through her as he held her at arm's length, his gaze roving boldly over her.

"Do you always dress that way?" he demanded. "You look fine enough to wait upon the king."

Madeline was not foolish enough to mistake this for a compliment. She smoothed out the folds of the shimmering apricot silk.

"I would not have taken such pains for the king," she said.

"You did it for me?"

"Yes."

"It was a waste of effort and money."

"I clearly perceive that," Madeline replied.

"If we are to get along, in future, you will not be so extravagant in matters of dress." He dropped her hand, pointing above her neckline. "Does that thing come off?"

"What thing?" Madeline grumbled. "My head?"

"No. That blasted mountain of flour."

"Yes, certainly it comes off. It's only a wig."

"Good. Remove it."

"Here? Now?" she asked, startled.

"Of course now."

She was inclined to refuse his blunt demand. But there was a dark impatience in his eyes that warned her if she didn't comply, he would remove the wig himself after his own rough fashion. Just as he had done with the portrait earlier, Madeline thought, feeling the bruise on her neck where the ribbon had snapped.

Expelling a gusty sigh, she reached up to dislodge the hairpiece. It proved a messy proceeding. Her gown would only let her stretch her hands up so far, so she had to bow her head. Powder and hairpins flew everywhere, and she lapsed into a fit of sneezing by the time she got the wretched thing off.

Unperturbed, Anatole plucked the wig from her grasp. Holding it away from him as though it were a dead rat, he flung it amongst the ashes in the fireplace.

A choked gasp escaped Madeline as he calmly dusted off his hands. The practical side of her nature wanted to protest such a waste. But she supposed it made no difference. It was not as though she had any desire to wear the thing again, either.

But now her own hair was exposed in all its mad red glory. Anatole had reacted so strangely before at the sight of one curl, she hardly knew what to expect from him now.

But there was little she could do but remove the rest of the pins and allow her hair to cascade about her shoulders in a fiery tangle. She tensed as Anatole stepped closer. He caught up one strand, brushing away the residue of powder. The curl lay stretched across his calloused palm like a skein of silken fire.

Madeline realized she was barely breathing. He stood so close, he overwhelmed her, dominating the line of her sight. There was no place else to look but at him, notice things she hadn't before. The hint of sun-bronzed skin at the open neckline of his shirt, the powerful cords of his throat, the way his thick lashes cast a shadow over his cheekbones when he lowered his eyes.

He feathered her hair with the pad of his thumb, his expression inscrutable. "Well," he pronounced at last. "It is most definitely the color of flame."

"Yes, I'm sorry," Madeline said, although she hardly knew why she was apologizing. Perhaps because she had spent most of her life expressing regret for the red hair that marked her as so different from the rest of her golden blond family. She rescued her hair from his grasp, brushing it behind her shoulders with a defensive gesture. She took a step back, putting enough distance between them so that she felt able to breathe again.

"I'm sorry you don't like it," she repeated miserably.

"I didn't say I didn't like it. I prefer your real hair to that ridiculous wig. The color will just take some getting used to. I daresay you'll look better when you've been brushed."

"I could say the same for you, sir," Madeline said, eyeing his unkempt mane.

But her tart remark seemed to roll right past him. Propping his chin in his hand, he continued his leisurely study of her. This time he reached out to pluck at her gown, raising up the hem to expose her ankles.

With an outraged gasp, Madeline snatched her skirt away from him. Unperturbed, he demanded, "What have you got on your feet?"

"A simple pair of shoes with heels."

"I thought as much from the way you mince about. Totally impractical. You'll break your neck on our steep stairs. Get rid of them."

Now? Madeline started to ask, then realized it was a foolish question. She leaned for support on a pedestal table, easing out of her shoes. Her height dropped by several inches. Without wig, without heels, she barely came up to the middle of Anatole's chest.

"Is there anything else you want removed?" she asked testily.

She regretted the question as soon as it was out of her mouth. Something wicked flashed in his eyes, his gaze drifting down to linger on the region of her bodice.

But he said, "No, I'd be afraid to take anything else off. There would be nothing left of you."

Her lack of inches had always been a sore point with Madeline. Her cheeks stinging, she bridled. "If we are to get along, sir, you will refrain from making disparaging remarks about my size, especially my—" She crossed her arms defensively over her breasts. "I am large enough for all practical purposes."

"Agreed." But his lips twitched in a sardonic smile.

Madeline continued in injured tones, "I realize you are far more attracted to strapping females like my cousin Harriet, but you will have to learn to restrain yourself. At least in my presence."

Anatole's smile dissolved into a mighty scowl. A hint of red crept into his cheeks. "*If* we are to get along, madam, I prefer to forget that particular incident, and I desire you to do the same."

"Agreed." But the remembrance of the wholehearted way he had kissed Harriet fretted at Madeline, like a pebble lodged in her shoe. "Of course, it is not an easy thing to forget . . . my bridegroom pouncing upon another woman."

"It was a simple mistake, damn it! Do I have to hear about this for the rest of my life?"

"I don't intend to bring it up again. It is only that Harriet and I are both well-bred women, not tavern wenches. We are not accustomed to such behavior. Neither she nor I had ever been kissed before. I still haven't been."

"Is that a complaint?"

"No, certainly not."

"It sounded remarkably like it to me," he said, an undercurrent of warning creeping into his voice.

But Madeline had never been able to let any argument rest until she made her final point. "I am only saying that it was disconcerting watching you embrace my cousin under my very nose when you never even thought to kiss me."

"Fine! Allow me to remedy that." As Anatole started toward her, Madeline realized too late that she had goaded him too far.

With a squeak of alarm she whisked herself out of his reach, putting a leather-covered armchair and a heavy pedestal table between them.

But he kept coming, a look of fierce determination darkening his face. Madeline gasped as the furniture flew out of his path, and he barely seemed to have touched it.

Panicked by a display of such savage strength, she bolted for the door. She grabbed for the handle, but to her horror, it refused to turn. It wasn't as though the door were merely locked, but jammed. Almost as if the knob was held fast by some powerful invisible hand.

Tugging at it frantically, she felt Anatole's hands close over her shoulders. He wrenched her around to face him.

"No, please," she cried, her heart thundering in her chest. She flung up both hands to ward him off. "I—I'm sorry. I won't mention that kiss again."

"Damned right you won't," he growled. Whipping her hands behind her back, he held her wrists fast in the grip of one iron hand.

With his other he seized the back of her neck, dragging her closer. For one dizzying instant the warlike profile of his face hovered above her own, paralyzing her with the glittering intensity of his eyes.

Then his mouth clamped down on hers. Hot, hard, and ruthless. Crushed against the wall of his chest, she couldn't breathe, couldn't stir. She could only submit to a possession that was at once terrifying and exhilarating. A whimper escaped her that was partly the plea for some mercy and partly the urging of a darker longing she scarce understood. And still the kiss went on, bruising her lips, bruising her to the depths of her very soul.

When his mouth released her at last, she felt her knees threaten to buckle beneath her. She understood now why Harriet had swooned. She just didn't know why her cousin had screamed.

Anatole's dark eyes glinted down at her, his breath coming short and quick.

"There!" he said. "I trust there will be no more complaints about kissing."

Numbly Madeline shook her head.

He released her so abruptly, she had to clutch at the door for support. He stalked a few steps away from her, his hands braced on his hips.

When he turned to face her again, he looked detached and composed. Obviously she was the only one who felt so shattered by the embrace.

"You may go and tend to your cousin now and see about getting settled into your rooms. I have more important matters to take care of, but you may hand Trigg whatever orders you like. If he gives you any trouble, tell him he will obey or he shall have to deal with me."

"But—but I can't get out," Madeline faltered. "The door is jammed."

An odd smile touched Anatole's lips. "No, it isn't."

"Yes, it is." She jiggled the knob only to have it turn easily in her hand. Feeling like a complete fool, she let herself out of the room without another word.

Only when she was safely out of Anatole's sight did Madeline pause to press her hands to her burning cheeks. She was still trembling.

Steady, she told herself. Don't be an idiot like Harriet. No matter that it had been her first kiss. What was it after all but the pressing together of two pairs of lips? There was no reason that she should be feeling this devastated.

Except that there had been no tenderness in Anatole's embrace. He had kissed her the same way he had Harriet, the same way he would kiss any other woman. Rough and ruthless, like some marauding Celtic warrior seeking recreation between battles.

She would simply have to become accustomed to it, Madeline thought forlornly. She doubted she would receive such attention from her husband very often. She wondered if he would even have kissed her at all if she had not goaded him into it.

Touching one finger to her tender lips, Madeline resolved to take great care never to goad Anatole St. Leger again. Especially not on their wedding night.

The thought of Anatole seeking out her bed hovered in Madeline's mind like a shadow, dreadful, terrifying, and in some dark way, intriguing. But she refused to think of that now, or she would reduce herself to a useless puddle of quivering jelly.

More practical matters required her attention. Since her bridegroom could not be bothered, Madeline realized that it was up to her to see that she and Harriet were comfortably settled. She did not look forward to encountering the redoubtable Trigghorne again, but if she ever meant to be mistress of this household, she had best begin acting the part.

Stiffening her shoulders, Madeline made her way back to the entrance hall. She fully expected Trigg to give her more difficulty and was therefore surprised to discover the little man already busy, having Madeline's trunks and portmanteau carted up the wide oak stairs.

Trigg growled out orders to a lanky youth whose straw-colored hair hung over his eyes like thatch on a cottage roof. "Put your back into it, Will Sparkins. I don't want to spend me whole day a-haulin' ladies' geegaws."

Trigg hoisted one heavy trunk up on his own shoulder with a wiry strength remarkable for a man of his years and size. Straining under its weight, he shuffled toward the stairs, when he caught sight of Madeline. He cast one startled glance at her red hair, then began to complain, "Lord a'mercy, mistress. What'd you bring from Lunnon with you? The paving stones?"

"No, Mr. Trigghorne," she said calmly. "That trunk is full of my books."

"Books!" Trigg all but dropped the trunk. It landed on the marble floor with a heavy thud. "Why, what'd you bring those for? We got no use for more books here."

"One never knows," Madeline muttered. "More furniture might need balancing."

"Eh?" Trigg scowled, uncomprehending.

But Madeline swept past him, offering a smile to the lad called Will Sparkins. His crusty skin had probably only ever experienced the benefits of water when he got caught in the rain, but at least he showed more respect than Trigg. He bobbed his head and blushed whenever Madeline glanced in his direction.

Folding her hands in front of her, she proceeded to issue her instructions. "The trunks of books can be left down here for now until I am more familiar with the parlors on this floor. In the meantime, Mr. Trigghorne, I shall require three bedchambers prepared—"

"Three!" Trigg interrupted. "One oughta be enough."

"Three," Madeline repeated firmly. "I am not accustomed to sharing a bedchamber with my cousin or my maid."

"Those other two sniveling females? You don't have to worry about them. They're gone."

"What?" Madeline asked. "What do you mean—gone?"

"Those two ladies left with the rest of all those bewigged gents in their fancy breeches. They unloaded your trunks and off they all went, back to Lunnon."

"That's impossible," Madeline faltered.

"Seen 'em go with my own two eyes," Trigg said. "Didn't you, Will?"

Will nodded vigorously.

Madeline stood, stunned to silence as she took in the full impact of Trigg's words. All fled, back to London? She could believe that of the servants. Something about Castle Leger had frightened all of them from the coachmen to Madeline's flighty French maid.

Breton retainers had never been noted for their loyalty. Estelle especially had been a feckless creature. But Harriet . . . Madeline could not believe that her stalwart cousin would desert her in such a fashion.

Yet a disquieting memory intruded, of Harriet as Madeline had last seen her, clutching the back of the carriage seat and wailing. *I won't set foot in that man's house, Madeline. I can't stay in this godforsaken place a moment longer.*

A feeling of dread churned in Madeline's stomach. Lifting up her skirts and heading for the front door, she dashed past the astonished Trigg. Flinging it open, she bolted outside and across the portico to the top of the stone stairs.

The wind whipped her hair across her eyes but she brushed it back, scarcely knowing what she hoped to find. That Trigg merely played some malicious jest on her. Or perhaps even a glimpse of the last carriage lumbering away while she still had a chance to call after it, hail it to return.

But the courtyard below her was empty. Likewise the drive that stretched into the distance. The elegant coaches, the cavalcade of outriders, the teams of spanking bay horses. All vanished, whisked away as though by some sorcerer's hand.

"Damnation!" Madeline groaned, biting down upon her lower lip. She realized then that her bridegroom had already had a profound effect on her. He had taught her to swear.

It was the final daunting realization in a day that had been full of them. She sagged against the stone post at the top of the stairs, resting her forehead upon the cold rough concrete.

She didn't realize that Trigg had joined her until his voice proclaimed with triumph, "Told you they had all gone. But you didn't believe me."

Madeline raised her head long enough to give the old man a bleak look.

"Those fancy coaches set off back down that road like the devil hisself was after them." Trigg gave a wicked chuckle. "But then, master's been known to have that effect on people."

"I'll wager he has," Madeline said dully.

Trigg angled a sly glance at her. "Perhaps you wish you'd a gone with them, mistress."

There was no perhaps about it. But Madeline still possessed enough spirit to straighten, and face Trigg down with a haughty stare.

"I have no intention of returning to London, Mr. Trigghorne. I am the new mistress of Castle Leger, and I am here to stay. You may as well learn to accept that fact."

Trigg's smirk faded. "Whatever you say, ma'am."

It was only as the sulking old man returned to the house that Madeline allowed her brave facade to crumple. She tried to remind herself of how often, during the long journey, she had longed to be free of Harriet's fussing and nagging tongue. But that had been before she had been left stranded in this strange place, in a houseful of unfamiliar servants, all of them male. Sweet heaven, she didn't even know how she would manage to get undressed for bed tonight.

But that seemed the least of her problems when she thought of coping on her own with the dark, brooding man who was her husband, without a single friendly face to console or encourage her. She didn't weep, but she felt overwhelmed by the bitter irony of it.

She had come so far, hoped for so much, seeking to escape the loneliness that had haunted her in London. But as she gazed back at the forbidding aspect of Castle Leger, she had never felt more alone in her life.

Chapter Five

Past midnight . . . the hour by which anything mortal at Castle Leger had long since sought out their beds. But Anatole St. Leger often wondered which existence he more belonged to: the world of normal men or the one of the unquiet shades of his ancestors. Tonight he felt more like one of those restless spirits, haunting his own bedchamber.

Ranging before his night-blackened windows, he tugged at the neckline of his half-open shirt, fighting the urge to go consult that blasted crystal again. Fighting the even darker urges of a St. Leger male who had waited for his bride too long already.

Now she was here, and it hardly seemed to matter that she wasn't the woman he had wanted. Not at quarter to two with the cartel clock on the wall ticking off the minutes in a way to drive a man insane, with the candles guttering low in their sockets, with the night pressing against the panes of his window as though dawn would never come again.

Not with his own blood pumping so hot in his veins.

Anatole stifled a low groan. Another dark of the moon. Another dark night of despair, unendurable loneliness and longings fierce enough to bring a man to his knees. Another night of sleepless hell.

He raked both hands back through his hair. He didn't need to go seek out more visions in the crystal to know his future. The damned woman was undoing him already.

He could actually hear the thudding of his own heart, the quick intake of his breath and . . . the infernal ticking of that clock.

Spinning about, with one glare, he wrenched the delicate timepiece from the wall, levitating it a few feet into the air. Somehow he stopped just short of dashing the clock to bits against the fireplace hearth. He whumped it down upon his feather-tick mattress instead. Mercifully the ticking ceased.

Dizzy with the pain that little outburst of temper had cost him, Anatole leaned against the bedpost for support, cursing his own folly. As his head cleared, his eyes were drawn to the far end of his bedchamber.

The silver branch of candles on his bureau sent a soft glow over his crimson bed hangings, stretching fingers of light toward the door lost in shadow. The door that connected to the room where *she* lay.

She had retired there much earlier in the evening, pleading exhaustion. Retired? *Barricaded* would be a better word. Locked herself in there to escape him.

Madeline . . . his perfect bride as Fitzleger insisted upon calling her, all that Anatole could ever desire in a woman. All that he could ever *dread,* Anatole thought bitterly. Fair and fragile, frightened half to death of him. And Anatole had not even told her the complete truth about himself as yet. He'd been too much a coward for that.

He continued to stare at the door in brooding silence, attempting to delve past the barrier, sense Madeline's movements in the way he could do with everyone else at Castle Leger. But it was useless. Even when he strained to the full extent of his power, Madeline continued to elude him. She remained outside of his range, as mysterious and unfathomable as the night that darkened his windows.

Anatole expelled a breath of frustration and baffled defeat. Curse the woman! If she was his true bride as Fitzleger claimed, then surely Anatole should be able to link himself to every breath she took, every beat of her heart, even from a league away. Instead he didn't think he could divine her presence if she was under his very nose. And this was the woman that he was supposed to face on the morrow, make to her the most sacred vow any St. Leger could give.

The pledge of his heart and soul not only for this lifetime, but the next.

"Damn you, Bride Finder," Anatole muttered. "You had best be right about her."

It was as much a prayer as it was a curse, because if the old man was wrong . . . Anatole scarcely dared think about the consequences, the agony of an eternity bound to the wrong woman, one who moved him not at all.

At least not the spiritual part of him. As for the physical side of him—he clenched his teeth. That was another matter.

The one kiss alone he'd forced from the woman had been enough to . . . The feel of her mouth beneath his, all honeyed and warm—even just the memory of it could—Damn!

Anatole rushed over to the washstand. He didn't pause for the niceties of pouring the water from the cream-colored pitcher into the basin. He splashed the cold liquid directly from the jug onto his flushed face.

And still his breeches and shirt felt too tight for his skin. He all but wrenched off the buttons, peeling open the white linen to lay his chest bare, spattering water over his heated flesh, dampening the dark mat of chest hair until he looked like a man racked with fever, soaked in sweat.

Maybe he was. Maybe he should dump what remained in the jug over the lower part of his anatomy. He couldn't believe that he lusted after Madeline this way, with an unbridled hunger that bit deep into his vitals.

She wasn't even a proper armful for a man like him. The truth was he'd simply gone without a woman for far too long. He had touched no other female since last winter, when he had sent the Bride Finder off on his quest. No matter how painfully his desires had raged, he had sought out none of the usual ways of easing his man-needs, foolish chits from the village who got some kind of dark thrill from bedding the dread lord of Castle Leger, jaded wenches who would have diddled the devil himself for enough coin.

He'd wanted no more of them with their practiced caresses and empty sighs. He had been able to hunger and dream of no one else but the woman that Fitzleger would find for him. His one true bride who would meet him as his equal, mate her fire to his, two halves of the same whole. The wife who would bring ease not only to his flesh, but perhaps to his troubled soul. . . .

What a fool he was. Anatole compressed his lips in a self-mocking sneer. What a complete and utter fool to have ever succumbed to the legends of Castle Leger, to believe that such a bride could exist when she didn't. Not for him.

All those long agonizing nights of abstinence, of burning, hoping, waiting. And all for what? Madeline Breton, the bride who shrank from the sight of him. She had actually bolted for the door rather than be kissed by him. When he'd spun her around to pull her into his embrace, her great green eyes had been luminous and pleading, begging him not to. But he wasn't sure he could have stopped even if he had wanted to. What had begun in anger, in a desire to demonstrate to her who would be master under this roof, had ended in pure, simple desire.

At least on his part. She had just looked bruised and scared. Yet the woman did not wholly want for courage. Anatole had caught glimpses of an irritating stubbornness and a spirit that belied her fragile appearance. Madeline could be brave enough as long as he didn't want to touch her.

But that was just the trouble. He did.

His ancestor Prospero would never have had this trouble with a woman. It was said that but one whisper from that cursed spell-caster had been enough to bring any female running naked to him.

But Anatole did not want to have his bride through witchery, mesmerization, and dark magic. He wanted her in the way of ordinary men. And the longer this hellish night wore on, the more he didn't see why he shouldn't have her.

Gazing at Madeline's closed door, a surge of hot bitterness rushed through him. She had agreed to stay here, be his wife. For all intents and purposes, she was already legally his. He'd paid out a handsome sum on the marriage settlement. That made her not so different from the other women he had bought and paid for, only more costly.

The thought was like acid to his soul and helped to stir his angry resolve. Why shouldn't he have her? Now. Tonight. Would she be any less afraid of him if he waited until tomorrow night? A thousand nights from now? Why not put an end to both their torments, the agony of her anticipation and his just plain agony?

The blood pumping darkly through his veins, Anatole started toward the door. He paused to glance back at the candles. A brief pain flashed behind his temple, and one taper lifted up and floated across the room.

It settled into his hand with a splash of hot wax on his thumb. Anatole stifled a curse at the clumsiness of his power. But perhaps his power was not to blame so much as the fact that his hand had begun to tremble in very human fashion.

Steadying it, he reached for the door to find it wouldn't open. But locked doors had never posed any problem for Anatole St. Leger. With a single moment of concentration, he slid back the bolt on the other side, and the door swung open.

The candle shine spilled into the room before him, and Anatole cupped his hand around the flame, not wanting to startle Madeline awake.

Assuming that she slept. Perhaps she knew no better rest this night than he did. It was impossible to tell, for the heavy brocade curtains were drawn around the four-poster bed, obscuring Madeline from his sight.

His pulse gave an erratic beat as he crept into the chamber, settling the candle into a brass holder upon the dressing table. He nearly barked his shins up against one of Madeline's trunks. They stood in a row, stacked against the wall, unopened and unpacked.

The only signs that a woman occupied this room were the petticoats and gown draped neatly over a ladder-back chair.

The thought of Madeline stripped of these garments made his mouth go dry. He fingered the silken fabric of one discarded stocking and felt like some kind of disgusting voyeur, an intruder here.

Which was absurd. This room was as much his as any other part of Castle Leger. As much his as the woman hidden behind that bed curtain.

Whipping about, Anatole stalked closer to the bed in the center of the room. It was so damnably silent in here. The kind of silence that reminded him of certain nights in his youth when his mother had barred herself in her bedchamber after another of her bouts of hysterical sobbing.

His father had paced the hall below, bowed down by the weight of his wife's misery, doing penance for sins he could not help. The sin of being born a St. Leger.

Anatole had watched these little dramas played out, a quiet specter in the doorway, forgotten by both of them. Sometimes Anatole wondered which parent's rejection had cut him the most deeply.

He only knew that he would never allow himself to become the kind of man his father had been, a victim of love and of the dulcet tyranny of a woman's tears.

His hand tightened on Madeline's bed curtain. He stopped himself just short of wrenching it open. He didn't want to be dominated by his wife, but he hadn't come here to terrify her, either.

No, by his mother's grave, that was the last thing he wanted to do. Slowly he eased the heavy drapery aside, exposing the shadowed recesses of the mammoth four-poster bed. For a moment it hardly looked as though she was there. By god, that old jest about being able to lose such a woman amongst the sheets hadn't been far from the truth.

He had to shift the candle closer, before he could clearly make out Madeline's form, huddled in a ball in the center of the bed, the coverlets dragged up to her chin.

She hugged the pillow to her head with both arms, her fiery red hair tumbled half across her face. Her golden-tipped lashes rested against the curve of her cheeks. She didn't look like a woman who had sobbed herself to sleep, but she appeared pale and unhappy for all that, even in the depths of slumber.

As he studied the set of her chin, it occurred to Anatole that Madeline never would be the sort of woman to give way to hysterics. She was more the kind to let her heart break one tear at a time, all shed quietly into her pillow, where no one would ever see or know.

Swallowed up in that great big bed, she looked small and lost, with a childlike vulnerability. He felt a strange emotion stir deep inside him, far deeper than any of his physical burnings. It had been so long since he'd experienced such a thing, it took him awhile to recognize it for what it was.

Tenderness. The urge to draw her into his arms and hold her for a long time until she felt quite safe.

As though she sensed him hovering over her, Madeline stirred. Anatole retreated a pace as she shifted position, a tiny furrow marring her brow. She didn't appear to be enjoying the most comfortable repose.

As she squirmed again, the coverlet fell off her shoulder, and Anatole saw what the trouble was. She was still trussed up in her damned corset. He scowled. Whatever would possess a woman to lace herself into such a torture device in the first place, let alone wear the fool thing to bed—

But he broke off his mental tirade as an uncomfortable thought struck him. Madeline had likely worn the thing because she'd had no choice. There had been no one to help her out of it.

He had shown her scant sympathy earlier when she had reported to him the defection of her maid and her cousin. A woman had no need for a fancy French maid in the wilds of Cornwall, and as for the swooning Harriet . . . Anatole had been glad not to encounter her again, to be spared the embarrassment of tendering some awkward apology for that unfortunate kiss.

Yet Madeline had never seemed to ask for his sympathy. She'd been quite calm about the whole thing. Only now did he fully realize what it had meant to her, being abandoned in a household full of strange men.

Silently cursing his own stupidity, Anatole's first impulse was to wake her and strip her of those wretched stays. But even as he reached for her, he hesitated.

She looked so damned exhausted, so damned innocent. It seemed profane somehow to be thinking of touching her while she slept, unawares. He could imagine too clearly how she would start awake, the fear that would cloud her eyes when she found his calloused hands upon her, read the lustful purpose in his face.

A long frustrated sigh escaped him. He started to back away from the bed. He had waited this long. He could surely manage to suffer through one more night.

But he couldn't leave her this way, either. She flopped over on her back, her eyes never opening, but a small sound of discomfort breached her lips. It was a wonder the woman could even breathe. He glanced down helplessly for a moment at his own large, awkward hands.

Then, hesitantly, he focused his gaze upon the lacings of her stays. He had never tested out his powers upon anything quite so fine. The silken strings were already in a tangle from Madeline's own futile efforts to free herself. For a man of his impatience, it was all Anatole could do not to yank at the garment with the same force that had brought his clock flying off the wall.

Gulping deeply, he gentled his mind, his thoughts whispering over the lacings, undoing them slowly . . . so slowly beads of perspiration dotted his brow. His temples throbbed from such a long-sustained effort. By the time the last string tugged free, he felt almost weak.

He took a deep breath to gather up his reserves, before looking again to ease the garment away from her body. Madeline didn't awaken, but she issued a long grateful sigh. The corset trapped beneath her, she wore nothing now but a loose flowing shift.

His efforts had dislodged that as well, tumbling it off her shoulder, partly exposing her back. The damned corset had left cruel red marks upon her delicate white skin. Anatole caressed her with his eyes. Sighing again, Madeline rolled over onto her back, nestling sensuously against the pillow. One arm still buried beneath it, she slung out the other like a woman beckoning a lover to her bed.

Her linen shift was thin, low-cut, exposing the globes of her breasts, small, perfectly shaped, with rose-colored tips. A shudder racked through him. He felt his thoughts dangerously close to getting away from him.

Clenching his teeth, he shut down the power of his mind. But he couldn't shut down the desire as well. It flared to new life inside him, a dark, hungry thing, needing consummation, to mate with Madeline Breton as he had never mated with any woman before.

The desperate longing seemed to pulse from his flesh, throwing off heat as a roaring fire would do. It almost seemed that Madeline could feel it, too, even lost in slumber. She stretched her body languorously, moistening her lips. Anatole felt something inside him snap. Trembling, he bent over the bed, telling himself he could be gentle. He *would* be gentle.

Bending closer, he intended to kiss her softly awake, like the prince arousing the maiden from her hundred-year sleep. But as his shadow fell over her, Madeline shifted again, freeing the arm cradled behind the pillow. She had something clutched in her hand.

Anatole froze. The sight of the blue ribbon entwined about her fingers had more effect on his passion than a jugful of cold water. She still had that

God-cursed miniature. Not only had she retrieved it, but she had fallen asleep cherishing the thing as though it were some sort of precious treasure.

Anatole stared at the portrait, a painful reminder of the folly of his youth when he had made himself nigh sick with longing to be that man painted upon the ivory, handsome and serene, his mind clear of all tormenting family legacy, of powers too dark and strange for any human being to understand.

Instead . . . Anatole straightened, catching sight of his reflection in the mirror hanging above the dresser. A shadowy figure, he looked more of a beast than a man as he hovered over Madeline with his shirt undone, his hair a black tangle, his eyes a dark glitter, marking him for the true son of St. Leger that he was.

An anguished cry escaped him. It didn't disturb Madeline, for he trapped it deep within his soul. He stared down at her, realizing he was as much a fool now as he had been at the age of fifteen when that portrait had been made. Imagining that he could make her desire him when she already had her prince, caught up in ivory, ribbons, and dreams.

Let her keep her dreams, Anatole thought bleakly. At least for one more night. He'd have to rob her of them soon enough.

Stealing one final longing glance at his fiery-haired bride, Anatole drew the coverlet back over her. Then he turned and crept from the room.

A moment later and the bolt clicked again, locking the door. It was that sound that finally awoke Madeline. Her eyelids fluttered, but she resisted, trying to cling to sleep, to the dream that was already slipping out of her grasp.

It was the most delicious dream she'd ever had, sensual, yet somehow poignant. Anatole had come into her bedchamber. Not the harsh man whose bold rough kiss had left her bruised and shaken, but *her* Anatole, the one from the portrait.

He'd been warm and tender, helping her to undress, undoing the lacings of her corset with such loving patience. His fingers had moved over her back, stroking, caressing. She'd reached out to him, and he'd smiled down at her, worshiping her with the magic of his beautiful dark eyes.

He had seemed to be trying to tell her something.

I only want to love you, Madeline. Let me. Show me the way.

Then he'd bent toward her, and she had sighed, waiting for a kiss that had never come. It was like reading a book and coming to the most wonderful part of the story, only to lose one's place. And try as hard as she might, Madeline could not seem to find it again.

She gave up at last, allowing her eyes to drift open, the last vestiges of sleep and her dreams vanishing. She awoke to the empty confines of an unfamiliar bedchamber, her lover reduced to nothing but paint strokes on the ivory she cupped in her hand.

A haunting sadness swept over her, a sense of loss so strong she could hardly account for it. She felt bereft, abandoned all over again. Tears trickled down her cheeks until she dashed them aside, telling herself not to be a fool.

There was no reason for her to lie here blubbering like a babe. She'd had a dream, not a nightmare.

No, the nightmare was reserved for her waking hours.

But she refused to allow herself to think self-pitying nonsense like that, either. Stuffing the miniature beneath her pillow, Madeline rolled over, determined to think no more of dreams or nightmares. To simply go back to sleep.

Closing her eyes, she snuggled deeper under the covers, shoving her corset farther out of the way.

Her corset? Madeline's eyes flew open wide. Sitting upright, her hands groped over her own body, feeling nothing but the thin shift and the softness of her breasts. Peeling back the coverlet, she found her stays beside her, the once snarled strings curling freely across the sheets.

She could scarce believe it was the same garment she had struggled for a full half hour to shed, if the corset was not so clearly illuminated by . . .

By the light someone had left burning on her dressing table.

Jolted fully awake, her heart thudded. She noticed the melting candle just in time to watch the flame gutter and go out.

For a long time she sat bolt upright in the darkness, barely breathing. Her gaze roved fearfully around the shadowy corners of her bedchamber before she could convince herself she was alone.

At least she was now.

Drawing the blankets clear up to the level of her eyes, Madeline sank back against her pillows.

But not to sleep.

Chapter Six

"... And if any of ye know of an impediment as to why these two should not lawfully be joined in matrimony, speak now or forever hold your peace."

The Reverend Septimus Fitzleger's words echoed around the church, from the bell tower to the rood loft, fading to silence as his warning must have done hundreds of times before. But it was the first time Mr. Fitzleger ever feared an objection might be raised by either the bride or the groom.

The vicar's gaze flicked from Madeline to Anatole and then back again. The bridegroom remained stonily silent but Madeline's gloved fingers clutched her bridal bouquet tighter as she fought to keep from crying out.

Yes. There were a dozen reasons why she shouldn't marry Anatole St. Leger.

Because the man used books to prop up his furniture. Because he was dark-tempered, rough, and dangerous. Because he despised everything about her, and she would never know a moment's tenderness from him.

Because his castle by the sea was a place fraught with dust and desolation. Because the single night she'd spent beneath his roof had been one of little sleep and much terror, one she'd spent starting up at every sound, fearful that the phantom that had melted out of the woodwork and undressed her was going to come back again.

A dozen reasons for not becoming Madeline St. Leger? A hundred more likely, but none that would sound rational. Not with the sunshine spilling through the tracery of St. Gothian's arched windows like the clear white light of reason.

And Madeline reminded herself, she was, above all else, a reasonable woman.

Fitzleger dove back into his prayer book and rushed ahead with the services. Behind her, Madeline could hear the witnesses settling back on the front pew. There were only two: Mrs. Beamus, the vicar's ruddy-cheeked housekeeper and old Darby, the church sexton.

Kindly people, no doubt, but completely unknown to Madeline. She longed for the support of Harriet's presence, despite her cousin's annoying tongue. She even found herself missing the rest of her noisy, heedless, and cheerful family: Papa, Mama, Jeremy, and the girls.

But perhaps it was appropriate that there were only strangers present at her wedding. Because she was marrying a stranger. Peeking from beneath the brim of her bonnet, Madeline risked a glance up at her formidable bridegroom.

At least he looked somewhat tamer this morning in his suit of velvet, a somber shade of midnight blue, the long coat falling past the knees of his breeches. The unrelenting darkness of his attire was only relieved by the white frills of his shirt, the lace that spilled over his cuffs.

The style was a little old-fashioned but very elegant, except for the leather belt that strapped his sword to his side. Madeline had been disconcerted by the presence of the weapon ever since she had watched him buckle it on before setting out for church. She'd asked no questions, but what sort of man came armed to a wedding?

Only one like Anatole, whose features spoke more of an ancient warlord than a proper country gentleman. His ebony hair glossed back into a queue left his face mercilessly exposed, the brow with its slashing scar, the uncompromising nose, the mouth, hard and intimidating.

His was not a face one would ever call handsome. But she had to admit it was a compelling one, capable of forcing its way into a woman's dreams; although, he had not been in hers last night.

But had he been in her bedchamber?

Someone certainly had, defying the locks on her doors, to leave behind a lighted candle, undoing her corset strings. She didn't believe in ghosts, phantoms, or unquiet spirits. But what about unquiet bridegrooms? Was it possible that Anatole had gained access to her room and—no, that was equally ridiculous.

He'd shown so little consideration for her welfare, she could not imagine those rough hands of his gently undressing her without awakening her. If he'd had any interest at all in her last night, it would have been to kick in her bedroom door like the barbaric warrior he was and—

Madeline checked the disturbing thought. One should hardly imagine being ravished in church, the holy altar itself but a few feet away.

No, there was only one reasonable explanation for last night. She must have left the candle burning on the dresser herself and forgotten it. Her corset strings must have come loosened with her tossing and turning, and the garment had fallen off by itself. *The only reasonable explanation.* Then, why didn't it satisfy her?

A silence settled over the church so profound it penetrated even Madeline's preoccupied thoughts. She became aware that both Fitzleger and Anatole were staring at her. For one awful moment she feared she had voiced her speculations aloud. Her heart skipped a beat, then she realized Fitzleger had been speaking. He had obviously been addressing her, and awaited an answer.

Mama had often accused Madeline of being woolly-headed and letting her mind wander off in the midst of balls and suppers. But Madeline had never imagined she'd do such a thing at her own wedding. Her cheeks fired with mortification as Mr. Fitzleger repeated himself with infinite patience.

"Wilt thou have this man to be thy wedded husband?"

Would she? Madeline swallowed hard, trying to gather her scattered wits. Beneath her gown, she felt the miniature she had persisted in keeping, pressed close to her skin, like the gentle weight of the dreams she was abandoning, of the perfect companion and friend, the perfect love.

"Well, I—I," she faltered. She saw Mr. Fitzleger's face wax anxiously, and Anatole shifted impatiently. Had his hand dropped beneath his coat, nearer to the hilt of his sword? Perhaps that was why he'd brought the weapon, to prod vows from a reluctant bride.

Madeline's gaze drifted toward Anatole's face. There was one thing about the man that would never be tame and that was his eyes, fierce and mesmerizing with dark facets. He had no need of any sword, not with those eyes. They bored deep into hers, compelling her answer.

"I will," she blurted out. She felt a little dazed, as though with those two simple words she had just surrendered everything to Anatole St. Leger.

The rest of the ceremony passed in a blur, Anatole's own vows, the reblessing of the rings, the final prayer, the fateful closing words.

"I now pronounce thee husband and wife." Fitzleger's voice held a mingling of relief and triumph. He closed his book with a snap and mopped his perspiring brow. Then he gazed expectantly at Madeline and Anatole.

When neither made a move, Mr. Fitzleger prompted, "You may kiss your bride, my lord."

"I know that," Anatole growled. He turned and reached for Madeline. She stiffened, bracing herself for the onslaught of one of his savage, knee-buckling kisses. Her alarm must have showed in her face because Anatole hesitated.

His arms dropped awkwardly back to his side. Something flashed in his eyes that might have been irritation. It could hardly have been regret. He ran two fingers across his brow, staring at her with brooding intensity.

He did not seem to even bend forward, and yet Madeline could have sworn he kissed her, his lips grazing her cheek, soft, warm, and gentle. As he turned away, she pressed her hand to her face in confusion, beset by an urge she scarce understood. To reach out to him, to call him back to her side.

But it was not as though her reluctance had wounded her bridegroom's feelings. He fetched his cape from where he had tossed it on the front pew, coolly swirling it about his shoulders like a man who'd done what he came for and was now impatient to be gone.

Mrs. Beamus and Mr. Darby skittered to attention, making their obeisance to him from a safe and respectful distance. It was Madeline that they crowded closer to, offering felicitations.

But even as she accepted their good wishes, she remained aware of Anatole in the background, a proud figure, cloaked in shadow, standing isolated. And alone.

Mr. Fitzleger stepped forward to claim her hand, squeezing it with the vicar's usual sweet enthusiasm. "Oh, my dearest Madeline, I hope you will be very happy."

She thanked Fitzleger for his kindness and for the flowers that had been his gift to her.

"Oh, tush, 'twas nothing, my dear. I am sure that Anatole would have himself if—if—" The vicar lowered his voice, casting an anxious look in Anatole's direction. "There is a good reason why he would not think to offer you flowers. You see he—he—"

"It is all right," Madeline said. "You don't have to make excuses for him. I have fully recovered from all my romantic delusions."

She glanced toward Anatole herself. He had taken to pacing before the altar, running his fingers absently along the carved rood screen. Even the quiet beauty of this tiny village church seemed incapable of touching his rough and restless spirit.

"I must simply learn to accept Anatole St. Leger for what he is," Madeline murmured.

"Ah, my dear." Fitzleger sighed. "That would be the most wondrous gift you could give him."

Madeline doubted that Anatole would want anything she had to offer, but she kept such lowering thoughts to herself. The sexton fetched forth the parish register to record the marriage.

Darby presented the ledger first to Anatole with that mixture of fear and deference that Madeline noted all the villagers accorded him. Shaking back the lace at his cuffs, Anatole scratched his name across the surface of the open page before passing the quill to Madeline.

She was surprised to see that her husband wrote in a beautiful hand, bold and flourishing. Set beneath it, her own signature seemed insignificant.

She tried not to feel as though she had just signed her name with her heart's blood, chiding herself for such melodramatic nonsense. Darby whisked the ledger away, and Mrs. Beamus headed back to her kitchens. Even Fitzleger excused himself, retiring to the sacristy to remove his vestments. As the last of the vicar's footsteps faded, Madeline laid her flowers upon the altar stone.

There could be nothing more solemn than being left alone in an empty church. Except she was not alone. Her new husband was with her. Anatole stood a short distance away, but the aisle that separated them might as well have been full fathoms wide. His eyes raked over her from the hem of her petticoats to her curls, which she had dressed loosely beneath her bonnet. Though she could detect no sign of approval on his features, at least the contempt of yesterday was absent.

They had scarce spoken more than a dozen words to each other from the time she had crept downstairs that morning until their short journey in the coach to the church. Madeline wondered if she was condemned to a lifetime of being lost in the man's silences. A grim fate for a woman who had been accused of talking too much in some of the finest salons in London. But then, so many gentlemen disliked hearing their opinions proved wrong by a lady.

Lifting the hem of her gown, a confection of ivory silk embroidered with roses, Madeline crossed over to Anatole, her petticoats rustling about her ankles.

To cover her nervousness, she said cheerfully, "Well, my lord, I thought the service was quite nice. Mr. Fitzleger managed it very quickly."

Anatole tugged at his cravat as though the finery were choking him. "Were you anticipating some more elaborate affair?"

"Oh, no. I did not come to Castle Leger expecting any grand wedding."

His lashes swept down. "I *know* what you came here expecting, Madeline." There was a bitterness in his tone that surprised her, making her feel self-conscious of the portrait hidden beneath her gown. It was almost as though she had betrayed Anatole with another man, which was absurd. There was no love between them to betray.

When Anatole raised his eyes, his customary sardonic expression had returned. "So. You managed to survive both the wedding and your first night at Castle Leger. My congratulations, madam."

Madeline winced but retorted, "Survived is a very apt word, my lord."

"Did you not sleep well last night?"

"Well enough."

Taking a step closer, he raised one finger and traced the bruised hollow beneath her eye. His brows arched skeptically almost as though he *knew* exactly what sort of night she'd spent. Her suspicions about what had happened in her room flared anew.

"And you, my lord?" she challenged. She could likewise have touched the shadows beneath his eyes if she had been bold enough. "How did you fare last night?"

His hand fell away from her face. "I slept like the dead." He amended. "I mean . . . like a rock."

"Truly? At one time I thought I heard you stirring about in your room."

She had heard no such thing, but a shade of unease crossed Anatole's features.

"You might have heard me when I was resetting my clock. I trust I didn't disturb you?"

"No, but there was a question I wanted to ask you."

"Yes?" His tone was not encouraging.

Did you slip into my bedchamber and undress me?

Unthinkable to give voice to such a suspicion with Anatole's fierce gaze upon her. Unthinkable and impossible. Madeline fought back a hot blush. To cover her confusion, she stammered out the first question that came into her head. "I was wondering about the age of the church. St. Gothian's seems so very old."

Was it her imagination or did the set of his shoulders relax? "The church has been here in one form or another since the reign of Edward the Confessor. The original building was said to have been built on the site of a pagan altar."

Madeline's gaze roved about the chancel and nave, admiring the church's serene beauty anew, the finely carved rood screen with its organ loft, the magnificent stone relief depicting the Gift of the Magi.

"It's amazing so much of this has survived the years," she said. "The Puritans destroyed such things elsewhere."

"My ancestors could not save the stained-glass windows from Cromwell's army, but they disassembled the reredos and the cross, hiding them away."

"That was a dangerous thing to do."

"Both the church and the village fall within our lands. St. Legers protect their own."

"And I suppose that now includes me?"

"Aye."

Madeline had meant her remark as a jest, but Anatole's reply seemed deadly serious.

"Do you mean that if any man offered to harm me that—"

"He would be dead," Anatole said in a deceptively soft voice that both chilled and warmed her. It was not quite the same as being loved and cherished, but to have a husband so willing to protect her was no small thing.

She wandered along the main aisle, running her glove over the edge of ancient pews that seemed permeated with the scent of incense and the salt tang of the nearby sea. For once Anatole appeared not quite so impatient, content to watch her, allowing her to satisfy her curiosity.

She couldn't help noticing that unlike many benefactors of a church, his family had no private enclosed bench set aside for them. When she remarked upon it, he said, "The villagers have always preferred to have the lords of St. Leger out in the open where they can be seen. It makes the local folk more . . . um—comfortable."

Madeline could well understand that. Anatole made her far less nervous when he was in her sight, not standing behind her as he was now. She could sense his presence as much as if he had taken that great black cloak of his and enfolded her in it, gathering her to the heat of his powerful frame. It made the hairs at the back of her neck tingle. If his ancestors had been anything like him—

It suddenly occurred to her that Harriet was right. She knew nothing about this man's family.

Turning to face Anatole, Madeline gestured toward the empty pews and remarked, "I had hoped . . . that is I thought that perhaps some of your relatives might have attended our wedding."

"Oh, they're here."

His dry remark puzzled her until Anatole pointed toward the church floor. Glancing down, Madeline saw what she had failed to notice before, the names carved into the worn stone.

The practice of burying bodies beneath a church was not unusual, but Madeline felt suddenly uneasy. She skittered back from the memorial she had heedlessly been trampling.

"St. Legers have long been buried here instead of in the churchyard," Anatole said. "The hope being that the added weight of the building might keep them in their graves."

"What!"

He hastened to add, "I mean because it's holier ground. They can better rest in peace."

"Oh!" Anatole had a disconcerting way of explaining things. "Are your parents also—"

"No!" A shadow crossed his features. "My mother . . . and my father lie elsewhere."

Madeline sensed from his tone she had blundered upon a painful and forbidden subject. With great delicacy she drew back from it, returning to her study of the floor. The names extended to the enclosed porch itself, one small marker carved into the space beneath the bell tower.

"Deidre St. Leger," Madeline murmured, noting the dates. "She died quite young. How sad."

"One of my more unfortunate ancestresses," Anatole said, trailing after her.

"She must have been a very petite woman considering . . ." Madeline gestured, noting the Lady Deidre's narrow resting space.

"No, actually according to the family records, Deidre was a regular Diana, tall and strong. Only her heart was buried here in a small casket."

"Her—her heart?"

"Supposedly Deidre wanted it that way. She said that since her family had trampled so much over her heart during her life, they might as well continue to do so after her death."

Madeline shuddered, repulsed, but fascinated by the tale. "She sounds like a most unhappy woman. Why did she die so embittered?"

"The Lady Deidre was foolish enough to fall in love."

Madeline glanced wistfully at her husband's stern profile. "Do you find that so foolish, then, my lord?"

"It is for a St. Leger. We have always been bound to marry only the one who is selected for us."

"You mean like you sent Reverend Fitzleger to find me?"

Anatole nodded.

"I know Mr. Fitzleger is a venerable, aged man. But he could not possibly have been around in Deidre's time."

"There was another Bride Finder before him. And another before that. But Deidre chose to disregard our family custom. Because she had given her heart to another, she rejected the man her Finder had provided. If she could not have the man she desired, she vowed to have none at all. She thought she could defeat the curse by remaining unwed. It didn't work of course."

Anatole scowled down at Deidre's memorial. "She met with death and disaster, the lot of all St. Legers who refuse to wed their chosen mate."

For a moment Madeline's mind boggled with what he was telling her. She had an image of generations of white-haired little men, scouring the countryside for mates to save St. Legers from their doom. A quaint family legend, but patently ridiculous.

An uncertain laugh escaped Madeline. "My lord, *you* cannot possibly believe in such things as curses. You cannot honestly think—"

She broke off at Anatole's black frown. It was obvious he did believe in the legend of the chosen bride, or else she would not be here. Someone needed to inform the poor man that the dark ages were over, that a new era of reason had dawned, at least in the rest of the country beyond Cornwall.

"Such superstition is not rational," she said. "What empirical proof could there be for such a thing?"

"Proof, madam? I do not have to look further than my own parents for such proof. My mother was not a chosen bride. She was damned from the moment she arrived at Castle Leger until the day she—"

He broke off, his jaw clenching. The same darkness clouded his eyes as when he had spoken of his mother before. This time Madeline could not stop herself from asking, "What happened to her?"

"She died young. Just like Deidre St. Leger. I was but ten years old at the time. Losing my mother so broke my father's spirit that he followed her to the grave within five years' time."

"Then, you have been the master of Castle Leger since you were but fifteen?"

"I've been my own master even longer than that."

"I'm sorry." Madeline wanted to touch him, but Anatole was not the sort of man to readily accept sympathy. "How did your mother die?"

"She was killed by fear and sorrow."

That was impossible, Madeline had to bite her lip to keep from pointing out. People did not die merely from misery or terror. More likely the poor lady had suffered from consumption or a weak heart. But as she stared at Anatole, something in his face made her swallow the remark. Instead she said gently, "Oh, yes, I see."

"You don't see anything at all. You don't understand a damn thing about me. Or my family." Anatole struggled for words to explain and finished by biting out, "I don't want you to share the same fate as my mother."

"I won't. After all, I am the chosen bride, aren't I?"

Madeline looked solemn enough, but a coaxing light shone in her eyes.

Anatole glowered at her. The infernal woman was humoring him, curse her hide! The same as he had done with Will Sparkins the day the lad came tearing up from the beach with some faradiddle about spotting a sea monster.

He dragged his hand back through his hair in pure frustration, dislodging several strands from the queue. "You don't believe a blasted word I've been telling you, do you?"

"N-n-o-o-o," Madeline admitted, but was quick to add, "there are better reasons—you don't have to fear my being doomed to an early grave. I am as strong and healthy as a farm girl. Most unladylike, my mother would say. I could not produce a maidenly swoon if my life depended upon it."

She gave his hand a pat, as though she considered the matter settled. With a soothing smile she drifted off to study the statue of St. Gothian she had spied set back in its niche. Anatole stared after her, not knowing whether to be more annoyed or dumbfounded. He had dreaded this moment all morning, knowing that at some point he must reveal to his bride his strange family heritage. Her question about Deidre had given him his opening, and so he had begun to explain to Madeline the dark legacy of the St. Legers and his own accursed share in it.

He had envisioned dismay, rejection, the kind of fear and revulsion that had haunted his mother to her grave. But it had never occurred to him that Madeline might simply refuse to believe any of it.

She looked so demure beneath her bonnet, tendrils of auburn hair wisping about her delicate face. Her silken gown billowed about her lithe figure, all warm, all natural womanhood, her soft pink mouth set in a line so . . . so . . .

So sunnily obstinate, so cheerfully opinionated!

Anatole folded his arms across his chest. So the lady demanded proof, did she? Otherwise she'd set him down as a superstitious fool, to be treated with the sort of kindness she might have shown the village idiot.

He could offer her proof aplenty that the St. Legers were a breed set apart from other men, beginning with his own peculiar talents. All he had to do was levitate the candles from the iron wall sockets or send the poor box floating down the aisle.

Or what about the nosegay of bluebells and wild heather she'd left on the altar? a voice taunted inside him. Why didn't he whisk those up into the air and dance them before Madeline's eyes?

Because the mere thought of it was enough to make his blood run cold. His fingers strayed to his scar, and he wondered bleakly if he was the only one in the world who connected something as innocent as flowers with pain . . . and death.

His gaze swept back toward Madeline, her face tipped up in delight as she studied the carvings of cherubs set above the baptismal font. Sunlight streaming through the lancet windows bathed her winsome profile with a radiance that took his breath away, her green eyes so clear, so calm, so *sane*.

Anatole expelled a deep sigh. Though he damned himself for his weakness, he knew he would not be offering his bride any proofs of his demon's heritage. At least not this day.

His sigh, soft as it was, echoed around the church, capturing Madeline's attention. She glanced back at him with a tentative smile.

"Does my lord grow impatient to be gone, or are we waiting for Mr. Fitzleger's return?"

"No."

"Then, perhaps we should go back to Castle Leger."

He would have been happy enough to have escorted Madeline from here. The solemn peacefulness of St. Gothian's always oppressed him, making a mockery of his own restlessness. He would not have lingered at the church to wait upon Fitzleger or to allow Madeline to become acquainted with the bones of his ancestors or even to explain his own mad family history.

He had another reason, and he was dreading it. He would as soon forget about what was expected of him, but he couldn't. Perhaps because he was exactly what Madeline thought him—a superstitious fool. But he had avoided his unpleasant task long enough.

When Madeline started to skirt past him, he blocked her path. "Wait! There is one more thing we must do, a brief tradition that the heir to Castle Leger must honor when he marries."

"Another family tradition?" Madeline faltered. She was beginning to look wary of St. Leger customs, which well she might. The wariness changed to downright alarm when Anatole eased back his cloak and drew forth Prospero's sword from its scabbard.

The length of steel gleamed in the light, the crystal mounted upon the pommel flashing bright rainbows against the pews. Anatole deliberately avoided looking at the mesmerizing stone. That would be all he'd need on top of everything else, one of his damnable visions.

"Is this ceremony absolutely necessary?" Madeline asked weakly.

"Yes, I'm afraid it is." He held up the weapon for her closer inspection. "This is the sword of my ancestor, Lord Prospero St. Leger, who—"

"Prospero? What an unusual name." For all her unease, Madeline tipped her head to one side like an inquisitive sparrow. As she studied the sword, her eyes lit with that curiosity Anatole was beginning to recognize as so much a part of her. "Do you mean like the Prospero in Shakespeare's *Tempest*?"

No, he meant Prospero like in the devil from hell. But Anatole choked back the uncomplimentary description of his ancestor.

"I don't know anything about Shakespeare," he said. "All I know is that the first lord of Castle Leger was called Prospero, and this was his sword—"

"I didn't see any Prospero amongst the names on the floor," she interrupted again. "Did he not want to rest in peace beneath the church like all the others?"

"The blasted rogue never wanted to rest in peace anywhere," Anatole muttered under his breath. Aloud, he said, "He's not buried here because he died in a fire. His ashes were scattered over the sea."

Before Madeline could ask any more awkward questions, Anatole rushed on, "Prospero's sword has always been handed down to the ladies of the St. Leger family."

"The ladies?"

"Aye, no one is quite certain when the custom began, but it has always been the duty of the St. Leger heir to surrender the sword to his wife, along with his pledge to—to engage in no duels with her kinsmen."

"But you have no quarrel with my family," Madeline said reasonably. "You don't even know them."

"I am speaking figuratively, Madeline. Every St. Leger has made war against the world in one fashion or another."

"And what is your war, my lord?"

"Well, I—I don't have one," Anatole blustered. "That is not the point. There are three conditions imposed upon the man who inherits this sword. One, he must only use its power to fight a just cause. Two, he must never shed the blood of another St. Leger.

"And third, he must surrender the sword to the woman he lov—" Anatole broke off gruffly. "I mean to his wife."

"But if you give me the sword, how can you use it to fight a just cause or—"

"Damnation, woman! If you keep questioning everything I say, we will never get finished with this business."

Madeline flinched at his angry tone. Retreating a step, she subsided, regarding him with great reproachful eyes. Anatole smothered another oath and splayed his hand back through his hair, wreaking havoc on what remained of his queue.

Curse it all! He had not meant to roar at her again. But he felt like enough of an idiot without Madeline pointing out to him how illogical this was.

Seizing her by the hand, he dragged her back toward the altar, ignoring her faint protest. He realized his ferocity stemmed partly from the knowledge he was once again being less than honest with her.

Hell! The ceremony was not about the surrender of swords, as much as it was of hearts, the promise that every St. Leger made to his bride, to be true to her not only in this life, but in the next.

Clenching his jaw, Anatole positioned Madeline opposite him. As he dropped to one knee before her, he wondered grimly if he wasn't about to make a bigger fool of himself than he had last night, when he had hovered over her bed like some lovesick youth.

One glance up at Madeline's face told him all he feared. She gaped at him, her eyes widening to their fullest extent. Anatole felt a red flush begin to creep up his neck.

Ah, damn! Why couldn't he have had a family with normal marriage customs, like wedding feasts, bridesmaids, and ribbon favors?

He didn't know how he was going to go through with this, pledge Madeline his devotion for all eternity when he did not even think he could make her a good husband in this lifetime. Not when she feared him so, tensed at his every touch. He'd be fortunate if he did not have to spend the rest of his days making love to her only with his mind.

She was so cursed beautiful, gold-tipped lashes fringing green eyes that held all the warmth and sweetness of the kind of gentle springs that never touched his hard lands. Beneath her bonnet, she'd allowed her hair, ringlets of fire and silk, to cascade down freely after the old-fashioned wedding custom that showed she was still a maiden pure and true.

All in all, a most perfect bride. For any other man in the world but him, Anatole thought bitterly. As he gazed up at her delicate porcelain features, the words that he knew he was supposed to say stuck in his throat.

Instead he balanced the sword across his palms and all but thrust it up at her, growling, "Here! Take it!"

Madeline only stared at him. Of all the strange things she had experienced since coming to Castle Leger—and the list was growing long—this was by far the most disconcerting.

Her proud, arrogant, and powerful husband, surely the most unromantic and ungallant man she'd ever known, was kneeling at her feet like some bashful swain. She had to stifle an urge to break into nervous laughter.

His much abused queue had finally come undone, his hair swirling black and wild about the granite-chiseled planes of his face. With his warrior's scar, his cape pooling off his broad shoulders, he could well have been some medieval knight paying homage to his lady. If it had not been for his ferocious scowl.

"Here!" he repeated tersely. "Take the God-cursed sword, Madeline."

She had no choice but to obey. Holding out her hands, she gingerly accepted the heavy blade, blue steel glinting against the white cushion of her gloves. She found herself fascinated in spite of herself. She had never realized a sword could be so elegant, its beauty almost mystical with the wrought gold hilt and sparkling crystal.

As soon as the sword was safely in her hands, Anatole leapt to his feet.

"Is this all?" Madeline breathed. "Is the ceremony over?"

"Yes," he snapped. "I—I mean no." He ducked his head, his cheeks stained a dull red. "I'm supposed to say something like, 'Lady, I surrender to you my sword and my—my . . ."

The rest of his words were lost, muttered between his clenched teeth.

"Your sword and your what?" she asked timidly.

He muttered again, and still she could not hear him. When she cocked her head inquiringly, he shot her a baleful glare.

"Damn it, I *said,* I surrender my sword, my heart, and my soul for all eternity!"

Beautiful words. Or they would have been if they had not been bellowed at the top of Anatole's lungs. If he had really meant them.

Madeline fingered the sword in dismay. "But—but what am I to do with it?"

"The sword or my soul?"

"Either." The weight of both threatened to lie heavy upon her hands.

"Just accept the blasted thing."

Madeline shifted the sword awkwardly in her hands. Grasping it by the hilt, she rested the tip against the stone floor.

"Thank you," she murmured. "It's very nice, but—"

"But what?"

Madeline fretted her lower lip, wishing that just once she could suppress the practical side of her nature. "I was thinking that it would be helpful if the sword-giving custom also included a scabbard to keep it in."

Fearing she might have offended Anatole, she hardly dared look at him. But after a moment of stunned silence, he flung back his head and laughed. Not with his usual sardonic mirth, but a hearty male laugh that lit his eyes and carved deep, generous lines about his mouth.

"By my faith, you are quite right, lady." He proceeded to unbuckle his scabbard and then cinched it about her waist. Taking the sword from her, he eased it inside the leather casing himself.

She suddenly realized how close Anatole stood, his hand lingering at her waist. She could feel the heat and vitality of the man pulsing through those long, bronzed fingers, even through the layers of her gown.

"Better?" he asked, still smiling.

"Y-yes," she stammered, although she was not entirely sure it was. Not with her pulse skipping out a rhythm so different from its usual calm beat.

The rigid planes of his face relaxed into a softness she would not have imagined him capable of. The darkness of his eyes mellowed to a rich golden brown, and the timbre of his voice became almost gentle as he said, "I'm sorry."

"For what?" she asked in astonishment.

"For inflicting upon you all this St. Leger insanity, all of my family's strange beliefs and customs."

"I daresay I'll grow used to them in time."

"Will you? I hope so, lady. I know we have made a most awkward beginning, but truly I do not desire to make you unhappy—" He swallowed deeply. "Or afraid."

Too late, Madeline thought. Not be afraid? After tales of family curses, sword ceremonies, and hearts buried beneath the church floor?

And yet despite everything, she felt an urge to reassure Anatole. She had never seen him look so vulnerable, a haunting sadness in his eyes.

She brushed the ebony strands back from his face, her fingers grazing his cheek. "I am a most sensible woman, my lord, not easily frightened."

The muscle in his jaw jumped at her touch. He looked a little confused, as though he knew no more what to do with her gentleness than she did his sword.

"You do not always seem this brave," he said.

"Indeed, sir, after what I have been through, I think I must have the heart of a lion. Most women abandoned at that castle of yours would have succumbed to strong hysterics."

"I'm not talking about your fear of Castle Leger. I'm talking about your fear of me."

Madeline found that harder to deny. She lowered her head, but he crooked his fingers beneath her chin, forcing her to look up, the feel of his hand warm and disturbing against her skin.

"You do fear me, don't you, Madeline? Yesterday when I wanted to kiss you, you fled across my study as though the devil were after you."

"You alarmed me. You were too ferocious. That is not the way you should have kissed me."

"One kiss, and you've become an expert on the subject?"

"I may never have been kissed before. But I always dreamed." Madeline smiled sadly as she recalled just how much she had dreamed. "I always knew just how it should be."

"Then, show me."

"What?"

"Show me how you want to be kissed."

He could not possibly be serious. But one glance at the determined look on his face told her he was. Madeline's gaze flew to his mouth. The mere thought of pressing her lips to his was enough to make her heart miss a beat. She eased his hand away from her face, flushing.

"Oh, n-no. I couldn't possibly," she said, backing away.

"Why not?" he demanded, stalking after her.

"Because I—I—" She stumbled, the weapon tangling in her skirts and tripping her. She was so short and the blasted sword was so long. Regaining her footing, she retreated until she bumped up against the edge of the front pew. Anatole loomed before her, his broad shoulders blocking her view of all else.

"Because," Madeline blurted out the first foolish thought that popped into her head. "You're too tall. You are out of my reach."

"I can bend." Bracing his arms, he trapped her against the side of the pew and leaned closer. All trace of mellowness had vanished from his face. His eyes darkened with that inner fire that never failed to both intrigue and frighten her.

"Show me, Madeline. Show me how you want to be kissed."

He was fierce. He was harsh. He was demanding. Yet how could she ever expect him to be otherwise if she could not find the courage to teach him? He was offering her the perfect opportunity. Her gaze dropped to the full sensual curve of his mouth, and she swallowed hard.

"I can't do it with you staring at me," she whispered.

After a brief hesitation Anatole closed his eyes and waited. Silence stretched out for what seemed an eternity before Madeline summoned up the nerve to rest one hand on his sleeve.

Beneath the velvet's soft deception, she could feel the strength of his arm, tense and steely with the same latent power as the sword strapped to her side. Her heart hammered uncontrollably. She rose up on tiptoe, intending to do no more than brush her lips against his. But suddenly she felt as though some unseen force shoved against her, like a powerful wind or the thrust of a mighty wave.

Tipped off balance, she collided against Anatole's chest, her lips melding with his in a kiss of unexpected sweetness, a kiss whose heat shivered through her, leaving her all warm and trembling. Rousing in her an impulse to twine her fingers in his dark masses of hair, to press herself closer to the hard, unyielding contours of his body, to explore the mysteries of his all too yielding mouth with greater urgency—

Shocked at herself, Madeline wrenched free, rocking back on her heels.

"Th-there," she panted, though she was no longer sure of what she had just proved, of exactly who had been giving the lessons in kissing here. "That is how a kiss should be. More gentle."

Anatole's eyes fluttered open with a sultry languor that did little to douse the strange fire that seemed to have flickered to life deep in her belly. His chest rose and fell in a quick, even rhythm.

"Lady, you could kill a man with such gentleness," he murmured.

She didn't know what he meant by such a complaint. Only one thing seemed clear.

"Then, you don't like the way I kiss, either?"

"I never said that."

His eyes never leaving hers, he took her hand and slowly upended it. Nudging her glove aside, he pressed his mouth to the delicate vein that pulsed in her wrist, searing her with his heat. A tremor coursed through her, and she was dismayed to realize that even when he attempted to be gentle, Anatole was capable of melting her very bones.

"Perhaps tonight we will find some manner of compromise. Between your kisses and mine."

"Perhaps," she whispered. Mesmerized by the low rasp of his voice, by the darkness of his eyes, she would have agreed to anything he said at that moment.

It was only when he released her and levered himself reluctantly away, only when she was able to breathe again, did the full import of his words strike her.

Tonight we will find some manner of compromise.

Madeline's heart dipped down to her toes.

Tonight . . .

Their wedding night.

His tricorne tucked firmly beneath his arm, the Reverend Septimus Fitzleger emerged from the sacristy door into the churchyard just in time to observe the distant figures of Madeline and Anatole heading down the lane. With his long strides Anatole reached the waiting carriage before it occurred to him that his bride was not keeping pace. He turned back impatiently to scoop her off her feet and thrust her up onto the seat of the curricle with all the finesse of a man hauling sacks of grain. Then jumping up beside her, he nodded to his groom to stand aside before whipping up the team of horses. The servant barely had time to leap to his post on the back of the vehicle before Anatole set it thundering down the lane. Madeline clutched her bonnet for dear life with one hand, the side of the curricle with the other.

Perhaps not the most gallant or romantic start to a marriage, Fitzleger thought with a sigh, but at least Master Anatole had not driven off and forgotten his bride entirely. As he watched the carriage vanish in a cloud of dust through the sleepy, sun-drenched village, Fitzleger fought the urge to sink down upon the church steps in a fit of weariness and relief.

Never had he performed any wedding service as fast as he had this one, fearing that at any moment, either the bride or groom would change their mind and bolt for the door. There had been that one heart-stopping second, when he had been certain Madeline was about to—

But never mind. She hadn't and he hadn't. And the Lord bless them, they were now as officially wed as two people could be. Septimus's part in the affair was done, and a good thing, for he felt purely exhausted. At the age of seventy-two, he feared he was getting too old for this bride-finding business.

But then, Anatole St. Leger's match had proved more difficult than most, and Septimus should have expected as much. Anatole had always had a wilder kick to his gallop, even for a St. Leger. He'd been forced to walk his own path at too tender an age, alone, untamed, and . . . unloved.

Poor boy, poor lost boy. It still grieved Fitzleger's heart to think on it. What a world of pain and bitter memory the young master concealed beneath his hard and gruff exterior. It would take a very extraordinary and patient woman to pierce the armor in which Anatole had encased his heart. But Septimus believed, *nay, he knew* all the way down deep to that special corner of his bride-finding soul, that Madeline had to be the one.

So why, then, did he not feel a greater sense of satisfaction at this moment? Ever since leaving the young couple alone in the church, Fitzleger had been overcome by a sense of melancholy that had only increased as he had laid aside his vestments.

Perhaps it came from the realization that this might be the last match he would ever be called upon to make. Anatole's cousin, the arrogant young Roman, had a foolish disregard for the old St. Leger ways. Most of the other St. Legers were already happily wed, and Septimus did not expect to live long enough to perform his service for the next generation.

So, then, who would?

That very question had worried him for sometime. Neither of his sons evinced the slightest sign that they had inherited his gift. Who would be left to save future St. Legers from disaster and guide them down the path to wedded bliss? No one, Septimus feared.

For a moment the thought saddened him, but his natural optimism was quick to reassert itself. His youngest daughter-in-law was about to be brought to bed with child again. Perhaps this time it would be a grandson instead of another girl. And perhaps that little chap might prove to be the next Bride Finder.

Comforted by this notion, Septimus clapped his tricorne upon his head and set off down the well-worn path through the churchyard that led to his snug rectory. But he had gotten no farther than the lych-gate when he was arrested by a sound that disrupted the serenity of the morning, ringing out above the shush of the oak trees being ruffled by the wind.

The sound of a sob, harsh and deep, as though torn free from the depths of someone's soul. Startled, Fitzleger turned and glanced behind him, trying to track down the source of the distress. As he squinted from the porch steps of the church to the low stone fence that rimmed the yard, he saw nothing at first.

Then a movement caught his eye, the flutter of an ankle-length cloak that all but obscured the person who mourned over a grave near the back of the church. Hood pulled forward, the coarse brown garment nearly blended with the broad old oak that overshadowed the church, making it small wonder that Fitzleger had failed to notice the poor creature sooner. A woman, he believed it was.

She bent over one of the headstones, another shuddering sob racking her, the cry as thick with rage as it was with grief.

Ah, no, Septimus thought sadly. Not poor Bessie Kennack come to weep over her mother's grave again. He'd been worried about the girl for some months now. She was far too consumed with her sorrow and her bitterness, still blaming Master Anatole for predicting Marie's death. Heaven knows, Bess could not curse the man any more than he did himself.

But clearly the girl was in need of words of comfort, even though Septimus scarce knew what more he could say, how to reason with her. Praying for some divine inspiration, he shuffled back across the churchyard toward where she stood. But he'd not even come within speaking distance when Bess stiffened as though sensing his presence.

She bolted behind the broad oak with the speed of a frightened fawn.

"Bessie, wait. Come back," Fitzleger shouted, hastening forward.

"Bess?" he called more uncertainly this time, puzzled by her behavior and by something else as well. As he had drawn closer to the caped figure, he was no longer sure it was Bess Kennack.

Reaching the end of the yard, he peered cautiously around the tree to find . . . no one.

No alarmed young woman cowering behind the wide trunk. No distressed woman scrambling over the stone fence. No cloaked woman fleeing down the lane. No woman of any kind, anywhere.

Septimus leaned one hand up against the tree as he glanced uneasily about him, feeling more than a little disconcerted. Such mysterious vanishings he might have taken in stride up in the old hall at Castle Leger, but not in his own tidy little churchyard.

Where could the creature have got to so fast? Why did she run? And most important of all, who was she? Septimus was fairly certain by now that it had not been Bess. If he were not growing so old and forgetful, he would have remembered that Marie Kennack was not even buried in this part of the churchyard.

The only one who had been laid to rest in this older section during the past few decades was . . .

Fitzleger stiffened, a sudden chill coursing through him. He turned slowly, his gaze tracking past the well-worn monuments to the one that was recent by comparison, the marker that now had a single bloodred rose laid across it.

The chill inside him deepened, icing all the way to the marrow of his bones. He read the single word carved into the headstone with all the arrogance and infamy of the man who lie buried there.

A single word . . . a name.

Mortmain.

Chapter Seven

Anatole prowled before the gallery of windows in the dining room. Black hair tumbled dark and wild about his features, his coat and waistcoat discarded across one of the ladder-back chairs. Cravat stripped from his throat, the lace wrenched from his cuffs, he felt more himself than he had all day.

Forcing open one of the casements, he allowed the breeze to penetrate the stuffy chamber, undoing several of the topmost buttons of his shirt in an effort to cool his heated flesh. The night air seemed heavy with the scent of flowers, the wet tang of the sea, and a hundred nameless longings.

Beneath the starlit sky the garden stretched out before him, a wilderness of azalea bushes, primroses, bluebells, and rhododendron trees. They had been planted in the last century by the lady, Deidre St. Leger, who had had the uncanny ability to make things grow. Legend had it, the blossoms had been watered by her fierce tears, nourished by the spot where her blood had been spilled.

The garden continued to thrive in spite of Anatole's neglect. He avoided it for the most part, the fragrance of the flowers like poison to his soul, infecting him with bitter memories and regrets, the mood of black self-pity that he so despised.

But tonight, for the first time that he could remember, he did not feel weighted down by the past, the strange legacy that haunted his family with tragedy and sorrow.

Anatole glanced at the ormolu clock on the mantel. How long had it been since his blushing and nervous bride had vanished upstairs to prepare herself for bed? For *his* bed. Five minutes ago? Ten?

Long enough for Will and the other footman Eamon to have nearly cleared away the remains of the bridal supper. Crystal, china, and tarnished silver that had not seen the light of day for years littered the surface of a mahogany table vast enough to have banqueted King Arthur and every one of his blasted knights. Dragging all that finery out had been a waste, along with the many courses of food congealed in the dishes.

The supper had gone mostly untasted. Madeline had picked at her food like a sparrow. As for himself, Anatole was usually an excellent trencherman, but this evening, he found he had little appetite.

At least not for food.

He scooped his brandy glass up from the table. Cradling it between two of his fingers, he took a long swallow. The golden liquid sent a rush of heat through his veins. As if he needed it. His blood had been fired with impatience ever since leaving the church, so much so that he wondered what prevented him from setting all consideration aside and rushing upstairs. Taking his bride the way his thundering pulses demanded that he do.

His promise, he supposed, and the memory of a pair of wide green eyes, the slight tremor in Madeline's voice when she had complained that he was too rough with his embraces. The criticism had stung him to challenge her into demonstrating her notion of a kiss.

Damnation! It hadn't even been a proper kiss at all, so chaste, just a hint of what sweet warmth lay beyond the barrier of her sealed lips. Not enough to satisfy a man's hunger, only to tease it. And yet . . . he'd been strangely moved by her kiss. Other desires had stirred inside him, confusing and unsettling. The urge to gather his delicate bride into his arms and to woo her, to please her, to offer her any manner of rash promises. Like the pledge that they would find some compromise between them. He, who had never compromised with anyone in his life, man or woman.

To compromise with gentleness? It was not even a vow he was sure he could keep. Anatole drained his brandy glass and set it down with a sharp snap. Christ, he felt so raw and edgy, anyone would think that he was the one about to lose his virginity tonight.

Perhaps he should have done a few things to ready himself. He rubbed his fingertips along the square line of his jaw, frowning at the hint of bristle, then held both of his large hands palm-upward to examine them. They were more the hands of a groom or a farm laborer than a gentleman. Couldn't he have done something to soften those blasted calluses? Applied a poultice perhaps? And what about a night shift? He was so used to sleeping in the raw, it had never occurred to him to purchase such a garment and—

And what in sweet hell was he thinking of? Anatole lowered his hands, stunned by the direction his mind had taken, wondering where these fool notions were coming from.

As if he didn't know, he thought, clenching his jaw. They were coming from her. Madeline. His chosen bride. His woman of flame. If he didn't take care, the next thing he knew—

Anatole stiffened, checking his discomfiting thoughts about Madeline as his keen inner sense honed in on a fresh disturbance. Footsteps in the outer hall. Someone moving through the castle who did not belong there this time of night. Anatole pressed his fingertips to his forehead, concentrating.

It was . . . Fitzleger. Anatole's brow furrowed into a deep scowl. What the deuce was the Bride Finder doing here, tonight of all nights? He tracked Fitzleger's shuffling steps toward the imposing double doors that led to the dining room. With a quick glance Anatole flung open one of them just as the old man reached the other side.

Will and the other footman looked up from their work, mildly surprised to see the vicar suddenly silhouetted upon the threshold. But most of the servants at Castle Leger were inured to stranger things. With a shrug the two lads went back to their task of loading soiled dishes onto trays.

After a nod of greeting, Fitzleger skirted past them and headed down to the far end of the chamber where Anatole awaited him with locked arms and a far from welcoming expression.

Hatless, his wings of hair ruffled by the night wind, the little vicar lacked his usual air of serenity. He appeared ill at ease, bursting out before Anatole could even speak.

"Your pardon for this intrusion, my lord. I did not like to disturb you, but a matter has arisen that has been worrying me all day. I could not rest easy until I consulted you."

"Now?" Anatole demanded. "Could it not wait until the morrow? Damn it, man, this *is* my wedding night."

"I am aware of that. That is why I am so relieved to have caught your lordship before—before—" A hint of pink stole into Fitzleger's cheeks. "Before you became preoccupied."

Anatole wished fervently that were the case. His eyes drifted again to the clock. Did Madeline now lie trembling in her bed, her supple warm body pressed between cool sheets?

He stifled a low curse and heartily wished Fitzleger at the devil. With an exasperated sigh Anatole said, "All right, old man. I can accord you fifteen minutes, but no more."

"In privacy. If you please," the vicar added meekly.

Anatole turned toward the footmen and bellowed out, "Will! Eamon!"

Catching the two lads' attention, he ordered them to finish their work later and motioned them out of the room. As soon as the door closed behind them, he all but thrust Fitzleger into one of the side chairs at the table and poured him out a glass of wine.

He barely gave the old man a chance to taste the burgundy liquid before saying, "All right. So what the devil's amiss?"

"I hope nothing more than an old man's foolish fears, but . . ." Fitzleger fortified himself with a swallow of the wine before continuing, "Something odd happened at the church this morning."

"So it did. I was married."

But Anatole's quip evoked no response from Fitzleger. The vicar stared into his wine cup, shadows darkening his saintly blue eyes, like storm clouds shifting through heaven. The old man *was* troubled about something. Deeply troubled.

Anatole drew up a chair beside him and sank into it.

"Tell me what happened," he commanded in gentler tones.

Fitzleger set down his cup, a tremor coursing through his frail hands. "After you and Madeline left this morning, my lord, I remarked a strange woman passing through the churchyard. Cloaked, hooded, I never saw her features. Only what she was doing. Mourning over a grave. She left a rose on the marker of Tyrus Mortmain."

Both of Anatole's brows shot upward. *Mortmain*—a name he'd been taught to fear and loathe from the cradle, ancient enemies, a treacherous, scurrilous tribe that had ever coveted the lands of Castle Leger. The blood feud between the St. Leger and Mortmain families had become almost legendary, spanning the centuries. Whenever Anatole's grandfather had heard the name mentioned, he'd been wont to turn and spit upon the floor.

Anatole didn't spit. He merely cursed. "Tyrus Mortmain! That black-hearted bastard? Who would weep over his grave except for a God-cursed fool or—or . . ."

"Or another Mortmain," Fitzleger finished the grim thought for him.

The notion gave Anatole pause for a moment, but he was quick to reject it.

"Nay, impossible. The Mortmains are all dead, the last of them destroyed years ago. I was always told that after the murder of my Uncle Wyatt, my grandfather tracked Sir Tyrus back to his manor house to put an end to his villainy. You were there yourself that night, Fitzleger, were you not?"

"Aye, I remember too well. Rather than be taken and brought to justice, Tyrus set his own house afire, trapping everyone inside, his servants, even his own wife and daughters."

"And none could have survived?"

"From that terrible conflagration?" Fitzleger shuddered. "No, only Tyrus was pulled from the rubble, alive, but badly burned. He lived long enough to repent, asking to be laid to rest in the churchyard. Your grandfather was angry with me for granting the request, but how could I do otherwise?"

Fitzleger sighed. "I held a simple service for Sir Tyrus to which no one came. So who could this unfortunate creature be that would come sobbing over him now? After all these years. She vanished so quickly when I approached, I almost feared she might be a . . . a ghost."

"Unlikely, Fitzleger. My Uncle Hadrian always says that was the only decent thing about Mortmains. When they're dead, they stay that way."

"Then, who might this woman be?"

"I don't know." Anatole sagged back in his chair, rubbing a tense spot between his shoulder blades. He'd had enough trouble all these years, just contending with his peculiar St. Leger heritage. But at least he'd been spared dealing with one torment. Mortmains. He was damned if he'd be plagued with them now.

"The woman was probably no one," he muttered. "Some wandering gypsy or half-witted wench stumbling about the churchyard who couldn't read and found the wrong grave."

With great reluctance he offered, "But if it makes you feel better, Fitzleger, I will check further into the matter."

"Thank you, my lord. It would greatly relieve my mind if you did so as soon as possible."

"I trust you don't require that I set out immediately?" Anatole asked dryly.

"Ah, no. The morrow will be soon enough." Fitzleger smiled, some of his serenity restored. He shifted to the edge of his chair, preparing to rise. "Now, you will forgive me, my lord. I have kept you away from your good lady long enough."

"Indeed you have. I ordered her up to bed some time ago."

Fitzleger sank back in his chair, his eyes flying wide with shock. "You—you *ordered* her?"

"Aye."

"Like one of your servants?"

Anatole caught the faint note of censure in the vicar's voice and stiffened. "I am accustomed to rapping out commands. I cannot change my habits for one small wife."

"But, my lord, some things must change when a man marries."

"Such as?"

"Well, your household for one. I was most distressed when I heard about the abrupt departure of Madeline's maid and cousin."

"It wasn't my fault. It's not as if I chased those fool women off with a loaded blunderbuss."

"I'm sure your lordship didn't need to," Fitzleger murmured. "But you must see that now that you have a wife, you are going to need more servants."

"I have plenty of servants."

"I mean female servants."

"No! I may have been forced to take a bride, but I'm not going to have this castle overrun by hoards of bickering, gossiping women."

"But you cannot expect Madeline to live in an all male household."

"Why not? I've managed to do so quite comfortably all these years." But Anatole was being unreasonable, and even he knew it. Resisting the suggestion a moment longer, he conceded with a gesture of defeat. "Very well. One chit from the village if you can find one brave enough to come here. One wench to wait upon Madeline and act as her maid, but that is all."

He shoved to his feet, casting an impatient glance toward the door. "Now, is there anything else?"

"Yes, I fear that there is. Much more that you need to understand about ladies, my lord. They are very different from men."

"Isn't it a little late for this kind of lecture, Fitzleger?" Anatole drawled. "You should have come around with it when I was thirteen."

"When you were thirteen?" Fitzleger looked aghast. "You mean that was the first time you—Never mind. I don't want to know." The vicar flung up one hand as though to ward off any possible answer.

"What I am trying to say, my lord, is that when a man is in an amorous mood, to him there is only the present. But a lady's receptiveness at her bedchamber door often depends on how she has been treated during the day."

"What do you think I've been doing to Madeline? Beating her?"

"That would have been difficult, since I gather that you were not even with her this afternoon." Fitzleger eyed him sternly. "You went out riding, sir."

"Have you set spies upon me now, old man?"

"No, my sexton happened to notice you galloping along the shore and mentioned the fact to me."

"What of it? I often do so."

"But on your wedding day? To thus abandon your bride?"

"I might have been able to take her along with me," Anatole reminded him tersely, "if you had found me a bride that wasn't terrified of horses. Instead you brought me one whose idea of a pleasant afternoon is sipping tea and discussing dead poets. I don't have the least notion what to do with a female like that—well, except for one thing. But I hardly think you would have wished me to cart Madeline upstairs and set upon her like a rutting stag in the middle of the day."

"I wouldn't want you setting upon her that way at any time," Fitzleger replied.

Since that was the thought uppermost in Anatole's mind at the moment, he felt a guilty flush sting his cheeks. He paced down the length of the table, smacking the backs of the chairs with his palm.

"What more do you want from me, Fitzleger? You know Madeline was never the sort of bride I wanted, but I went through with the marriage anyway. I even gave her the damned sword."

That at least appeared to please the old man. "And how did Madeline respond?"

"She was damned surprised, as any woman in her right mind would be." Anatole was forced to add with a certain grudging respect, "However, I'll wager she was the first St. Leger bride who ever had the wit to ask for the scabbard to go along with it."

Fitzleger beamed. "Ah! There, you see. I told you Madeline was possessed of a great, good sense. You must realize now that all your fears about revealing to her your family heritage were groundless."

Anatole compressed his lips, avoiding the old man's eyes.

"My lord?" Fitzleger asked anxiously. "You did finally tell her everything . . . didn't you?"

"I tried. But it didn't do a damn bit of good. The cursed woman has an answer for everything. She doesn't believe a word I say."

"Your lordship has the means to make her believe."

"I didn't see any reason for forcing the issue."

"Didn't see any reason? My lord, if you continue to guard your secrets, keep your distance, how do you expect Madeline to learn to love you?"

"I have no desire to be loved! It will be enough if she doesn't fear me."

Anatole rounded on the old man. "Don't you see that Madeline's skepticism can be a good thing? It might protect her from ever having to deal with this St. Leger madness. Her disbelief will act as her shield."

"Her shield or your mask?"

A most gently voiced question, but Fitzleger's eyes were far too perceptive, probing deeper into the truth of Anatole's motives than he wished to go himself.

"Have done, Fitzleger. You fulfilled your part of the bargain. You found me my bride. How I choose to deal with her is my concern."

Signaling that he wished to hear no more, Anatole flung the door open and preceded Fitzleger through it. Snatching up a lantern, he lighted the way out to the stable yard himself, pausing to frown up at the sky. Strange what lectures and mention of Mortmains could do to blacken a man's mood.

The night that had seemed velvet with promise suddenly appeared vast and threatening, the moon's brilliance dimmed by smokelike wisps of clouds. Even the stars looked cold and unfriendly.

Anatole ordered one of his burly grooms to saddle up and escort the vicar home. The rutted path to the village could be treacherous enough at the best of times.

Not, he assured himself, because he was the least worried about the old man. No, he just wanted to make sure Fitzleger and his infernal sermons were returned safely to the rectory and stayed there.

Even as he helped the vicar into the saddle, the little clergyman had to have one last word.

"You will try to be gentle with the girl?" Fitzleger pleaded.

"As much as my nature will allow," Anatole slapped the mare on the rump and sent the vicar lurching into the night, hard followed by Anatole's groom. As Fitzleger vanished into the darkness, Anatole wondered what had really brought the Bride Finder to his door tonight? Concern about Mortmains? Or concern for Madeline?

Shaking his head, Anatole returned to the house, extinguishing the lantern and setting it on the side table. The hall was almost eerily silent at this hour. Madeline of a certainty must be ready for him by now. In fact . . . Anatole grimaced. He'd be fortunate if she hadn't fallen asleep waiting.

As he strode toward the stairs, he heard the soft clicking of paws on the marble floor behind him. He glanced around to find Ranger hard on his heels.

Like Fitzleger, it was a rare thing for the old dog to stir himself from his position by the fireside at this time of night. Safe from prying eyes, Anatole hunkered down to indulge the animal with a show of attention. Scratching the hound behind his shaggy ear, he said gruffly, "What do you want, eh?"

Ranger gazed up at him, a world of devotion and canine wisdom gleaming through his single good eye.

Anatole's cousin Roman St. Leger had recommended more than once that the old hound be put to cliff. But as Ranger's tongue bathed his hand with rough affection, Anatole smiled and thought that he'd far rather tie the all too elegant Roman in a sack and toss him into the sea.

He rumpled the dog's dome-shaped head and murmured, "So I suppose you too have come after me with advice on how I should be handling my bride."

"Oh, no, my lord. I would never presume." Will Sparkins's startled voice echoed down the hall as the lad emerged from the back stairs leading to the servant's quarters.

"I was talking to the dog, Will," Anatole said, straightening and feeling foolish.

But the earnest young footman only gave a solemn nod. "I heard tell how Mr. Caleb St. Leger often speaks to animals."

"Yes, but the alarming thing about my cousin is that he insists they answer him back."

Will grinned, then asked, "Is it all right if I finish clearing off the dining table now, sir?"

"Yes, I was just on my way upstairs."

"Aye, I figured you'd be heading up to bed soon. To—to sleep," Will added hastily. One of the older boys or the stable hands would likely have risked a smirk. Young Will merely blushed fire red.

Anatole wondered irritably if everyone at Castle Leger and in the village was taking such keen interest in the master bedding his bride tonight. Feeling somewhat self-conscious, he ordered Will to keep Ranger from following him. As Will collared the dog, Anatole turned to mount the stairs. He had not gone more than a few steps when he felt a tingling sensation.

A sensation that had nothing to do with his anticipation of Madeline's charms, but one that was all too familiar and far more disturbing. An ominous prickling behind his eyes. A warning. And this time the source of it was . . . Will.

No! Not now, damn it! Anatole ground his fingertips against his eyes. He could not be going to experience another bout of his curse. Not tonight of all nights.

He took another step up the next riser, determined to ignore it. But the feeling only intensified, pins and needles of fire jabbing inside his head.

"Will!"

The lad was urging Ranger toward the dining room, but he froze at once, glancing back. "Sir?"

Anatole glanced down into his youthful features and knew a sense of sick dread. Let the boy go, a voice inside him pleaded. Whatever was to be, Anatole would as soon not know. The pain would recede after a while if he could but just ignore it.

But it was like trying to ignore the need to breathe. Anatole trudged back down the steps and spoke in a voice dulled with the resignation of bitter experience.

"Come here, lad."

The footman approached and stood before Anatole as trustingly as Ranger would have done. Anatole brushed Will's straw-colored hair from his eyes, the ache now more in Anatole's heart than in his mind.

It needed the crystal and a deliberate effort on his part to see his own future. But for others, the visions often took him unaware, and he had to look no further for the devil's medium than his own fingertips.

Laying his hand upon Will's brow, Anatole brought his gaze into focus, delving deep into the pupils of the boy's eyes. Prospero was said to have had the power to mesmerize this way, to take over the mind. Anatole's talent was more simple and more devastating. To rob someone of their future.

He felt himself dwindling, telescoping into Will's eyes, and then the vision came hard and fast in a sickening blur. Will at the woodpile. The sharp gleam of the axblade. The slip of the fingers. Will's shriek of agony. The crimson stain blossoming over his leg.

As the image faded, Anatole felt drained. His hand shook as he dropped it from the boy's brow.

"Stay away from the woodpile," he rasped.

Will paled, but asked for no explanations. None of Anatole's servants would have dared to do so. The lad wrung his ungainly hands and quavered, "But—but, sir, Mr. Trigghorne will have my hide if I don't tend to my chores, chopping wood and—"

"Damn you, boy. I'll have your hide if you disobey me." Anatole seized Will by his shirtfront, hauling him close until the lad's frightened face was only inches from his own. "If you set one foot near an ax, I'll take a whip to you. I'll lock you in the tower until you're an old man. I'll—"

Anatole paused for breath, the wildness of his threats only equaled by his despair, by the knowledge that no matter what he did, what commands he gave, nothing could be prevented. He had as much chance of saving Will's leg as he'd had of saving the life of Marie Kennack.

The fury ebbed out of him as quickly as it had come, leaving only the sense of helplessness. He released Will's shirt, smoothing out the coarse linen, his unsteady fingers coming to rest on the boy's shoulder.

"Just do as I tell you," Anatole said hoarsely. "All right?"

Will stepped back and nodded, his fearful eyes never leaving Anatole's face as he stumbled away, disappearing into the dining room to finish his chores. Only when Will had gone did Anatole permit his fierce facade to crumble, sagging against the newel post of the stair for support, burying his face against his arm.

He was just damn glad no one else had been about to witness his weakness or this most recent display of his damnable St. Leger gift. Especially not his bride. He'd meant what he'd said to Fitzleger earlier. He intended to protect Madeline from this aspect of himself for as long as he could.

But the Bride Finder's question came back to haunt him.

"Her shield or your mask?"

Aye, his mask, then, Anatole admitted bitterly. For it was clear he needed one. What manner of man was he to be possessed of such black powers?

Not a man at all, but a monster. He had that on the best authority. His own mother.

Something cold nudged Anatole's hand, and he became aware of Ranger beside him, whining softly, bewildered, but trying to offer comfort.

Anatole thrust the dog away from him. All he wanted was Madeline. Needed her with a depth and ache that alarmed even him, needed to drown himself in the sweet, clear reason of her eyes. To lose himself in the soft smiles of a woman too rational to believe in ghosts, legends, or family curses. To pretend for just a little while that she was right.

Bolting up the stairs, Anatole stalked through the upper hall. As he paused outside Madeline's bedchamber door, it was all he could do not to thrust it open.

He forced himself to knock instead and waited, his pulse quickening.

But there was no answer.

He knocked again, a little more sharply this time. Still no response. He scowled, trying to probe past the barrier with the power of his mind, but he had no more luck divining Madeline that way than he had ever had.

The only presence he detected was Trigghorne's, the surly old servant lurking at the far end of the hall, watching him.

"Your lady ain't in there, master," Trigg called out, sounding somewhat surprised and reproachful. "I thought you'd have known that."

Anatole turned to glower at him. "What do you mean she's not in there? Where else would she be?"

Trigg stepped forward, his scrawny chest puffing out with righteous indignation. "Why, she's gone back to where she spent most of the afternoon. The library. Your lady is book mad. I heard tell about such Lunnon women. They're called bluestockings, young master, and if you don't put a stop to such nonsense right now—"

"I don't need any more advice from anyone regarding my wife," Anatole bit out through clenched teeth. Shoving past Trigg, he charged back down the hall.

Taking the stairs two at a time, he descended, humiliation fueling his mounting anger. He'd spent all this time, pacing, waiting, curbing his impatience. And all the while, Madeline had been off somewhere, her nose shoved in a book. Well, that's what a man got for attempting to be sensitive and considerate. Damnation!

Storming toward the back of the house, Anatole fetched up outside the library, the door looming up before him like a wall of bitter memory. It was a room he seldom entered, that selfsame door too often in the past shut in his face.

After his mother's death, the library had become his father's refuge, the place where Lyndon St. Leger had hid himself from the world, but mostly from his own son.

The words of accusation had never been spoken, but Anatole had always seen it there, darkening his father's eyes.

"If not for you, your mother might have lived. . . ."

But the gentle Lyndon had never been one to rage, to pour out his grief and sorrow. He had merely retreated from life, shutting himself up with his books, closing Anatole out.

It had been painful enough having his father do that, Anatole thought, clenching his jaw. He'd be damned if he was going to have a wife who did the same thing.

CHAPTER EIGHT

The library was an unexpected treasure trove of shelves reaching from floor to ceiling, books crammed into every available wall space, even above the doorway. The place filled Madeline with the first delight she'd known since her arrival at Castle Leger. Despite the stale odor that clung to the chamber, the cobwebs of neglect clinging to the volumes, she felt at home here, surrounded by old and trusted friends. Chaucer, Milton, Shakespeare, Dante . . .

From now on she'd make certain the room was aired, a fire lit here every day, the books dusted. But for tonight . . . She cast an anxious glance toward the candles flickering in the wall sconce, burning lower, burning her time away along with them.

Perched on the top of a tall ladder, she yanked down another volume, the dust tickling her nostrils. She ran her hand lovingly, almost reverently, down the leather-bound spine. Books, her best companions, the one true solace through much of her life.

But she had a sinking feeling that for once the knowledge she sought was not to be found pressed between any of these pages. A simple basic knowledge such as exactly what was a woman to do with an ardent bridegroom on their wedding night? The question alone was enough to stir flutterings in her stomach, a stomach largely empty.

She'd spent most of supper with her hands clenched in her lap, sitting in state opposite her new husband. Anatole had been lost at the far end of that incredibly long table, making a natural flow of conversation impossible.

As if it wouldn't have been in any case. Her husband was a man of few words, but he'd spoken volumes with his eyes. Those uncanny eyes of his that had never seemed to leave her face throughout the meal. Dark, hungry, searching, rousing an odd warmth in her, dewing her skin with a fine sheen of perspiration. Even though her mind had no notion what to do with such a bold, strapping man, it was as if her body possessed a knowledge all of its own.

Now, if only her body would be good enough to share that information in more specific terms. A wry smile crooked Madeline's lips. Her sister Juliette had warned her she'd come to this pass eventually. Juliette had always teased, "You're going to be sorry someday, Mad. Wasting all your time reading instead of paying attention to more worldly matters. Someday you're going to need to know things that aren't stuffed in one of your precious books."

Incredibly it seemed that Juliette had been right. Madeline skimmed through the pages of Rabelais with despair, her eyes no longer focusing on the words. If only she'd had the comfort of one other woman in the house tonight. Preferably an older, more experienced female.

Or, Madeline thought even more wistfully, if only Anatole had turned out to be the gentle bridegroom Madeline had expected. Ah, but he hadn't, and she was foolish to keep fretting over that fact. She squared her shoulders. The man was what he was, and she would have to learn to deal with him as such. He was not the complete ogre she'd initially thought him to be.

There had been that fleeting moment in the church after that strange sword ceremony when Anatole had been almost gentle. The kiss they'd shared had been soft, sweet, and even though Anatole had complained about it, he'd said that they could find some manner of compromise between his fierce ways and her need for tenderness.

That thought was all that kept her from fleeing into the night in a state of total panic. Sighing, Madeline replaced the Rabelais, but she couldn't resist trying just one more volume. A folio of Shakespeare's *Antony and Cleopatra*.

She was easing the book from the shelf when the library door flew open with a loud crash. The reverberations caused the ladder to tremble beneath her. Madeline clutched at both the book and the topmost rung to keep her balance.

Her gaze flew to the doorway, and her heart turned over. Her bridegroom loomed in the threshold, casting a long shadow into the room.

And the expression on his face looked far from compromising.

"Anatole," she gasped.

He stepped inside the room, his black hair flowing back from the taut angles of his face, his heavy brows crashed together like a peal of thunder. The door seemed to slam closed behind him of its own accord.

"What the devil are you doing in here?" he asked.

"Why, I—I—" Madeline stammered, feeling as guilty as though she'd been caught stealing books. She knew an absurd urge to hide the one she held behind her back. "I am doing what one usually does in a library, my lord."

It occurred to her that he probably didn't know what that was, so she added, "Reading."

Anatole glowered up at her. He stalked toward her with a warrior's stride, hands planted on the flat plane of his hips. Madeline clutched the top of the ladder, feeling like a kitten treed by a great snarling mastiff. Now, what had happened to make him so angry, she wondered in dismay? Would there ever be any comprehending the man's black moods?

She went on desperately, "You have an excellent library here, my lord. I was so surprised. It didn't seem like anything that you would—I—I mean . . ."

"Anything that I would bother with? It isn't. This was my father's world, not mine," Anatole said with a bitterness Madeline was unable to understand.

"Well, it's wonderful," she concluded weakly. "I can see myself spending many happy hours here."

Anatole's eyes flashed dark fire. The ladder must have been more unstable than she'd imagined, for it began to sway wildly beneath her. With a startled cry Madeline grabbed for the shelves, sending books flying as she tried to maintain her balance, but to no avail.

She tumbled from the rung only to be caught hard against Anatole's body. She felt giddy, helpless for a moment, held suspended against his powerful frame. Then he plunked her down on the carpet, his hands still gripped possessively about her waist.

"You won't be spending any time here at all," he growled. "Not if it means neglecting your duties as my wife."

"What duties?" she asked in astonishment. "What have I neglected?"

"My bed."

His bluntness brought the fire to her cheeks. Her eyes roved over him, taking in the details of his appearance. Clad only in his breeches, boots, and shirt, the topmost buttons were undone to reveal a disturbing glimpse of hair-roughened chest. Like a warlord who'd started stripping himself for action, only to find the enemy flown.

But she wasn't his enemy. She was his wife.

"I'm sorry," she said. "I came into the library, and I fear I lost track of time. I wasn't tired."

"I didn't want you in my bed to sleep."

"I know that." Madeline raised her head, meeting his gaze with a calm she didn't feel. "And so you've tracked me down to fling me over your shoulder and cart me upstairs?"

His hands on her waist tightened. "If necessary."

"It won't be," she said sadly. "I am fully prepared to—to submit."

"Good." He hauled her into his arms, taking her mouth in a kiss that savored more of conquest than any sweeter emotion. So much for all his promises to be more gentle, Madeline thought, her heart breaking.

But she held herself still, offering herself up to his embrace as rigidly as any martyr consigned to the flames. Her lack of response only seemed to fuel his passion. He breached the seal of her lips, his tongue invading her mouth with a fierce desperation that stirred strange, conflicting desires inside her, the desire to flee, the desire to melt closer against him.

But when he reached up to cup her breast, alarm won out; it was a touch too intimate, too new. Struggling wildly, she managed to break free and backed away. But the bookcase behind her allowed her little room for retreat.

Anatole stalked after her, pinning her with his brooding gaze.

"I *will* have you, Madeline," he said. "I've waited and dreamed of this night for far too long."

"So have I," she cried. "But our dreams were not the same."

"Obviously not."

Madeline gasped as he plunged his hand down her bodice, but only to draw forth the miniature portrait and dangle it accusingly before her.

"Why do you continue to wear this God-cursed thing?"

How had he even known that she still had it? Madeline wondered. Remembering how brutally Anatole had treated her cherished portrait last time, Madeline snatched the miniature away from him, cupping it in her hands.

"I continue to wear it because I like it," she said. "It's a lovely painting."

"I won't have my wife mooning over the image of another man." His hand closed over her wrist as though he meant to pry her fingers open.

Desperately Madeline tightened her grip. "It's not another man. It's a likeness of you."

"Don't be a fool, damn it! You can see plainly that it's not."

"Then, you should curse the artist instead of me."

"I have! Ever since I painted the—" Swearing under his breath, Anatole broke off what he'd been about to say.

But it was too late. Madeline had heard enough to gape at him in astonishment. "You painted the portrait yourself?" she asked, taking no pains to conceal her incredulity.

He didn't answer her. Shame washed over his features. He released her wrist and stepped back. Madeline slowly uncurled her fingers, trying to reconcile the delicate brush strokes of the painting with Anatole's large rough hands. Was it possible a man as fierce and ruthless as Anatole could have created the face that had captured her heart and imagination? The expression exquisitely gentle, the mouth so sensitive, the eyes filled with a haunting sorrow the way . . . Madeline's breath caught in her throat. The way Anatole's eyes were now.

The barrier of his pride was down, allowing her a glimpse of a far different man. Lonely, vulnerable, unsure of himself.

Then he turned away, flinging up one hand as though he would shield himself from her searching gaze.

"Never mind," he muttered. "Keep the damn portrait, and let your dreams warm your bed. I wish you joy of them."

He strode toward the door. He was offering her a reprieve. Madeline should have been grateful, and yet . . .

She stared at the miniature, the Reverend Fitzleger's words echoing through her mind. *'Tis the portrait of his soul.*

"Anatole!" she cried out. "Wait!"

He didn't turn around, but he hesitated long enough for Madeline to lift her skirts and rush after him. All anger had drained from his face, leaving only an expression of great weariness.

She held the portrait out to him and said, "You really did paint this?"

"Aye," he replied dully.

Dozens of questions rushed into her head, but how could she possibly ask him what she most wanted to know? Why? How, with such incredible skill, had he come to depict features so different from his own?

"You intended it to be a self-portrait, then?" she inquired hesitantly. "You did it by looking into a mirror?"

He gave a harsh laugh, raking back his black tangle of hair, touching his scar. "Does it look as though I had?"

"I only thought . . . well, you might have painted this when you were younger."

"I was but fifteen, but I never resembled the face in that painting, even then."

"Fifteen!" Madeline exclaimed in awe. She'd known many acclaimed artists in London whose work did not display half as much talent. "Dear heavens, you were a prodigy."

"I was a fool," he said. "Wasting my time painting images of the man I could never be. The sort of man that . . ." He reached out to touch her hair, his calloused fingers snagging on a silken tendril, his eyes darkening with a hopeless longing. He allowed his hand to fall back to his side.

"The sort of man who wouldn't terrify his bride into hiding in the library on their wedding night."

"I wasn't hiding. And I'm not terrified of you."

"No?" A sad smile touched his lips.

"Well, not *that* terrified," she amended. "I only came to the library seeking information."

"What kind of information?"

"About our wedding night." Madeline tussled with her own pride before blurting out, "I don't have the least notion what I'm supposed to do."

When Anatole's brow knit in confusion, she ducked her head, her voice coming out in accents of muffled embarrassment. "I don't know how to—to consummate our marriage."

She braced herself, waiting for Anatole to break into a gale of laughter. But a silence settled over the room, one that stretched out for so long, she was forced to risk a peek at him.

He stood frozen, completely thunderstruck. He opened his mouth as if to speak, then closed it again, finally protesting, "But surely your mother must have explained matters to you."

"My mother was always too busy selecting a new gown or attending the latest salon to ever be bothered explaining anything."

"But your sisters. Fitzleger told me you had married sisters. Surely they—"

"Louisa and Juliette?" Madeline said, appalled by the mere suggestion. "They are younger than I. I have always been the one to give advice. I could hardly go to them and admit that—that—"

"That there was something you didn't know?" Anatole filled in dryly.

"Exactly!"

"Then, what in thunderation were you planning to do?"

Madeline supposed this was not a good time to remind him that she'd expected her husband to be a different sort of man, tender and patient about initiating his bride into the mysteries of married life. She moved past him, fidgeting with the ribbon that held the portrait.

"I was hoping that my maid Estelle might have been able to give me a hint or two. Frenchwomen seem born knowing about such things. But since she is gone, I had no choice but to come to the library to research the problem."

Anatole gazed about him, appearing to study his library with a new respect. "I have books about *that*?"

"No," Madeline said glumly. "At least, nothing specific enough. The best I found was a reference in Chaucer to something he called 'a merrie fit.' But that's not at all helpful."

"No, I suppose it wouldn't be." A thoughtful frown creased his brow.

Madeline had expected him to be amused by her predicament. Or else impatient and annoyed. The last thing she'd expected was that he might be as nonplussed as she was. An awful thought struck her.

"Dear Lord," she murmured. "You're not a virgin, too, are you?"

"Of course not! However, my experience with well-bred ladies is not wide. I have never bedded a woman innocent of the ways of men."

"Will it be so very different, then?" Madeline asked anxiously.

"If I've never bedded a virgin before, how the deuce should I know?" He took to prowling about the room, restlessly fingering the books she'd discarded. He fetched up in front of the window, shoving back the heavy must-laden draperies to stare out into the night.

As Madeline watched him, realization dawned on her, one that flooded her with amazement. Beneath all his fierce male bluster, Anatole was as nervous and uncertain about tonight as she was. Only while she had sought her answers in books, he seemed to be seeking his in the darkness of the land beyond the glass.

Candlelight limned his profile, somehow rendering his harsh features more vulnerable than she'd ever seen him before. Despite the broad reach of his shoulders and his towering height, she found herself thinking instead of a fifteen-year-old boy that had once wandered the rooms of this vast empty house. So lonely, he'd spent his time with watercolor and brush, trying to redesign his own face.

What dark forces had shaped that boy into the man that now stood before her, this man with his scarred face and haunted eyes, who loved horses and hated books, whose mind seemed a battleground, torn between his own imperious will and ancient superstitions? There was obviously much more to the fierce-tempered Anatole than Madeline had ever imagined. So much about him that she did not yet understand. But if he was ever truly going to be her husband, she needed to try.

Gazing down at the portrait one last time, she slowly removed it and laid it upon the library table. Drifting closer to Anatole, she touched him lightly on the sleeve. Gathering up her courage, she said, "We are two reasonably intelligent people, my lord. Surely we can find some way to muddle through this wedding night of ours."

She summoned up a smile, her hand remarkably steady as she held it out to him. "It is getting late. I think that it is time that we went to bed."

Anatole stared at her proffered hand as though afraid if he dared reach for it, it would be withdrawn. Then slowly, carefully, he engulfed her fingers in the warm strength of his own.

"Aye, lady," he said huskily, raising her hand to his lips.

Picking up a candle to light the way, he escorted her from the library with a solemn courtesy. Hand in hand, they crossed the silent hall to face the dark at the top of the stairs together.

Madeline's bedchamber already seemed to have taken on the aura of her presence, her fragrance lingering in the air, the dresser strewn with ivory-handled hairbrushes, ribbons, and other female lacy things, as soft and mysterious to Anatole as his bride herself.

Madeline stood near the foot of her bed, facing him, the glow of a single candle illuminating her look of shy expectancy. Anatole realized it was up to him to make the next move. After all, he was the one who was supposed to know what he was doing here.

But all he seemed able to do was stare at her, clumsy as some awestruck peasant lad. He flexed his hand, still warm from the gentle imprint of her fingers. He couldn't remember the last time anyone had dared reach for his hand. Perhaps no one ever had.

The gesture left him shaken. He'd spent so much of this day imagining taking her, it had never occurred to him that Madeline might end by taking him, in some subtle way he did not fully understand.

As the minutes stretched out, Madeline became nervous beneath his regard. Fretting with the trim on her gown, she asked, "Should I fetch my nightgown now?"

"No," he said hoarsely. "You won't be needing one."

"But what am I to wear to—Oh!" Her cheeks flamed bright red as realization appeared to strike her.

Wonderful. Anatole grimaced. Why didn't he just announce that he wanted her naked under him and be done with it? He closed the distance between them, slipping his arms around her in what he hoped was a reassuring manner. But his hands felt wooden and awkward, daunted by the sheer weight of her innocence. She understood nothing of the kind of desire that burned inside him. One wrong move on his part, one rough caress, and he'd shatter the tentative bond beginning to form between them.

He'd cursed himself for a fool earlier when he ended up blurting out to her the secret of that portrait. But in some odd way, it had made things better. She'd left the miniature downstairs on the library table, forgotten. It was almost as though he'd vanquished a rival.

Although she was tense, Madeline nestled closer against him. Her breasts grazing his chest proved a sweet torment, and he longed to devour her face with fierce hot kisses.

Instead he forced himself to brush his lips chastely against her forehead. Running his hands over her back, he began to tug at the laces that held her gown.

"Wait!" she said, bracing her hands against his chest and glancing up at him. "Could you explain first?"

"Explain what?" he murmured, intoxicated by her sweet feminine scent, by the feel of soft womanly curves only a bit of silk and lace away.

"Explain what it is we're going to do."

The blood that had been warming so nicely through Anatole's veins turned to ice. He stared down at her in horror. No. She couldn't possibly be expecting him to talk about *that,* could she?

But it was obvious from the earnest expression in her eyes that she could and did. Anatole stifled a groan. Only Madeline would want a rational explanation for something as irrational as the mating process, the primal urges that drew men and women together.

"Please," she added as though sensing he was about to bluster out a refusal. "It would make me feel so much better."

Anatole stilled his hands at her waist and swallowed hard. He had no trouble discussing the most bawdy facts of life with his grooms and stable hands. Why was the prospect so much more intimidating with his own wife?

"Well," he said at last. "What happens between a man and a woman . . . It is just something natural."

"Yes?" Madeline nodded encouragingly when he hesitated.

Anatole's eyes roved about the bedchamber, seeking inspiration. He racked his brain, trying to remember how he had obtained his first awareness of what his own father had always delicately referred to as "country matters."

"Surely at some time you must have observed the behavior of bitches?" he asked in pure desperation.

"Bitches?" Madeline repeated weakly.

"Hunting hounds. The way they breed."

"We never had any hunting hounds. Only a little King Charles spaniel." A worried furrow appeared in Madeline's brow. "However, Muffin did have the strangest affinity for the butler's leg."

"I don't have any interest in your legs," Anatole hurried to reassure her. "At least not that way."

Pacing a few steps away from her, he blew out a gust of breath and tried again. "What about horses, then? Have you ever—" An unfortunate image rose in his mind of the violent way his own stallion mounted a mare when put to stud.

"No, never mind about that," he said hastily. This was ridiculous, he thought, dragging his hand back through his hair. He was actually starting to feel beads of perspiration gather on his brow. He'd never been much of a man for talking, always favoring the more direct approach.

Setting his mouth in a grim line, he said, "Madeline, I think it would be best if you simply allowed me to show you."

Before she could argue with him, he sank down on the edge of the bed and began doggedly tugging off his boots and hose. His shirt quickly followed. When his hands lowered to the buttons of his breeches, he heard Madeline's soft gasp. But, although he'd often been foolish enough to regret the imperfections of his face, he was not the least bit modest about his body.

Peeling off his breeches and discarding them, he turned, fully prepared to peel Madeline's fingers away from her face. He was not as prepared to find her staring at him, round eyed.

Madeline thought she should avert her face or at least lower her eyes. But, although she was blushing hotly, she couldn't seem to do either. Curiosity had always been her besetting sin.

Her only acquaintance with the male form was through her brother's sketches. On his grand tour Jeremy had gone through an artistic period, trying to copy the European great works of art, most of his efforts seeming to center on classical nudes. But pen and ink was one thing, six feet two inches of naked male flesh quite another.

Anatole had seemed daunting enough with his clothes on. Seeing him out of them left Madeline feeling breathless and weak. He was a large man in every respect. From the broad reach of his shoulders, his muscular chest dusted with dark hair to the flat plane of his stomach and hips, his thighs and calves, tautly honed, not an inch of softness about him anywhere.

Madeline's gaze centered on the area between his legs, so very different from the statues her brother had sketched.

"You look swollen," she whispered in horrified fascination. "Does that hurt?"

"Only if it's left unattended to," Anatole said with a wry smile. He paced toward her, the fire in his eyes adding to the peculiar fluttery sensation stirring inside her rib cage.

"Now it's your turn," he murmured.

"Oh, no!" She backed away, folding her arms protectively across her bosom as though she'd already been stripped. "Please, I—I can't."

He cornered her against the bedpost, stroking one finger softly through her hair. "If we are going to accomplish anything tonight, my dear, you have to."

Although spoken gruffly, it was the first time Anatole had ever made any attempt at endearment. To be termed his "dear" spread a warm glow through her, even if it didn't quite remove her embarrassment.

She forced herself to lower her arms. "You're going to have to put the candle out."

"But I want to see you."

"No, you don't," she said miserably, remembering his previous disparagements about her size. "You'll only be disappointed. You've already said that you don't find me buxom enough."

"Then, I was a nearsighted idiot. Stripping you out of that blasted corset, I found I was much mistaken."

"When did you ever—" Madeline broke off, the suspicion she'd entertained that morning crystallizing into a dead certainty. "You *were* in my room last night."

For a moment she thought he'd try to deny it, but he shrugged and said, "I found you asleep tangled up in that damn corset. I only sought to make you more comfortable."

"But how did you get into the room?"

"There is a door that connects our two chambers."

"I know that, but it was bolted from my side. Are you some kind of phantom that you can walk through a door?" she asked with a half smile.

He didn't smile back.

An uneasiness skittered up her spine, and she began to question him more closely, an urgency coming into her voice she couldn't explain. "How were you able to undress me without waking me? And why didn't you just wake me? What were you doing in my room at such—"

"Enough," Anatole growled. "You will drive me to distraction with all these questions. There is one thing you should understand about lovemaking. It is best accomplished in silence."

"But—"

"No more talk." He stopped her mouth with his kiss, not harshly, not roughly, but his lips firmly sealing hers.

Strangely, in that instant, the candle flickered as though caught in a draft, the light snuffing out. She thought Anatole would move to relight it, but he didn't. He now seemed to prefer the darkness himself.

Just as the man preferred silence to questions.

Madeline tried to relax, telling herself she was making too much of the incident in her bedchamber. Anatole had obviously done nothing more than creep into her room, attempted to make her more comfortable. A considerate act, surely. Then why did the notion of him hovering over her bed, watching her sleep with his intent brooding eyes make her so nervous? As though there was something more, something that the man wasn't telling her.

And that *something* seemed to press between them like a heavy cloak of secrecy. He whispered kisses across her face, hinting of a hunger that made her quiver, his face masked by shadows, the black fall of his hair.

As he turned her about to undo the laces of her gown, Madeline changed her mind about wanting the candle out. She now would have welcomed a flood of light despite the fact that Anatole was undressing her. The darkness only made him seem more of a stranger, as though he were indeed a phantom lover, his fingers whisking over the bindings that came undone far too easily.

One by one her garments pooled to her feet, until only the thin protection of her shift remained, leaving her with a sense of panic, of events moving too fast, beyond her control.

She kept silent as long as she could. But then she simply had to speak. "Anatole, I can't do this without knowing. Without you telling me . . . things."

But exactly what things she wanted to hear him say, she wasn't even sure herself.

He eased her shift down one shoulder, and she felt the heat of his mouth press against her bare flesh, his voice a warm rasp that sent shivers through her.

"Some things can't be explained, Madeline. Only experienced. Like riding a horse at a five bar gate. You simply have to throw your heart over."

"I've never been much of a horsewoman," she murmured with a weak laugh. And throwing her heart over was what had gotten her into this situation in the first place. Being undressed, preparing to do who knew what with a man she didn't know, who seemed more shadow than substance, his features lost in the darkness.

Anatole peeled away her shift, and she was left naked, trembling, feeling more vulnerable than she had ever been in her whole life. Slowly he turned her to face him, his eyes no more than a mysterious gleam, a phantom's eyes.

He drew her against him. Madeline gasped at the shock of her bare flesh meeting his, and the illusion of any phantom lover ended. The male body pressed to hers was hard, real, pulsing with life and heat.

His lips found hers in a kiss that began soft and built to complete possession, his tongue invading her mouth, melting, teasing, tasting. An odd notion flitted through Madeline's head that she now knew how Eve must have felt when she sampled the forbidden fruit of knowledge. Frightened, but intrigued.

A whole new awareness, a world of new sensations rippled through her. Anatole's fingers roved over her back, molding her softness to his unyielding strength. Despite her ignorance, Madeline had a few vague notions regarding the mating process. She knew enough to guess that their bodies must fit together in some fashion if a child were ever to be planted in her womb.

As Anatole's hands slid down, cupping her buttocks, pressing the most intimate part of her closer against his heated shaft, she suddenly knew. Knew with startling clarity just how this coupling would be brought about.

The idea should have terrified her. And it did. He was such a large man, and she had never felt so fragile. But her fear ran at odds with the inexplicable heat pooling deep inside her, sweet and heavy.

She dragged her mouth away from his, her voice coming out in a soft quivering sigh. "Anatole, please. You must allow me one last question. Is—is it going to hurt?"

His breath, which had been coming quickly, seemed to still in the darkness.

Anatole cradled her face between his hands. In that moment he wished that he were either a better lover or a better liar.

"Yes," he said at last. "The first time I believe there will be some discomfort for you. I'm sorry."

Her hands came up to curl about his wrists, as though she were seeking to brace herself, her fingers all too slight and fragile. Just like the rest of her.

"Then, perhaps it would be better," she whispered. "If we did this quickly before my courage fails me."

He tangled his fingers in her hair, caressing back the silken strands, but he had run out of words to reassure her. All he could do was guide her toward the bed. He tumbled her down to the mattress, settling himself close beside her, aware of the tension in her, not knowing what to do about it.

In that moment Anatole made a mortifying discovery. He'd bedded many a wench, but he didn't know how to make love to one. Not really. His bed partners had always taken from him what they wanted as he took from them. Now his bride lay next to him in the darkness, frightened, expectant, waiting for something he didn't know how to give.

Carefully he drew her closer, brushing a tentative kiss across her lips. He'd doused the candle, but not even a St. Leger could banish the moon. Its silvery glow crept past the curtains, invading the bed in a sliver of light that afforded him tantalizing glimpses of Madeline's naked beauty. The tangled fire of her hair, the soft swell of her shoulder, the teasing hint of her rosy-crested breast, the ivory curve of her hip.

Her body was perfectly formed, but dauntingly small and delicate compared to his hulking frame. The hand that he fit to her breast seemed far too large and rough, and he cupped her as gently as he could.

He handled her as carefully as if she were spun from the finest cut crystal, but to his frustration, she still tensed at his lightest touch, his most fleeting caress.

When he parted her thighs, seeking out her most intimate softness, he felt her tremble, and bit back a silent curse at the inconvenience of maidenhood.

It wasn't supposed to be this way. Tales of St. Leger men and the fiery desire they aroused in their chosen brides were as legendary as the passion of Lancelot and Guinevere. Virgins or not, those women were rumored to have been as hot-blooded as the men that claimed them.

Prospero was said to have once seduced a lady away from another man at the very altar. Anatole's own grandfather, it was whispered, had disappeared into the bedchamber on his wedding night only to emerge three days later with his wife still sighing for more.

But as Anatole clasped his nervous bride in his arms, he felt less of a legend than a mere mortal, a man being driven close to the brink by his own throbbing needs. Perhaps Madeline was right. Perhaps this first time, it would be better simply to get it over with.

Easing her onto her back, he cradled himself between her legs. Braced on both arms, he poised above her, trying not to look too deep into her wide, frightened eyes.

"Are you ready?" he whispered.

A foolish question. The woman stiffened beneath him like a defeated duelist braced to receive the fatal thrust.

But Madeline nodded bravely.

Gritting his teeth, Anatole positioned himself to ease inside her, fighting against his baser male instinct to plunge hard and deep into her welcoming warmth, trying to be as gentle as he could.

But by the sweet fires of heaven, the woman was so tight. He had no choice but to thrust, severing her maidenhead in a single swift stroke. The feel of his flesh joined to hers was incredible, but Madeline's soft cry of pain nearly unmanned him.

Holding himself as still inside her as he could, he asked, "Are you all right?"

She nodded again, but he couldn't help noting how she dug her hands into the mattress on either side of him.

Anatole grimaced. With more heroism than he ever knew he possessed, he rasped, "Do you want me to stop?"

There was a pause in which he felt she held his entire sanity in her hands. Then her reply came to him, so soft he barely caught the word.

"N-no."

The kiss he bestowed upon her was more grateful than passionate. With a low groan he settled himself deeper inside of her. Holding her breath, Madeline released it and seemed to relax a little beneath him.

Was it possible that after the initial pain, the passion could still come? That if he began slowly enough, with all the skill he possessed, he could yet coax his bride into some semblance of desire.

Hovering over Madeline, he trailed kisses along her neck, with a grim determination, attempting to set a rhythmic stroking. But he'd been too long without a woman, and Madeline sheathed him like a velvet glove, tight and warm and perfect. He thrust harder and deeper, the pressure building inside him to the point of pain, the kisses he pressed to her face growing ever fiercer, more feverish.

He broke over her with all the fury of the storms the sea often lashed at his lands, the suddenness taking him unawares. Shock waves of sensation shuddered through him, racking his frame. He emitted a hoarse cry as he spilled his seed deep inside of her.

The release left him spent, exhausted, and he collapsed, panting for breath. He lay that way for a long moment, chagrined by his loss of control. A chagrin that became worse when he realized that Madeline was pinned beneath his full weight.

Horrified, he dragged himself off of her. She'd gone so still, he half feared that she lay crushed, broken.

"Madeline?" He tugged at her shoulder. She quivered at his touch, but didn't answer him, her fiery hair tumbled across her face. Damning himself for a careless brute, Anatole brushed the strands aside with awkward fingers.

The eyes that Madeline had been holding tightly closed fluttered open. "Is it over?" she asked, gazing uncertainly up at him.

"Yes," Anatole said hoarsely.

Wincing a little, she sat up slowly, dragging the coverlet over her breasts to cover her nakedness.

"Am I permitted to talk now?"

He half dreaded what she might say, but he nodded. She had every right to upbraid him for his brutality, his lack of self-control, his clumsiness. If only she didn't start weeping. He prayed to heaven she wouldn't do that. He was already feeling enough of a monster.

Madeline tilted her head to one side, the way she always did when considering something. Anatole braced himself.

"What we just did . . ." she began. "Is it possible? I mean . . . am I now with child?"

A child? As usual, Madeline managed to take him by surprise with her questions. Getting her with child had been the last thing on his mind when he'd taken Madeline into his arms tonight.

He felt an unexpected curling of dread, imagining that at one time his own mother must have been very like Madeline at this moment. All soft and dreamy-eyed with hope, contemplating the prospect of bearing a child. Then he had been born. . . .

"It doesn't always happen right away," he said quickly. "Usually it takes many more couplings."

"Oh. You mean we're going to have to do this again?"

Her dismay was so evident, it was like a slap in the face.

"Well, not right away," he said.

"Good! I don't think that I could."

"Did I hurt you so badly, then?" he asked bleakly.

"Oh, no. But I am a little sore in some rather unusual places." Looking rather embarrassed by this confession, she adjusted the covers more tightly around her. "And so what do we do now?"

"Go to sleep, I suppose."

"In our own beds?"

He understood at once what she was hinting at.

"Of course," he said. He swung his legs over the side of the bed and began groping for his discarded clothing. He jammed himself back into his breeches, gathered up his shirt and boots. By the time he'd done so, Madeline was already stretched out underneath the covers, apparently not even daring to fetch her night shift while he remained in the room. She burrowed against the pillows, watching, waiting for him to be gone.

Anatole didn't know why the notion should bother him so much, but it did. Heaven knows, when he'd bedded other women, he'd always been impatient enough to take his leave when the lovemaking was finished. Why should it be any different this time?

Perhaps because he couldn't help wondering if Madeline would have been so anxious for him to quit her bed if he had possessed more of the attributes of Prospero. Or of the handsome face he'd created in that damnable portrait.

But no. He was only Anatole, rough, scarred, and unrefined. His lips twisted bitterly. The monster . . .

"Well . . . g'night," he said awkwardly, and backed away from the bed. But as he approached the door connecting to his own chamber, he was arrested by the sound of her voice.

"Anatole?"

He paused, glancing back. She was sitting up in bed, haloed by moonlight, her hair rivulets of dark fire cascading over the pale outline of her shoulders. He was appalled to realize how much he wanted to stay with her, just to touch her, hold her a little longer . . . how little it would have taken to make him want to love her all over again.

He swallowed thickly. "Yes? What is it?"

"About tonight . . . I just wanted you to know . . ." She plucked at the bed-coverings. "It—it wasn't nearly as bad as I'd thought it was going to be."

Anatole flinched. Not nearly as bad as she'd thought it would be? The smile she offered him was shy and sweet. But he still felt as though she'd just poured acid over what remained of his pride. Without another word he left her room and returned to his own bedchamber.

Only when he had gone did Madeline stretch out, nestling against her pillow. The tension of the last hours, nay the last few days caught up to her at last, and she felt exhausted, too tired to even fetch her nightgown.

Besides, there was something deliciously sensual about the brush of the sheets against her bare skin. Sleeping naked made her feel somehow bold and daring, more aware of her own body than she had ever been before.

Hugging the coverlets close to her, she thought of the thing that Anatole had just done to her. A rather strange and wondrous thing, the way his body had joined with hers. And not nearly as terrifying as she'd imagined.

It had hurt at first, just as he'd said. But Anatole had been amazingly considerate, almost shy in his caresses, his efforts to be gentle. Beyond the discomfort she had experienced something—she could not describe just what it had been. A feeling, a promise, a hope, that the next time there might be something more. . . .

It astonished her to discover that she would ever consider doing *that* again. But she was considering it . . . a great deal.

And why not? she thought, hugging her pillow to her with a soft smile. She was no longer the innocent virgin, the naive spinster. She'd feigned a lofty indifference when her younger sisters had whispered and giggled over "married lady matters." But it had filled her with a certain wistfulness, a sense of melancholy.

She'd always felt so much an outsider, so much at odds with her sisters, indeed all the rest of her sex. While she had read and philosophized about the nature of life, Juliette and Louisa had experienced it, flirted, married, possessed themselves of secrets as old as Adam.

Now those secrets were Madeline's as well. She'd ever been a quick study, and she flattered herself that she had learned a great deal about men tonight, about Anatole. She was finally, in truth, a wife. And possibly before the year was out—Madeline's hand drifted over the region of her womb—possibly in nine months' time, she could be a mother.

The thought filled her with awe. Her eyelids grew heavier, and she yawned, imagining a bright-eyed child. One child swiftly became half a dozen precocious moppets, clustered about her knee. She would superintend their education herself, of course, rewarding her darlings with sweetmeats and sugar nuts as they lisped out their Latin verbs and recited Homer in flawless Greek.

Madeline's lashes drifted down, and she fell asleep dreaming of her scholarly brood of children all staring up at her with their father's magnificent dark eyes.

She slept on, unaware when Anatole crept back into her room hours later. Although dawn had yet to fully lighten the sky, he already stood booted, dressed, his riding cape slung over his arm as he prepared to slip out to the stables to saddle his horse. The last minutes of the night he'd anticipated for so long ticked relentlessly away, his wedding night slipping quietly toward morning.

But what had he expected, he thought with a scowl. Roman candles? Sky rockets? Cannon fire? No, he hadn't been that much of a fool.

But he had expected surcease from the dull aches, the loneliness, the longings that had plagued him all these months. Yet the restlessness, the emptiness, the torment that kept him awake and pacing like a caged beast for the better part of the night were still there.

He wanted to curse the day he'd ever sent Fitzleger to find him a bride, the fate or the folly, whichever it was, that had brought Madeline Breton to his doorstep.

But as he gazed down at his sleeping bride, somehow he couldn't. She'd kicked off the covers in her sleep and lay curled on her stomach, her head pillowed on her arms. Her hair shimmered, a softer fire now, curtaining the smooth white skin of her shoulders. She was laid out for his hungry eyes in all her naked beauty.

He'd begged the fates for an ordinary woman, and instead destiny had mocked him and sent Anatole a faery queen.

Aye, he thought. That's exactly how he would have painted Madeline. That is, if he had not given up his painting long ago as an occupation fit only for a foolish dream-ridden boy, not suited to the harder nature of a man.

But if he did still wield his brush, he would have painted her as a fairy, gossamer wings rising out of her back as she slept soundly curled up on a flower, innocent in her nakedness. But nothing so fragile as a primrose or lily. Not for his practical Madeline. Oh, no, she would have selected for herself a nice sturdy dandelion.

Anatole smiled ruefully at his own nonsense, but he was coming to know his little bride rather better in spite of himself. And he ought to have been satisfied with her. So she wasn't the great, strapping wench he'd hoped for. But for all her air of delicacy, she had borne up pretty well under him.

She hadn't wept. She hadn't shrieked for him not to touch her. She'd steeled her courage and endured their mating. And that's all he'd ever asked for in a wife, wasn't it?

That's what he'd told Fitzleger. That it would be enough for Anatole if Madeline learned not to fear him.

I have no desire to be loved, he'd insisted.

"And I still don't," Anatole told himself fiercely. But the words rang strangely hollow, as the predawn darkness hung like a gray curtain outside the window, as Madeline slept on, blissfully unaware of his existence. Five o'clock in the morning . . .

What a desperately lonely hour to discover that he had lied.

Chapter Nine

Morning mist drifted in from the sea, enveloping Castle Leger in a world of white. The fog half obscured the path that cut through the cliff face, the surf pounding against the jagged rocks below the dizzying heights where Anatole guided his mount.

But he urged the stallion forward with an iron hand at the reins and the confidence of one long familiar with every rock, every crevice that marked his lands. He'd often played along this cliff side as a boy, alone, but then the rugged path had been dotted with a hundred imagined companions, pirates, and smugglers, knives clutched in their teeth as they had scaled upward to where he'd waited, brandishing a willow sword.

Or sometimes he had retreated into the wild garden of primroses and bluebells that tumbled almost to the cliff's edge, hiding behind the rhododendron trees, playing at seek and dare with the elves who lived in the heather.

That, however, had been before his mother's life ended in such tragic fashion, taking away with her both pirate king and elfin lord forever, ending his boyish delight in such imaginings, in the terrible beauty of his own lands, the cruel rocks, vast sea and sky.

But in all the years since he'd become master of this place, he'd never once been driven to flee Castle Leger as he was doing now. Riding out. Running away. From her.

Madeline. His bride. His lady of flame.

Anatole reined in his horse, glancing back in spite of himself. The home that he both loved and hated was still visible in the distance. The towering battlements and ancient turrets rose up from the haze as though the castle were no more than a shimmering image conjured from a wizard's book of spells.

He could barely make out the window behind which his bride still lay sleeping, another part of the enchantment, her flame-colored hair spilled against the pillow, the memory of her beauty tempting him to return. Calling to him like a siren's song, beckoning him back to her bedchamber. To kiss her gently awake, take her in his arms, and . . .

And do what? a voice inside him mocked. Repeat the failure of last night? He still didn't have the slightest idea how to move her, to inspire her with the great passion and undying devotion a St. Leger bride was supposed to feel.

Anatole swore softly, the curse laced with as much despair as frustration. Christ! He didn't even dare face her this morning for fear of what she might see in his eyes, the hopeless longing, the madness that had begun stealing over him.

He'd gone unloved for most of his life. What insanity could possess him to crave it now? He didn't know. All he knew was that he had to get away from Castle Leger for a while until he had time to sort out these strange feelings and fears in his own mind. Until he'd regained some command over himself.

And though he damned himself a coward for fleeing from one small wisp of a woman, Anatole spurred the stallion forward. Questing after a threat to his peace of mind that he far better understood.

Mortmains.

The mist persisted, damp and colder down by the shoreline. Perfect weather, Anatole thought wryly, for tracking down a phantom woman who was likely no more than the product of an old man's imagination or his failing eyesight. And there was no more perfect place to come looking for the ghost of an enemy he'd thought long dead than here. . . .

Anatole drew rein, peering through the drifting wisps of fog at the cove stretched out before him. The tide was out, the powerful sea becalmed, little more than a cold gray froth leaving dark stains upon the shore.

It was a barren sweep of coast, isolated, dangerous, with jagged rocks barely visible beneath the surface of the water, the shore streaked with patches of sand more golden than the rest and more deadly, the kind that could give way beneath a man, swallowing him from sight forever.

No snug cottages nestled in the bare hills beyond, no fishermen's nets sprawled out to dry in the sun, there was nothing here but some half-dead oaks exposed to the salt wind of the sea and the scorched remains of a formerly magnificent manor house.

Once the estate had been known by some fancy French name, but over time the local fisherfolk had come to call it Lost Land because of its black reputation for wrecked ships, murdered sailors, and hapless travelers who'd simply vanished, whether victims of the dangerous shifting sands or some more sinister hand. Land as treacherous as the Mortmains themselves.

A chill worked through Anatole that had nothing to do with the dampness of the day. A pervading sense of evil clung to this place that touched the outermost borders of his own land. The Mortmain estate could have been a million leagues away and still not be distant enough as far as St. Legers had always been concerned.

He urged his horse cautiously along a narrow path that led up from the shore cutting through a marshy meadow. Tension settled between his shoulder blades. He'd never seen a Mortmain in his lifetime. And yet the closer he drew to the ruined manor, the more conscious he became of passing into the shadow of the enemy.

They'd been his family's most bitter enemy for generations. Who was it that had had Lord Prospero condemned and burned for witchcraft? A Mortmain. Who'd led the Roundhead Army that had once attacked and despoiled Castle Leger? A Mortmain. Who had been behind the murder of Deidre St. Leger? A Mortmain.

And so on down to present times, to the illegal execution of his own father's younger brother, Wyatt St. Leger, hung by Sir Tyrus Mortmain on a trumped-up charge of smuggling and treason to the crown. Hung without proof or trial, an act of injustice that had spurred the final confrontation between Sir Tyrus and Anatole's grandfather. A confrontation that had ended here on this hillside in a night of fire and fury.

Anatole's stallion whickered and shied back, his nostrils flaring as though the light haze that swirled about them still bore the acrid tang of smoke. The horse balked, tossing his head to one side, veering away with an animal's uncanny sense for avoiding a site of death and destruction.

Giving over the struggle, Anatole dismounted and tethered the uneasy stallion to a stout branch of one of the dying oaks. He continued the rest of the way up the hill on foot.

The remains of Mortmain Manor towered before him, only a few walls still standing, blown-out windows staring at him like gaping eyes and mouths. A blackened monument to all that remained of the Mortmains' ruthlessness and cruelty. Vaulting ambition and vengeance reduced to nothing more than rubble and ash.

Anatole hesitated before picking his way carefully through what had once been the manor's front door. He went only a few steps, fearing one wrong move might bring what remained of the building crashing down on his head.

The interior was a pile of collapsed stone, ash, and fallen timber, anything of value long since scavenged away. Where the roof should have been was nothing but misty clouds and pale gray sky. Little stirred except for the strident cry of some rooks nesting in the remains of one of the chimneys.

Anatole frowned. He didn't know what he'd hoped to achieve by coming to Lost Land except that if there was a chance any Mortmain remained alive and had returned, the most likely place he'd find some sign of it was here.

But a sign like what? Someone attempting to hang curtains in the crumbling window frames, spread out Aubusson carpets over the debris? With a look of disgust Anatole dusted off the fine powder of ash that had already collected on his leather gloves.

Convinced that he'd come on a fool's errand, he turned to go. But he hadn't taken more than a step, when he realized that he was no longer alone. The sensation crept over him, as though the mist itself had suddenly thickened around him, seeping into his bones.

Anatole tensed, listening. He neither saw nor heard anything, but he felt it. A presence somewhere nearby. The hair at the back of his neck lifted, his special inner sense going off like a watchman's rattle.

His sense didn't function as well here as it did at Castle Leger; it was as though it were cloaked by the mist, by the ruined manor's own powerful aura. He couldn't tell the who or the where, only that someone was drawing closer. The sensation grew stronger by the second, almost suffocating. A feeling of hostility. Dangerous. Threatening.

Anatole silently cursed himself for not having the forethought to bring a loaded pistol. He had only a rapier strapped to his side, but the weapon would have to do.

He unsheathed the sword as quietly as he could, straining with all his senses to detect some movement, some sound that would tell him where his enemy lurked.

There, he thought, every nerve pulsing, every muscle flexing. Just outside the walls of the ruined manor, someone crept, waiting.

The blood pumping through his veins, Anatole set his mouth in a grim line and stalked forward. He had just breached the opening in the smoke-blackened wall when the attack came.

The sword seemed to come out of nowhere, arcing toward him with a deadly hiss. He deflected it with his own blade and spun around, thrusting. He came within inches of piercing his attacker's heart. The only thing that saved the man was his agility and the fact that Anatole froze, the shock of recognition setting in.

Sword suspended, he stared at the familiar masculine face. Ash gold hair waved back from patrician features cast in lordly beauty almost too perfect to be human, a fine-chiseled jaw, an aquiline nose, wing-tipped brows, the sullen mouth of a demigod who'd been denied Mt. Olympus.

Roman St. Leger. The last person Anatole would have expected to encounter here. Or wanted to.

Roman's frigid blue eyes locked with his for a long tense moment, fixing Anatole with a challenging stare that Anatole returned unblinking. It was Roman who finally yielded, withdrawing his sword. With a laugh he backed off, shoving his rapier back into a long cane until it resumed the appearance of a harmless gold-tipped walking stick.

"Well, cousin. This is a first. Imagine me being able to take *you* by surprise."

Anatole lowered his own sword, the tension coursing through him, fast giving way to anger.

"You bloody damn fool! What do you mean by attacking me that way?"

Roman's brows shot upward. "I didn't know it was you, now, did I? Not being possessed of your unusual gifts of perception. For all I could tell, you might have proved to be some wandering brigand."

"You should have been more careful. I might have run you through."

"And that would have been a tragedy." Roman's smile mocked him. "*The St. Leger who sheds the blood of his own kin is himself doomed.* Isn't that how the old legend goes?"

Roman had no respect for any legends, St. Leger or otherwise. But Anatole had always felt a strong urge to put this particular one to the test, especially where Roman was concerned, even if he did risk his own destruction.

He'd come close to it once in the more hot-blooded days of his youth, but then there had been cooler and wiser heads present to separate him and Roman. There was nothing to rely on here except his own good sense.

Clenching his teeth, Anatole slid his sword back in its sheath before Roman could goad him into doing something stupid. His cousin possessed a remarkable gift for that.

Roman bent to fetch his hat, which had flown off in the scuffle, a dapper tan felt with a low crown and narrow brim. It matched the French-style frock coat he wore, its collar tricked out in velvet, the enameled buttons decorated with hunting devices. His cream-colored breeches were protected by spatter dashes, his jockey boots blackened with polish and gleaming. The complete attire was far too elegant to be wasted riding through this back country, but it was difficult to imagine Roman in anything less.

While Roman settled the hat back on his head, Anatole demanded, "So what the devil are you doing here?"

Roman took his time about answering, jamming his hands back into a pair of fawn-skin gloves. "I might ask you the same thing, cousin. From what I've heard, congratulations are in order. Isn't your bride due to arrive any day? I expected you would be mighty preoccupied preparing for your wedding."

"I already had it. Yesterday."

Roman stilled. "I see," he said. For a moment something ugly seemed to simmer in the depth of his eyes. Then the expression was gone as he stretched the second glove into place. When he spoke again, it was in his usual light mocking tone.

"You had the wedding and didn't trouble to ask me? Tsk, tsk. Obviously you've never heard the story of the bad fairy who wasn't invited to the family gathering and then decided to wreak a good deal of mischief."

Anatole stirred uneasily at Roman's thin smile. That was one of the most irritating things about the damned man. You could never tell whether he was serious or jesting.

"I didn't invite any fairies to the wedding. Good or otherwise," Anatole said. "It was a very private affair."

"How like you," Roman muttered. He paced a few steps away, abandoning the pretense of his negligent pose. "You might at least have had the courtesy to inform *me*."

"I didn't realize I was obliged to account to you."

"You're not, but you know that I have always—" When Roman broke off, compressing his lips together, Anatole finished for him.

"You've always considered yourself to be my heir."

"Yes, I rather fear that I did."

"Then, you're a damned fool."

"Undoubtedly."

"You couldn't have seriously ever expected to inherit Castle Leger. We're the same age. What made you think you'd outlive me?"

"A man can always hope, can't he?" Roman asked with a smile whose softness never reached his eyes.

Anatole supposed he should have been disconcerted to discover his own cousin wished him dead. But it was a sentiment he'd returned toward Roman on more than one occasion. By some strange coincidence, they'd been born on the same day, almost at the same hour. The enmity that simmered between them seemed to have existed from the cradle.

Perhaps, Anatole thought, it was because they were such different kinds of men. Roman, with his silken manners and elegant clothes, belonged to assemblies, salons, ballrooms, while Anatole was more at home in the stables, on the cliffs and moors.

Or perhaps it was because Roman was one of those rare St. Legers who had been left untouched by the family curse, devoid of any peculiar talents, a blessing that Anatole bitterly envied.

But perhaps his dislike of Roman was rooted in something far more simple. Something as basic as . . . doors. Library doors, parlor doors, doors to Anatole's own home that had been shut in his face as a lad, but had always been open and welcoming to Roman. . . .

Anatole shoved the painful memories aside and faced his cousin squarely. "I'm sorry to disappoint you, but I intend to live a long time and father a good many strapping healthy sons."

"No doubt you will," Roman said, eyeing Anatole's large frame with an expression of distaste. "Though, I must confess. I never really believed you would marry."

"You mean you never believed any lady would have me."

"You are a rather alarming prospect as a husband, cuz. But then, there is supposed to be a chosen bride out there for every St. Leger. I presume you sent the *Bride Finder* out to fetch her?"

"Yes," Anatole said, anticipating Roman's sneer.

His cousin's upper lip did indeed curl. "Somehow I thought you'd be more intelligent than that. Like me, full of too much good sense to be taken in by the family's hoary old legends. But you actually did trust that half-witted, half-blind old man to find you a wife."

"Fitzleger's wits are still as keen as yours. And he sees well enough. When he wears his spectacles."

"I do hope he had them on when he selected your lady. Where did he find her?"

"London."

"London?" Roman's eyes widened. "Another surprise. I more envisioned you plighting your troth to one of our local Amazons. And just who is this paragon Fitzleger chose for you?"

Anatole felt reluctant to tell him, which was ridiculous. Roman could find out easily enough.

"Her name is Madeline Breton."

"One of the Honorable Gordon Breton's daughters?"

"Yes, I believe so."

"A good enough bloodline. The old man is third or fourth cousin to the Earl of Croftmore. But the Breton line of the family is rather profligate, always in debt. I don't imagine this bride of yours brought you much of a dowry."

Anatole's eyes narrowed with suspicion. "And just how the blazes do you happen to know so much about my bride's family?"

"My dear cousin, unlike you, I haven't spent my life buried in Cornwall. I frequently get up to London and out in Society. Though I don't recollect ever meeting your Madeline at any of the functions I attended. What manner of creature is she?"

"She's a woman."

"I could have guessed that much. I mean is she accomplished? Charming? Is she very beautiful?"

For some reason Roman's soft-voiced questions made Anatole feel uneasy. Like a miser with thieves inquiring too closely about the size of his treasure.

"She's tolerable enough," he said.

"Tolerable enough?" Roman chuckled. "That sounds rather lukewarm. What of the grand passion that's supposed to exist between a St. Leger and his chosen mate? I'm astonished to find your bride has permitted you to stray from her side so soon. According to the old legends, she should be practically begging you to return to her bed."

That would have been difficult, Anatole thought, considering that his bride was likely still peacefully asleep, not even noticing that he was gone. Memories of Madeline's assessment of his lovemaking rose unbidden to his mind.

It wasn't nearly as bad as I thought it was going to be.

Talk about being damned with faint praise. Anatole was annoyed to feel a hint of red creeping into his cheeks, a telltale sign that his keen-eyed cousin did not miss.

Roman donned a look of mock solicitude. "I trust nothing has gone amiss already, Anatole. Or that Fitzleger has not inadvertently paired you with the wrong woman. It's conceivable that even a Bride Finder could eventually make a horrible mistake."

"No mistake has been made."

"Of course not," Roman said in such soothing tones Anatole longed to break his jaw. "But just in case, maybe you'd better wait a bit before you do that little ceremony where you hand over the crystal sword, surrendering your heart and soul for all eternity."

Anatole felt his face wash an even deeper shade of red.

"Oh, dear. You've already gone and done it." Roman's smile assumed a crueler cast. "Tell me. Have you yet thought to offer her any flowers as well?"

The jab found its mark, and Anatole flinched. He now recollected the real reason he despised Roman. If his cousin possessed any St. Leger gift at all, it was an uncanny knack for discovering the most vulnerable spot in another man's heart, thrusting his knife in, and giving it an added twist.

Anatole's hand tensed, not with the urge to reach for his sword, but to press his fingertips to his brow and do something far worse to his cousin. Only Roman had ever tempted him to make such black use of his power. The only thing that restrained Anatole was the realization that his cousin would derive some twisted pleasure from sending him over the edge.

He stared back down the hill toward where his stallion had found a few blades of grass to nibble, to where the distant outline of the shore was lost in haze. Only when he felt in complete control of himself did he turn back to face Roman.

"Never mind about my bride," he said coldly. "She's no concern of yours. You've avoided ever answering my question with all this idle chatter. What are you doing here at Lost Land?"

"Alas, cousin. Your bride is none of my concern. What I'm doing here is none of yours."

His amusement in goading Anatole apparently at an end, Roman sketched an insolent bow and strode away, disappearing around the side of the half-crumbling manor walls. Swearing, Anatole followed hard after him, discovering where Roman had tethered his own mount.

A sleek gray gelding pawed the ground restively near the gate of a low stone cottage, which at one time had been the steward's house. Roman headed toward the horse, but Anatole easily outdistanced him with his longer stride. Getting there first, he assumed control of the reins himself, preventing Roman from going anywhere.

Roman pulled up short, favoring Anatole with a haughty stare. But Anatole ignored him, repeating his demand with strained patience.

"I asked what you're doing here, Roman. Did you also come looking for some sign a Mortmain has returned?"

The hostility in Roman's eyes dissolved into a look of genuine surprise.

"Good Lord, no! I'm not some credulous peasant, believing people can return from the dead."

"There's a chance that not all of the Mortmains are dead. Certain information has reached me, indicating that someone might possibly have survived the fire that night. A woman. Perhaps Sir Tyrus's daughter."

"I certainly hope not. That would prove damned inconvenient." Roman reached for the gelding's reins, but Anatole only tightened his grip.

"Then, if you're not looking for Mortmains, what the hell are you doing here?"

Roman's mouth twitched with annoyance, but he finally conceded with an irritated sigh, "Surveying."

"Surveying what? Mortmain land?"

"No, *my* land."

Anatole was astounded enough to loosen his grasp. Roman took advantage of his shock to snatch the reins from him, startling the horse into skittering sideways.

"What the blazes are you talking about?" Anatole asked.

"I thought I made myself pretty clear," Roman said, stroking the gelding's nose and making soft noises to soothe it. "I've bought Lost Land. I signed the deed yesterday afternoon."

"Bought it? From whom?"

"From a distant relative of Sir Tyrus's wife who inherited the place after there were no more Mortmains. He's a London banker who was happy enough to be rid of the place. I got it fairly cheap."

"Have you entirely lost your mind?"

"I don't believe so."

"Then, what devil possessed you to buy this—this accursed land?"

"Maybe because I was not fortunate enough to have inherited property the way you did, cousin," Roman said, a trace of acid bitterness creeping into his voice. "My own father left me little more than that run-down farm and those ridiculous fossils he was always collecting. I've always had the urge to be master of a bit more than a few straggly sheep and some old rocks."

"But to purchase Lost Land . . ." Anatole glanced about with a troubled gaze at the blighted landscape, the ominous aspect of the ruins themselves, the whisper on the wind that seemed to linger here, haunting, threatening.

"This place, the men who lived here have been a bane to our family's existence for generations. For a St. Leger to own Mortmain-tainted land. No good can possibly come of it."

"You're starting to sound as bad as old Fitzleger. A superstitious fool," Roman scoffed. "You forget who once owned your precious Castle Leger, cousin. You also forget that I don't require your approval."

Roman swung into the saddle, wrapping the reins around his gloved fist. "Now, if you'll excuse me. I have a great deal else to attend to this morning. I'm meeting with the architect who's going to rebuild the manor house for me."

Anatole would have liked to argue the matter further, but he had no choice but to stand aside as Roman nudged the gelding forward.

"As always, a pleasure to see you, cousin. Feel free to return to my lands anytime you like. Next time I promise you a far better reception."

Roman's teeth flashed in a wolfish grin, and he kicked the gelding into a gallop. Instead of heading down toward the cove, he vanished into the mist-ridden hills beyond.

Anatole fought a strong urge to ride after Roman and pound some sense into the man. His cousin was either a reckless fool or a smoothly calculating bastard. Even after all these years, Anatole had yet to decide which. The notion of Roman owning Lost Land left him with a sense of dread. Even though Roman had been right about one thing.

Mortmains *had* once owned Castle Leger and most of this stretch of West Penrith. The ambitious lords had determined to carve for themselves a duchy out of Cornwall, but their treachery to a king had caused them to be stripped of everything save this barren property. The most prized section of their estates had been awarded to a strange young knight named Prospero. . . .

It seemed like fate, the magnificent castle set high upon the stark and rugged cliffs had been destined to become Castle Leger, the place of St. Legers while this wretched cove, these low hills, this . . . this Lost Land. It was most definitely *Mortmain.*

Anatole pulled a wry face at the illogic of his own musings. Likely Roman had been correct to term him a superstitious fool. Even more likely his unease about Roman buying Lost Land had little to do with the land itself and far more to do with the prospect of having Roman settling so near to the border of Castle Leger. 'Fore God, he'd almost have preferred a Mortmain.

There was bound to be trouble, and when Anatole returned home, perhaps the first thing he'd better do was to consult the damned crystal and—

And Anatole cursed, remembering. He couldn't consult the crystal anymore because he'd surrendered the sword to his bride. Scowling, he plunged back down the hillside, heading toward where his stallion awaited him.

He tried not to think of all the gibes Roman had flung out to him about

Madeline, but Roman's taunts had a way of getting under a man's skin like an infection of the blood.

You're rather an alarming prospect as a husband, cuz. . . . What of the grand passion that's supposed to exist between a St. Leger and his mate. . . . I'm astonished your bride permitted you to stray from her side. . . . Even a Bride Finder could make a horrible mistake. . . .

Gritting his teeth, Anatole mounted his horse, trying to still those insidious whispers, that voice breathing doubt in his ear. But he galloped out from Lost Land, not quite able to shake off the fear that he'd surrendered both his sword and his soul to Madeline Breton far too soon.

He rode back toward the village and spent the rest of the morning there and among the outlying cottages, making inquiries after Fitzleger's mystery woman. He even directed his search among the fishermen down in the inlet, waiting to launch their boats with the tide.

But no one seemed to have noticed any strangers passing through recently, besides the foppish architect Roman had hired and Mad Lucy, the old charmer woman. Anatole didn't know why he continued to pursue the matter. Perhaps because the more he thought about it, the more he liked the idea of a Mortmain heiress turning up and keeping Lost Land out of Roman's hands. After all, how much trouble could a woman be?

How much trouble, indeed, he thought as he followed the track back to Castle Leger hours later. The mists of morning had dissolved into the gloom-ridden skies of late afternoon. Tired and dispirited, Anatole kept the stallion to a trot, feeling as though he'd accomplished little.

He hadn't solved the mystery of Fitzleger's churchyard visitor, and he hadn't sorted out the far more troubling puzzle of his own heart, the exact nature of his feelings toward his bride.

But as his horse passed beneath the shadow of the old castle keep, Anatole felt his blood quicken with anticipation. Anticipation simply because now *she* was there. As he cantered into the courtyard, he found himself glancing up eagerly at all the tall latticed windows.

Almost as though he expected to see Madeline looking for his return, ready to bound down the stairs flinging her arms wide, tilting her lovely face up to receive his kiss, offering him a warm welcome the likes of which he'd never known. Make him feel for the first time in years, perhaps the first time in his life, that he really had come home.

Bah! Anatole reined in the stallion, feeling partly wistful, partly filled with self-disgust. What sort of fool was this woman turning him into?

Someone looked out for his arrival, but it wasn't Madeline. Anatole heard his name hailed from the portico above, and the next instant Lucius Trigghorne came half flying, half stumbling down the stone steps.

Anatole had never seen the surly old man look so agitated, almost as though a thousand tiny demons nipped at his heels. Now what? Anatole wondered as he slung himself off the back of the horse. What sort of disaster could have befallen in his absence. He'd had no premonition of anything lately except that business last night with . . .

Will.

A sick feeling churned in Anatole's stomach. But no, damn it. He'd warned the boy again only that morning to stay away from the woodpile when he'd entrusted Will with the task of kenneling Ranger. The wretched hound nigh broke his heart trying to tear after Anatole whenever he rode out, and the poor old fool was getting far too ancient for that.

But perhaps, Anatole thought when he caught sight of the wild look on Trigg's face, perhaps he should have kenneled Will instead.

Trigg staggered down the last of the steps, the old man wheezing for breath, leaning up against the stallion for support.

"Oh—oh, master," he gasped. "Thank God . . . you're home. S-something terrible—"

Anatole seized the old man's arm, alarm and impatience sharpening his voice. "Catch your breath, man, and tell me. What's happened. Is it Will? Goddamn the boy to hell. Why couldn't he listen—"

But Trigghorne interrupted him with another wheeze. "No. Not Will. The house . . . been invaded."

Invaded? Anatole looked at the grizzled old man as though he'd gone quite mad. Castle Leger hadn't been overrun by anyone since the days of Cromwell's Roundhead Army.

It was ridiculous to think such a thing could happen simply because Anatole had ridden out and . . . and left his new bride alone and unprotected.

Anatole felt a clutch of fear the like of which he'd never known. He spun around wildly, already groping for his sword.

"Invaded? By whom?" he demanded fiercely of Trigg. "Smugglers? Brigands? Mortmains?"

"No," Trigg moaned, sagging down to his knees with a groan. "By . . . by women."

Chapter Ten

Madeline removed the apron that protected her bright yellow gown, and laid it over the back of the library chair she had just polished. It now gleamed, as did the table and most of the bookcases that lined the walls. There was still much cleaning left to be done, but she'd made great progress here in the library, along with many of the other parlors in this wing of the house. She and her army of village ladies.

The Reverend Fitzleger had helped her to recruit some half-dozen able-bodied women to work at Castle Leger, and the lower hall had become a hive of activity, humming with sights and sounds that Madeline was certain had not been seen or heard at Castle Leger for many a day.

The softer lilt of women's voices, the bustle of skirts, the swish of brooms vigorously applied. Lucius Trigghorne had taken himself off somewhere to sulk at what he'd bitterly termed "a petticoat invasion." But Will and the other young footman, Eamon, had pitched in eagerly to help, driving back the dust and neglect of many years.

Madeline had insisted on reclaiming the library from the cobwebs herself. As the afternoon shadows lengthened, she looked at the rows of books now arranged so tidily upon the shelves, and she felt a sense of keen satisfaction. Tomorrow she would begin sorting and cataloging them, but for now . . .

She ran a weary hand across her brow. Warm from her recent exertions, she slipped outside for a breath of air. The wild tangle of garden that sprawled along the back of the house lay hushed and still before her. Gnarled rhododendron trees and azalea bushes poked their branches upward through the afternoon haze. A mad carpet of bluebells and golden heather seemed to fight for possession of the path, the sweet fragrance mingling with the salty tang of the sea.

It was as though the flowers bloomed in sheer defiance of this hard land, the damp breath of the fog, the distant dragonlike roar of the sea. And as Madeline plucked a pink-blushed rhododendron from one of the trees, she began to believe there was a chance she might be able to bloom here, too.

After last night.

She didn't fool herself into thinking that any great love had flourished between her and Anatole. Not the kind she'd always dreamed of. But what had happened in that bedchamber proved that they could at least deal, well, *reasonably* with each other.

Although . . . A slight frown creased Madeline's brow as she bent to pick a few of the bluebells, a handful of heather. She had to admit she'd been far from reasonable when she awakened this morning to find that her bridegroom had simply vanished, without leaving word where he was going, without even bidding her farewell. Hurt had sluiced through her, as powerful as it was unexpected.

She'd had to take herself to task for being so foolish. Of course, Anatole could not be expected to dance attendance upon her. The man was used to going his own way, roaming wild and free, accounting to no one. And it was not as if she did not have enough to keep herself occupied in his absence.

Civilize the house first, she told herself with a smile as she plunged farther down the garden path, adding more blossoms to her bouquet. Then she'd see about civilizing the man.

And it became obvious a few moments later that the man greatly needed civilizing. She tensed, listening as a bellow carried to her ears coming from the direction of the house.

Anatole . . . shouting her name. He'd come home at last. Madeline's pulse began to beat a little faster. Strange how swiftly things could change. Only yesterday morning, she would have dreaded encountering her formidable bridegroom. Now she felt both shy and eager at the prospect of seeing him.

But she was not about to be summoned to him the way he called for one of his dogs. She forced herself to remain calm, waiting until Anatole appeared at the end of the path, his travel-stained riding cloak draped over his stalwart shoulders, his black hair flowing wild and loose about his face.

He looked out of place in the garden, like some dark warlord who'd lost his way, wandering out of a far-distant time.

Her dark warlord. Madeline's heart tripped over itself with an unexpected and fierce pride in him. Then she gave a horrified gasp as she recollected her own appearance, her hair still tucked up in the mobcap she'd worn while cleaning.

Ducking behind a tree, she wrenched the thing off and ran desperate fingers through her disorderly tumble of curls.

Anatole nearly missed her entirely.

"Madeline!" His voice sounded sharper now, almost alarmed. He struck off on a path that led in the opposite direction.

Madeline stuffed the lace-trimmed cap in the pocket of her gown. Still clutching her bouquet, she darted after Anatole, plucking the back of his cape.

"Here I am," she said somewhat breathlessly.

Anatole whipped around like she'd loosed a pistol shot off behind him, his face strangely pale. But the color ebbed back into his cheeks as his astonishment swiftly gave way to anger.

"Hell's fire, madam! What'd you mean by hiding from me that way?"

"I—I wasn't," Madeline stammered, taken aback by this grim reception. "I never meant to startle you."

"You've done a fine job of it all the same. What the devil has been going on here in my absence? Why is my house overrun with wenches?" His glower caused Madeline to retreat a step, clutching her bouquet even tighter.

"They—they are women. From the village."

"I know that. What are they doing here?"

"I engaged them to help with the cleaning."

"And who gave you permission to do that?"

"You did."

When Anatole stared at her as though she'd lost her mind, Madeline added hastily, "When Mr. Fitzleger called upon me this morning, he said that you'd told him I could have a girl to—"

"*A* girl. That means one," Anatole said. "I never intended to have the castle stuffed with women."

"I don't call four or five maids *stuffing,*" Madeline replied indignantly. "I only thought—"

"I know what you thought! The same as every other woman from the beginning of time. That as soon as you are married to a man, you can charge into his house and start changing everything."

"I thought it was supposed to be my home as well." She didn't add that she'd also thought his reaction to all this would be far different. When she'd first arrived, he'd believed her to be such a useless creature. She'd wanted to show him just how sensible, how efficient she could be as mistress of Castle Leger. She'd hoped that he might learn to be proud of the wife he'd chosen.

But that was the thing that she seemed to be in danger of forgetting. Anatole hadn't chosen her. The Bride Finder had.

"Fine," Madeline said, swallowing past the hard lump that rose in her throat. "I'll just return to the house and put all the cobwebs back where I found them."

She spun away from him in a swirl of petticoats. The flowers drooping in her hand, she marched back through the garden, her steps hastened by wounded pride and hurt feelings.

"Madeline. Wait!"

Ignoring his command, she kept on going, but Anatole closed the distance between them in several strides. His hand shot out, closing over her arm. She had no choice but to turn back and face him, although she held herself rigid beneath his touch.

His expression had softened a trifle, but his jaw worked in a grim struggle before he was able to get out the next few words.

"I . . . I'm sorry."

It was not the most eloquent apology Madeline had ever heard, but surely the most sincere. And the most hard-won. She gave a gruff nod to show her acceptance, relaxing a little of her stiffness.

"It's just that you are constantly taking me by surprise," he continued. "From the very first. I—I am not accustomed to it. So many changes."

"Neither am I."

His hand slid down her arm to grasp her hand, and she finally detected some trace in his harsh features of the man who'd taken her to bed last night. The kindness. The gentleness.

Her breath stilled as she imagined he might now offer her a warmer greeting. He wanted to. She thought she could see it in his eyes, those compelling eyes that seemed to lure her into his arms by the sheer power of his gaze. Madeline took a hesitant step forward, when the look vanished. Anatole's lashes swept down, and he released her, leaving her more confused than ever.

"So what were you doing out here all alone?" he demanded.

It took Madeline a moment to remember. She'd been so certain she was about to be kissed, she'd even readied her lips. Battling aside her chagrin and embarrassment, she said, "It was the garden. There is something almost magical about it."

She eagerly held out the lush bouquet for his inspection, but Anatole regarded the flowers with as much enthusiasm as if they'd been a bundle of deadly nightshade.

Feeling more foolish than ever, Madeline withdrew her offering. "I have never seen flowers bloom this way so early in the year."

"You shouldn't have been doing that. It's dangerous."

"Picking flowers?"

"No," he said tersely. "Meandering about this garden. The path slopes downward, eventually ending at the cliffs. I don't want you wandering off alone again."

"All right," she agreed with some reluctance. Although she appreciated his concern, she wanted to argue with him, tell him she was not a careless child or a china doll that needed to be stored safely on a shelf.

But something about his expression kept her silent. He stalked a few paces away from her, leaning up against a tree, staring broodingly at the tangled path he claimed led to those dangerous cliffs, the drop-off to the sea. Madeline noted for the first time how weary he looked, deep lines of exhaustion carved into his face.

She imagined he was one of those iron men, born to the back of a horse who could spend long hard hours in the saddle without it having such an effect on him. So what in the world could he have been doing that left him looking so worn down?

When she ventured to ask him, the only reply she received was brief and dismissive. "It was about some estate business. Nothing of any great interest."

Then why did he look so troubled that she longed to brush the hair back from his brow, caress his warrior's scar, and tell him everything would be all right? Except that she didn't have the least idea what everything was, and it was clear he had no intention of telling her.

Sadness and frustration warred within her. Considering the intimacies she and Anatole had shared, she had thought things might be different. Her husband surely could not continue to remain such a stranger to her. Not after last night.

But the set of his shoulders appeared as stiff and untouchable as ever, his expression closed against her. Whatever his grim thoughts were, he seemed to snap out of them himself. Straightening away from the tree, he said, "About those women from the village. You can keep them and do whatever you like to the house. As long as you leave my study alone."

"As you wish, my lord," Madeline murmured, concealing her disappointment at the way he continued to shut her out. "Heaven knows, I have enough else to attend. There are still all the bedrooms, and after that the entire old wing of the house. I am sure the castle keep could use a good dusting and—"

"No!" Anatole snapped with such vehemence Madeline gaped at him.

"You are not to go anywhere near the old keep, do you understand?" he said fiercely.

"But why? I have a great curiosity about historic places, and I was looking forward to—"

"No! I absolutely forbid it."

Madeline stiffened at his peremptory tone. She was doing her best to be patient and understanding, but Anatole had a way of making it very difficult.

"Upon my word, sir," she said. "First, you told me to stay out of your library. Next it was the gardens, and now your castle. Am I your wife or your prisoner?"

"I am not used to anyone questioning my commands, madam."

"And I am not used to obeying unreasonable orders, sir."

"Is it unreasonable to want to keep you safe? The castle keep is old, dark, and dirty, full of—of spiders."

"I'd hardly be afraid of a few spiders. You make me feel as if you have some other reason. What are you hiding over there? Another wife?"

She'd meant the remark as a jest, but the uneasy expression that sifted over Anatole's features was far from reassuring.

"I'm hiding nothing," he said. "If you are so bent upon seeing the place, I'll take you there myself sometime."

"When?"

Her persistence caused his jaw to knot with vexation. "When . . . when we have been married a year and a day."

"But that is like something out of an old nursery story."

"Well, that's what you came here looking for, wasn't it?" He sneered. "A fairy tale?"

His sarcasm bit at her like the lash of a whip, flinging that folly over the portrait back in her face, hurting worse because she thought they'd laid that issue to rest. Perhaps she hadn't learned so very much about men after all. Certainly not this one.

Raising her eyes to Anatole's, she said with quiet reproof, "Perhaps I did come to you with some starry notions, my lord, but you are fast curing me of all of them."

Then she gathered up her skirts, heading back to the house before the fiery ball of dignity lodged in her chest dissolved into something foolish like tears.

This time Anatole made no effort to stop her. Though he wanted to. So badly that he ached with the need to gather her back into his arms, cover her face with a hail of kisses, carry her off to his bed, and lose himself in loving her. As a man should be able to do with his wife. None of these difficulties or shadows between them.

But all he could do was watch her go, the bright sweep of her skirts and fiery tint of her hair vanishing into the house. In that one moment it was as though all the color and warmth drained from the garden, leaving only the cold gray sky and bitter wind blowing in from the sea.

Anatole ground his fingertips against his eyes, feeling too wearied even to swear. He'd hurt her again, the last thing he'd desired or meant to do.

God, when would he ever learn to stop roaring at the woman like some demented beast? Even after that fool Trigg had alarmed all hell out of Anatole, even after he'd stormed into the house and found the place crawling with women, he'd tried to keep his temper in check. He'd intended to seek Madeline out, discuss the situation with her in firm but reasonable tones.

But then he couldn't find her in the garden, couldn't sense her whereabouts no matter how hard he strained his unique gift of perception. Panic had clawed at his heart, and he'd been able to see nothing but the path that led down to those accursed cliffs.

Heaven help him. The woman was making him raw and vulnerable in a way he hadn't been for a very long time. When she'd finally appeared, his relief had been so great, he'd had to cloak it behind blind, unreasoning anger.

And as if all that had not been bad enough, just when he'd mended his quarrel with her, she had to bring up what he'd been dreading all along. A wish to see the old part of the castle.

In the alarm of the moment he'd been unable to think of anything to do but play the tyrant. Forbidding her to visit the keep until a year and a day had passed.

A year and a day? Anatole winced. Where had that idiotic notion come from? Madeline was right. It did sound like something from a damn fool fairy tale.

But what else could he have said or done? Agreed to take her over to the old castle hall, let her make her curtsy to Prospero's ghost? Introduce her to the rest of his family legacy, equally as terrifying, including his own accursed talents.

Perhaps it would be best to do it and have it done with. He'd ever been a forthright man, and this constant need for secrecy was beginning to wear him down. The mask he was forced to wear had begun to chafe.

Maybe the time *had* come to tell Madeline the truth. What was the worst that could happen?

The answer unfortunately seemed to be littered at his feet. The nosegay of flowers Madeline had picked now lay strewn across the path. Anatole wondered if she'd even noticed them falling from her hand as she'd fled from him.

He bent down to retrieve a discarded azalea, annoyed by the way his hand trembled. He could picture too clearly how Madeline had looked when she'd first shown him the bouquet, her lips soft and smiling, her eyes shining with wonder as she'd talked to him about the magic to be found in flowers. He, who had never seen magic in anything.

But he was starting to see it in her, and that terrified him. He turned the azalea in his hands, stroking one fingertip along the silky white petals.

Roman's voice suddenly echoed in his head, Roman with his devil's gift for stirring up a man's most painful memories.

Have you yet tried to offer her any flowers?

Anatole compressed his lips, fighting against the images those words evoked. His ancestress Deidre had known how to distill an elixir from her blossoms, the kind of brew that could make a man forget. It was supposed to have been her parting gift to her lover as she lay dying.

Anatole had never wanted anything to do with his family's spells, but he'd often wished he had the secret of this one . . . the power to forget. But the sight of the single flower he held was enough to make his blood run cold with memory.

Anatole pinched the bridge of his nose, closing his eyes against the remembrance. But the mind that was so skilled in stripping away the mysteries of the future was equally adept at baring the misery of the past . . .

He was a child again, defying his father's stern orders, defying everything by creeping toward forbidden territory, the gilt-and-rose-draped sitting room that to him had seemed the abode of angels.

The door had been left ajar and peering inside he saw her, his golden-haired mother like the queen of the angels, perched upon the carved armchair that was her throne. Bent over her embroidery, with her supple fingers she plied her needle with a grace and skill that fascinated him.

Her blue eyes were clear. For once she had not been weeping. That fact emboldened him to squeeze a little farther inside the door and breathe, "Mama?"

Cecily's head snapped up; her serenity fled. The revulsion that sprang to her eyes was as immediate as the shudder that coursed through her.

"Stay away from me," she hissed.

Timidly he stretched out his hand, showing her the clump of wildflowers, roots, and weeds clutched in his grubby hand. "Mama, I only want to—"

"Stay away!" Her voice became more shrill. She leapt out of her chair, cowering behind it, her face turning almost savage in her fear.

His shoulders sagged. He had not expected to be allowed to touch her, or have her touch him as he saw other boys' mothers do, tousling his hair or gathering him close for a hug. He'd learned to accept the fact that there was something very bad about him that made him unworthy of her love.

He'd only wanted to show her that he was not evil. Not entirely. Glancing sadly at the bedraggled bunch of flowers, knowing he could not get any closer, he'd done the only thing he could. Concentrated harder than he ever had in his life and gently floated the bouquet across the room.

A horrible cry had escaped Cecily, and in the wildness of her terror, she grabbed up the first thing to hand, a crystal vase.

The memory of his mother's screams, the shattering glass cut through Anatole's head like a knife. Clenching his fist, he pressed it to his scar, until he was able to still the remembered pain.

The windswept garden came slowly back into focus. Something soft creased his palm, and as he slowly opened his fist, he realized what he had done. Crushed the delicate flower he'd held until nothing remained but broken petals drifting down to the hard-packed earth.

And he'd actually believed that he was ready to tell Madeline the truth? Anatole shuddered. No, it was more important than ever to keep her from finding out his dreaded secrets.

He needed more time to prepare her, to make certain she would not be afraid. More time to—to . . .

To do what? mocked a voice inside him that sounded strangely like Roman's.

To win her heart?

Aye, Anatole was stunned to realize. That was exactly what he was hoping for. He sagged back against the tree, a mirthless laugh escaping him at the irony. It wasn't Madeline who had fallen prey to fairy tales.

He had.

Chapter Eleven

The door stood at the end of a narrow stone passage carved in the shape of an arch. Made of ancient oak, the portal seemed steeped in mystery and superstition, legends of Bride Finders, family curses, and stranger secrets Madeline was beginning to fear lurked just beyond the barrier.

Lightning flashed through the rain-washed windows, illuminating the mural painted above the door, a dragon with vermilion wings outstretched, claws extended, rising up out of the lamp of knowledge. Like a fiery sentinel, the mythical beast appeared to glare down at Madeline with its golden eyes, threatening to scorch her if she dared venture too close.

She jumped half out of her shoes when another crack of thunder sounded, almost as though in warning. Warning her to leave this shadowed hall and return to the main wing of the house before she did something she might regret.

But it had taken her a full day to summon her courage and find the key that unlocked Anatole's forbidden castle. She cradled the cast-iron weight in her damp palm, knowing she should make haste. Her husband had ridden out again on another of his unexplained errands, leaving her alone for most of the day, but there was no telling when he might return.

She stole a nervous glance over her shoulder, the arched stone hallway gloom-ridden in the murky afternoon light, the rain driving against the leaded panes of glass in this older wing of the house. She was quite alone here, but still she hesitated to fit the key in the lock, although she hardly knew why.

Why should she feel so guilty about defying Anatole's arbitrary command? Almost as if she were about to betray him in some fashion. She wouldn't have been forced to this subterfuge if the man hadn't been so blasted unreasonable.

Ever since their encounter in the garden, the tension had remained rife between them. She had tossed on her pillow last night, half hoping he would steal into her bedchamber to apologize, to offer her some better explanation for his strange behavior. Hoping, she thought wistfully, for something more. But the door connecting her room to his had remained silent and closed.

Anatole might have surrendered his crystal sword to her in that peculiar ceremony, but he'd obviously held back on the heart and soul part, Madeline thought bitterly. She understood him no better now than the day she'd first arrived.

Telling her she wasn't allowed to set foot in the castle-keep until a year and a day had passed! What sort of sense did that make? And what could possibly be in there Anatole didn't want her to see?

Skeletons of men choked to death in one of Anatole's black tempers? Hoards of stolen treasure? Servants who'd gone insane chained to the dungeon walls? Or something even worse?

Madeline scolded herself for entertaining such lurid imaginings. Likely she would find no more than what Anatole had said. A dank old castle keep crawling with spiders. And his reason for forbidding her would turn out to be just another one of those . . . those St. Leger *things*, a belief in some sort of family curse that would be set loose, just as Anatole believed his mother had died young because she wasn't a chosen bride.

But Madeline had never allowed superstition to rule her life, and she wasn't about to start now. Reason and logic would provide answers to everything, including the enigma that was her husband.

Yet as she stepped closer to the forbidden door, an inexplicable shiver worked its way up her spine. The air seemed to have gotten suddenly colder, a chill caressing her skin. And she thought she heard something stir beyond the heavy wooden barrier. The creak of a footstep?

Madeline trembled, fighting an urge to scoop up her petticoats and run. She chided herself for being so foolish, allowing her nerves to get the better of her. Steadying her fingers, she eased the key into the lock.

"Madeline!"

Anatole's voice shot through her like a crack of thunder. She gave a frightened gasp, and nearly dropped the key. Her heart threatened to batter its way past her rib cage. Fighting for composure, she turned slowly around.

He stood where there had been only shadows before, a phantom of a man whose presence seemed to fill the narrow passageway. Bursts of lightning flashed over the eerie whiteness of his shirt, the rain-wet darkness of his hair, the hard contours of his jaw.

"Anatole, you—you're home already," she said, hoping she didn't sound as dismayed as she felt. She retained just enough presence of mind to slip the key from the lock and conceal it in the folds of her skirts.

"What are you doing here?" he asked quietly. Too quietly like the calm that presages a violent storm. As he stalked forward, she retreated. But there was no place to go, the rough barrier of the door pressing against her back.

"Well, I—I—" she stammered, then felt disgusted as she realized what she was doing. Behaving like some cringing schoolgirl caught out in mischief.

Madeline straightened, coming away from the door. "I'm sure you know quite well what I was doing."

Anatole said nothing. He merely held out his hand.

After a moment's hesitation Madeline sighed and relinquished the key into his outstretched palm. She stared down at the mud-spattered toes of his boots, more disconcerted than she cared to admit. She felt a little like a mouse who'd tweaked the whiskers of a mighty lion and now waited, dreading his roar.

He crooked his fingers beneath her chin, forcing her to look up, and Madeline braced herself. But the rage she'd expected to find was absent. The harsh planes of his face appeared battered, his eyes weary and sad. She'd never seen him look so solemn, and it made her even more uneasy. Somehow she would have preferred the roar.

"Have you ever read any Greek myths?" he asked.

"W-what?" she faltered.

"Greek myths like the one about Psyche and Eros. Are you familiar with it?"

Madeline blinked at him in surprise. Her imperious warlord had caught her defying him, and the man wanted to discuss *mythology*?

"Y-e-ess," she replied cautiously. "Eros and Psyche . . . that was the myth where the princess Psyche married a mysterious stranger who promised to give her everything she could possibly desire. There was only one condition. She was never to look upon his face, but—" Madeline broke off uncomfortably, suddenly realizing where this was leading.

Anatole continued for her, "But one night Psyche's curiosity and fear got the better of her. Terrified that she might have wed a monster, she armed herself with a dagger and stole into her husband's bedchamber. There she lit a candle and looked upon him while he lay sleeping."

Madeline tipped her chin to a defiant angle. "And she was so startled, she dropped the dagger, discovering that her husband was none other than Eros, the handsomest of all the Greek immortals."

"But because she'd broken the condition, she lost him."

"But she eventually won him back and became a goddess herself," Madeline said with a triumphant smile. "So the story turned out all right in the end."

"*But* so much misery could have been avoided if only Psyche had obeyed and trusted her husband."

"But how could she trust you . . . I mean how could I trust him when you are being so secretive. I mean *he* was . . ." She trailed off in frustration. Somehow she and Anatole seemed to be getting hopelessly tangled up in this myth. But unlike Eros and Psyche, Madeline was not at all sure they would find such a happy resolution.

"It's only a ridiculous story," she muttered.

"I used to think so, too, when Fitzleger first told it to me. But now I'm not so sure." There was a gravity to Anatole's voice, compelling her attention more surely than if he'd bellowed.

"I behaved badly yesterday, barking commands at you to stay away from this part of the house. But, Madeline, there are some things I can't explain to you as yet. All I can do is hope that you will trust me, believe that I'd never do anything that would hurt you."

He placed his hands on her shoulders, turning her to face the door. "Did you notice the mural above the arch?"

"How could I miss it?" That infernal dragon seemed to regard her with an evil glint in its eyes.

"It's a copy of the device on the St. Leger coat of arms. Did you also remark the words painted on the base of the lamp?"

"No." Madeline stood on her tiptoes, squinting closer. The light in the hall was very dim, but she was able to make out a phrase etched in Latin. She translated hesitantly, "He who has great power must . . . must use it wisely."

"It's our family motto. Yours now, too."

"But I don't have any power."

"Aye, but you do, lady. Far more than you could possibly imagine."

He turned her to face him again. "The decision lies with you. Obviously I can't watch you every moment of the day, nor do I wish to. I demand that you give me your word of honor, you will stay away from here."

Madeline felt more convinced than ever that her husband must be keeping some grim secret from her. The door, what lay beyond it, appeared all the more intriguing, compelling. But so were Anatole's eyes as he watched her, waiting. Almost as though his entire fate rested in her two hands.

"All . . . all right," she said at last. "Though I hope I'm not required to swear an oath in blood."

His lips twitched with the first hint of a smile. "No, your hand upon it will do."

She slipped her fingers into the calloused strength of his. "Very well. I promise. I'll stay away from the castle keep as long as you desire."

"Thank you." He bent swiftly, catching her hand to his lips, brushing against the delicate skin of her wrist. Her pulse throbbed at the unexpected contact, the heat of his mouth seeming to spear through her veins.

Then he raised his head, his black mane of hair falling back. The dark fire in his eyes made her forget everything. Forbidden castles, locked doors, frightening secrets. He slipped his arms about her waist.

Anatole had not kissed her since their wedding night, and Madeline found herself quickening with anticipation. He brushed his lips across her brow, her cheeks, the tip of her nose, finally tasting lightly of her lips.

He smelled of spring rain, of wild gallops across the moors, of the raging power of the seas. A thoroughly masculine scent. A quiver of excitement shot through Madeline, and she wished that she had not taught the man to be quite so gentle.

She longed for him to . . . she scarce knew what. Crush her in his arms and combine some of this tenderness with the fire and fury of the first kiss he'd ever bestowed upon her, the one that had nearly brought her to her knees. Astonished by these confusing desires, Madeline gazed up at him.

"Do you still find me such an alarming specimen?" he asked.

"No." She fingered the wild damp lengths of Anatole's hair, abraded her knuckles along the roughness of his jaw, shadowed by a day's growth of beard.

"Although, you could use a little taming," she said with a smile. "Nothing that a pair of scissors and a straight razor wouldn't cure."

"But there is nothing that can be done about *this*." He touched his fingers to the scar that tore a jagged line across his brow.

Madeline nudged his hand aside, gently tracing the ancient wound herself.

"It suits you somehow, your warrior's scar. Gained in some hotheaded sword battle, no doubt." She shivered. "It must have been a terrible wound. A few inches lower, and you would have been blinded."

"It happened so long ago, I scarce remember." Anatole captured her hand, kissing her fingertips, avoiding her eyes.

His warrior's scar . . . if his lady only knew how he'd really come by it. If she only knew his other wretched secrets.

And she'd come damned close to finding out all of them. If he'd been a few minutes later coming home—if he hadn't chanced to go into his study and discover the key missing.

Anatole's vast relief was tempered with apprehension. Despite the promise he'd wrung from her, how long could he continue to deceive her this way?

And would it ever be long enough to achieve what he wanted more than anything in this world? To have her love him with that kind of undying love all the St. Leger wives had shown their mates for ages past.

It was hopeless. How could he possibly imagine that a man such as he could ever win her heart? A man whose only knowledge of women had been how to lift their skirts and take his ease. Not that he couldn't have used that kind of *ease* from Madeline. His desire had only grown worse since he'd known the touch and taste of her, felt what it was like to bury himself deep inside of her.

He'd never sought advice from anyone before, but he found himself wishing there were someone, some wiser man he could consult about the arts necessary to enchant a lady.

The thought had no sooner formed in his head when Anatole felt an icy chill sweep over him. Gazing over the top of Madeline's red-gold curls, he was horrified to see the door handle rattle. He could sense Prospero's presence on the other side of the wooden barrier, could almost see the specter's wicked grin.

"Stay out of this, you old devil," Anatole said through clenched teeth. "I need no help from you."

"What?" Madeline looked up at him with wide-eyed puzzlement. "What did you say?"

"Nothing! Only that—that there's the very devil of a draft in this old corridor. We should get back to the main wing where it's safe—I mean warmer."

Wrapping his arm about Madeline's waist, Anatole hustled her away before Prospero took it into his head to do something worse. As they left the passage, Anatole hoped that he was the only one who caught the faint echo of laughter.

He hardly dared relax his stride until he had Madeline safely back in the new wing. The freshly polished marble floor, the gleaming wood banister in the front hall seemed so solid, so blessedly normal.

Madeline paused at the foot of the stairs, touching her hand shyly to the front of his shirt. "It's little wonder you took such a chill back there. You need to get out of these wet clothes. You're still damp from whatever wild adventure you were pursuing out in the storm."

Anatole sucked in his breath. Her touch, her suggestion to discard his clothes were as innocent as the spring rain, but the effect on him was like thunder. Visions of stripping her bare as well stormed through his head, molding her lithe naked form to his in a heated embrace, tumbling her down amongst the cool linen sheets and . . .

And no! He was resolved to be more the kind of man Madeline could love, something a little tamer, more civilized. And that didn't include ravishing her in the middle of the afternoon.

He was certain he now knew what he'd done wrong on their wedding night. Been far too blunt, too quick with his physical demands. She needed more time to respond with passion to his touch. Something no St. Leger bride had ever required before.

But then he was no Prospero, Anatole thought bleakly. He didn't even possess the charms of his own grandfather. Yet somehow he must learn to do better by her. Carefully he eased Madeline's hand away from his chest.

"I did ride farther than I meant to," he said, steering the conversation back into safer channels. "But it wasn't that much of an adventure. I only called in at the rectory to—to take tea with Fitzleger."

Another lie. Would he ever be able to offer Madeline anything but half-truths and falsehoods? He'd never drunk a cup of tea in his life that he could recall. What he *had* done was report to Fitzleger his complete failure to find any trace of the old man's mysterious churchyard visitor.

But his explanation appeared to satisfy Madeline. "Oh, yes," she said. "Mr. Fitzleger and I had many lively afternoon teas together in London, debating over everything from our differing translations of Virgil to our opinions on these new French philosophers."

"I fear that Fitzleger and I do less debating and far more arguing."

Madeline regarded him with troubled eyes. "You quarreled with Mr. Fitzleger?"

"Nothing of any consequence," Anatole assured her. It was all but impossible to quarrel with the saintly little man, but Anatole had been treated to another of the Bride Finder's soft-spoken lectures regarding Madeline.

Fitzleger had shaken his head after hearing of Anatole's recent encounter with Roman, including his cousin's disturbing curiosity about Anatole's bride.

"Ah, my lord, you must now see the risks you run by being so secretive. What if Madeline should have a chance meeting with Roman in the village or hereabouts? Or any of the other St. Legers she doesn't even know exist."

"There will be little possibility of that. Not if I keep her close to the house."

"My dear boy, you cannot keep your wife locked up in an ivory tower."

"I can certainly try," Anatole had replied stubbornly.

The old man had cast him a look of gentle remonstrance. "Women generally require a little more by way of society than a few servants and a pack of hunting hounds. You will only make Madeline unhappy if you shut her off from the rest of the world."

Madeline's unhappiness was the last thing Anatole desired. "So what do you want me to do? Throw a blasted ball in her honor?"

"You can start by simply making her known to the rest of the St. Legers."

"No!" Anatole had shot to his feet and taken to pacing about Fitzleger's tiny parlor.

"What is it that you fear?" Fitzleger asked. "That if you agree to this meeting, some of your family will tell Madeline things you do not wish her to know?"

Anatole wished that he could have said, yes, that was exactly what he dreaded, but it was only part of it. He might not be able to control Prospero, but he was fairly confident as head of the family, that he could command the silence of the living St. Legers.

His real fear went far deeper and was far more irrational. The fear that if he shared Madeline with anyone else, somehow he would lose her before she was even his.

But he could hardly explain something that foolish to Fitzleger. He had ended up by storming away from the vicarage instead, Fitzleger watching his retreat with sorrowful eyes. As usual, Anatole's irritation with the old man stemmed from the realization that Fitzleger was right. . . .

"Anatole?" Madeline's tug at his sleeve brought Anatole back to the present. She gazed at him questioningly, and he was chagrined to realize that he must have been standing there like a block of stone while he wool-gathered. Muttering some excuse about going to change his clothes, he made his escape up the stairs.

But his conversation with Fitzleger would give him no peace. Anatole had only gone halfway when he hesitated, turning back.

"Madeline!"

She'd headed off down the hall in the direction of the library, but she came back to stand at the foot of the stairs, one slender hand poised on the banister.

"Yes?" She looked up at him with that sweet expectant smile, which was fast proving his undoing, filling him with indescribable yearnings.

You will only make her unhappy if you shut her off from the rest of the world.

Anatole struggled with himself another long moment before confessing, "Fitzleger and I did discuss something of import today. He thought that perhaps—that is, I was wondering—" He clenched his jaw, then managed to get the words out. "I was wondering if you wished to be presented to my family."

"Your family?" Her smile wavered. "But . . . but I thought they were all in St. Gothian's under the church floor."

"There's at least one that should be," Anatole muttered, Roman's unwelcome image coming to mind. "But I do have an uncle or two, and many cousins yet living."

"Oh," Madeline said faintly. She should have been glad to hear that Anatole had some family, that he was not quite the solitary figure she'd imagined him to be. Why, then, did she feel so unsettled to learn there were more St. Legers running tame about Cornwall?

"I have never been that close to my family," Anatole said. "But I suppose I must introduce you to them."

"Of course. It is only natural your family should wish to meet your wife."

But there wasn't anything natural about any of this, Madeline thought. One might have imagined that these other St. Legers would have been present at their wedding. But Anatole hadn't even bothered to mention them. The question was *why*.

Madeline tried to still these troubling thoughts. The important thing was that Anatole had told her now. It was the first indication he might be willing to share some part of his life with her besides a bed, and Madeline seized upon it with all the eagerness of a starving sparrow pecking at crumbs.

"We should invite your family to Castle Leger at once," she said. "We could have a . . . a supper, a very informal one."

"A supper?" Anatole looked as wary as if she'd suggested some bizarre ritual. "Do you know how to go about such a thing?"

"Certainly. I arranged my mother's dinners and salons for her all the time." However, Madeline didn't add that after all the details had been taken care of, her mother had frequently begged her not to attend. Not that she could blame Mama, Madeline thought ruefully. She'd always been something of a social disaster, with a penchant for saying the wrong thing at the wrong time to the wrong person. But she could surely manage to mind her tongue for one evening.

"Very well," Anatole conceded. "I shall see that my family is summoned to Castle Leger."

"*Invited,* my lord," Madeline corrected gently.

"What? Oh, er—yes."

But after Madeline had bustled off, eager to begin laying her plans, all of Anatole's doubts returned in full force. Had he completely lost his mind?

It had been years since he'd asked anyone but Fitzleger to cross the threshold of his home, even his own family. The last time St. Legers had gathered beneath this roof had been for his father's wake. And that day had proved a bloody damn nightmare, with himself nearly killing Roman, roaring at the rest of them to get the devil out and leave him alone with his grief.

He had a vague recollection of bluff faces, kind eyes, hands that would have reached out to him in sympathy had he not turned away. But he'd sought his comfort where he'd always found it, wrapped in a mantle of solitude. Over the years he'd maintained that distance, except for chance encounters out riding on the moors, down on the beach, or at the local inn. Summoned or invited, perhaps this time his kin would tell him to go to the devil. And how would he explain that to Madeline?

Damn Fitzleger and his interfering advice to hell.

Anatole's misgivings only intensified as he wound his way upstairs. He approached the door of his own room when his extraordinary sense picked up another presence, one he was not familiar with beneath his roof.

He frowned, focusing in. A young woman, one of those dratted females Madeline had recently engaged. The girl lingered just down the hall on the shadowy landing of the back stairs.

Anatole liked neither being spied upon nor having servants who cowered away from his presence. Twisting in that direction, he commanded, "You there! Come out at once, girl."

He heard a soft intake of breath, then the young woman stepped out of the doorway. At first he could see little more than a clean apron tied over a worn gray dress. Then she crept closer, her face emerging from the shadows. Wisps of strawberry-colored hair curled out from beneath a maid's white cap framing a countenance too hard and embittered for one so young.

Anatole froze, staring into thin, sharp features he'd last glimpsed over Marie Kennack's grave, the girl's eyes reddened with her grief.

You killed her. You cursed my mother with your demon's touch, telling her she would die.

Anatole had stood with bowed head, not trying to defend himself, filled with unreasoning guilt, unbearable regret. Sometimes he was unsure himself whether or not the girl had spoke true.

He flinched back a pace as though even now Bess Kennack continued to hurl her accusations at him.

"What are you doing here, girl?" he asked hoarsely.

"I was but coming to collect the mistress's mending, sir."

"I mean—what are you doing here at Castle Leger?"

"I was told to come here because you were looking for maids, sir. And your good lady was kind enough to offer me a position. Unless—" Bess angled a glance at him that seemed equal parts fear and challenge. "Unless *you* don't want me working here."

Anatole certainly did not. Bess's presence could prove naught but a constant reproach, a painful reminder of the darkness his strange abilities brought into people's lives. But somehow he could not bring himself to turn the girl away.

"The selection of the female staff falls within my wife's province," he said with a stiff shrug. "But in future, girl, make yourself known and don't be hiding on the stairs."

"Yes, sir." Bess dipped into a curtsy that seemed respectful enough. Did he only imagine the look of pure hatred burning in those pale blue eyes?

Anatole watched uneasily as she vanished, a pale gray ghost slipping off down the servant's stair. Every instinct he possessed warned him that the girl was trouble, and God knows, he had enough of that looming in his life. He should dispatch her back to the village posthaste.

But if there was any kindness he could offer Bess Kennack, he more than owed it to her. Fitzleger had obviously been the one to send her here. The old man would hardly have done so if he hadn't thought it would be all right.

Perhaps Bess had finally forgiven Anatole for the part she believed he'd played in her mother's death. And if she had not? It scarce mattered, Anatole thought with a tired sigh.

He'd grown accustomed to being haunted in his own home.

Chapter Twelve

The night was streaked black with roiling clouds, the stars extinguished like so many snuffed candles trailing smoke. A brisk wind set the tree branches to clawing against the windowpanes, and even the moon had hidden itself away.

A perfect night, Anatole thought wryly as he upturned his face toward the sky, scenting another storm brewing. Restlessness, danger, and portents of disaster all blown in from the sea. Aye, a perfect night . . . for a gathering of St. Legers.

Stiff and uncomfortable in his best black frock coat and knee breeches, Anatole paced along the top of the stone stairs sweeping down to the carriage drive. Ranger trailed anxiously at his heels as though Anatole's own sense of unease had communicated itself to the dog.

The night wind threatened to wreak havoc with Anatole's neatly tied queue and cravat, but he was in no hurry to return inside the house. He took another puff from his pipe, a calming habit he'd learned from Fitzleger, but the night breeze had managed to extinguish that as well. Sighing ruefully, he tapped the tobacco out of the ivory-carved bowl and returned the pipe to his waistcoat pocket.

The smoking had only been an excuse anyway to escape the last-minute bustle of preparations. He'd had nearly a week to resign himself to the notion of this blasted supper party, and he thought he'd managed to do so, giving Madeline free rein to plan the event as she chose, staying out of her way.

But he hadn't counted on how strange it would seem, watching her open doors long closed. Lights blazed again from the chandeliers in the long gallery, and it gave him a queer tight feeling in his chest.

A few steps closer along the portico, and he had a clear view through the tall latticed windows. Inside, candle shine illuminated the mint green Spitalsfield silk that hung on the walls and the delicate sofa and chairs, the pattern on their cushions a potpourri of lavender and faded roses. The darkness had fallen back from the creamy expanse of carpet, the marble fireplace, and the cherry wood pianoforte.

The drawing room had witnessed many St. Leger events over the generations, christening suppers, wedding feasts, betrothal balls, birthday fetes, glasses lifted to toast a new king, to celebrate a successful harvest or the vanquishing of a Mortmain.

But the room had remained dark and silent for over a decade, the last person to have any use for the elegant chamber had been . . . his mother. Cecily St. Leger had played hostess to all manner of entertainments that had been the talk of the entire countryside, as though she'd been seeking in a desperate round of gaiety to banish the shadows that hung over her life.

For a brief time she had succeeded, filling the long gallery with light and music, laughter and dancing.

Not that he had ever experienced these marvels for himself, Anatole thought bitterly. Or at least not up close. Only from a distance those times he'd managed to escape from the care of his gentle tutor Fitzleger, from his room down at the gatehouse that Anatole regarded more as a banishment, a prison. Eluding the vicar's watchful eye, he'd fluttered through the night in his white shift like a small, pale moth drawn back to the great house. Drawn to the blaze of lights, the tinkling of crystal, the scrape of violins, the chorus of laughing voices.

His mouth thinning, Anatole stared at the beckoning windows, and it was almost as if he could see the phantom boy he'd once been, creeping closer, crouching there behind the pillar trying to remain invisible while he peered inside.

The brilliant scene had unfolded before his wondering eyes like some theatrical spectacle, the ladies in their gowns and jewels, the gentlemen in their stiff brocades and lace cuffs, all too beautiful and perfect to be real.

But none had been more magnificent than the young couple by the pianoforte. Cecily St. Leger's graceful fingers had rippled over the keys of the pianoforte, her sweet soprano joined to his father's bold tenor, Lyndon St.

Leger gazing at his wife with rapt adoration as they united in some tender ballad.

Listening to them in the darkness, huddling his bare feet beneath his night shift, Anatole's young heart had swelled with longing and a humble sense of pride, that these magnificent beings were his own mother and father. That although it was never openly acknowledged, in some small way they belonged to him.

All too soon the call to dinner would come, and the wonderful music ended. One by one, the couples had linked arms and vanished into the dining room beyond. Anatole had pressed his nose against the glass in a desperate effort to obtain one last glimpse of his mother before his father escorted her from the chamber. The double doors would close, leaving Anatole staring like an audience at an empty stage, feeling more alone and forgotten than before.

Then a rage would sweep through him, an anger he scarce understood but so strong it made him long to shatter the glass windows. But Fitzleger had managed to teach him something of self-control.

So he'd shrunk down beneath the sill, hugging his knees to his chest, allowing something to shatter inside himself instead. . . .

Ranger's cold nose nuzzled Anatole's hand, the hound's whine drawing him back to the present. Anatole blinked the images of the past away, startled to realize that in his musings, he'd drifted closer to the drawing room. The memory had been so strong, he half expected to see that trembling child huddled beneath the windows. But there was no child, only the grim-visaged man reflected eerily back to him in the glass.

Muttering an oath, Anatole drew back into the shadows, ashamed that a mere childhood memory could still have such power over him, to haunt, to compel . . . to hurt. Damnation, he was no longer some grubby-faced boy to be skulking around out here in the dark. He was the dread lord of Castle Leger, the master of all these lands, these walls, every being who dwelled within them, including his new bride.

Why then did he feel a need to remind himself of that?

He leaned up against the house's stone facade, Ranger pressing close to him, pawing at his knee, the old hound as ever not understanding his master's dark moods, but eager to offer solace.

Anatole rested his hand lightly on the dog's head, knowing an urge to kneel down the way he had used to as a lad and fling his arms about Ranger, burying his face in the familiar warm comfort of the dog's neck.

He half started to bend when Ranger tensed, letting out a sharp bark, alerting Anatole that someone else had come out of the house. He straightened sharply, not having to turn around to see who it was.

There was only one person at Castle Leger capable of catching him off guard this way. Madeline. In a whisper of silk and a cloud of rose-scented perfume, she glided toward him across the portico.

Ranger ambled over to her, and she murmured a low greeting to the dog, before calling, "Anatole?"

He clenched his teeth, wondering with dread how long she might have been watching him, how much of his recent folly she had observed.

He turned slowly to face her with a stiff nod. "Madam."

The night breeze caused her gown to billow out around her. Fashioned of brilliant green silk, the hem was caught up with rosettes to reveal a dauntingly feminine froth of petticoats. A lot of dress for one small woman, rustling and shimmering with her every movement as she came closer, her face a pale oval in the soft glow of the porch lantern.

She cocked her head to one side in that curious puzzled gesture that had become so familiar to him over the past week.

"Is anything wrong?" she asked hesitantly.

Wrong? No, nothing much, except the woman had been flinging open too many damned doors since her arrival at Castle Leger. And not just ones leading to closed-off rooms, but to places deep inside of him until his heart felt like a rusty gate being forced open. An often painful sensation . . .

"What the deuce should be wrong?" he forced himself to reply.

"I don't know. It's just that I couldn't find you anywhere in the house, and I was worried."

She'd remarked his absence and had been worried? Enough to have come in search of him? It was far more than his own parents had ever done. He scanned Madeline's face eagerly, but the hope that had flared within him died.

The smile she offered him was her usual one, so cheerful, so sensible. Of course, she'd come to look for him. She'd have gone to look for anyone she thought might be missing and in distress, from simple Will Sparkins to the kitchen cat. Besides being the most practical of souls, Madeline was unfailingly kind. But it was not her kindness he wanted.

"There was little to worry about," he said. "I merely decided to give Ranger a run before taking him down to the kennels. I assumed you'd want all the dogs out of the house tonight."

"Yes, thank you, but not Ranger."

Anatole's brows rose in astonishment, even more so when despite the danger to her fancy gown, Madeline bent down to stroke the old hound's dome-shaped head.

So his lady harbored a soft spot for shaggy, scarred old beasts, did she? Then, perhaps there was some hope for him yet. She sifted her slender fingers through the animal's fur, and Anatole watched with an avid kind of hunger.

Damn, a man had sunk to a low pass when he found himself envying his own dog. The candle shine from the house brought out the fiery highlights in her hair. Caught up in some elaborate topknot, it cascaded over one shoulder in a ripple of long curls, exposing the delicate nape of her neck. His fingers itched with the urge to caress, to test the silkiness of those tendrils, the soft warmth of her skin, but he knew one touch would never be enough, so he kept his hands in fists clenched tight at his side.

He'd tried so hard to be a gentleman these past days, so much so that he scarce knew himself. Never raising his voice to a level of a bellow. Never approaching her when he still smelled of the stables. Never cursing in her presence, not even when he'd discovered that in her enthusiasm for cleaning, she'd tossed out his favorite old pair of hunting gloves.

And above all else never touching her except to help her rise from her seat after dinner or to give her a chaste kiss when he bade her good night each evening. Determined to seek no more from her until she seemed willing to grant it. So respectful. So considerate. So civilized.

It was damn near killing him. Did the woman even notice his clumsy efforts to woo and win her? The constant ache in his loins, the fire in his St. Leger blood berated him for a fool. Win her, be damned! She was his wife, blast it. It was his right to take her whenever and wherever he chose.

And Madeline would submit, cheerfully gritting her teeth like the most practical woman that she was. That thought was the greatest agony of all.

With a final murmur to the dog, Madeline straightened, glancing up at the ominous sky with its shifting shadows.

"I hope none of our guests get caught in a storm," she said. "The wind sounds so unusual, almost wild and mournful. It promises to be a passing strange night."

Anatole grimaced. Possibly more strange than Madeline could even guess, but he would take great care to see that didn't happen.

She shivered, rubbing her half-bared shoulders, a most innocent invitation for a man to wrap her in his arms, hold her fast until he warmed her blood.

And his own. Spreading fire from his mouth to hers, melding what was soft in her to all that was hard in him. Until the next thing he'd be doing was stripping that elegant gown from her shoulders and taking her right here beneath the drawing room windows.

Anatole shuddered, steeling his jaw, subduing the beast in him the only way he was able. By turning away.

"We should get back to the house," he muttered. " 'Tis far too chilly out here for you."

"Oh, no, I'm fine—" Madeline began, but Anatole was already striding toward the front door. She bit down on her lip, stifling the rest of her protest.

She would have liked to linger, discover why he'd really been out here in the darkness. For a brief moment her formidable husband had appeared like some lost boy, alone and forgotten, waiting for someone to reach out to him, invite him inside.

But whatever thoughts had tormented Anatole, they were destined to remain like so much else about the man. A mystery. Madeline felt the familiar tug of despair. She'd had such high hopes for tonight, unreasonable ones perhaps. Her marriage to Anatole had gotten off to a most strange beginning, but hosting a supper for one's new relatives was such a *normal* thing to do. Surely it would help to draw Anatole and her closer together. Perhaps he would learn to share more of his memories, his dreams, those troubling secrets that ever kept a barrier between them. But the more light she brought to the man's home, the deeper he seemed to retreat into the shadows.

His reclusive nature made life difficult for her, especially this evening when she could have used a little reassurance. She was about to hostess her first supper party, and she still knew so little about the guests she was supposed to entertain.

She'd plagued Anatole with questions all week, but he'd neatly evaded most of them. Beyond telling her that his one uncle was in the shipping trade, the other invested in tin mines, he'd had little to say. Any discussion of the other St. Legers seemed to be just like the old castle keep. Forbidden.

Trust me, Anatole had demanded.

And she was trying. But it would have been far easier if her husband had been a little less distant. Like the most cunning of enemies, her doubts seemed to attack hardest at night, when she had nothing to do but stare up at the canopy of her empty bed and fret that she might as well have remained a spinster for all the difference being married had made in her life.

She was still alone in the night, left only to dream of the tender lover who'd whisper such sweet things in her ear, his kiss arousing new passions within her, desires of which she'd only experienced the slightest taste.

She'd been glad of a little respite after her first encounter with Anatole, but now . . .

Did her husband ever intend to return to her bedchamber? Of course her interest in the matter was purely practical, she assured herself. Anatole needed heirs, she needed babes to love, her little band of scholars.

Was there something more about the mating ritual she'd yet to understand? Perhaps it couldn't be performed every night. It had appeared to be far more demanding of Anatole's physique than hers. Perhaps he could only do it once a fortnight. Or even once a month. There was only one way she could know for certain.

Ask him.

But her heart quailed at the thought as she glanced to where he awaited her beneath the portico's swaying lantern. There was nothing of the lost boy about him now as he stood impatiently holding the front door open for her, a tall and magnificent figure in his evening clothes, the frock coat trimmed with gold braid, the satin breeches clinging to his powerful thighs. A veritable dark prince with his jet-black hair, angular features, and warrior's scar.

When he beckoned imperiously, Madeline lifted the hem of her skirts and rustled toward him. Ranger had already vanished inside. But Madeline paused on the threshold. Summoning up her courage, she rested her hand on her husband's sleeve.

"Anatole, could I ask you a question?"

The familiar wariness crept into his eyes, though he gave a rueful smile. "You ask far too many questions, madam. What is it this time?"

"I was just wondering why—that is—" Madeline swallowed hard.

Why don't you ever come to my bed?

The embarrassing question hovered on the tip of her tongue, but she couldn't quite get it out. Staring up into the velvet night of his eyes, her courage failed her. She finished lamely, "I was just wondering if you think your family will approve of me?"

Her question left him nonplussed for a moment, then he replied, "Certainly. Why wouldn't they?"

His tone heartened her until he added, "After all, you are the bride Fitzleger chose for me."

"Oh, *that*. Yes, of course." Madeline lowered her eyes to conceal her disappointment. She'd hoped he'd been about to say that his family would approve of her . . . because he did. Foolish of her.

"So all the rest of your family also believe in the Bride Finder?"

"Aye . . . well, most of them do."

"And your uncles and cousins also gave their wives swords for wedding gifts?"

"No," he said. "As the heir to Castle Leger, I was the only one who had to do that."

His reply further dampened her spirits. *Had* to. That was very different from wanting to and—

Madeline brought herself up short. What man in his right mind would want to give his wife a sword? Her logical way of thought seemed to have become muddied with confusion since her arrival at Castle Leger.

"Now, madam, may we go inside?" He took her by the arm, urging her past the door, when suddenly his fingers clamped down in a grip that was almost painful.

With a gasp of protest Madeline glanced up to find the most extraordinary expression chasing across his features. Nostrils flared, eyes narrowed, every line of his body stiff and alert. There was something raw and primitive about her husband, like a beast scenting danger.

"Anatole? What is it? What's wrong?"

He didn't even seem to hear her. Releasing her, he whipped about to stare into the darkness.

At last he pronounced hoarsely, "They're coming."

"Who—" Madeline began, then her heart skipped a beat as she realized what he meant. The St. Legers. She could scarce believe she'd allowed herself to become so distracted as to forget.

Her own eyes swiveled in the direction of the night-blackened road leading to Castle Leger.

"Did you spot the light from a coach lantern?" she asked.

"No." Anatole winced, pressing his fingers to his brow. "It's just that when so many St. Legers travel together, they—er—create quite a stir in the night."

Madeline listened intently, wondering why she did not also detect something, the clatter of carriage wheels, the rumble of horses on the drive. But she supposed Anatole must be right. She had noticed on more than one occasion that his hearing was far more acute than hers, almost eerily so.

She drew in a deep steadying breath. She'd promised herself she would be the perfect hostess tonight, charming, gracious, and above all else, calm. But it would have been easier if her husband hadn't appeared so grim, hands braced on his hips, like an embattled knight of yore steeled to repel invaders.

Was it her imagination or had the wind picked up sharply, the night sky waxing just a trifle darker? A sense of unease skittered up her spine.

She still didn't know what to expect from Anatole's family, but she had a sinking premonition they were going to prove far different from her own cheerful dithery relations.

Madeline had hoped to fortify herself in the front drawing room before her guests arrived, greeting them with regal dignity as each was properly announced in turn. But somehow she might have known these St. Legers would manage to overset her plans.

She had darted upstairs long enough to repair the damage the night wind had wrought upon her hair, to fetch her fan. But by the time she descended to the hall below, she could already hear the rumble of voices in the long gallery.

She fought back an unreasoning urge to dart back into her bedchamber and bolt the door. There was no sign of her husband; the only person stirring about the lower hall was Lucius Trigghorne.

Madeline frowned at the sight of him. She'd managed to spruce up most of the other male servants for this evening, get them thrust into clean livery. But the unrepentant Trigg still ambled about in his greasy breeches and yellowed shirt, his grizzled hair not even combed.

As Madeline came down the last of the steps, the old man flashed his teeth stumps in a malevolent grin.

"Company's here, missus," he said, jerking one dirty thumb in the direction of the drawing room.

The little gnomelike man never missed an opportunity to try to disconcert her, but this time, Madeline vowed not to rise to the bait.

"I am aware of that, Mr. Trigghorne," she said, concealing the tremor in her fingers by smoothing out her gloves. "Has my husband come down yet?"

"Master's already in the parlor."

"Good, then, you may be about your business, sir. I'm sure they could use some extra help down in the kitchens."

"What for? You be already set to serve up them St. Legers their favorite dish."

"Truly?" Madeline asked, puzzled. "What do they like to eat?"

"New brides."

Madeline shot him an indignant glare, but Trigg shuffled off toward the servant's stair, cackling at his own jest. At least Madeline hoped the horrid little man was jesting.

Steeling her spine, she crept over to the drawing room door and inched it open a crack. Through the narrow sliver of space, she could see no one but Anatole, his arms locked behind his back in a rigid posture.

"It's been a long time, boy," a gruff voice was commenting.

"Aye," Anatole agreed.

It pained Madeline somehow to see Anatole looking so stiff and uncomfortable. She'd often been at odds with her own family, but however little they understood her, she knew she'd always be welcomed back into the fold with warm hugs and noisy greetings.

It had never occurred to her that she might be obliged to come to Anatole's rescue this evening, but the thought gave her the courage to fling wide the door and slip gracefully inside.

The chamber fell silent at her entrance. Madeline plastered a smile on her lips and started to dip into a curtsy until she focused on the room full of faces staring back at her.

She froze midway down, her mouth dropping open.

Dear Lord! She'd just sashayed into a . . . a towering forest of men!

They surrounded her, masculine forms in all different shapes and apparel, but all possessing Anatole's stature, his stalwart limbs. The same fierce eyes, the same hawklike nose marked some half-dozen countenances, all of them decidedly male.

She swayed and might have tottered over completely had Anatole's hand not shot out to help her regain her balance. Numb with shock, Madeline scarce made sense of the introductions he began to fire at her.

"This is my oldest uncle who is in the shipping trade," Anatole said, indicating a great bear of a man. "Captain Hadrian St. Leger."

Shipping trade? Madeline thought as she summoned up a timid smile. Uncle Hadrian bore more the look of a wily old pirate, bluff, weather-beaten, his full beard shot through with gray. When he grinned, he displayed a set of large, handsome teeth that appeared capable of devouring a new bride in one gulp. And as for his sons, two sandy-haired youths Anatole introduced as Frederick and Caleb St. Leger, they both gawked at Madeline as hungrily as shipwrecked sailors who hadn't seen a woman for months.

Far less alarming was Anatole's other uncle, Paxton, who'd made his fortune in the tin mines. Modestly attired in a somber brown frock coat and gray powdered wig, he had the brisk manner of a London merchant. His son Zane, however, was another matter. The young man's disheveled clothing and bristling mop of black hair gave him the flyaway look of someone who'd recently been struck by lightning.

Yet by far the most disturbing member of the group stood a little apart from the others in the shadows pooling by the window curtain. Lean and ascetic, so pale, Madeline wondered how any man could appear so drained of life and yet survive.

"My cousin, Marius St. Leger," Anatole said. "One of the few skilled doctors hereabouts. He trained at the physician's college in Edinburgh."

The gaunt man favored Madeline with a solemn nod.

"And this is my wife, Madeline," Anatole concluded with a fierce glance, as though daring anyone to challenge the statement.

Clinging to Anatole's arm, she managed a curtsy that was more weak-kneed than graceful. An awkward pause ensued in which she was thoroughly inspected by six pairs of intent male eyes. It was all she could do not to disgrace herself by hiding behind Anatole's broad back.

To her relief, attention shifted to the slender doctor at the back of the throng.

"Marius?" Captain Hadrian said, the growl both questioning and prompting.

The others all fell back as Marius St. Leger came forward. He glanced up at Anatole as though soliciting his permission for something.

A permission her husband appeared reluctant to grant. But after a tense pause, Anatole pried Madeline's hand from his sleeve and offered it to Marius. The young man wrapped Madeline's fingers in the cool strength of his own.

He had the most melancholy eyes Madeline had ever seen. Disquieting eyes that left one reluctant to stare into those dark depths for fear of—of Madeline scarce knew what. Yet his touch was strangely calming. He looked into Madeline's face for a long moment, then smiled.

"Fitzleger has chosen well."

"I knew it. The old man never fails." Hadrian gave a guffaw of triumph. Before she had time to draw breath, Madeline was snatched away from the shelter of her husband's side, embraced by one sinewy pair of male arms after another. Hugged and bussed on the cheek until she was left blushing and gasping for air.

Even Anatole could not escape the tide of exuberance, his hand wrung with congratulations, his back slapped until Madeline's formidable husband was left as gruff and embarrassed as a blushing schoolboy.

Madeline should have been pleased with her hearty acceptance into the St. Leger family. And she was, except for one thing—the puzzling absence of any softer greetings.

She'd only heard two members of the female side of this family ever mentioned, she reflected uneasily. One of those had her heart buried under the church floor, while the other . . . How was it that Anatole had described his young mother's death?

She died of fear and sorrow.

In the midst of the general hubbub, Madeline tugged anxiously at her husband's sleeve. Drawing him aside, she whispered, "Anatole, are there no ladies left living in your family?"

Anatole scowled, glancing about him as though he'd just noticed himself the absence of any women. He gestured, summoning his youngest cousin.

Caleb St. Leger ambled over, a gangly boy of about fifteen. He possessed a sunny, if somewhat vacant smile.

"Where are your women?" Anatole demanded.

Caleb looked bewildered, and for a moment Madeline feared the boy meant to check his waistcoat pockets. He scratched his neck, blushing deeply. "Well, cousin Anatole, you know Da doesn't hold with us taking mistresses. He says we can damn well wait until we are married before—"

"He means our mother and sister, you dolt!" his brother Frederick cut in. With all the wisdom of his seventeen years, Frederick rolled his eyes and offered Madeline a look that seemed to apologize for the folly of his younger brother. "Mama and Elsbeth are at home."

"Why aren't they here?" Anatole demanded.

Frederick shrugged. "Didn't know they were invited."

Anatole muttered a vexed oath. But before he could say anything more, his uncle Hadrian stepped into the breach.

"I'm sorry, lad," he said. "But the command you sent requesting our presence was not all that clear. And it has been a long time since any ladies were welcome at Castle Leger."

"Or anyone else for that matter," Caleb mumbled under his breath, provoking his older brother into giving him a sharp nudge in the ribs.

"However," Paxton spoke up, "my wife Hesper will be pleased to wait upon your good lady whenever it may be convenient." He favored Madeline with a courtly bow.

"And my wife as well," Zane St. Leger added.

"And mine." Hadrian nodded his agreement.

"I shall look forward to making their acquaintance," Madeline said, turning impulsively to the doctor. "And your lady, too, sir."

There was a tense pause before Marius replied, "Alas, my dear cousin, I fear I no longer have one."

"Oh, I—I'm sorry," Madeline stammered.

"So am I," Marius replied quietly, making Madeline wonder with dismay what tragic story lurked in his past, what family curse or tradition he might have run afoul of. These St. Leger men seemed to be pure hell on their women. . . .

Whatever lay behind Marius's sad smile, Madeline was relieved when Caleb piped up, "Well, I'll be happy to send my wife along as soon as ever Mr. Fitzleger gets me one."

Which remark earned him another scornful jab from his brother, but the older men laughed, even Marius, and the tension was broken.

The matter smoothed over, the gentlemen ushered Madeline toward one of the settees and gathered around her like a swarm of bees surrounding honey. Anatole stationed himself by the fireplace, maintaining a watchful eye as his male relatives barraged Madeline with eager questions, trying to draw her out, learn more about her.

But at least they were doing it by more conventional means than Marius used. Anatole's gaze flicked to the pale figure of his cousin, who spoke little, listening gravely to whatever was said as was the doctor's habit.

As cursed as Anatole often thought himself, he'd always been grateful he possessed no share of the talent Marius had inherited. Marius . . . the one who could make even other St. Legers uneasy. No man should be able to strip another's soul bare, and slip past the most carefully guarded secrets of the heart.

Anatole wondered why he'd allowed it, permitted Marius to take Madeline by the hand, stare into her eyes, violate his bride in that fashion.

Perhaps because of his own lingering doubts, though it shamed Anatole to admit it. The fear that somehow a mistake had been made, that he was about to go the way of his own father, yearning after the wrong woman to the point of tragedy and destruction.

Fitzleger has chosen well.

What a world of relief there had been in those four simple words, enough so that Anatole felt he might actually survive this evening.

Surely the worst moment was over, that initial acceptance of his bride. And while his uncles and cousins might not approve of his demand for their silence regarding certain family matters, he was fairly confident he could trust them to respect his wishes.

The misunderstanding over the ladies being invited had been awkward, but Madeline seemed to have accepted it with a good grace. Any trace of her nervousness vanished behind an eager smile when Mr. Fitzleger finally put in his appearance.

He was greeted by the rest of the St. Legers with all the warmth and deference due him as the Bride Finder. And although Fitzleger returned their greetings with equal pleasure, the old man seemed out of breath, as though he'd run all the way from the village.

Smoothing down his white wings of hair, he bestowed a courtly bow upon Madeline, apologizing for his lateness. "My little granddaughter Elfreda arrived today far earlier than I had expected her. Mrs. Beamus and I have had much to do to get the child comfortably settled. It has been a long time since we've had a wee one at the vicarage."

"But what a joy it must be for you, Mr. Fitzleger," Madeline said. "Will the child be with you long?"

"I believe so. The air of London has not been agreeing with the poor child and her mother, my youngest daughter-in-law, Corinne is much preoccupied, preparing for her confinement."

"I hope she brings forth a son," Hadrian said. "A boy with the gift. We'll be needing another Bride Finder for the next generation."

"I am sure Corinne will do her best, sir."

"Well, tell those sons of yours to put their backs into the task." Hadrian's ribald comment caused Madeline to color, and Anatole was surprised it did not earn his burly uncle one of Fitzleger's gentle rebukes.

But Fitzleger bore an air of distraction about him, and Anatole didn't think it was entirely owing to the unexpected arrival of one small girl. He knew that particular expression on his old tutor's face far too well.

Now what the devil's amiss? Anatole thought grimly.

He was not kept in suspense for long. When the general flow of conversation resumed, Fitzleger wasted no time in drawing Anatole aside for a private word in his ear.

"My lord, on my way here, I noticed something that has me much troubled."

"Not another mysterious cloaked woman," Anatole said with a wearied sigh.

"No, thank the Lord, but something equally as disturbing." Fitzleger raised troubled eyes to Anatole's face. "I did not realize until this evening that you had taken Bess Kennack into your service."

"And so? Did you not send her to me for that very reason?"

"No, I most certainly did not."

Fitzleger's emphatic reply caused Anatole to frown for a moment. Then he shrugged, "Someone else from the village must have done so, then."

"But do you think it wise to have her here under your roof? I know you only meant to be kind, but—"

"Kindness has nothing to do with it. It's called guilt, Fitzleger."

"Guilt for which there is no reason. You are not responsible for the death of that girl's mother, no matter what poor Bess thinks in her bitterness." Fitzleger shook his head, saying earnestly, "Send the girl to me. If Bess needs employment, I will find it for her. This situation seems fraught with disaster, considering how the child feels about you."

"The *child* thinks I'm a demon from hell who should have been put to the torch at birth. But it is not an opinion I am unfamiliar with."

"My boy—" Fitzleger began, resting his hand upon Anatole's sleeve.

But Anatole rejected both the old man's gentle touch and his advice. "Have done with your fretting, sir. As long as Bess performs her duties and pleases my wife, I have no complaint. I could not be in any serious danger from a chit of a girl."

Especially not when danger seemed to approach from a far different source. Anatole's senses came to full alert, the footsteps of someone's imminent arrival stalking through the corridors of his mind.

Yet as hard as he tried to focus, he couldn't seem to hone in on the identity. He hadn't been exaggerating before when he'd told Madeline that many St. Legers in one place produced a disturbance in the atmosphere. The combined power of so many forceful personalities clouded his inner sense, made him feel as though he groped through a fog.

Could it possibly be his steward? Warford had been concerned of late about some poachers and—Anatole sucked in his breath, cringing at the stab of pain behind his eyes. He rubbed his fingers across his forehead.

No, it wasn't Warford's warm blustery aura he detected. This felt colder, sharper, like a blade of steel lifting his scalp.

"Roman!"

The name escaped Anatole in a curse, startling Fitzleger. Brushing past the old man, Anatole prepared to bolt toward the hall. But it was already too late.

The long gallery doors swung open, and Roman St. Leger swept into the room. Conversation trailed away to nothing, all eyes turning in his direction, for as Anatole had often remarked bitterly, no one knew better how to make an entrance than Roman.

Doffing his chapeau bras and multi-caped cloak, he swirled toward Bess Kennack, who stood behind him in the shadows. Tossing both garments into her arms with a careless grace, he chucked her under the chin, causing the dour girl to blush and gaze up at him with an awed expression.

As the girl backed away, Roman faced the assembled company with an elegant bow. Attired in a frock coat of ivory brocade and matching breeches, his blue waistcoat was shot through with silver. Roman's golden hair waved back from his perfect features, the silken lengths secured at the nape of his neck by a dark velvet bow. Shaking out the lace at his sleeves, he glanced up at Anatole, his eyes dancing with malice.

The forgotten bad angel, the evil fairy come to make mischief . . .

Anatole's gut knotted with apprehension, and he stalked forward to bar Roman's path. Roman raised his quizzing glass and eyed Anatole's black frock coat with a mocking stare.

"Merciful heavens, cousin. Who has died?"

"No one. *Yet*."

An amused smile curved Roman's lips, but Anatole was aware of movement behind him at the far end of the room. His cousins springing to their feet, his uncle Hadrian stiffening to an alert stance, Marius taking a hesitant step forward.

Anatole was certain they all remembered too well the last confrontation between Roman and himself within the walls of Castle Leger.

It had been the day of Lyndon St. Leger's wake, when grief and tensions were high, years of rivalry and resentment simmering over. He and Roman had gone for each other's throats like a pair of mad dogs, and it had taken the combined efforts of the entire St. Leger tribe to end their deadly struggle.

And all because of a watch, his father's watch, that by tradition should have passed down to a much-loved son. But it had been bequeathed to Roman instead.

His cousin still wore the cursed thing. With a gesture that was slow and deliberate, Roman retrieved the timepiece from his waistcoat pocket and flicked it open, affording Anatole a glimpse of the miniature of his mother mounted in the casing.

"Dear me," Roman murmured. "My apologies, cousin. It appears I am a little late for these festivities."

"Late?" Anatole said, struggling to conceal how much the sight of that cursed watch still affected him. Keeping his voice low so that it did not carry back to the others, he demanded, "What the devil are you doing here at all?"

Roman sighed. "That question is getting to be a tiresome habit with you, cousin. I have come to join this little family gathering."

"I don't recall that you were invited."

"I should have been. To the best of my memory, I am still a St. Leger."

"A fact that I do my best to forget."

Something brittle and dangerous flashed in Roman's eyes. "Then, perhaps it is up to me to remind you."

Anatole tensed, bracing himself for anything when Fitzleger rushed forward, the old man insinuating himself between them.

"Gentlemen, please!" he said in that same distressed tone he had been accustomed to scold them as boys. "This discord between you must end. St. Legers have ever stood together. Master Roman, if you wish to remain, you will behave yourself accordingly."

The tension faded from Roman's perfect features, replaced with his usual languid air of amusement. "Oh, aye, certainly, sir."

"And my lord." Fitzleger turned to Anatole, speaking softly. "Think of your good lady. You would not wish to distress her with an unpleasant scene."

Anatole scowled, but his gaze traveled to where Madeline stood surrounded by the tense forms of his uncles and cousins. Her face was alight with a mixture of innocent curiosity and uneasy bewilderment.

No, Anatole thought, he did not wish to distress his bride. In fact, it amazed him to discover how far he would go to avoid doing just that. Even so far as to dance with the devil himself.

Stepping close so that no one else could see, Anatole caught Roman's arm in a hard grip.

"If you stay," he said tersely, "you'll mind that adder's tongue of yours. My bride knows nothing of my unusual heritage, and for the moment I intend to keep it that way. At your own peril, you do anything to defy me in this matter."

Roman's brows arched in surprise, but he said, "Why, cousin, far be it from me to do anything that would displease you."

Wrenching his arm free, he smoothed out his sleeve, his lips curling in a smile that Anatole mistrusted. Every instinct he possessed urged him to use his power as he'd never done before. One good blast, and he could fling Roman back out those doors and straight to hell.

Aye, and he could also terrify his bride to death, condemn himself forever in her eyes as something strange and savage, an uncivilized monster.

Clenching his jaw, Anatole could only do what he'd so often been obliged to do for his cursed cousin. Stand aside.

Roman sauntered past, and Anatole could see the other men relax. He exchanged some bantering words with his young cousins, but his gaze fixed on Madeline. His eyes widened with something far different than his usual sardonic appraisal, and Anatole well understood the reason for it.

His bride, he thought with a mixture of pride and despair, had never looked more lovely than she did this evening.

"Anatole," Roman murmured, his rapt gaze never leaving Madeline's face. "I trust you do plan to present me to your wife."

Something twisted in Anatole's chest, an emotion so foreign he scarce recognized it for what it was. Fear.

"Madeline," he said. "My cousin. Roman."

It was hardly the most polished introduction, but Roman, damn him, more than made up for it by the smooth way he bowed over Madeline's hand.

"Madam." Roman raised her fingertips to his lips. "Forgive my neglect in not welcoming you to the family sooner. Had I known what beauty awaited me, I assure you, I would have visited long before now."

"Thank you," she murmured, looking flustered, the sort of effect Roman always had on women. Had Anatole truly hoped his sensible Madeline might prove different?

A hollow sensation lodged deep in his chest as he listened to Roman pour silken compliments into her ear, telling her how enchanting she looked this evening, how charming.

All the things Anatole realized he should have told her himself. Things he'd desperately wanted to say, but had been prevented by the weight of his own rough tongue. Now all he could do was stand by helplessly and feel himself dwindling. Back into that awkward boy with his face pressed against the glass.

Desolation warred with more primitive impulses, the desire to yank Madeline away from Roman, haul her possessively into the circle of his arm. Fighting against the urge to play the jealous fool, Anatole scarce noticed the stirring of another arrival filter through his consciousness.

Not until a discreet cough sounded from the doorway. Anatole flicked an impatient glance in that direction and froze at the sight of the bizarre apparition hovering there. A painted man . . . his face lost beneath a layering of dead-white cosmetic and rouge, a patch affixed to the corner of his thin mouth. He seemed to be all powdered wig and lavender silk, the wasp-waisted frock coat he wore flaring out from his slender hips and padded shoulders.

"What the deuce—" Anatole's exclamation drew the attention of the others, his own astonishment echoed in the dark mutterings of his uncles.

"Who the devil is that?" Paxton said, staring.

"Never mind *who,*" Hadrian grumbled. "*What* the devil is it?"

Madeline slipped close to Anatole and whispered, "Is that another of your cousins, my lord?"

"Hell, no!" Anatole replied feelingly, insulted by the mere suggestion of such a thing.

The only one who appeared unperturbed was Roman. He aimed his quizzing glass idly at the man in the doorway and drawled, "Ah, Yves. Your pardon, sir. In my exuberance at being clasped to the bosom of my family, I had entirely forgotten you."

He beckoned, and the man crept inside the room. Anatole wondered that he had not detected his presence sooner, but the creature had a weak aura, the weakest he'd ever known in any man yet living. He was swallowed up in the shadow of Roman's far more powerful one.

"Gentlemen, my sweet cousin, Madeline," Roman said, with a languid wave of his hand. "Allow me to introduce Monsieur Yves de Rochencoeur."

The fellow dipped into a flourishing bow, and Anatole's nostrils curled with distaste. The Frenchman reeked of some cloying scent, worse than a sailor's backwater whore.

Roman continued, "Yves is a dear friend of mine. I took the liberty of fetching him along with me to dine."

Liberty was far too mild a word, Anatole thought, outraged. Bad enough that Roman had had the insolence to show up uninvited without bringing one of his foppish friends along with him. But before he could vent his own annoyance, his youngest cousin chimed in.

"Damn, Roman," Caleb said, with all the bluntness of youth. "But this is a family supper."

Rochencoeur's eyes widened with dismay.

"*Milles pardon,* messieurs, madame," he said. He had an odd raspy voice that grated along Anatole's nerves like an iron file dragged across metal. "I did not *comprende. Certainement* had I but known, I would have not the intrusion made."

The Frenchman backed toward the door, and Anatole would have been well content to let him go, but with a soft cry Madeline hastened forward.

"Oh, no, monsieur, pray do not go," she said. "We should be honored to have you join us, should we not?"

Her appeal was met with stone-faced stares, only Fitzleger offering an encouraging nod.

"My lord?" She turned imploring eyes toward Anatole. "There is more than enough room at the table. Please tell monsieur that he is welcome."

Anatole folded his arms across his chest and squirmed, aware of the grim silence of the other St. Legers, fully understanding the reason for it. He possessed a Cornishman's instinctive mistrust of all strangers himself, but he wasn't proof against the plea in Madeline's large green eyes. He had already agreed to Roman's infernal presence. What was another aggravation more or less?

"Well," he said, "the fellow doesn't look as though he'd eat much. I suppose he may stay."

"How gracious of you, my lord," Roman purred, but Caleb shot him a look of pure betrayal.

"Anatole—" the youth began only to be cut short by a stern frown from Mr. Fitzleger.

"That'll do, lad." The vicar came forward to offer Rochencoeur his hand. "You are more than welcome, sir. Tell me, do I detect the hint of a southern accent in your voice? The lilt of Gascony?"

"You have the keen ear, monsieur," the Frenchman replied. He still looked ill at ease, but he managed a thin smile. "I was born there, in a little village. But now I spend most of my time in Paris."

"So what the blazes brings you to England?" Anatole asked.

Before the man could reply, he was cut off by Roman, "Monsieur Rochencoeur is a most talented *artiste*. I have great need of his services."

"Here in Cornwall?" Hadrian growled. "What the deuce for?"

"Why, Uncle, did I fail to mention that?" Roman said with one of his silky smiles. But it was Anatole's gaze that he met and held, as though anticipating the effect of his words.

"Yves is my architect. He is the man who is going to resurrect Lost Land."

Chapter Thirteen

Branches of candles glowed the length of the mahogany table, the burning wicks reflecting in the crystal goblets and the whimsical china designed by Anatole's own grandfather. The St. Leger dragon breathed fire from the center of each plate, cup, and saucer.

Will Sparkins filled the wineglasses, strutting about in his new powdered wig and gold-trimmed black livery. The lad had cleaned up to be quite a comely young man, his thatch of hair trimmed away to reveal a pair of sweet blue eyes.

The transformation of Will was at least one good Madeline had accomplished since coming to Castle Leger. Perhaps the only one, she feared.

She tried to relax, to smile at her guests, but she'd never been much good at this sort of thing. She sought to remember everything she'd observed in her mother about playing the role of gracious hostess. However, Mama had never held a dinner quite like this one, with dragons snarling out from the china, her only companions a cadre of men who looked more apt to dive for their swords instead of their forks.

There was a tension in the air that threatened to rival the storm gathering outside. Dark undercurrents swirled all about Madeline, which she scarce understood, only felt.

She picked at the fricandeau of veal on her plate, her gaze traveling to where Anatole sat at the far end of the table, his face cast in shadows as he sipped his wine in brooding silence.

She thought wistfully back to the other suppers they'd shared this past week, alone. Detesting formality, Anatole had dragged his plate down to her end of the table. He'd eaten heartily, allowing her to talk, which she feared she had done in abundance. But that companionable silence was far different from the grim one he'd adopted now, making him more remote from her than ever.

Somehow the tension seemed to have crept in, clinging to the coattails of one man. The glittering gentleman seated to her left.

Roman St. Leger.

Madeline scarce knew what to make of Roman, with his handsome face, smooth manners, and smiles that never quite melted the winter in his eyes. He was different from the other St. Legers, she thought, studying his flawless profile.

From Anatole down to young Caleb, they all had an otherworldly quality about them, an arresting, unforgettable *something* that Madeline could not quite define. A something that Roman lacked.

Becoming aware of her intent regard, his eyes met hers across the rim of his wineglass, his mouth twitching with amusement.

"Shall I turn the other cheek, cousin?" he asked. "So you may study my left profile as well?"

"Oh, n-no." Madeline lowered her gaze, blushing furiously at being caught out.

"But you were staring at me with such a confused frown on your lovely face. Is there something about me that puzzles you?"

A great deal, Madeline thought, if she were permitted to speak the truth. Such as why Anatole had appeared reluctant to admit his own cousin to the house? And why had the mention of the mere words *Lost Land* set all the St. Legers on edge, made Anatole look ready to strangle both Roman and his unfortunate friend Yves?

"I'm sorry," she said. "I did not mean to stare. It was rude."

Roman leaned closer, lowering his voice to an intimate timbre. "Not at all. It is a most agreeable thing for a man to find himself the object of interest to such a beautiful pair of green eyes. Are they more the shade of emerald or jade, would you say?"

"I—I don't know," Madeline stammered, uncomfortably aware that Anatole's fierce eyes were trained in her direction.

She had never been adept at receiving such flattery or engaging in light flirtation. Her sister Louisa would have known how to handle a man like Roman, laughing, fluttering her lashes, making the most of any opportunity to drive her young husband wild with jealousy.

Madeline recoiled at the notion of even attempting such a dangerous game with Anatole. There could be no jealousy where there was no love. Whatever hostility existed between Anatole and his cousin sprang from some ancient grudge, another part of his past that she was not to be permitted to know.

"Your eyes are more like emeralds, I think," Roman persisted, leaning even closer. "The same brilliant fire and luster—"

"Indeed, sir, they are neither emerald nor jade. They are just plain green."

Roman's brows arched in surprise. "Do my compliments offend you, cousin?"

"No, I would simply prefer it if you spoke to me like an honest, sensible man."

Madeline winced. She'd been too blunt as always. Roman's eyes narrowed.

But the wintery expression passed, and he laughed, murmuring, "Ah. The lady is as wise as she is beautiful."

He settled back in his chair, much to Madeline's relief. Appearing to have accepted her rebuff with good humor, he obliged her by changing the subject. Roman could be an engaging companion when he chose, speaking to her of London, the theater, and a dozen other mutual interests.

But as the second course was served, it seemed more prudent to direct her attention to Roman's friend, Yves. The Frenchman was all but forgotten by the rest of the party. Mr. Fitzleger, who might have been kind to him, was seated at the far end of the table, next to Anatole. And the rest of the St. Legers talked amongst themselves, excluding Rochencoeur.

The Frenchman appeared to be the sort of dandy that Madeline would have avoided herself, and had often done so in London drawing rooms. But she felt an unexpected sympathy for the man.

Perhaps because the two of them were both outsiders here amongst this overpowering St. Leger clan. It was almost cruel the way Roman had thrust his friend into this awkward situation, bringing him to a supper where he had not been invited or wanted. Roman should have known that Rochencoeur was exactly the kind of man that would most incite the contempt of his forthright relatives. The nervous Frenchman seemed to shrink back in his seat as though determined to draw as little attention to himself as possible.

Yves did not give the appearance of any great intelligence, his pale-colored eyes empty, as devoid of animation as a china doll. Yet Roman did not seem to be the sort who would suffer a fool gladly as his companion. It puzzled Madeline greatly how the two men could ever have become friends.

She curbed her curiosity while she made certain the Frenchman's wineglass and plate were kept refilled. It amused her to note that Anatole's prediction regarding Yves's eating habits were wide of the mark.

Most of the St. Legers had lusty appetites, but Madeline would have wagered that Monsieur Rochencoeur could have eaten any of them under the table, even the burly Hadrian.

She watched in amazement as the Frenchman worked his way through several helpings of the wine-roasted gammon, pigeon pie, and green peas. But he had the most exquisite table manners she had ever seen in any man, his hands even more slender and graceful than her own.

As Rochencoeur paused for a swallow of wine, she ventured, "So you are an architect, monsieur?"

"Not *précisément*, madame," Yves said with a modest smile. "I have merely the passing interest in the building of fine houses."

"You have come a long way for a passing interest," Madeline exclaimed. "You must be a great friend of Roman's to travel so far to offer him your aid."

Rochencoeur's gaze flickered uncertainly to where Roman had fallen into conversation with Zane St. Leger. "Ah, *oui,* but in truth, I came to England more in the service of a lady."

"Your wife, sir?"

"*Non.* Alas, my wife is gone these many years. I spoke of my noble patroness, Madame la Comtesse Sobrennie."

Madeline knew she was betraying an impertinent curiosity, but Yves had her intrigued. She had to wait patiently while he sampled the blancmange and the curry of rabbit, but the man was not loath to talk about his noble patroness.

"It is most difficult for a younger son to find his fortune, especially a man of my meager talents. Madame la Comtesse has been so kind, so generous. She has helped me to make my way in society. She has even undertaken the education of my only son Raphael."

Yves put down his fork long enough to display the miniature attached to his watch fob, a portrait of a chubby-faced lad with cherubic curls and steady blue eyes.

"What a handsome little boy," Madeline said.

"Oui." A spark of pride momentarily lit Yves's expressionless eyes. "He has only the eight years but already promises to be the grand gentleman all due to *la comtesse*. Such a gracious lady. So clever, so charming, so . . . so *belle*."

Madeline nodded and smiled at the Frenchman's enthusiasm for the countess. But she steered him back to the subject of far greater interest.

"It is fortunate your service to the countess allows you the time to help Roman with . . . what was the name of his estate?"

"Le Pays Perdue."

"Lost Land. Surely a rather bleak name for a gentleman's property?"

"It is a bleak place, madame. Lost and forgotten, a noble house reduced to ashes. But that will all change when—"

"I fear you are boring my fair cousin, Yves." Roman leaned across the table, cutting in suddenly with an unpleasant smile. "You are a good fellow, but you do have this unfortunate tendency to go prosing on about my affairs."

Madeline's eyes widened at such blatant rudeness. She glanced anxiously to see how Yves took it, but if the Frenchman resented Roman's insult, he gave no sign of it, other than an almost imperceptible tightening of his fingers about his wineglass.

Lowering his eyes back to his plate, he said quietly, "I was not *prosing*, monsieur. Madame St. Leger merely expressed a curiosity the most natural about your new estate, and I was attempting to answer her."

"If my cousin is so curious about the place, she must ride over and see it for herself. You are fond of riding, are you not, my dear Madeline?" Roman purred.

It was Madeline's turn to be discomfited. Her nervousness around horses had always been a sensitive point, even more so since her marriage to Anatole.

Only a few days ago her husband had insisted upon taking her on a tour of his stables, displaying his hunters with a fierce pride. She'd been far too intimidated by such massive beasts to even stroke their glossy manes. Anatole had finally sent her back to the house, and Madeline had gone with a heavy heart, knowing she'd disappointed him greatly.

But of course it was impossible that Roman could know any of this.

She forced herself to answer his question as lightly as she could. "Alas, no, sir, I fear I am not that good of a rider."

Unfortunately her remark carried to the opposite end of the table, drawing the attention of the rest of the men.

"Nonsense, my dear," Paxton St. Leger said with a genial smile. "All St. Leger women are bred to the saddle."

"One would certainly suppose that Anatole's bride would be," Roman added.

"Well, she is not," Anatole said. "And there's an end of the matter."

"Likely that is because of the great strapping brute you force her to ride. A lady requires a more civilized mount."

There was an unfortunate quality to Roman's voice whenever he spoke to Anatole that made everything he said sound fraught with some meaning that escaped Madeline. She watched in dismay as her husband's eyes darkened to an ominous hue.

Young Caleb intervened, leaning forward in his chair to say earnestly to Madeline. "You don't need to be afraid of Anatole's horses, cousin. They are fine fellows. I am sure if I talked to them, I could persuade one of them to carry you gently."

"You talk to horses, monsieur?" Yves asked with a chuckle.

"Aye, sir." The boy leveled the Frenchman a glance of lofty scorn. "It is my own special gift. The same as my cousin Anatole can—" Caleb clapped a hand to his mouth, looking horrified, as though he'd been about to blurt out something he shouldn't.

"The same as Anatole can what?" Roman prodded softly.

Caleb cast a glance at Anatole, appearing fearful of incurring his displeasure. And her husband was looking mighty displeased, but more with Roman.

"I—I—" Caleb said. "I only meant that I can communicate with horses the same as Anatole is—is good at riding them."

That was not at all what the boy had first meant to say, Madeline was sure of it. Much to her disappointment, Caleb went back to gnawing on a partridge wing, clearly determined not to speak another word.

She had hoped this evening, through Anatole's family, she might learn more about the man she had married. But the St. Legers appeared to be as guarded when mentioning Anatole as were his servants or any of the villagers she had chanced to meet.

It was as though a spell had been cast over Castle Leger, a spell of silence. The only one who seemed unaffected by it was Roman St. Leger. Toying with his wineglass, he returned to the distressing subject of horses as smoothly as though he'd never been interrupted.

"Perhaps I shall send Madeline something from my own stables. I have a gentle mare that would be perfect for her."

"No!" Anatole snapped before Madeline could reply.

"You may consider it a belated wedding present—"

"I said no!"

Madeline had no desire for the horse or any other gift from Roman, but she feared the offer could have been refused more graciously.

Roman's lips thinned. "Perhaps you should let your lady decide for herself."

"I can see to the mounting of my own wife, thank you," Anatole growled.

"We assumed you would have already taken care of that, lad," Hadrian said with a wicked twinkle in his brown eyes. It was obvious the captain only sought to break the tension that simmered between Anatole and Roman, but the seaman's ribald comment brought a fiery blush to Madeline's cheeks.

"Captain St. Leger!" Fitzleger cried.

Hadrian shot him an unrepentant grin. "Now, Vicar. All newlyweds must put up with a bit of teasing, isn't that right lad?" He gave Anatole's arm a playful jab. "So tell us. Did you break your grandfather's record of making love for three days?"

Anatole did not reply, his face firing as red as her own, his expression far more strained.

"Th-three days?" Madeline said, mortified. That certainly answered her question about how often a man could come to his wife's bed. If he had any desire at all to do so. Her heart sank as she realized there was far more wrong with her marriage to Anatole than in her innocence she had ever supposed.

"Aye," Hadrian chuckled. "You mean you have not yet heard the tale of how my father, Grayson St. Leger, whisked his bride away to the bedchamber directly after the ceremony, and she would scarce allow him out of her arms long enough to eat his breakfast—"

"Hadrian!" his brother Paxton groaned. " 'Tis our mother you are speaking of."

"And a fine lusty woman she was, too. Nothing to be ashamed of. 'Tis a glorious thing the sort of passion St. Legers inspire in their chosen brides."

"Aye," Zane said, and he quoted softly, " 'Two hearts brought together in a moment, two souls united for an eternity.' "

Paxton relaxed into a reluctant smile, and the rugged faces of all three men were transformed with an unabashed tenderness, their thoughts obviously drifting off to the wives awaiting them at home. But when Madeline's gaze sought Anatole's, he refused to even meet her eyes.

"But surely," Roman said, "there is no need to be telling Anatole's bride about such grand love and passion. Madeline must have experienced it all for herself, have you not, my dear?"

Madeline was spared the necessity of a reply by Anatole slamming his fist down on the table hard enough to make the silver plate jump.

"My bride's experiences are none of your blasted concern. Now, talk of something else, damn it!"

He cast a savage glower around the table that momentarily reduced everyone to silence. Madeline looked distressed by his flare of anger, but it was the last thing he needed, Anatole thought, for any of his lusty St. Leger relatives to guess that far from three days worth of loving, Anatole had only bedded his wife the once—and that with no great success. His pride would never recover.

Mercifully they all returned to their dinners, even Marius appearing unaware. Only Roman continued to regard Anatole with his insolent eyes and damnable smile.

Anatole clenched his teeth, fighting to keep himself under control. He'd vowed he would not allow Roman to push him into losing his temper tonight. But it was proving difficult, Roman taunting him with that subtle malice only Anatole could see, those double-edged remarks that only he could feel sting.

Past enmity mingled with the present as he watched Roman coax Madeline out of her embarrassment with that insidious charm of his. Anatole gripped the edge of the solid oak table so hard, it amazed him the wood did not splinter.

It had been a mistake allowing Roman across his threshold, as he'd known it would be, even without the man's silken barbs. Anatole had no social graces to compete with his cousin or the likes of that French dandy.

The pair of them now had Madeline engrossed in talk of some blasted poet Anatole had never heard of, making him disgustingly jealous of every word, every smile his bride bestowed upon Roman and that damned Frenchman. The discussion brought an animated sparkle to her fine green eyes that Anatole reflected bitterly he had never been able to put there.

But then, he had no conversation besides his horses, his hunting, or the farming on his estate. A man had little need of more when he took most of his meals in the company of his dogs and footmen. He'd never been ashamed of his ignorance until now.

That was just one more terrifying thing Madeline was doing to him. She was making him forget how to be alone.

Thunder rumbled outside, striking closer to the windows, and Anatole stirred in his chair, wishing this supper from hell would come to a swift end. The prospect of such a storm would have sent lesser men scurrying for their horses, but there had never been a St. Leger born troubled by anything so paltry as a lightning bolt, and that infernal Frenchman looked unlikely to rise from the table while there was still a pastry left.

Anatole stifled a curse when Mr. Fitzleger further prolonged the meal by insisting they drink a round of healths to the new bride and groom. But there was no gainsaying the gentle old man's affectionate good wishes.

Beaming, Fitzleger shoved to his feet and lifted his glass. "To Madeline and Anatole," he said, saluting them each fondly in turn. "Long life and much happiness."

"Here, here," Zane St. Leger seconded.

"To their continued prosperity," Marius added softly.

"And may they be blessed with many children," the irrepressible Hadrian put in.

"And bad 'cess to all Mortmains," Caleb sang out the traditional toast of St. Legers for generations.

Anatole tossed down his wine with impatience, thinking no more of the matter than he ever did. Until he saw Madeline tilt her head in that curious expression he had learned to dread.

"What's a *Mortmain*?"

"A parcel of black-hearted, scurvy bastards," Hadrian said. "Fit to murder all of us St. Legers in our very beds."

When Madeline's eyes widened in alarm, Anatole directed a repressive scowl at his uncle.

"The Mortmains were merely another Cornwall family who feuded with ours for generations," he said quickly. "You don't need to worry about them, Madeline. They are all long dead and gone."

"But if there are no more Mortmains, why do you still drink toasts to their ill fortune?"

More to the point, why did Madeline always have to have a logical explanation for everything? Anatole thought in sheer frustration.

"Well, because—because—"

"Because it is merely another ridiculous family tradition," Roman cut in, scornfully. "Just like our custom of sending out an old man to select our brides for us."

Anatole felt Roman's icy contempt saw at the remaining threads of his patience.

"Have a care, Roman," he said. "I'll tolerate no insult to Mr. Fitzleger beneath my roof."

"You misunderstand me, cousin. I intend no disrespect to the good vicar."

"I should hope not," Paxton told him sternly. "You will be needing the Bride Finder's services yourself one day."

"Oh, I think not. I have made my own arrangements." Roman's eyes flicked from one face to another, flinging out his next words like a man tossing down a gauntlet.

"Monsieur Rochencoeur is going to act as my marriage broker."

A stunned silence followed this announcement broken by Paxton's strangled gasp, "What!"

"Damnation!" Zane exclaimed, a sentiment swiftly echoed by the others.

Hadrian came half up out of his chair. "First the lad buys Lost Land and now this! He couldn't be more bent on mischief than if he was turning into a damned Mortmain."

The room dissolved into a cacophony of angry voices, and Anatole cursed Roman himself. He had a grim feeling this was what Roman had intended all along, merely biding his time, waiting to set them all by the ears.

His cousin lounged in his chair, clearly enjoying the sensation he had caused while Anatole fought to restore order.

"Quiet!" he thundered.

Everyone fell silent except for Roman's idiotic friend.

"It is only the most innocent bit of matchmaking," Monsieur Yves's hands fluttered as he sought earnestly to explain. "My patroness, *la comtesse,* you see she is a widow."

"A very beautiful and rich widow by all reports," Roman murmured.

"Her own papa was an English milord, and so she has the desire to marry again in the country of her birth. And I thought that if I could bring Monsieur Roman and *la comtesse* together, perhaps—"

"I said, *quiet!*" Anatole glowered at the Frenchman, and this time the fool had the wit to subside.

"Have you entirely lost your mind?" Anatole demanded, turning back to his cousin.

"I don't think so," Roman said, coolly shaking out the lace at his sleeves. "Is it madness for a man to seek a wife?"

"But, my boy," Fitzleger broke in, "if the time has come for you, if you are indeed ready to marry, you know you can rely upon my services."

"No offense, Bride Finder. But I don't have as much confidence in your abilities as some members of my family. I wouldn't want to end up as obviously mismated as . . ."

Roman trailed off, his eyes traveling significantly in Anatole's direction. Anatole tensed, his hard stare daring Roman to continue.

After a long moment his cousin appeared to think better of it.

"I wouldn't want to end up like Marius," Roman finished instead. "Wedded to a grave."

It was a cruel thrust. Marius flinched and said, "The tragic loss of my bride was none of Mr. Fitzleger's doing."

Madeline had remained grave and silent during the entire heated exchange, thinking she was far wiser to stay out of what was, after all, a family quarrel. But she could not refrain from turning to the pale doctor and asking gently, "What happened?"

"I delayed too long," Marius said. "Mr. Fitzleger wrote to tell me he had found my bride. But I denied the promptings of my heart, my very blood. Nothing was so important to me in those days as completing my medical studies. In my arrogance with my unique gifts, I believed I should learn to cure the world."

A shadow passed over Marius's gaunt features, not one of bitterness, only one of aching sadness. "By the time I journeyed south, my Anne was so ill of the typhus, there was nothing I could do to save her. She . . . she died in my arms."

Marius's quiet words had a sobering effect on the entire room. Madeline felt her eyes grow moist with sympathy, but Roman's lip curled in scorn.

"That was over ten years ago, but my cousin remains a bachelor, grieving for a woman he barely knew. According to our precious family tradition, *poor* Marius must end his days alone until he joins his dear Anne on the other side of the grave."

"But that's dreadful," Madeline said.

"Is it not, indeed?" Roman twisted in his seat to fix her with his ice blue stare. "But surely as a chosen bride yourself, you must ascribe to the powers of our Bride Finder."

"Well, I—I—"

"You must believe that some magical fate singled you out to be Anatole's bride, to love only him for all eternity. Or is it possible that you have some doubts on that score?"

Madeline slunk back in her chair, wishing that she had stayed out of this. Roman's question focused the attention of the entire room on her, and none awaited her answer more tensely than her own husband.

She met Anatole's eyes across the table, and her heart quailed. She knew full well his convictions regarding the Bride Finder tradition, his belief that his mother had died cursed because his father had defied the custom. Heaven knew, she had no desire to mock his family's superstitions or to take Roman's side in anything, but she could be no less than honest.

She spoke hesitantly, choosing her words with great care. "The legend of the Bride Finder, the idea that there can only be one man, one woman destined for each other is—is wonderfully romantic, but—but no, I cannot believe in such a thing. It defies all common sense.

"I see no reason why Marius may not in time find happiness with someone else. Nor why Roman should not be permitted to marry his wealthy countess."

She braced herself, fully expecting Anatole's anger. What she did not expect was the depth of pain in his eyes, as though she'd hurt him in some way she didn't understand.

The other St. Legers exchanged astonished then outraged glances. A sick sensation stirred in Madeline's stomach, and she thought she now knew how Spanish maidens must have felt, daring to defy the Inquisition by giving voice to heresy.

Only Roman grinned at her with approval. He gave a triumphant laugh.

"Ah, finally someone in this misbegotten family who is as cynical as myself. I do believe Mr. Fitzleger has made a mistake this time. You should have been my bride, cousin."

Rising gracefully to his feet, Roman raised his glass to her in salute. But as he prepared to take a sip, Anatole's eyes flashed darkly in his direction. Roman's hand jerked, dashing the wine back into his own face.

He sputtered a curse, dropping the glass. Madeline gasped, shrinking back as it shattered on the table.

"Mon Dieu!" Yves leapt up from his seat, plying his friend with napkins. But to Madeline's astonishment, Roman struck the Frenchman's hands aside and rounded on Anatole.

He backhanded droplets of wine from his chin, his eyes blazing with fury.

"Damn you and your tricks," he rasped, as though somehow his own clumsiness was Anatole's fault. "I'd call you out for that if you weren't possessed of the devil's advantage."

"It's an advantage I'd willingly set aside," Anatole said.

"Then, I am for you unless you are too much a coward to meet me on a plain man's terms."

Anatole's face went white. He shoved to his feet with such force, his chair clattered to the floor. Madeline's cry of dismay was lost in the protests of the other men as Anatole flung himself around the table.

"Is this plain enough for you?" he snarled, driving his fist into Roman's jaw.

Roman staggered back into the table, sending glass and china flying. Dimly Madeline felt Yves drag her to safety, but her eyes locked on Roman with horror. Recovering himself, he snatched up a carving knife.

She screamed as he lunged at Anatole. Anatole seized his wrist, deflecting the blade inches from his throat. He and Roman locked in a deadly grapple, slammed back into the mantel, sending the fire irons crashing.

The next few seconds were a blur of uproar and confusion as the other St. Legers leapt in to separate the two men. It took the combined efforts of Hadrian, Zane, and Caleb to drag Anatole off while Marius and Frederick fought to make Roman release the knife.

Hadrian cursed and Paxton pleaded. But it was Mr. Fitzleger's voice who rang out above the rest.

"For the love of God, gentlemen. Stop this! Have you both forgotten there is a lady present?"

Madeline feared the old man's words would have no effect. Anatole's queue had come undone in the struggle, his dark hair tumbled wildly about his face as he continued to strain against Hadrian's burly arms.

But then his gaze flickered in her direction. He took a deep shuddering breath and forced his muscles to relax.

Marius forced Roman to drop the knife, and it clattered harmlessly to the floor. Roman wrenched himself away from his cousins, striving to recover his usual sangfroid, smoothing out his hair, straightening the wine-spattered lace of his cravat.

A terrible silence ensued, and Madeline realized that her heart had begun to beat again, leaving her trembling all over. She still did not quite understand what had happened.

One moment Roman had spilled his wine; the next he and Anatole were trying to kill each other. And while distressed, the other St. Legers did not appear particularly surprised.

It made no sense at all. Only one thing was terrifyingly clear, and that was the red stain she saw seeping through Anatole's sleeve.

"Anatole," she cried out. "Your arm."

Anatole glanced down at his sleeve with indifference. But as Hadrian released his grip on Anatole, the burly man gaped with horror at the blood staining his hands.

The expression was mirrored in the faces of the other St. Legers. Roman's lips twisted in a faint imitation of his usual sneer.

"Dear me," he said, his voice not yet quite steady. "Now I've gone and done it. Shed the blood of another St. Leger. Doomed myself for all time."

"Hold your tongue, Roman!" Hadrian snapped.

Recovering from her shock, Madeline galvanized herself into action. Snatching up napkins from the table, she shouted for someone to bring her some water.

Bustling over to Anatole, she prepared to remove his frock coat, dreading what she might find. But Anatole jerked away.

"Forget about it. It's nothing," he muttered, his face lost behind the black fall of his hair.

"I am sure it is," she said soothingly. "But you must let me—"

"Leave it alone." He whipped from her, presenting her with the indomitable line of his back.

"Please, Anatole, I only want to—"

"This cursed supper party is at an end. You may retire, madam."

"But, my lord—"

"Go to bed, Madeline," he said savagely, twisting to look at her, and she finally saw his eyes. Hard, remote, they seemed to thrust her away as surely as if he'd taken both hands and shoved.

She glanced about her for some support, but was dismayed to discover the others shrinking from her as well. Hadrian, Caleb, Paxton, all of them stone-faced, looking anywhere but in her direction. As though she had been the one to cut Anatole with the knife instead of Roman. But she had obviously committed a far worse sin in their eyes, debunking their cherished myth of the chosen bride.

Even Mr. Fitzleger appeared sad and disappointed in her. Only Monsieur Rochencoeur dared to offer her a sympathetic glance. A sympathy that was almost her undoing. Hot spots of color burning in her cheeks, she swallowed back a hard knot of tears.

Salvaging what remained of her dignity, she picked her way toward the door through shards of dragon's wing china and broken crystal.

Just like her hopes for this evening. Completely shattered.

Anatole stared at the first dark droplets of rain bleeding down the windows as his family began to take their leave.

Roman and the Frenchman were the first to go. But why not, Anatole thought bitterly. Roman had as usual accomplished what he'd come for, driving Anatole to the brink of madness, leaving discord and disaster in his wake.

The last of Anatole's anger drained away, leaving him weary, scarce aware of the burning pain in his arm where Roman had cut him. He was aware of little beyond self-disgust and a sense of shame that once more Roman had gotten the whip hand of him, forced him to snap.

He could hardly bear to face the rest of his family, willing them away. If they had failed to guess before that there was something amiss with his marriage, they certainly all knew it now. The echo of Madeline's words seemed to linger in the room.

The idea that one man, one woman could be destined for each other is wonderfully romantic, but I cannot believe in such a thing.

It was something that no St. Leger bride would have said, at least not one who had found true passion in the arms of her husband. It must be as obvious to the rest of his family as it was to himself how greatly he had failed with Madeline.

He could sense the weight of their concern pressing against him, and his pride felt stripped as raw as his heart. He knew they would have stood with him against any enemy, those tall stalwart men, shoulder to shoulder, sword to sword.

But this trouble with a woman, his own chosen bride. This left them baffled, discomfited, as helpless as he was himself. One by one, they muttered their farewells and drifted out the door, even Fitzleger trailing out, the old man's faith, for once, badly shaken.

All gone until only one remained, but unfortunately, he was the one that Anatole would have most wished gone.

As the seconds ticked by, he drummed his fingers impatiently against the glass before turning to glare at his cousin, Marius.

"Is there something the matter with your horse?"

"No," Marius said. "I simply thought you might have need of my services."

Anatole gave a harsh laugh. "I don't think my bride's heart requires any more looking into, do you? She made her feelings quite plain enough."

"I was referring to my medical services. You know I don't enjoy the exercise of my peculiar powers any more than you do yours."

Anatole compressed his lips at the quiet rebuke, and turned away when he saw Marius fetching the medical bag that always traveled with him.

"I don't need any cursed medical attention."

"The choice is yours, my lord. If that trifling wound should become infected, if it should become necessary to amputate, likely it is of no account. You always have another arm, and I daresay that in time you will learn to shoot as well with your left hand as you—"

"All right, damn it! You may attend me," Anatole bit out through clenched teeth, stripping out of his frock coat. "For I suppose there will be no getting rid of you otherwise."

"You suppose rightly, cousin," Marius said, concealing a slight smile.

Anatole peeled back his sleeve, cursing when the linen stuck to the wound. He ripped the fabric free, setting his torn skin to bleeding afresh.

It was a clean slash down the back of his forearm, but Marius frowned as he mopped at the blood with a damp towel.

"It does not appear deep enough to need stitches," he said. "But it's an ugly wound for all that. Roman has much to answer for."

Anatole shrugged, then flinched when the movement caused his split skin to crack wider.

"I offered him provocation enough," Anatole admitted grudgingly. "It was an unworthy trick, using my power to fling the wine in his face. I should never have so lost control."

"I thought you showed admirable restraint." Marius rummaged around in his medical bag, producing a jar, some healing ointment of his own concoction. "You could have used that unique gift of yours to send us all crashing through the windows."

" 'He who has great power must use it wisely,' " Anatole quoted dryly, then sucked in his breath with a sharp hiss. Whatever Marius put in that cursed ointment of his, it stung like hell.

Marius offered him a rueful smile, and for one brief moment, Anatole felt a rare bond with this cousin who had always rendered him so uneasy. It was strangely comforting.

But the feeling didn't last long, not with the evidence of tonight's disaster strewn before his eyes. Overturned chairs, shattered china, spots of wine and his own blood staining his mother's elegant Aubusson carpet.

He expelled a deep sigh as Marius proceeded to bandage his wound, images obtruding that he had blocked from his mind before in the haze of his fury. Mostly of Madeline's face. So earnest as she'd dashed what remained of his hopes by declaring her disbelief in eternal love, so frightened when he'd gone at Roman like a savage dog.

And so hurt when he'd snarled at her to get away from him. But at such a moment her kindness and concern had stung worse than Marius's ointment.

He cursed the day he'd ever agreed to this stupid supper party. Any progress he'd made with her during the past week, his efforts to be more civilized, had all been undone in moments. This evening had gained him nothing except to confirm his bride in her bad opinion of him, to show her that he was something not fit to be turned loose in society and to earn him another night in an empty bed. Both his loins and his heart ached fiercely at the thought.

Marius paused in the act of pulling the bandage taut to glance up at him. "Er—I think you should just forget what happened here and make peace with your lady. Go to her bed."

Anatole jerked his arm away as though Marius wielded a knife instead of gentle healing hands. He glared at him accusingly. "I thought you said you didn't like to exercise your power, cousin."

"I don't. But when emotions are as strong as yours at the moment, they fairly shout in my ears, whether I want to hear them or not." He gave an embarrassed smile, the expression quickly replaced by one far more serious.

"Anatole, I don't know what mistaken pride or fear holds you back from your lady. But you need to set it aside."

"You're not exactly the man to be giving me such advice, are you, Marius?"

It was a cruel remark, worthy of Roman, and Anatole regretted it the moment it passed his lips.

The sadness in Marius's eyes deepened, but he said, "On the contrary, I am uniquely qualified to tell you. Don't make the same mistake I did. Go to your bride before it is too late."

A rare surge of emotion thickened Marius's calm voice. He made a brisk show of repacking his medical bag.

Anatole averted his eyes, made uneasy as all St. Legers were by Marius's grief. The one hitch in their family legend, the reminder that even with the skill of the Bride Finder, things could go awry. Happy endings were not guaranteed.

Anatole flexed his arm, astonished to find it already feeling somewhat better. He hoped now his cousin would be satisfied and be gone.

But Marius lingered, his brow knit into a frown. "I know you do not care for my advice, cousin," he said. "But there is one more thing I must say to you."

Anatole tensed, wanting no more talk about his difficulties with Madeline, but Marius went on, "It is about Roman."

"Roman?" Anatole relaxed in his surprise. "What about him? I can well imagine what you've been seeing in his heart. My head mounted upon one of the old castle pikes."

Marius grimaced. "If only Roman's thoughts were that simple. But he is far too complicated. Between this strange business of his purchasing Lost Land and now wanting to marry this French countess, I cannot figure what he is about."

"You have been trying to read him, then?"

"I confess that I have and to no avail. Venturing into Roman's heart is like descending into some twisted labyrinth. He is so clever at disguising his own motives and feelings, I'm not sure he understands them himself half the time. He's always been different from the rest of us."

"Aye," Anatole said. "If my aunt had not been such a virtuous lady, I would have suspected Roman of being a bastard in more ways than one."

"That is impossible. St. Leger women are never unfaithful to their men."

Never? Anatole wondered bleakly. Not even in their hearts?

Marius continued, "We all know that occasionally there have been St. Legers born devoid of our unusual gifts. Roman is simply one such."

"The fool should count his blessings," Anatole muttered.

"But he never has. I have often felt his pain over this. Being a St. Leger by name and blood, but not in spirit. Perhaps this is why Roman has always been so bitterly jealous of you."

"Of me?" Anatole echoed in disbelief.

"Aye. Envious of your powers, your position as head of the family, your lands and fortune, especially considering how little he inherited himself."

"And so what are you getting at, Marius?" Anatole asked impatiently. "That I should feel sorry for the cursed man?"

"No." Marius sighed. "I am only trying to tell you that envy can eat at a man's soul far faster than any disease can ravage his body. It can make him more dangerous than the worst sort of madness. And I greatly fear Roman is beyond all hope of cure."

Marius regarded Anatole with grave eyes. "You need to be careful of him, Anatole. Very careful indeed."

And on this final note of warning, Marius took his leave.

Chapter Fourteen

Sleep was impossible.

Long after Madeline had gone upstairs, she sat in her nightgown, half-heartedly brushing her hair before the mirror, all the while listening for the creak of a floorboard, the tread of a footstep, the slamming of a door. Any sound from the adjoining chamber that would alert her that Anatole had come upstairs, that the stubborn man had not bled to death on the dining room carpet.

Though, after the humiliating way he had rejected her, she didn't know why she should care. But she did, and she continued to listen even though she despised herself for it.

But it was difficult to hear anything other than the thunder pealing over the house. The storm battered against the windows of her bedchamber, the wind rattling the glass, the rain striking like a hail of arrows. It was as though the land of Castle Leger itself rose up like an avenging fury, raging against the woman who had presumed to refute its most cherished legend.

Stalking over to the windows, she flung open the heavy brocade draperies and gazed out into the rain-washed night with defiance. If she had unleashed any curse with her heresy, she dared it to come and get her, strike her down.

It could hardly be any worse than what she had just gone through downstairs, being shunned by the other St. Legers, sent up to bed by her husband like an errant schoolgirl.

She lingered by the windows, tempting her fate, but nothing happened but the disapproving grumbling of thunder, lightning flashing against the sky like bursts of cannon fire, illuminating the dark landscape with its twisted trees, the ribbon of road leading away from Castle Leger.

Did it ever do anything but storm in this part of the world? she wondered bleakly. She didn't envy the St. Legers their journey homeward on such a black and bitter night. Most of them must have gone by now unless Anatole's uncles had lingered over port to commiserate with him on his unfortunate marriage. For she doubted that any of the St. Legers still thought that Fitzleger had chosen so well.

She'd known so little warmth and genuine acceptance that the loss of their good opinion pained her, but not so much as the memory of the look in Anatole's eyes when he'd thrust her away from him.

And all because she had been reckless enough to agree with Roman about the Bride Finder. But what other sensible reply could she have given to Roman's prodding about eternal love and the St. Leger destiny? How was it Zane had described it? Two hearts brought together in a moment, two souls united for an eternity. A lovely romantic notion. But it must be as obvious to Anatole as it was to herself. A good many moments had already passed, and they were not passionately in love with each other or ever likely to be.

So what had Anatole expected her to say? She didn't know, but she feared she had disappointed him. Not that that was anything new. She had been nothing but a disappointment to the man ever since he'd first clapped eyes on her, not at all what a St. Leger bride was supposed to be.

Not bred to the saddle, not able to inspire a man with passion, three days' worth or otherwise. Not even able to share his family's beliefs.

Leaning her head against the glass, despair threatened to overwhelm Madeline at last, cracking through the shield of her own anger and indignation. But she blinked fiercely, determined not to cry.

The world was wet enough tonight without her adding to the deluge. If she could not face the emptiness of her bed, she could find something more sensible to do than streak the window with her tears and work herself into a raging headache.

With a final sniff she began to pick up the clothing she'd strewn about the room in her struggles to undress. She had never bothered to send for the girl she was training to act as her maid.

Bess Kennack was a deft young woman, but her intense eyes and dour manner occasionally discomfited Madeline. Her spirits were oppressed enough without gazing upon Bessie's gloom-filled countenance.

Retrieving her green silk gown from the chair by the fire, Madeline attempted to jam the dress back into her overcrowded wardrobe. In her struggles she dislodged several bandboxes and something hard, which came tumbling out, startling her. She leapt back in time to save her bare toes as the heavy object thudded to the carpet.

She pulled a face when she saw what it was. The St. Leger sword embedded in its leather sheath, the crystal in the pommel winking up at her like some capricious eye. She had never known quite what to do with the blasted weapon ever since Anatole had given it to her. Tuck it up amongst her parasols or bury it beneath her petticoats? It was constantly in her way.

Gingerly she bent down and tugged the heavy weapon upright, sliding it out of its scabbard. Candlelight played over the length of naked steel, the wrought gold hilt, the sparkling crystal.

Her heart softened a little as she remembered how gruff and embarrassed Anatole had looked when he'd been forced to kneel and present the sword to her on their wedding day. Almost endearingly so.

Perhaps he had never gotten around to surrendering his heart and soul along with the blade, but she realized now he had offered something else instead.

His pride. And that of all the St. Leger lords who had gone before him. She feared she had rather heedlessly trampled over both tonight. It wasn't a comfortable thought.

But she had never asked for anything to be placed in her hands. It was far too heavy a burden. All she had ever wanted was a simple country life, a scholarly husband, a library full of books, and a nursery full of children.

She'd never bargained for legends, forbidden castles, and swords. The blade was a strange gift for any woman, let alone one like her whose heart had never beat faster at the sight of a soldier in his regimentals or at the thought of a knight in armor. She'd always been an admirer of the gentler arts: poetry, music, philosophy.

And yet there was something amazingly beautiful about it. She turned the sword in her hands, studying the elaborate decoration on the hilt. The crystal possessed a clarity that was mesmerizing, infusing the sword with a strange allure and power.

Enough to make a woman forget poets and dream instead of warriors . . . the kind of iron-fisted man who'd band his sinewy arm about a maiden's waist and snatch her atop his fiery steed. Challenge her to brave his fierce facade, and drive the darkness from his wearied eyes.

They'd ride like the wind past sea and shore, rocks and hills to a field of heather, where he'd tumble her down among the sweet-smelling flowers to work his wild magic upon her . . .

The image brought a dew of perspiration to Madeline's skin, stirred an unbearable heat deep inside her. She scarce heard the knocking at her door until it came a second time, a little louder.

"Madeline?"

Anatole's voice, low as it was, cut through the haze of her thoughts. Madeline blinked, wrenching her eyes from the crystal like one snapping out of a trance, wondering what had just come over her.

"Madeline? Are you already abed?"

"No," she replied, nearly dropping the sword again in her haste to thrust it into the sheath. Feeling as guilty as a child caught toying with the fire, she hurried to jam the weapon back into her wardrobe.

She'd barely managed to do so when the door connecting her chamber to his swung open.

Part of her was still angry and hurt by the way he'd dismissed her, but she felt relieved to see him standing tall and upright, recovered from his wound. A fresh shirt stretched across the broad span of his shoulders, the outline of a bandage visible on his forearm beneath the fine linen.

"May I come in?" he asked. His hair was still battle-tossed from his violent struggle with Roman. Deep lines bracketed the hard set of his mouth, the darkness in his eyes.

She nodded, a little surprised that he would bother to ask her permission. If it had been anyone else but the fierce lord of Castle Leger, she would have described his manner as hesitant.

He stepped inside the bedchamber, half forgetting to close the door behind him. Madeline braced herself, uncertain of his mood. He no longer appeared angry, but there was a strange restlessness in him for all that.

He came as far as the end of her bed, twisting his fingers around the elaborately carved post.

"You are well?" he asked abruptly. "I did not rouse you from your sleep?"

"No."

"But I knocked several times, and you did not respond."

"I—I was preoccupied," she said. Too busy playing with his sword and entertaining foolish fantasies of him making love to her in a field of heather.

Madeline suppressed both the thought and the telltale blush that threatened to rise to her cheeks.

"Why?" she demanded. "Did you come to make certain I had obeyed your command to go to bed?"

"No, I only thought that you might be distressed after that damned uproar downstairs."

So that was the reason for the man's discomfort? He had expected to find her dissolved in a puddle of tears?

Madeline stiffened proudly. "Why would I be distressed? I assumed it must be a Cornish custom for the men to try to murder each other after dinner. Or perhaps only a St. Leger one."

"I am sorry," he said. "Such a thing will never happen again. Roman will not set another foot on Castle Leger. Not while I live."

His words sent a shiver through her. She remembered all too well the savagery of Roman's expression when he had slashed at Anatole with the knife. It filled her with a protectiveness toward Anatole, though she scarce knew why.

In any contest of strength Anatole would certainly emerge the victor, yet Roman, she sensed, would always possess a marked advantage over her husband.

Roman knew how to be cruel.

"Then, you were not able to mend your quarrel with your cousin before he left?" she asked anxiously.

"No, by God!" Anatole's fingers strayed to his injured arm. "Our quarrel is well past mending this time."

"I am still confused by what happened. Do you think Roman was a little drunk? It was so odd the way he spilled his wine and then—"

"He wasn't drunk." Anatole prowled over to the dresser, scowling at his own reflection in the mirror. "The hostility between us has always been there. Roman and I have hated each other since the day we were born."

"But why?"

"It's not important."

"But I should so like to understand."

"If only you could," he muttered.

Madeline crossed over to him, laying a hand on his arm. "Then, tell me," she pleaded.

He cast her a measuring glance, something haunted in his eyes, making her want to stroke soothing fingers across his brow, tame some of the wildness from his hair . . . from his heart.

She had a feeling that he desperately needed to tell her something, far more than about Roman. But he lowered his eyes and brushed past her, leaving her raw with disappointment.

"I don't want to talk about Roman. Not tonight," he said. "We can continue this discussion another time perhaps."

"When?" she asked bitterly. "In a year and a day?"

"All you need know is that you are never to receive Roman or speak to him again. Is that clear?"

No, it wasn't, Madeline wanted to argue, but she recognized the inflexible set of his jaw all too well. What had happened with Roman was to be added to the list of things she was not to worry her pretty head about, like forbidden castle rooms and Mortmains.

"Is that clear, madam?" Anatole prodded when she failed to answer.

"Perfectly, sir." She sighed. There seemed little point now in trying to broach a far more painful subject, the discord between Anatole and herself, the way she had offended his family and wounded—well, if not Anatole's heart, at least his pride.

But if she had, the man was not about to admit it to her. He didn't wear his vulnerabilities well. A profound sadness swept over her as she watched him pace toward the door, preparing to leave, a stiff proud figure. Forever maintaining his distance, keeping his secrets, guarding his heart.

But how was she to change that if he constantly refused to allow her any closer to him? Why had he come to her tonight if this was all he had to say?

And why did he linger, one hand poised on the doorknob, his dark silence filling the chamber, pressing against her like a heavy weight?

As the seconds ticked by, she wondered if she was the only one aware of the lateness of the hour, the fire dying on the hearth, the inviting reaches of the bed that loomed behind her.

Unable to bear it any longer, she finally asked, "Was there something more you wanted, my lord?"

She feared he had not even heard her, then he muttered, "Yes," the single word sounding wrung from him.

"What is it?"

"I want you!"

Madeline's breath caught in her throat. It was the last thing she'd expected him to say, but completely like him to be so direct. No impassioned declaration, no tender plea. Just three simple words that shot through her like a bolt of lightning.

"You—you mean you want to do *that* again?" she asked, fearing she must have misunderstood him.

There was no mistaking his expression as he stalked toward her, his eyes a strange mix of apology and desire.

"I won't hurt you this time. It will be better, Madeline. I swear it. You don't need to be afraid."

Her heart pounded madly, but not from fear. She felt as if she had been waiting forever for this to happen, for Anatole to return to her bed. She just hadn't expected it after a night like this one, full of tension, quarrels, and knife fights, when the gulf between them had never seemed greater.

As he slipped his arms around her waist, she braced her hands against the wall of his chest, gazing up at him.

"But—but why?" she asked.

"Why what?" He grazed his lips against her temple, his breath quick and warm against her skin.

"Why do you want to make love to me?"

"Because you're my wife."

"But why now? This moment. After the way—"

"For the love of God, Madeline. Must you have a reason for everything?" he said, his voice part groan, part weary laugh. "No more questions. Not tonight."

He bent swiftly, sealing her mouth with the firm warmth of his own. The kiss was meant to silence her as much as anything else, but she could not remain impervious as his lips sought hers with increasing hunger.

It had been so long since Anatole had kissed her this way, full on the mouth, molding her frame to his, making her aware of the heat, the raw power that pumped through the man's veins. She'd half forgotten the seduction of his lips, the sensual mysteries of which she'd only had the barest taste on their wedding night. Her body quickened with an anticipation she could not control.

If only she could have fully trusted to the magic of it, this sudden flare of desire. But she continued to wonder, to doubt. What had finally prompted Anatole back to her arms? Had he been goaded into it because of the boasting of the other St. Legers, the passion they'd found in their chosen brides?

Or was Anatole only making love to her for the same reason he'd surrendered his sword? Because it was expected of him? Breaking the heated contact of their lips, her eyes fluttered open, seeking the answers to her questions in his face. But to her astonishment, she found the room plunged into near darkness. At some point during that searing kiss, the candle had blown out.

Anatole's expression was lost to her, the hard contours of his face barely visible with only the glowing embers of the fire left to illuminate the bedchamber. Madeline thought she knew how poor Psyche must have felt in that myth, being embraced by a man she could never see, never fully understand.

Anatole strained her close, breathing fervent kisses against her hair. She felt so slight, so fragile in his arms, he half feared he was crushing her. She made no sound of protest, and although she was yielding enough, he sensed a reluctance in her, a wariness that drove him half wild.

She still wasn't eager to have him in her bed and heaven knew, he never intended to force himself upon her, not after how roughly he had already treated her tonight.

He'd only come to her bedchamber to apologize, nothing more. But the sight of her had dissolved all chivalrous intentions, her womanly curves draped in the innocence of that white nightgown, her hair shimmering about her shoulders, soft and fiery gold.

She was all that was beautiful, all that was calm and reason in a world too often riddled with storms and the St. Leger brand of madness.

And, God, how he wanted her, Marius's words of warning continuing to pound through his brain.

Go to your bride before it is too late . . .

Anatole cupped her face between his hands, devouring her face with his kisses, his caresses fueled as much by desperation as desire.

Damn it! He was a St. Leger, and she was his chosen bride. He would make her tremble with need for him. He would! He swept her off her feet so suddenly, a faint gasp escaped her.

Cradling her high in his arms, he carried her over to the bed. Half stumbling in the darkness, he cast her down upon the mattress.

He started to strip the shirt from his body when a flare of lightning illuminated the room, affording him a glimpse of Madeline's wide eyes.

He cursed softly, knowing he was on the verge of repeating all the mistakes of their wedding night. Alarming her with his nakedness, falling upon her too fast and furious.

He'd already behaved like a savage at supper. The least he could do was be civilized in bed. His body ached and burned with needs too long denied, his chest heaving with the exertion it took to suppress such raging desire. But he gritted his teeth, managing to gain some mastery over himself. Leaving his clothing on, he stretched out carefully on the mattress beside her.

He reached for her in the darkness, his hands trembling from suppressed passion, rendering him clumsy as he traced the line of her cheekbones, the curve of her jaw, the column of her throat.

Madeline lay stiff and unresponsive. A little breathless from his first fiery onslaught, she was only left further confused by this abrupt change in him. She clutched at his shoulders in the darkness, but even his body seemed veiled from her. She found herself oddly disturbed by the feel of rough linen instead of smooth warm skin.

Anatole's hands roved over her, caressing her through her nightgown, always stopping short of where she most ached to be touched. She squirmed beside him with an embarrassed impatience.

Did he not want her to remove her garments as he had insisted upon that first night? Did he not want to make himself naked? The man hadn't even bothered to remove his boots. Could they not light at least one candle so that she could see what he was doing?

It was on the tip of her tongue to ask when she remembered Anatole's ironclad rule for lovemaking. It was to be done in silence.

When he offered her another chaste kiss, she suppressed a frustrated sigh, thinking she had to be the most unreasonable woman in the world. This was all that she had ever wanted, wasn't it? A gentlemanly lover, modest and considerate.

Why, then, did her mind keep drifting back to that strange vision she'd had earlier, of Anatole riding off with her across the meadows, tumbling her down into the heather, embracing her with a desire so strong, it robbed her of all rational thought, leaving her blissfully weak and delirious?

She caught a taste of that fantasy in the warmth of Anatole's mouth as he kissed her again, but only enough to tantalize, not to fulfill—Anatole's restrained caresses a painful contrast to her imaginings.

She was no expert on lovemaking by any means, but something was terribly wrong here. Madeline submitted as he eased up the hem of her nightgown, inching down his breeches so their bodies could lock in the darkness. There was no pain this time as he entered her, the ache purely in her heart as she wondered how a man could seek such intimacy from a woman and still hold so much of himself back from her.

She longed for the sound of his voice, one endearment, one tender murmur of encouragement. But all she heard was the quick intake of his breath as Anatole labored over her, setting up a rhythm she couldn't match, a sweet fulfillment just out of her reach.

She battled against a hot stinging sensation behind her eyes. But by the time he'd finished with her, her tears spilled over, trickling down her cheeks. He collapsed beside her, his muscular body still shuddering from his exertions.

Madeline wiped at her eyes, furious with her own foolishness. Anatole had not hurt her. The man could not have been more careful with her if she'd been made of finely wrought china. Then, what the blazes was the matter with her? Why was she left with this hollow ache in her heart, her tears continuing to flow?

She was glad now of the concealing darkness, especially when Anatole propped himself up on the pillow beside her. Scarce taking time to recover his breath, he hovered over her.

"It—it was better this time?" he panted.

"Y-yes." For once in her life, she managed to lie.

"And . . . ?" he prompted, eager for her to say something more, but she had no notion what.

"It was very . . . pleasant."

"Pleasant?"

She could sense rather than see his frown in the darkness. He reached out to stroke her cheek, his fingers stiffening as they came in contact with the damp tracks of her tears.

"If it was so damned pleasant, why are you crying?" he asked.

"I don't know," she said miserably.

"Did I hurt you?"

"No."

"Then, for God's sake, Madeline. What is it?"

"I don't know," she repeated. "I just have this feeling that—that something isn't right."

"Something not right? With the way I make love to you?"

From the edge to his voice, she could tell she was treading on dangerous ground here, but she'd gone too far to turn back.

"It seems to me that there should be more to all this than two people merely touching. In silence. In the dark . . ."

She trailed off, feeling herself sinking in deeper with every word. An ominous quiet settled over the chamber so awful, even the storm raging outside seemed to hold its breath.

Then Anatole gave vent to a violent oath, causing her to cringe. He all but flung himself out of the bed, dragging his breeches back up over his hips.

"Anatole, I'm sorry," she faltered, struggling to a sitting position. But she doubted he ever heard her as he stormed out of the room, slamming the door behind him.

A low groan escaped her, and she scarce knew what she most wanted to do. Go after him. Try to explain. Pummel her pillow in sheer frustration, or simply burst into tears all over again.

What was wrong with her? After waiting all these nights for him to come to her bed, what must she do but drive him out of it again?

And after he'd been so gentle, so thoughtful. Performing his husbandly duty with all the decorum any reasonable woman would require. What more did she want from the man?

Three days, a voice whispered inside her. *Heather and hillsides. A warrior's kiss. The kind of passion St. Legers inspired in their women.*

Madeline hugged her pillow to her chest, appalled by her own thoughts. This could not be happening to her. *She* could not possibly be falling prey to the infamous St. Leger legend.

She plunked back down on the mattress, dragging her pillow over her head, to shut out all such irrational notions. It worked, but only partly. She still wasn't ready to believe in any St. Leger magic, but she was convinced of one thing.

This tame way of taking a woman was not Anatole's. She'd glimpsed enough fire in the man's eyes to know that he was capable of far more, that there was a wealth of tenderness and passion locked in his heart for the woman who knew how to draw it out of him . . . the right woman.

But it was obvious, Madeline thought, fresh tears burning her eyes.

She was not the one.

Doors burst open before Anatole with scarce more than a flash of his eyes. It was as though the house itself knew enough to get out of the way of the master of Castle Leger this night. All trace of the civilized man of the days past was gone.

Torchlight flickered over his hair snarling wildly about the savage planes of his face, his eyes black with barely contained fury. His boots rang out on the stone floors as he stormed along the arched corridor leading to the old castle keep. The last barrier rose up before him. He ground his fingertips against his brow, and the locked door trembled and gave way with a resounding crash. His head throbbed from such furious mental exertion, but it was as nothing compared to the pain and humiliation lancing his soul.

Outside the storm raged against the castle walls, but the only sound Anatole was aware of echoed within his mind, the memory of Madeline's soft hesitant voice.

There has to be more to this than two strangers touching. In silence. In the dark.

Something more? He'd made love to the woman with all the care and finesse he was capable of. He had held back so much of his own needs, it had damned near killed him. Bloody hell. What more did the woman want from him?

Grinding his teeth, Anatole slammed his way into the old hall, smashing the door closed behind him. As he jammed the torch into an iron sconce, light pierced the chamber with its cold stone walls and rustling tapestries.

The portraits of his ancestors gazed down dispassionately upon his anger. Prospero the sorcerer, Deidre the healer, Derek the dragon raiser, Simon the shape shifter, on down to Anatole's own grandfather, Grayson, the all-seeing one.

And someday, Anatole thought blackly, there would be one more portrait joining these legendary ranks.

Anatole St. Leger. Ah, yes, wasn't he the one who didn't know how to make love to his own wife?

He stalked the length of the hall, slamming over ancient carved chairs, giving the heavy banqueting table a mighty shove, thumping the rough walls with his fist, until he almost reopened the wound on his arm, his hands aching as badly as his head.

Only then did the frustration burning inside him give way to the cold weight of despair. He uprighted one of the chairs he'd overturned and sank into it, burying his face in his hands.

There was only one good thing about what had happened tonight. No St. Leger could ever be conceived from a mating as tame as that one, and that was all for the best. He wanted no child born as accursed as himself.

Oh, God! He'd done everything he could think of to win Madeline's love. Been patient and forbearing and so damned civilized. Holding that blasted supper party, enduring Roman's insolent presence beneath his roof.

He'd tried to make love to his wife with all the gentleness at his command, and all he'd succeeded in doing was making her cry. What the hell else could he do?

Sagging back in the chair, Anatole raked his hands through his hair. Maybe Roman and Madeline were both right. Maybe the legend of the chosen bride really was a pack of nonsense.

Or maybe, for once in his life, Fitzleger had made a mistake. It didn't matter anymore, for Anatole knew he was as lost as his father had been before him.

Tonight's failure had only branded that realization deeper into his heart. He had to have Madeline, had to possess her love, no matter what the cost. No matter what . . .

His brooding gaze tracked to the far end of the hall, the shadowed door half hidden behind one of the tapestries. The door that led to the most forbidden part of Castle Leger . . . Prospero's tower.

His mind recoiled from where his eyes were leading him. No! He'd spent his whole life rejecting the strangeness of his heritage: the magic, the sorcery, the powers for which there was no explanation. He'd be damned if he'd willingly seek to embrace it all now.

But as he rose to his feet, he knew that it was far more than his blind rage that had propelled him to this part of the castle tonight.

Desperate men seek the darkest of solutions.

Fetching the torch, Anatole moved slowly forward. Thunder hammered at the narrow windows, bursts of lightning illuminating the figures cunningly woven into the tapestry, the St. Leger dragon in full flight, escaped from the lamp of knowledge to wreak havoc upon a village of terrified peasants. A dire reminder of the St. Leger motto.

He who has great power must use it wisely.

But wisdom no longer played any part in a man's life when a woman entered it, Anatole thought grimly. He hesitated for only a moment before shoving the heavy tapestry aside.

The door behind it yielded almost too easily to Anatole's touch, the torchlight flickering over a curving stair that seemed to wind up into the night itself.

Holding the torch aloft, Anatole mounted the worn stone steps with great care, expecting at any moment to feel the icy blast of Prospero's disapproval. He'd already come farther than most St. Legers had ever dared, much farther than he'd ever wanted to.

As he trudged up the endless stairs, he recalled the things he'd heard about Prospero's bedchamber, the place rumored to be cast under some strange enchantment that left it untouched. Unchanged through centuries of wars, social upheavals, natural disasters, Mortmains . . .

Anatole had never truly believed it. That is, not until now when he emerged upward into the tower room itself. The chamber was quiet, as though even the storm that howled outside of Castle Leger had no power to penetrate here.

The massive bed, with its rich brocade hangings, the small wooden writing desk, the bookcase lined with ponderous-looking tomes—all appeared much as it must have been the last time Prospero had left it, riding forth with his usual cynical humor to surrender his life to an unreasoning mob, the charges of witchcraft, and a fiery death.

Awed in spite of himself, Anatole ran his fingers over the bedpost, which was curiously free of all dust and cobwebs. The intricate carving with the mysterious symbols was said to be the work of Prospero himself. He had made his own bed, hewn it out of a druid tree, the wood steeped in ancient mysticism.

Was it this, then, that gave Prospero the sensual power he'd exerted over women, winning hearts with his own brand of dark magic and passionate spells?

What was the old devil's secret? Was it bound up somehow in the carving of this bed? Or did the spell lie buried in one of those books over there? Anatole cast an uneasy glance over his shoulder, but his torch did not flicker with the slightest hint of Prospero's presence.

Emboldened, Anatole fixed the torch into the wall and crossed over to the bookcase to examine the volumes lined up haphazardly. Illuminated manuscripts. Strange mystic scrolls. Prospero had dabbled in everything from alchemy to blacker arts that Anatole had never wanted to think of. Until now.

He pulled down manuscript after manuscript, scroll after scroll, pages that seemed to crackle with ancient forbidden knowledge, written in French, Italian, Arabic, and other languages Anatole couldn't begin to identify.

"God curse it," he said. "Isn't there a one of these damn things written in plain English?"

He cracked open the last, only to find the pages filled with indecipherable Oriental symbols. Swearing, he jammed it back on the shelf, realizing he'd never be able to accomplish what he'd come for without Prospero's help.

Anatole glanced around the silent bedchamber and heaved a defeated sigh. "All right, you old devil," he muttered. "Where are you? You're always quick enough to plague me when I have no need of you."

His complaint evoked little response except for . . . the rustling of the bed curtains. Striding forward, Anatole wrenched them aside.

Nothing.

But he could feel it now, the prickling at the nape of his neck, the disquieting sensation that told him he was no longer alone. Perhaps he had never been.

Whipping about, he snapped, "Show yourself."

The only answer was the rattling of the bedpost.

"Damn it, Prospero! Come here! From whatever reaches of hell you lurk in—ooff."

Anatole's words were cut off by a warning rumble, a chilling blast of air that struck his stomach like a gigantic fist, driving him back. A brilliant light burst before his eyes, momentarily blinding him.

And then Prospero appeared in all his magnificence, a scarlet mantle flowing from his shoulders, his knightly frame garbed in a tunic embroidered in iridescent threads. Nothing of the pale phantom about him, he was all light and color. Even death had failed to rob him of his swarthy complexion, his neatly trimmed beard, and hair as black and lustrous as ever.

He appeared far too substantial to be a specter, but it was all an illusion as Anatole well knew. Once in the more uncontrolled days of his youth, he'd been goaded into leveling a blow at his irritating ancestor. He'd ended up by breaking his fist against the wall, much to Prospero's great amusement.

But Prospero appeared far from amused at the moment. It was not often that he deigned to make himself visible to mere mortals, even his own progeny. His exotic tilted eyes narrowed with the full weight of his displeasure.

"What mean you by this intrusion, boy?" he growled at Anatole. "What by all the gods do you want of me?"

Realizing that he was still backed against the wall where Prospero had flung him, Anatole slowly straightened. It was the hardest thing he ever had to admit in his life. He swallowed the thick lump of pride clogging his throat.

"I want . . . I need your help."

"Indeed? You did not seem so eager for my assistance the other afternoon. What was it you said? Let me think. . . ." Prospero stroked the ends of his beard, as though in effort of memory. "I believe it was something like *stay out of this, you old devil. I need no help from you.*"

It was clear that Prospero did not intend to make this easy for him. But then, Anatole had hardly expected anything different.

He paced over to the bookcase and fidgeted with the manuscripts, straightening them to avoid his ancestor's mocking gaze.

"My situation has grown worse," Anatole said grudgingly. "Things do not go at all well with me and my bride."

"I'm hardly surprised, with you tramping about the castle, raising a ruckus instead of where you should be. Warming the lady's bed."

Anatole felt his face fire. "That's part of the problem. You know what should be taking place between Madeline and me . . . in the bed."

"I've a fair notion," Prospero drawled.

"Well, it isn't happening. None of the fire, the passion. The kind of loving that is supposed to occur between a St. Leger and his chosen bride according to the legends."

"Ah, yes, the legends." Some secretive gleam of amusement shimmered in Prospero's eyes.

But Anatole ignored it and went doggedly on, "Something has gone very wrong with Madeline, and I don't know what the deuce to do about it."

"Perhaps you should have taken greater heed of the crystal's prophecy. Beware the woman of flame."

"As if I ever had any choice in the matter," Anatole said bitterly. "In fact, I am not at all certain that this disaster is not your fault."

"My fault?"

"Aye, you take such delight in tormenting me. It was you that tampered with the list I wrote out, stating my requirements for a bride. Maybe you tampered with Fitzleger as well, deliberately muddled his bride-finding talents."

"No, lad. It would take far greater magic than mine to tamper with a heart as wise and true as your Mr. Fitzleger. But if you are convinced your marriage has been a mistake . . ." Prospero shoved back his sleeves, dramatically raising his hands like a sorcerer about to perform some terrible magic. "I suppose I could use my black arts to spirit Madeline out of your life."

"No!" Anatole shouted, terrified Prospero might be powerful enough to do such a thing. He leapt to wrench Prospero's arm down and clutched at nothing but empty air.

Prospero drifted away from him, lowering his own hands with a smile. "It would seem you are not so convinced of a mistake after all."

"It doesn't matter anymore. All I want from you is . . ." Anatole hesitated, then blurted out, "I want you to give me a spell."

"A spell?" Prospero stared at him as though he'd run mad, which was not surprising, for Anatole had grave doubts about his own sanity at this moment.

"What kind of spell?" Prospero asked.

"You know. The kind that you used on women. The one that made them desire you beyond all reason, rendered them hopelessly in love with you."

"Ah, that one." An odd pensive smile played about the corners of Prospero's mouth. "You'll never find it pawing through those musty old books. It took a very special brand of spell."

"Then, give it to me."

"You wish me to simply hand over the magic it took me a lifetime to learn?" Prospero's brows arched at his imperious command.

"Please," Anatole managed to add.

Prospero studied him, thoughtfully stroking his beard, the ghost's expression inscrutable, leaving Anatole in agonies of suspense. Just as he'd begun to fear his request was to be denied, Prospero gave a careless shrug of his shoulders.

"Very well. I shall have to write it down for you. Fetch out pen, ink, and parchment from that desk."

Anatole hastened to comply, struggling to hide his eagerness. "Make sure you write it in English. It is the only language I know."

"I am well aware of that," Prospero said, rolling his eyes. Brushing his mantle back over his shoulder, he swirled over to the desk and seated himself behind it.

Anatole leaned anxiously over his chair as the sorcerer reached for his quill pen. Prospero paused to twist around and frown at him.

"Do you mind? I cannot concentrate with you hovering over me."

Reluctantly Anatole drew back a pace.

"This is a most delicate spell," Prospero said, dipping his quill into the ink. "I must take great care to get it right, or it could prove dangerous."

"Dangerous?"

"Aye, boy. There are always perils to be faced when you meddle with a woman's heart."

What a blasted disturbing way to put it, Anatole thought. The image of Madeline's sweet wistful face rose in his mind. He experienced a twinge of guilt at what he was about to do to her, rob her of her free will, force her to want him as desperately as he did her. But damn it! She was supposed to be his. Had not the Bride Finder said so?

While Prospero finished sanding down the incantation he had written, Anatole fought to quell any misgivings. Rolling up the parchment, the specter turned to hand it to him. Anatole all but snatched it from his grasp.

His hands trembled as he unfurled the paper to reveal a single line of script. He frowned. "This seems a rather short spell."

"But 'tis a passing powerful one."

"How do I use it? How does it work?"

"You will understand as soon as you have read the words."

Anatole stepped closer into the pool of torchlight, holding the manuscript up. Prospero's dashing flow of letters was almost indecipherable. He feared the old devil had forgotten and jotted down the spell in Latin or some such. But as he squinted closer, he was finally able to make out the words. There were only three of them.

"Simply . . . simply love her," he read aloud.

Simply love her? Anatole scowled in bewilderment.

"What the deuce kind of spell is this?" he asked, whipping about to face Prospero. But in a whisper of air, his ancestor had vanished.

"Prospero!" he roared as the realization slammed through him. He had just been made into the most spectacular sort of fool. The wily sorcerer had been toying with him as usual, had never intended to grant his request for a spell. Outrage and disappointment knifed through him, made all the sharper by the edge of his own despair.

"Damn you," Anatole choked. He rent the parchment into a thousand bits and flung them on the floor.

"I should have known better than to come to you for help. Thank you so much for bloody damned nothing!"

Snatching up the torch, he stormed out of the tower. The laughter that followed him was hearty and deep. But not entirely unsympathetic.

Chapter Fifteen

The thunder of the night gave way before the calm of morning, the light of day glistening on the dew-moistened flowers, the tangled grasses obscuring the path that led from the cliffs behind Castle Leger.

But Anatole scarce noticed the sun warming his skin as he trudged homeward, heart weary, his muscles sore and aching from a night spent out in the open, exposed to the wind and the rain, falling into an exhausted sleep just before dawn.

It was what he'd often done as a wild boy when his misery had threatened to overwhelm him. Run off into the night to lose himself in the very eye of the storm, much to poor Fitzleger's consternation and horror.

Sometimes only the sprawling landscape of the cliffs, harsh beneath a sky blackened with thunder, had been large enough to contain his youthful griefs. His pain at being unloved and unwanted, feared and despised. His terror of being forever outcast, alone.

In the midst of the driving rain, boyish tears could fall unremarked. He could let loose the dread force of his mind, and be afraid of harming no one save himself. While the sea had battered at the shore below, he'd often used his power to batter at the rugged cliff face, hammering at the immovable stones with all the grief and fury he possessed. Lashing out until he had collapsed into a fit of unconsciousness. Only to be found the next morning by Fitzleger and carried tenderly back to the gatehouse, having achieved a temporary sense of peace.

But he'd found no peace out on the cliffs last night, Anatole thought, wincing as he pressed one hand to his aching back, his sun-stiffened shirt raw and scratchy against his skin. Maybe because he'd grown too old to batter uselessly at rocks, too old to cry, even in the rain. He'd spent most of those dark hours simply standing at the edge of the cliffs, getting wet and miserable. Playing out in his head over and over that painful scene with Madeline in the bedchamber, hearing again Prospero's mocking laughter, being tormented by those three cryptic words.

Simply love her.

With that useless advice had ended his last best chance of winning Madeline's heart. No spell. No charm. No love potion. Then, for him, it was quite hopeless. Sighing wearily, he raked the damp black mat of hair from his eyes, now wanting only one thing.

To salvage some remnant of his dignity. To slip back into Castle Leger unseen, without anyone noticing the full extent of his folly, just how low he had sunk.

Limping carefully along, he managed to avoid the bustling stable yard and the curious eyes of his grooms. He plunged up the worn footpath leading to Lady Deidre's garden, when he was dismayed to see someone emerging from the house.

The last person in the world he wished to encounter.

Madeline. His wife.

A flush of shame mounted to his cheeks, and he bit back a curse at the woman's ability to take him by surprise. Moving with a swiftness he would not have thought his stiff muscles capable of, he ducked behind a stand of rhododendron trees.

It was a familiar hiding place from his childhood, although he'd fit much better as a lad. But he crouched down beneath the leafy branches, holding himself perfectly immobile. He still remembered the arts of concealment. He'd been so good at it as a boy.

It had become the only way he could get near his mother, ever look upon her face. Sadness washed over him to think that he had been reduced to this again.

Striving to curb his impatience, he prayed that whatever had brought Madeline out into the garden would take her swiftly back again. Lord, he hoped she wasn't bent on one of her merry flower-gathering expeditions. Each morning the woman filled the house to bursting with the wretched things.

But as Madeline meandered farther down the path, there was little of merriment in her steps. She moved with a certain listlessness, the straw basket she carried banging against her knee. The shawl that trailed over her shoulders was half slipping off, and she seemed unaware of it.

Craning his neck, Anatole strained to catch her expression, but her features were hidden beneath the wide brim of a deep green bonnet.

Finally she lifted her face to the sky, blinking as though astonished to discover the sun was shining. Her winsome face was so damnably pale. All her bright curiosity about the world seemed to have quite drained away. And her eyes . . . even from this distance he could see they were red-rimmed and swollen. Had she spent the whole night weeping after he'd left her?

His heart ached with such longing to go to her and draw her into his arms that he had to clench his fists to stay the impulse. For how could he offer comfort when he knew he was the source of her unhappiness?

She stood there, observing the garden for what seemed an eternity. Ducking her head, she emitted a heavy sigh and returned to the house, her flower basket left empty.

To Anatole, watching her go, it seemed as though a shadow had fallen across his lady, one that he recognized all too well. He'd seen it creep slowly over his own mother's gentle features, robbing her of her joy, her very reason until she had . . .

Oh, God! Anatole pressed his face against the rough tree bark, his blood iced with a chilling fear. He should have obeyed his instinct, sent Madeline away that very first day.

Now it was too bloody late. What in fiery hell was he going to do?

Simply love her Prospero's persistent words pounded through his head.

"Damn you," Anatole whispered hoarsely. "I don't know how."

Why don't you start by telling her how you feel, you young clod?

Prospero's voice sounded so close, so real, Anatole straightened away from the trees and cast a wary glance over his shoulder. But the specter's power had never extended beyond the old tower. Anatole had to be imagining he'd heard such an insane suggestion.

Tell Madeline how he felt? By thunder, he'd rather face an entire army of kill-crazed Mortmains. When was the last time he'd ever shown anyone what was in his heart, made himself so vulnerable? He couldn't even remember.

But his fingers drifted up to trace the outline of his scar. Perhaps that was the trouble. He could remember, all too well. Confess his foolish longings to Madeline? Impossible, he could never do it.

Coward!

The epithet cracked in his ears, and he spun about wildly. The voice was real enough this time. But he was no longer sure if these thoughts came from Prospero or somewhere deep inside of himself.

He stepped from his hiding place and plodded up the garden path, strangely conscious of all the fragrant blossoms Madeline had left ungathered. His gaze dropped down to the daisies strewn across his path, perky white petals he usually trampled in his haste to get down to the stable yard.

But for some reason, his bride seemed particularly fond of those simple flowers. Anatole stared at them for long moments, then swallowed hard. His stiff joints throbbed in protest as he bent down and began to uproot the daisies one by one.

He was appalled to see the way his big hands shook, but it had been a long time since he picked flowers for a lady. A very long time. He gathered up a handful in great haste, not daring to pause, to question what fresh madness had come over him.

Hurrying toward the house, he slipped through the French doors leading into the grand dining room, the way Madeline had gone.

The chamber stood empty, but Anatole shrank back, startling himself as he caught sight of his own reflection in the glass mounted above the mantel.

He looked like something out of those tales the village women used to affright their wayward children. Stories of a black-visaged goblin king who crept from beneath his rocky lair to snatch away naughty boys and girls.

He scraped one hand along his beard-roughened jaw. He desperately needed to shave, bathe himself, don fresh clothes before he went in search of Madeline. He buttoned up his shirt and made a pathetic effort to finger comb his hair, when he heard someone approaching the room.

Not Madeline. His inner sense told him clearly who it was, the familiar cold weight of guilt settling over his heart as Bess Kennack whisked into the room.

She bore an empty tray, intent upon cleaning up the remains of a breakfast that had gone uneaten. But at the sight of Anatole, she reared back with a gasp, nearly dropping the silver platter.

Her eyes widened with momentary shock, then she recovered herself with a shrug that seemed to say it was not that astonishing to see the master of Castle Leger looking like a demon spewed up from the depths of hell.

"Good morrow, sir," she said in her toneless voice.

Anatole ignored the greeting. "Where is your mistress?" he asked. "Has she gone upstairs?"

"No, sir. She is in the front parlor, receiving a visitor."

A visitor? Anatole slapped his hand against the mantelpiece in pure frustration.

"Blast Fitzleger," he said. "He would pick this particular time to come calling."

He didn't even realize he'd spoken aloud until Bess replied, "No, m'lord. 'Tis not Mr. Fitzleger, but that there French gentleman who came to dinner last night."

Rochencoeur? Roman's ridiculous little toady? Anatole scowled. "What the deuce does he want here?"

"I believe he came on an errand for your cousin, sir. Mr. Roman St. Leger."

Roman. The mere mention of the name caused Anatole's gut to clench. "What kind of errand?"

"Why, Master Roman sent the mistress the most glorious bouquet of roses I have ever seen." Bess's gaze dropped scornfully toward the brace of daisies Anatole held crushed in his fist.

He felt the sting of red in his cheeks, and he snapped, "You can be about your business, girl."

When Bess moved to clear the table, he added with a snarl, "Elsewhere."

She backed away with a respectful curtsy, but as she quit the room, a thin smile curled her lips. A smile that splintered in his heart like a shard of glass.

He glanced down at the daisies he clutched, and was not at all surprised to find the blasted things crushed in his hand.

Madeline arranged the lush red roses in a crystal vase, jerking her hand back when she pricked her thumb on a thorn.

Pulling a rueful face, she sucked at her injured fingertip, thinking it appropriate that of all flowers, Roman St. Leger would choose to send roses. Exactly like the man himself, beautiful but somewhat treacherous.

The flowers had come with a charming note expressing Roman's regrets for his conduct at the supper party. But Madeline feared she should have accepted neither the roses nor the message. Anatole had expressly forbidden her to have anything more to do with his cousin.

She ran a grave risk of courting Anatole's anger, and matters already stood badly enough between her and her husband. But Roman had been clever, sending his poor friend as his ambassador.

Monsieur Rochencoeur looked ill at ease to find himself back at Castle

Leger. Madeline didn't have the heart to distress the Frenchman further by thrusting the flowers back at him and showing him the door. She could always dispose of the roses later when Yves had gone.

While Madeline arranged the fragrant blossoms, Yves paced about the parlor, the stiff satin of his breeches crackling with every step. Powdered, patched, and perfumed, he should have been a gentleman in waiting at Versailles instead of paying a morning call in the backwaters of Cornwall.

The rugged St. Leger males would no doubt have sneered at the Frenchman's effeminate mannerisms, but Yves's elegance made Madeline conscious of her own bedraggled appearance, her hair straggling from beneath the lace cap tied under her chin, her gown as gray as her mood.

Though it took great effort, she summoned a smile and motioned Rochencoeur toward a chair.

"Pray, monsieur, do sit down and allow me to offer you some refreshment."

"Oh, *non,* Madame is *tres gentille,* but I must not detain you. *Certainement* you have many affairs of the more importance. Your husband . . ." Rochencoeur's throaty voice faltered a little as his eyes flicked toward the door. "He will be wanting you, *oui*?"

After what she'd said to him in bed last night? Madeline winced. No, not likely.

"My husband is not here, monsieur," she said. "He is out attending to estate business."

Madeline thought the lie fell awkwardly from her tongue, but Yves appeared too relieved by Anatole's absence to notice.

She felt glad, for it would have been mortifying to confess the truth to a stranger, that she had not the least notion where her husband was.

After Anatole had left her, all efforts to cry herself to sleep had proved to be in vain. By the time the first light of morning had broken over her windowsill, she'd waxed desperate enough to brave the uncharted reaches of Anatole's bedchamber, to apologize.

But all she'd found was his bed, not slept in. Sometime during the night, the man had vanished. Out in the darkness, out in the storm, and on foot. He hadn't even bothered to saddle his horse.

No one at Castle Leger had any notion where he'd gone or when he might return. Madeline had gone nigh frantic imagining him lost out there on the moors or fallen from one of the cliff paths, his body broken and bleeding. And it would be entirely her fault.

But none of Anatole's household dared question the master's actions, let alone brave his wrath by presuming to go in search of him. Torn between fear and frustration, Madeline had worked herself up into such a state, even the surly Trigg had taken pity on her.

"There's no sense frettin' yerself, mistress," the old man had said. "Master has a habit of going off by himself. He'll return when he's good and ready. You'll just have to get accustomed to it."

Accustomed to it? That she never would.

Damn the man, she thought bleakly. Was he going to run off this way every time he made love to her?

Forgetting all about her guest, she drifted over to the parlor window and plucked back the curtain to peer out at the carriage drive, as she had done more than a dozen times already that morning. Staring down that long road leading to Castle Leger, so desolate even in the bright sunlight.

It filled her with a certain bleak amusement to note that Anatole's old hound was doing the same thing. Ranger perched atop the portico steps forlornly awaiting his master's return.

She let the curtain fall back into place with a soft sigh, cursing herself yet again for her blunt tongue. When would she ever learn to curb it? When would she ever learn, especially with men, to stop being so blasted honest?

Ah, Madeline. She could almost hear her brother Jeremy's voice, torn between amusement and vexation. *You ever must speak your mind. That is because you think that you have all the answers, that you know everything.*

No, Jemmy, she mused sadly. Not anymore. Coming to Castle Leger had proved a rough education for her.

She now realized how little she did know about other people. About being married, about being a wife . . . about being in love.

In love? Now, where had a crazed notion like that come from? She couldn't possibly be imagining she was falling in love with Anatole St. Leger. A man whose dark nature she barely knew and didn't begin to comprehend.

That would be as unreasonable as . . . as fancying oneself in love with a portrait.

"Madame?"

Rochencoeur's voice broke in on her reflections, reminding her of his presence. Madeline turned away from the windows and was chagrined to realize how she had been neglecting her guest.

The Frenchman had lowered himself into the chair.

"Perhaps I could stay for the visit *brief,*" he said.

"Wonderful," Madeline murmured, though she now regretted that she had not allowed Yves to go when she'd had the chance. She needed to be alone with these new and disturbing thoughts about Anatole.

But she settled on the sofa opposite, determined to play the gracious hostess. It had been a little easier last night. Monsieur Rochencoeur had been more voluble then.

Today he, too, seemed pensive, as though wanting to speak but not quite able to make up his mind to do so.

At last he stretched in his chair and said, "I trust I shall not seem too forward *madame,* but I should very much like to make you the present of my own."

He reached beneath his frock coat and produced a slender volume, which he laid upon the tea table between them. When Madeline only stared at it, he urged, "Go on. Please to take it."

Madeline lifted the book and held it in her hands. It was exquisitely tooled in blue leather and gilt lettering, a French translation of the story of Electra and Orestes, the Greek drama of two children seeking revenge for the murder of their father.

The pages were well worn and had been lovingly pored over.

"Monsieur," Madeline said. "This must be one of your most treasured books. I cannot accept this."

"Non, non." He refused to take the volume when she tried to hand it back. "It was a gift to me from my dear patroness, and now you must have it. Like the Comtesse Sobrennie, you, too, are a lady with a great appreciation for the fine writing and the *philosophes.* It is rare, as rare as your kindness." His lips curled in a bitter smile. "And I have known far too little of that in my life."

Madeline did not doubt that, especially if Yves made a habit of choosing his friends from men of such stamp as Roman St. Leger. She felt awkward accepting the book, but she did so, murmuring her thanks.

While she studied the flyleaf, she became uncomfortably aware of Yves examining her, an unexpected shrewdness surfacing in the man's doll-like eyes.

"Forgive me, madame. But I cannot help remarking. You appear a little depressed today," he said. "The distressing events of last eve perhaps—"

"Oh, no," Madeline disclaimed quickly, unwilling to discuss her humiliation at that supper party, even with someone as sympathetic as Yves. "I am only a little tired, that is all and—and suffering from a touch of—of homesickness."

She forced a smile as she flung out the first excuse for her melancholy that she could think of. But she was a little ashamed to realize she had given very few thoughts to any of her family these past days. Ever since she'd first set foot out of that carriage, her world had been dominated by one person, one man. Anatole St. Leger.

It amazed her to discover how swiftly she had grown accustomed to his presence during the last week. The heavy tramp of his boots through the hall, the deep boom of his voice, the manly aroma of his pipe.

It was absurd. The man had only vanished for one morning, and yet she was missing him desperately.

She shoved the realization to the back of her mind, and tried to concentrate on what her visitor was saying.

"It is only natural that you should pine for your family back in London." Yves sighed. "I, too, know the pain of parting from a loved one."

"You are thinking of your son," Madeline said, glad to have the conversation deflected from herself.

"*Oui, mon petit* Raphael. It will be the long time before I see him again."

"Surely your schools in France have holidays?"

"*Mais* I am not permitted to return to France, to go near my son again until the task I have undertaken for la Comtesse Sobrennie is finished."

"You mean your commission to find the countess an English husband?"

Again, Yves nodded, a cloudy light filtering through his eyes. "Sometimes I think I should not be doing this, that I should go back to France before I set into motion that which can only end tragically. Perhaps I was wrong to choose Roman St. Leger. He is more cold and ruthless than I first perceived. But *la comtesse,* she is now determined."

"You'll pardon my saying so," Madeline said gently, "but this patroness of yours also sounds a little cold and ruthless. Keeping you parted from your son this way until you have done her bidding."

"If she is hard, the world has made her so. La Comtesse Sobrennie is—" Yves hesitated, clearly choosing his words with care "—a most determined woman. She has a great and generous heart, but she can be without mercy to those who stand in the way of what she wants."

He leaned forward in his chair, bending closer to Madeline in his earnestness. "I hope you will always remember that, my learned young friend. There is so much in this world of cruelty and despair that you do not know."

Yves's eyes glittered with an unnerving intensity, almost as though he were trying to warn her of something. Madeline tried to study his face, see past that absurd application of white powder and rouge, and she suddenly realized the truth.

Yves must be in love with this coldhearted countess himself. That was why he was so willing to do anything for her, even sacrifice being with his beloved son. The poor foolish man.

She laid her hand over his in a comforting gesture. "If you truly fear you are doing something wrong by forwarding this match between your countess and Roman, you should refuse. Advise her that she should not come here to wed him."

"It is already too late for that. But not too late for you."

"For me? What—what do you mean?"

Yves clutched at her fingers. "I do not believe your desolation is caused by the sickness of home, as you say. It is caused by your own husband. I have seen with my own eyes how he treats you, so hard and cruel."

"Monsieur! I know you must have received a dreadful first impression of Anatole, but I assure you that beneath his fierce exterior, he can be very gentle and—"

"Ah, bah! He is a St. Leger. They are all of a strangeness, these tall brutish men. I hear the tales of their history, much tragedy and sorrow for those *misérables* whose lives they touch." Yves's grip on her hand tightened, almost to the point of being painful.

"You should leave this place. There is no happiness for you here. Go home to your family, *cherie.* Go back to London."

Madeline gaped at him, shocked by such passionate and astonishing advice. But before she could even think of what to reply, the door to the parlor thundered open, and Anatole's wide shoulders filled the entryway.

Madeline leapt up with a glad cry, but her joy at seeing him home, safe, swiftly faded in horror at his appearance. He looked like some barbaric warrior, limping home from a battle he'd lost, mud spattering his boots and breeches, his shirt plastered to his chest, his damp hair matted to the granite planes of his face.

She thought the storm had ended last night, but she saw with dismay that Anatole had carried it home in his eyes.

An ominous silence descended as he stalked into the room. He slammed the door closed behind him with a resounding crack. Recovering from his shock, Yves bolted to his feet.

"M-monsieur St. Leger. I—"

"What the devil do you think you're doing here?" Anatole said.

Madeline moved hastily to insinuate herself between the two men. "My lord, Monsieur Rochencoeur has merely been kind enough to call."

But Anatole ignored her. Shoving past her, he stalked Yves across the room. The Frenchman backed away until he stumbled against the pianoforte, his hand crashing down on the keys with a jarring clang.

"Milord," Yves said. "I but came to deliver to madame the roses and the apology. From *mon amie* Roman."

Anatole's arm shot forward, and Madeline cried out, fearing he meant to seize Rochencoeur by the throat. But Anatole reached past him, snatching up the vase of flowers instead. Turning, he smashed the roses into the empty hearth, shattering the crystal with such force, both Madeline and Yves leapt back.

"There!" Anatole said, towering over the cringing Yves. "The roses are delivered. Now, get out."

Yves inched past Anatole toward the door. But despite the fact he was trembling, he paused long enough to bow over Madeline's hand.

"You will be all right, madame?"

"Yes—yes, of course, monsieur."

"Then, I will leave you. But you will remember all that I have said to you?" He dropped his voice to add, "I shall be only too happy to help you escape from this place. If you need my help, you will find me staying in the small cottage at Lost Land."

Madeline nodded, only anxious for the Frenchman to be gone before he did indeed provoke Anatole to murder.

Rochencoeur favored Anatole with a cold bow, then exited from the room with a remarkable degree of dignity for a man who was visibly shaken. The door closed behind him with a soft click, leaving Madeline alone with her husband.

She turned to face Anatole, quivering with indignation. She'd waited and worried her heart out over this man all morning. She'd even leapt to defend him when Yves had accused him of being a brute, and what must Anatole do but mortify her further by confirming the Frenchman's bad opinion.

"Sir! Your conduct is abominable," she said. "You terrified that poor man half to death."

"He's lucky I didn't break his neck. What the devil did he mean—that you should remember what he said? What's that fop been saying to you?"

"Monsieur Rochencoeur was expressing his concern for my welfare. It seems he fears that I am wed to some great barbarian who is likely to beat me. Though I cannot imagine where he could have gotten such a notion. Can you?" Madeline inquired too sweetly.

"The bloody impertinent fool. And was that his cursed excuse for holding your hand?"

"He only took my hand after I reached for his."

Anatole's eyes flared, and as he stormed toward her, Madeline thought she must be mad. This was like taunting the St. Leger dragon.

But she stood her ground, even though her chin all but brushed the wall of his chest. She raised her head to glare defiantly up at him.

"Monsieur Yves was feeling a—a bit distressed," she said. "And I only sought to be kind to him. Our hands touching was an innocent gesture. Certainly no reason for you to go snarling after him like a jealous lover!"

Anatole's face washed dull red at her accusation, but surprisingly, he made no attempt to deny it.

"I thought I made my wishes plain enough to you, madam," he said. "You are to have no contact with my cousin Roman."

"It was not Roman who came calling, but Monsieur Rochencoeur."

"It is all the same. That French dolt is Roman's creature, and I won't have him under my roof."

"Then, you should have stayed home to forbid him yourself!"

Anatole's hands jerked upward as though he would shake her. He clenched his fists instead, turning aside, delivering a savage kick to the chair where Yves had sat. "Why would you want to waste your time with that painted fool?"

"Monsieur Rochencoeur may be a trifle foolish, but he is one thing you are not, sir, and that is a gentleman."

Anatole flinched as though he'd been struck. "Maybe it was not the Frenchman's company you wanted so much as Roman's bloody roses and love note. Perhaps the next time my back is turned, I'll have you running off for a tryst with my cursed cousin."

Madeline gasped at the sheer injustice of such an accusation.

"I have no interest in your cousin or Monsieur Yves. I only received him because—because—"

"Because why?"

Madeline swallowed hard, but for once the turbulence of her emotions overruled her pride.

"Because you left me alone," she cried. "Vanishing without a word. Worrying me nigh ill. I was lonely and—and distressed. I only wanted some company. I—I—"

She faltered, feeling the tears start to burn her eyes. A silly habit she had indulged too often of late. Blinking furiously, she forced herself to continue.

"I just wanted a friend. Someone to talk to. Someone to share things with. That is all I have ever desired." Her voice broke on the last word, and she felt several salty droplets escape to splash down her cheeks.

"Damn!" She swore in self-disgust, groping for her handkerchief, which as usual she could not find.

Anatole regarded her fiercely for a moment before demanding, "Then, share it with me."

"What?" She sniffed, more concerned with halting the flood of her treacherous tears.

"Whatever you were sharing with that Frenchman. Share it with me!"

He glanced around, his gaze falling on the leather-bound volume Yves had given her. "Was it this book? Is that what the two of you were talking about?"

Madeline cried out in protest as Anatole snatched up the volume, alarmed that in his anger, he might end by ripping the book in two.

Tensing, she took a step forward, intending to rescue the slender book from his large, rough hands, but he cracked it open, studying the pages with hard concentration. He had not got much further than the flyleaf when his mouth tightened.

"It's in God-cursed French! I can't read such blasted stuff."

He flung the book down to the carpet with a savage oath and spun away from her. Madeline wasted no time in retrieving the precious volume, preparing to bolt for the peace and security of her bedchamber. Perhaps even farther, Yves's strange advice echoing through her head.

. . . Leave this place. There is no happiness for you here. Go home to your family, cherie. . . .

Perhaps not such strange advice after all, perhaps only the warning her own reason had attempted to give her all along.

Rustling to the door, Madeline stole a cautious glance over her shoulder, fearing Anatole might cut off her retreat. But he had stalked over to the windows and stared blindly out, his shoulders slumped, his posture one of total defeat.

She tilted her head to observe him with confusion. It didn't astonish her to discover he couldn't read French. But it was surprising that it seemed to matter to him so much, that he would even have made the attempt.

He did it for you, her heart whispered.

Impossible! Anatole had never shown anything but contempt for her interests. Why, all this past week he—

She frowned as a host of images from the past few days crowded into her mind. Anatole walking stiffly beside her through the garden, although he hated flowers. Anatole ordering the fire in the library lit, although it was the last place he wanted her to be. Anatole taking tea with her, balancing a cup and saucer in his huge hands, looking as uncomfortable as any man could.

Dear heavens! *Was* it possible? Could he, after his own gruff fashion, have been trying to please her? And she had been too stupid, too blind to see it. Even last night . . .

Her hand dropped away from the doorknob. Setting the book aside, she drifted closer to him. The sunlight streaming through the window was merciless, revealing every weary line of his hawklike profile, every vulnerability Anatole hid behind his granite facade. Wherever he'd run off to last night, it had done him little good. He'd found no more rest than she had.

He stared out the window, so lost in his thoughts, Madeline believed him unaware of her presence until he muttered in a voice thickened by pure exhaustion, "I am sorry, my dear. But it seems a hopeless business, does it not? You and I ever sharing anything."

Only moments ago Madeline would have been tempted to agree with him. But she was no longer so sure.

She settled herself beside him at the window, her sleeve bare inches from brushing up against his.

"I could teach you to read French," she offered.

"I fear I'm too stupid to learn."

"Oh, no, my lord. I'm sure you could learn anything you set your mind to."

He said nothing, merely cast her a doubtful glance that somehow went straight to her heart.

"Why do you hate them so?" she asked.

His brow arched in surprise. "Roman and his ridiculous friend? I would have thought that obvious—"

"No, I mean my books. Any books. Your own papa appears to have been a great scholar. Surely he must have encouraged you to read with him."

"The only thing my father ever encouraged me to do was keep my distance. He used his books to shut out the world. Especially me."

He turned his face back to the window, and Madeline fully expected him to retreat into one of his dark silences. But for once he seemed too worn down to maintain such dragonlike guard over his memories.

He dragged one hand across his eyes in a tired gesture and said, "After my mother's death, my father shut himself up in the library with his grief. He would scarce receive anyone, not even other members of the family. Except, of course, Roman."

"Roman!"

"Aye." Anatole's mouth twisted bitterly. "Both of my parents were very fond of my cousin, seeing in him the son they would rather have had. Handsome, clever, so blasted charming. Even when my father lay dying, it was Roman he sent for, Roman he wanted."

"Oh," Madeline said, thinking that explained so much, the enmity that simmered between Anatole and Roman, Anatole's scowling humor every time she wished to disappear into the library. Yet she was left with the feeling that part of the story still remained untold, bound up in the tragic marriage of Anatole's parents. Cecily St. Leger, the bride according to the family legend, who should never have been. Dying so young, mourned by her husband apparently to the point of madness.

"But how could your father have behaved so?" she asked. "Turning away from you, shutting himself off from the world. You were so young when your mother died. Who looked after you and the estate?"

"I had Mr. Fitzleger. He helped me learn my duties as the heir to Castle Leger."

"But you were not much more than twelve years old, were you not?"

"Little more than ten, but I aged quickly."

Too quickly, Madeline thought, noting the lines carved deep by Anatole's eyes, the brackets that framed his mouth, marks of care and sorrow that belonged to a much older man. She had never met the late Lyndon St. Leger, but she felt a strong resentment toward the man who could be so selfish in his grief, abandoning both his responsibilities and his son.

Her thoughts must have showed in her face, for Anatole rushed to his father's defense.

"My father did what he could to help on the days that he was stronger. Occasionally he would allow some of the villagers or Mr. Fitzleger to consult with him. My father had a—a unique knack for locating lost things. The only thing he never seemed to remember was where he'd misplaced his son."

Anatole attempted to jest, but the humor never quite touched his eyes. Madeline could see traces of the boy he must have been, hovering in the shadows, lonely, burdened down with responsibility too great for his years. Forever waiting for that library door to open to him. A door that never had.

She comprehended his pain all too well. She had never been the sort of daughter her parents wished for, either, with her love of books, blunt tongue, and mad red hair.

She longed to fling her arms about Anatole's waist and tell him she understood, to coax him to share more of his past with her. But this was the closest the man had ever allowed her to his heart. She hardly dared breathe, for fear of shattering the moment.

Gently she laid her hand atop his fist, where it rested upon the windowsill, for perhaps the first time in her life abandoning all words, trusting to her silence.

Anatole stared down at her fingers, as though such a gesture of comfort was an alien thing to him. Then slowly he turned his hand over. Unfurling his fingers, he intertwined them with hers one by one.

"Madeline, I—" he began, then broke off with a grimace. "Ah, hell! I've had to apologize to you so many times, you'd think I'd be better at it by now.

"About last night . . ."

He trailed off again, and a hot blush seared Madeline's cheeks. What had happened in her bedchamber or what had failed to happen was too raw and painful a subject for either of them to discuss.

Anatole rushed on instead, "I'm sorry for everything. For tossing your French friend out of here. I suppose I was jealous. I don't have his polished manners, and yesterday was such a damned mess. I have never been any good at supper parties and such like."

"Neither have I," Madeline said.

When he shot her an incredulous look, she nodded her head vigorously. "It's true. I have always had this awful penchant for saying the wrong thing at the wrong time. I have been dismissed in disgrace from far more elegant dinners than yours, Mr. St. Leger."

Her words wrung a smile from him.

"I never meant to offend your family last night. Or Mr. Fitzleger."

"It's not important."

"But it is. You were already estranged from your relatives, and now I have made it worse. I should never have said what I did about not believing in the Bride Finder."

"Why not? It is a damned fool legend. I don't half believe it myself sometimes."

She should have been glad to hear him say so. For Anatole to abandon his superstitions, to be more enlightened, that was what she wanted, wasn't it? Then, why did his words fill her with a peculiar kind of sadness?

"That's the dangerous thing about legends," she mused aloud.

"What is?"

"Sometimes . . ." She faltered. It was a difficult thing to admit, even to herself. "Sometimes even the most sensible person in the world can end up wishing the legend was true."

He carried her hand to his lips, his mouth lingering, warm against her skin, and there was nothing sensible about the way her heart responded, pounding madly.

"Perhaps we simply haven't tried hard enough," he said. "Perhaps even a legend requires a little mortal help."

"Perhaps. But you must own it is rather difficult with me curled up in the library, and you . . . you too often vanishing into a world where I cannot follow."

"I wish I could show you that world, Madeline. There's so much more here than you have seen."

"Like the old keep?" she asked hopefully.

"No, not the damned keep. I'm talking about the land itself, more power and magic woven into it than you'd ever find in my ancestors' moldering bones. The way the mist settles over the hills like the smoke from a sorcerer's kettle. Or the sea during a thunderstorm, the foam breaking like a herd of wild white stallions. Or the cliffs on a moon-spun night—"

Madeline had rarely heard him speak with such passion. But he checked himself looking sheepish. "I sound like an idiot. I'm a poor hand at explaining such things."

"Oh, no, you do it beautifully."

A poet's words, an artist's eye, and a warrior's battle-roughened voice. She found it an enchanting combination. "Please go on."

"It would be better if I could simply take you out with me."

"I wish you could. But you would not have much patience with me jogging after you on a pony or some sluggish old mare, which is the most I could manage."

He frowned, chafing her fingers in thoughtful silence for a moment. "There is another way," he said at last. "If you could but have enough faith that I would keep you safe. Could you do that, Madeline? Could you trust me?"

Trust him? He'd said that once before, demanded it of her, in fact. But this time he was asking with all the eloquence of his dark eyes, all the warm strength of his hand enfolding hers. She didn't have the least notion what he had in mind, but it didn't seem to matter.

"Yes, my lord," Madeline whispered, staggered to discover just how much she did trust Anatole St. Leger. Enough to follow him anywhere.

As Anatole led her from the library, all of Yves Rochencoeur's dire warnings were entirely forgotten.

Chapter Sixteen

The roan horse galloped along the beach, spraying up ocean and sand, the whitecap waters lapping against the animal's powerful legs. Perched before Anatole in the saddle, Madeline felt the hunter's muscles bunch beneath her, and she clung harder to her husband's neck.

The horse, Anatole had insisted, was one of his more gentle mounts, a sturdy gelding, noted for its endurance rather than its speed. Gazing up at the beast, Madeline had feared the great brute would prove more than fast enough. But Anatole had given her no time to think or reconsider. He had swept her up before him, carrying her off to his world, a land of lonely moors, stark cliffs, and sprawling sky.

Peeking from beneath the broad brim of the sensible bonnet she had worn to protect her easily burned complexion, the landscape seemed to pass Madeline by in a dizzying blur. And yet she felt more breathless than afraid, cradled between Anatole's hard thighs, protected by the strength of his arms, the ends of his black cloak enfolded about her, sheltering her from the stiff breeze raking in from the sea.

The sun had begun its downward arc, and they had covered a vast distance already. Over meadows, past fields dotted with sheep and dark stands of trees, isolated cottages, farms and gardens hewed out of places so rough, it seemed a miracle anything could survive, the people equally as rugged.

They had cantered along the dusty lane that snaked through the village, scattering chickens, causing old fishermen mending their nets to start up and take notice, grubby-faced urchins to point and shout. Past the Dragon's Fire Inn, where Anatole informed her bold cavaliers had long ago gathered to plot the ruin of Cromwell's army. Past the spires of St. Gothian, the old church built upon the spot where pagan Celts had once held their wild revels. Past the quiet rectory, with ivy clambering up its worn stone walls, where Mr. Fitzleger played on the lawn with his golden-haired little granddaughter.

Madeline had been allowed no more than time to wave at the astounded clergyman before Anatole had turned the gelding away from the village.

Heading down to the shore, he'd worked the horse up the steep paths carved into the cliffs and back out into the windswept hills again to show her the standing stone at the crest, rising up from waves of purple heather.

Like the famous Stonehenge in the south of England, Anatole told her, these mystifying monuments were scattered throughout Cornwall. No one knew from whence they came; they were obviously no trick of nature. The mass of granite that towered at the top of the hill appeared like something that had been cast aside by a giant's careless hand.

It didn't surprise Madeline to find such a strange object gracing Anatole's land. For if ever there had been a place destined to be marked by magic and mystery, it was Castle Leger.

In the shadow of the stone, Anatole offered both her and the gelding some respite from the pounding pace he'd set all afternoon. Swinging out of the saddle, Anatole lifted her down. Stiff from the long, bruising ride, she staggered like a sailor struggling to find his shore legs. Anatole banded his arm about her waist to steady her, at the same time releasing the horse. The gelding ambled off toward the straggling shade of some trees, cropping at tender shoots of spring grass.

It seemed the most sweet and natural thing in the world for Anatole to take her by the hand, and they strolled in companionable silence through the heather. All shadows, secrets, misunderstandings that stood between them felt far away, reduced to insignificance beneath such a canopy of azure sky.

With their backs to the standing stone, they looked out over the breathtaking slope of countryside. From these heights they could see all the way to the inlet that shimmered far below Castle Leger. Shrouded by a ring of jagged cliffs, the sparkling sea seemed to stretch on forever, its glass surface dotted with the white sails of fishing sloops, skimming the surface like gauzy butterflies.

"You have seen all of Castle Leger now," Anatole said. "Or nearly so. What do you think?"

The question was voiced with seeming casualness, but she could sense how anxiously he awaited her answer.

"Magnificent, my lord," she murmured.

His eyes gleamed with pride, but her gaze was more for the man himself than any vista of land, sea, and sky. Before they'd set out on this venture, Anatole had insisted upon bathing, donning fresh linen, tying his hair back. But the wind fought to uncivilize him again, tugging at the black flaps of his riding cloak, snatching away the thong that bound his queue, and Madeline felt grateful to it.

It suited him far better, the flow of hair whipping back from his proud shoulders, tangling about the swarthy contours of his face. Like his land, he was battle-scarred, weather-toughened, untamed, and free. Madeline wondered how she could have ever wished him otherwise.

When he glanced down at her, she lowered her gaze, embarrassed to be caught devouring the man with her eyes.

"It is all far more beautiful than I had ever imagined it could be when I first arrived here," she said. "Your—your land, that is."

"Your land now, too, Madeline," he replied softly. "You are the mistress of Castle Leger."

It was a fact she tended to forget, had never fully believed until this moment, standing with him on a heather-strewn hillside, her hand linked to his. She could almost feel the power, the pride of Anatole St. Leger flowing into her through his calloused fingertips, causing her heart to swell.

Their eyes met as they had done so often these past hours, only to dart away again like the wild gulls that circled up from the sea. Never had they been so much at ease in each other's company, yet at the same time, so self-conscious.

Easing her hand from his, she found it easier to direct her attention to the stone that loomed behind them, the gigantic rock towering above her. A circle had been worn smooth through its center like an enormous eye, large enough for a man to crouch down and pass through.

"It would have taken an amazing feat of engineering to have moved such a thing to the top of this hill," she said. "How do you suppose it came to be here?"

"I've no idea. Some believe it was the work of my ancestor Prospero. He was a . . . rather peculiar man." Anatole ran his hand over the rock's worn side. "But I'm certain the stone is far older than that. The monument to some ancient culture. The Druids, perhaps the altar stone of a priestess."

Madeline tipped her head to one side, considering. "No, I doubt this was the property of any woman. It seems too . . . well, too arrogant, too masculine."

Anatole smiled. "In any case, the villagers think there's magic in it. Crawling through the stone's eye is supposed to cure a man of anything, from the gout to being hilla-ridden."

"Hilla-ridden?"

"Beset with nightmares."

"And have you ever tried the powers of the stone?"

He looked sheepish as he confessed, "Perhaps once or twice. When I was a lad."

"Because you had bad dreams?"

"No."

"You must have been such a strong, strapping boy. I cannot imagine that there could have been much else ever wrong with you."

He said nothing, only smiled again, but this time it was tinted with sadness. Madeline was beset with an image of him, playing here by himself as a lonely child, creeping solemnly through the circle in the stone. Hoping . . . for what? To be healed of whatever it was that made him so unlovable in the eyes of his parents? Just as she had so often lingered before mirrors, wishing away the cursed red hair that marked her as so different from the rest of her family.

But there were no miracles to be found in wishing or in blocks of stone, no matter how mysterious. It was on the tip of her tongue to say so when something in Anatole's face as he gazed at the stone stopped her. Something a little awed, a little vulnerable.

She examined the rock again herself, allowing her sense of wonder to overcome her reason. Removing her gloves, she laid experimental hands upon the granite mound's cool surface. Then hiking up her skirts, she ducked down, struggling her way through the center of the eye. The toe of her kid boot caught on the edge, and she stumbled, clutching at the edge of the ring to keep from falling.

Anatole rushed to her rescue, his eyes lit by a tender amusement as he helped her through to the other side.

"Ow," she said, examining the raw skin where the rock had abraded the sensitive wrist area below her sleeve. "Your stone doesn't seem to have had a very healthy effect on me."

"That's because you didn't do it right. You have to crawl through it backward, nine times against the sun."

"I believe I'll defer that until a time when I am desperately ill."

Her words caused him to pale.

"God forbid," he said fervently. "That such a time should ever come." He drew her injured wrist to his lips and brushed his mouth lightly across her skin.

It was as unreasonable to believe healing could be found in a man's kiss any more than it could in a granite stone. And yet Madeline felt warmth that tingled to her innermost core, the throbbing pain displaced by a far sweeter ache that made her feel suddenly trembling and shy.

She retreated around the rock, cradling her hand to preserve the warm feel of his mouth, the kiss, like this golden afternoon to be pressed between the leaves of her memory forever.

Anatole made no effort to follow. He studied her through half-lowered eyelids in a way that was as unsettling as his kiss had been.

"Thank you," he said.

"For what?" she asked, somewhat unsteadily.

"For everything. For bearing my company this afternoon. For trusting me about the horse. For not telling me what a superstitious fool you think I am."

A guilty heat crept into Madeline's cheeks as she recalled how close she had come to doing just that, how little she deserved his gratitude.

"My cousin always said this stone was nothing but a blasted eyesore, and perhaps he's right," Anatole said. "If he had been the lord of Castle Leger, he would have found a way to tear it down."

Madeline didn't have to ask which cousin he meant. To even speak Roman's name threatened to invoke some evil spirit that would put a blight on the day, the newfound harmony between them.

"It is a good thing, then, that *he* is not Castle Leger's master," she said. "He could never be at one with the land or its people the way you are."

Anatole gave a wry laugh. "Meaning that I am as ignorant as any of my peasant farmers."

"No! But you do understand them, respect their beliefs. I suppose that is why they all adore you so."

Anatole looked as though he thought she'd lost her mind.

"Have you never noticed?" she asked. "I have, even in the short time I have been at Castle Leger. They all hold you in great esteem, your servants, your tenants, even the folk in the village. They fear and love and respect and . . . and are fiercely proud of you. You are ever their own dread lord."

He laughed outright in disbelief at her words, but a hint of embarrassment stained his cheeks.

"And you?" he prodded. "What about you?" He was still smiling, but his eyes were in earnest.

Madeline's heart skipped a beat, and she scarce knew how to answer him.

"You are my own dread lord as well," she said with a teasing smile, then ducked her head, lest he see something in her eyes she was not even sure of herself.

She drifted away from him, feigning a deep interest in a butterfly flitting amongst the heather. Anatole watched her go, suppressing a stab of disappointment. The day had been too perfect, the sun too bright, the sky too blue, enough to give a man unreasonable hopes again.

Yet he felt he had accomplished more with Madeline in this one afternoon than he had done with all his damn fool efforts at garden walks, teatimes, and supper parties. He should have had the wit to realize it sooner. If there was any place he would be good at wooing a woman, it was from the back of a horse.

She was looking happier than she had since her arrival at Castle Leger, the shadow that had so alarmed him, darkening her winsome features this morning had passed away, gone for the moment.

Wandering through the heather, she removed her bonnet, shaking loose her glorious fall of hair, recklessly tipping up her delicate complexion to the heat of the sun.

Swirling his cloak back from his shoulder, he leaned against the stone, content to watch her, drawing his pleasure from hers. He would give his very soul to keep her this way forever, smiling and unafraid, as vibrant and blooming as the wildflowers waving upon the hill.

Nothing else would matter, no, not even if she never desired him with all the legendary passion of a St. Leger bride. Nothing mattered as long as he could—

Simply love her . . .

The words sifted through his head like the lyrics of a familiar song, often heard, but never fully comprehended.

Until now.

Anatole stiffened, the meaning of Prospero's spell suddenly crystallizing in his mind with an almost painful clarity.

Forget the damned legends, the magic and spells, and the trying to capture the woman's heart as though it were a blasted prize.

Simply love her!

And, God, how he did.

Anatole blinked, the revelation staggering enough to bring him to his knees. Straightening away from the stone, he trembled with the force of it, his gaze eagerly tracking toward Madeline.

It was as though a heavy veil had been wrenched from some dark corner of his mind and he felt his power stir. He closed his eyes and . . . sweet heaven! For the first time he could feel her, truly sense her presence. Each beat of her heart, each breath, each movement a part of him, linked to her as he had never been to anyone before. It felt like holy light pouring into his soul through the stained glass of some vast cathedral.

"Anatole?" He heard the puzzlement in her voice as she called his name.

She was moving toward him, and he could *feel* it, each hesitant step.

His eyes fluttered open, and he released a long breath. Madeline paused a bare yard away from him. Cocking her head to one side, she studied him with concern.

"Are you all right?"

"Yes," he rasped. Well might she ask. He was certain he must be looking damned strange. He felt damned strange.

As she stepped closer, he drifted trembling fingers down the curve of her cheek, awe in his caress. Powerful emotion surged through him, and he wanted to laugh, to shout, to weep, to drop to his knees all at the same time.

Thank the heavens he was a St. Leger. For how else would he ever have managed to find her in all this wide, wide world? Madeline, his chosen bride . . . his love.

"God bless Mr. Fitzleger," he murmured.

"W-what?" She eyed him doubtfully. "Are you sure you are quite well, my lord?"

"Never better." He gave a shaky laugh, a man suddenly certain of his destiny. To love, to cherish, to protect this one woman forever. He plucked her bonnet from where it dangled from her other hand. "You should put this back on. The air is too rough for you up here."

He settled the bonnet over her bright curls, knotting the ribbons beneath her chin with a precision that would have done a seaman proud. Madeline submitted to his ministrations, although she did complain, "I am not made of china, my lord. You are far too protective of me."

"And I shall continue to be so. I would command the winds themselves to stay for you if I could."

"I almost believe that you could." Her nose crinkled in puzzlement. "You have this way about you I cannot explain sometimes."

"Yes, I do, do I not?"

To Madeline's astonishment, Anatole threw back his head and let loose a shout of laughter that echoed throughout the hills. She could not imagine what had come over him, the booming sound disconcerting and yet completely delightful. She had never seen him laugh thus before, hearty and free as though a great weight had just tumbled from his shoulders.

A startled gasp escaped her when he caught her beneath the arms and swept her off her feet. Lifting her so high, her face was at a level with his, he spun her around in a circle. Breathless, laughing in protest, she clutched at his shoulders. He whirled her around and around until she was giddy, begging him to stop.

He staggered to an abrupt halt, too dizzy to maintain his balance. Losing his footing, he stumbled over backward, taking her with him. They tumbled down into the heather, Anatole breaking her fall. She sprawled atop his chest, her bonnet slipping off to dangle by its ribbons about her neck, her hair as madly disheveled as his.

Panting, he gazed up at her with smiling eyes, their laughter mingling in a warm breath. Laughter that stilled as each became aware of their situation, the softness of her bosom pressed to the hard wall of his chest, their hearts pounding in unison, her tangled-up petticoats exposing her thigh, her skin brushing up against the taut fabric of his breeches.

She inched away, seeking a more modest position, but his arms encircled her, holding her fast. He murmured, "You were right, you know."

"About what this time?" she tried to jest, but her voice cracked.

"About what you said in bed last night."

"O-oh, no. I should never have said anything."

"But it was true. Something *was* very wrong between us."

"And now it isn't?" she asked wonderingly.

His mouth crooked in a seductive smile; he shook his head.

"Then, you think that the next time that we . . . we—" Her cheeks flamed as she realized what she was asking him.

He nodded, his gaze narrowing to a slow, simmering burn.

"Th-three days?" she faltered.

"And more, my lady. My grandfather's record is about to be broken."

His hand tangling in her hair, he cupped the nape of her neck, bringing her mouth down to his. Not tentatively, not roughly, but a kiss that was as sure and strong as the arms that held her.

He shifted her off of him, easing her beside him in the heather, his lips never releasing hers, his kiss waxing bolder, invading her with heat and tenderness.

Dazed, Madeline drew back, her breath coming light and quick.

Something . . . something had happened during these few moments they'd spent on this hillside, in the shadow of that strange stone. As though a powerful change had blown in on the wind, only to settle in Anatole's eyes.

He had looked at her with intensity before. He had even looked at her with heat. But never had he looked at her this way, as though she had become the entire sum of his being, the center of his world. As though he could reach deep inside of her and lay trembling fingers upon her heart.

He began to undo the ribbons that held her bonnet fast around her neck, his tanned fingers working the dove-colored satin with a tantalizing slowness, causing her body to quiver with anticipation. Slowly, carefully, he brushed the ribbons aside and pressed a kiss to her neck, the most sensitive hollow where her pulse had begun to race.

Tangling his fingers in the sun-warmed strands of her hair, he wooed her with kisses, rough and tender. She trembled with response, a delicious sensation of shock spiraling through her as she realized what he intended to do.

Make love to her. Take her. Right here, right now. In the midst of the sweet-smelling wildflowers, beneath the standing stone and the broad blue sky. And, sweet heaven, how she wanted him to, her body shivering with desires both new and achingly familiar.

As though she had known and felt all this before in a dream. Or in a fantasy obtained by gazing too long into a hypnotic shard of crystal.

Madeline's eyes flew wide as the memory struck her. All this was so much like what she had imagined last night, the breathtaking ride on horseback, the windswept hillside, Anatole's black hair falling about the warlike planes of his face. The strong feel of his arms, the fiery taste of his mouth as he'd laid her back into the heather. What was certain to follow . . .

She felt awed by the strangeness of such a coincidence and a little frightened. Not of all those wondrous things she knew Anatole was going to do to her, but that this magic might prove as ephemeral as her vision had been.

His hands caressed her back in sensual circles. But when he reached for the fastening of her riding jacket, she braced her hand against his chest, seeking to stay him.

"Promise me one thing first," she said.

His face was already flushed with passion, but he managed to smile. "And what would that be?"

"Promise me that no matter what happens between us this time, you won't leave me. You won't run away again."

"Madeline . . ."

"Promise!"

"I promise." Sweeping her hand away from his chest, he grazed his lips against the center of her palm. "As if I could ever run that far from you. I fear it far more likely that some day you might be the one to flee."

"That I never would. I was terrified last night when you vanished and I could not find you. Worried that something dreadful might have happened to you. At one moment I even had this foolish fear that—that—" She bit down on her lower lip. "I had driven you away, angered and disappointed you so much, you might seek out the bed of another woman."

"Foolish, indeed," he said gently. "Madeline, do you still not understand? I can only desire one woman, and that is you. My chosen bride for all eternity."

"Just like in the legend?"

"Aye, the legend you so stubbornly refuse to believe in."

"Then, teach me," she whispered. "Teach me to believe."

She felt a tremor pass through him in response to her plea. His dark lashes swept down, and he drew her close again in an embrace that was both reverent and passionate, sweet and dark with impending desire.

Time itself stilled, the sun hovering on the horizon, the heather no longer stirring with the breeze. His lips claimed hers with all the fierce tenderness any St. Leger had ever brought to his bride. It was a warrior's kiss, bold and demanding, breaching the soft defense of her lips, offering her no quarter until all she could do was sigh and surrender.

Melting into his caresses, she buried her fingers in the wild darkness of his hair, hungrily returning his kiss. Heat and fire and magic, his tongue teased hers with a primitive rhythm that made her shiver in his arms.

She knelt beside him in the heather, her arms wrapped about his neck, her cheek resting against his beard-roughened jaw, while he fumbled with her clothing. He had lost all patience for slow seduction, tugging, until riding jacket, dress, chemise, all drifted about her knees, leaving her naked to the raking of his eyes.

Yet she knew no urge to cover herself. All sense of shame, false modesty had been left far behind in that reasonable, prudent world she'd once inhabited. A world she could scarce remember.

The same breeze that had uncivilized him seemed to have wantoned her. Like any primitive maiden who had ever romped beneath the stone, she shook her cascade of hair back from her shoulders, proudly exposing the globes of her breasts. His eyes flared, and he unfastened the cordings of his black cloak, spreading it out to make a bed of midnight in the purple heather. Tearing at the buttons of his shirt, he stripped it from the hard contours of his chest, shucking his breeches, working off his boots.

He towered over her, sunlight playing over his powerful body, all golden-toned skin, taut muscle, and aroused male flesh. Like some pagan god bent on seducing a mortal maid, his long black hair tangling in the wind, the heat of his gaze skimmed over her with a strange, arousing power.

Madeline arched back with a sigh, her skin tingling in a dozen places. It could have been the warmth of the sun, the breeze stirring against her flesh. But she felt as though she were being stroked by long, supple fingers, sending the blood racing through her veins.

How was it possible, she wondered, for a man to make a woman feel so caressed with nothing more than the fire of his eyes? But as delicious as such imagining was, she longed for the reality of his touch.

When he dropped back to his knees beside her, she ran her fingertips over the broad slope of shoulders, the sinewy strength of his arms, skimming gently over the recent wound left by Roman's knife.

She sculpted her hands to the hard muscle that delineated his chest, tracing swirls in the dark mat of hair. He bore her explorations with a warrior's iron stoicism, but she could feel the way his heart jumped, his flesh quivered at each touch.

A purely feminine thrill shot through her at the realization that she could exert such power over this mighty indomitable male. Emboldened, her fingers drifted lower over the rigid plane of his stomach, toward the region of his body that still mystified her.

Twice she had felt the power of his thrusts inside of her, but never before had she dared to . . . Catching her breath, she closed her hand around him. Hot, pulsing, smooth velvet . . . fascinating.

With a low groan he seized her wrist to stop her.

"No, lady, not this time. I'll not be . . . driven to the brink before I work my magic upon you."

When he thrust her hand away from him, she emitted a cry of protest, but he suppressed it with his mouth slanting over hers in a fierce kiss. His hands whispered along the curve of her breasts, and she gasped at the shock of it, the heat of his palms a marked contrast to the cool air sifting over her skin.

His leather-toughened fingers splayed above her waist, holding her captive to the hunger of his mouth, the sweet torment of his thumbs abrading her nipples to a state of aching hardness. She quivered, a soft moan catching in her throat.

He tumbled her down onto the folds of the cloak, his powerful body poised above her, shielding her from the sun. He stared into her eyes, his own black with powerful emotion, desire shaded with deep regret.

"Ah, Madeline. You deserve so much more than my silence. If only I could tell you—I should have had the courage to do so long ago. I—I—"

"Shh," she said, soothing her fingertips over the troubled set of his mouth. "Whatever it is, it will keep."

"But I haven't even said how beautiful—How much I—What I feel for—" He broke off, swallowing thickly. "I have no words."

"Then, show me, my lord. Show me what is in your heart."

With a shuddering sigh he buried his face against her shoulder, searing her skin with the passion of his kiss. His hands moved over her, working their magic, no longer touching her as though he thought she would shatter. He suddenly seemed to know the secrets of her body better than she did herself, stroking, caressing, seeking out the warmth of her most intimate places.

Desire tightened deeper and hotter inside of her until it became an unbearable ache. She writhed beneath him, whimpering, her fingers scoring feverishly over the span of his back.

This . . . she was stunned to realize was what she'd longed for, waited for all those long nights alone in her bed. This was what she had traveled so far from London, home, and family to find.

Not some serene poet with dreamy gaze and golden words, but this rough plain man with his profound silences and deep strength, who came to her with calloused hands and a scarred heart, his eyes a well of hidden sorrows, his fierce mouth bearing an infinite capacity for tenderness.

He worshiped her with his lips, his touch, his gaze, and when he sought to part her thighs, she was more than ready for him. She opened herself to him eagerly, drawing him close into her embrace.

For one heart-stopping moment his eyes locked deep with hers, and she felt as though he could see into the very core of her soul, the aching center of her need. Then with one smooth thrust, he plunged himself inside of her. No pain, no disappointment, no despair this time, just a simple union of their bodies that was natural and right.

Caressing a kiss across her mouth, Anatole began moving, cupping her behind the knees, teaching her how to match his rhythm.

They rocked together as one, the tempo slowly building to something as ageless and primitive as the stone that loomed above them. His kisses becoming as fevered as his stroking, Anatole whispered her name, the single word a ragged prayer on his lips.

Like being caught up by a powerful tide, Madeline clung helplessly to his shoulders, allowing him to take her where he would, spiraling off into a world where all reason was left behind. Nothing remained but pure sensation.

The bright blue sky, the mammoth stone, the purple heather, all vanished until Madeline was aware of nothing but the man who labored over her, his chest glistening with sweat, his body trembling as though he fought to hold some mighty force in check. His dark eyes bored into hers, waiting, demanding some mysterious response of her with each thrust of his body.

A response that coiled tighter and deeper inside of her past the point of endurance. Digging her nails into his back, she arched high against Anatole, crying out in wonder and surprise as something exploded inside of her. Waves of pleasure, incredibly sweet, so intense, she felt lifted, hurled to the sky.

Her body shook with the force of it, and as the passionate throbbing faded to a warm glow, she drifted back to earth, staring up at Anatole with dazed eyes.

A fleeting smile touched his lips, of the deepest satisfaction. As though he had been waiting for just that moment, he relinquished all control. With one final thrust a tremendous shudder racked through his own frame. Closing his eyes, he arched his head back with a hoarse cry.

A sound that echoed throughout the hills, like a warrior's fierce shout of triumph. Panting, he sank down on top of her, covering her with the warmth of his body, taking care not to crush her beneath his weight.

For a long time the hilltop was silent, broken only by the rustling of the heather, the haunting cry of a gull winging its way back toward the sea.

Shifting to his side, Anatole strained Madeline close to him, his skin warm and damp from their recent bout of passion. The sun had crept a little lower in the sky, the breeze blew a little brisker, but Madeline felt none of it, still bathed in some strange afterglow.

But Anatole insisted upon tugging the end of the cloak over her. She nestled beneath it, snuggling her face against his chest, listening to his heartbeat resume its ordinary beat. But nothing could ever be ordinary again, she thought, overwhelmed by the shattering release she had found in Anatole's arms.

She had sensed long ago that the man was possessed of hidden fires, the need to love someone buried beneath his indomitable facade. Waiting for only the right lady to arouse him to such burning tenderness.

But she had never fully believed, had given up all hope that she would prove to be the one. Her eyes filled with tears of joy, gratitude, relief, but she blinked them away, fearing Anatole would only be disturbed by them. A rare expression of peace had stolen over his rugged features, stripping years away. He was looking mighty pleased with the world at the moment, with himself and her.

He glanced down at her upturned face and intoned a single word. "Well?"

She knew what he was asking her, but blast the man, she noted with amused tenderness. There was not a hint of anxiety in his voice, only a smug certainty.

"It was . . . tolerable."

Certainty vanished in an instant, a pained chagrin stealing into his eyes. Her heart melted with regret immediately, and she could not bear to tease him any further.

Rolling on top of him, she laid her arms upon his chest and braced her chin on her hands.

"You know full well all that you just did to me, sir," she murmured. "And now I know something, too."

"What is that, milady?"

"I understand why your grandmama wouldn't let her husband out of bed for three days."

Anatole's smile slowly returned, his teeth flashing in a grin of masculine triumph and pure St. Leger arrogance. And Madeline found it wholly adorable.

"I'm thinking of keeping you here naked on this hill for a whole week," she said.

A chuckle rumbled deep in his chest. "I have no objections, madam. But what about my horse?"

"We'll just turn him loose, and he can wander off and . . . and find his chosen mare."

"*He* is a gelding."

"Oh," Madeline mourned. "Poor horse."

Anatole laughed outright. His eyes smiling into hers, he framed her face, dusting a light kiss on the tip of her nose, and she realized exactly how much had changed between them.

They were no longer two desperately lonely people brought together by the offices of a saintly old man. They had become lovers in truth, sharing intimate murmurs, playful caresses, teasing jests all their own.

Anatole nibbled at her earlobe, nuzzling the sensitive hollow just beneath, and Madeline blissfully closed her eyes. Indeed, she *did* understand why all those other St. Leger women had been reluctant to release their men, if they had been anything at all like Anatole.

It wasn't just for those few moments of glorious passion, but all that came after. The laughter, the gentler touching, the tender kisses, being held safe and fast in a strong pair of arms. The thrilling consciousness of having tamed something wild and dark to one's side, the attentions of such a fierce magnificent man, hers and hers alone for the moment, the rest of the world so far away.

A world that threatened to intrude all too soon. Even as Anatole's mouth was a breath away from hers, he froze suddenly. Twisting his head to one side, he tensed, listening.

She had seen that strange alert expression on his face before, and it sent a ripple of unease through her. She tried to ignore it, determined that nothing should happen to ruin this magic afternoon.

Cupping his cheek, she sought to turn his face back to her, but he eased her off of him. Whipping to a sitting position, every muscle in his body went taut, his eyes intent, focusing on what, she had no idea.

"Damn," he swore at last, casting her a rueful smile. "If you're going to keep me naked, we'll have to do it back in the privacy of my bedchamber. Someone is coming."

Madeline strained with all her might, but she could detect nothing beyond the play of the wind through the grass, the distant whickering of Anatole's horse.

"I don't hear anything," she complained.

But Anatole was already scrambling to his feet, shrugging back into his breeches. "You'll have to trust me on this one, sweetheart. Quimby is at this moment riding toward us like the very devil. And while he may seem a rough old codger, he has the soul of a Puritan. I can't afford to scandalize the best head groom I've ever had."

Tossing her clothes down to her, he laughingly urged her to make haste. Although bewildered, she moved to comply, but she was still shifting the bodice of her riding dress up over her arms when she heard it for herself. The far-off thudding of hooves.

A rider appeared on the horizon, sweeping over the ridge of the next hill. Anatole wrenched her dress up the rest of the way himself.

But her attention was focused on the horseman, now swiftly closing upon them. Madeline squinted hard until she was able to make out the sun glinting off a balding pate.

Her jaw dropped open. "It *is* Quimby." She twisted around, turning astounded eyes upon Anatole. "How could you possibly know that?"

"Uh, well, that's—that's something I've been meaning to explain to you. And I will . . . back at the house."

Avoiding her gaze, he bent to retrieve his cloak, shaking off loose bits of grass and heather. Stalking down the hill, he waved his hand in greeting to the groom approaching at such a thundering speed.

"Quimby!" he shouted. "What the devil do you mean, riding one of my hunters as though a pack of Mortmains were—"

His words died away as Quimby reined the chestnut mare to such an abrupt halt, the horse all but reared back on its haunches. Even from the distance where she stood, Madeline could tell something was terribly wrong.

The elderly groom was breathing as hard as the horse. His voice carried up to Madeline in snatches. "My lord . . . Looking everywhere for you. We've sent for Dr. Marius. Something terrible . . . accident back at the house. 'Tis Will . . . Young Will Sparkins."

Anatole seemed to turn to stone. But he asked no questions, merely gave a stiff nod of dismissal. Quimby wheeled the mare about and galloped off as wildly as he had come. Pivoting on his heel, Anatole turned and headed for his own horse.

Madeline watched in dismay. He had forgotten all about her. Confused, a little frightened, she darted after him, panting to overtake his longer strides.

"Anatole," she called, shrugging hastily into her jacket.

He didn't even turn around. She didn't manage to catch up with him until he stopped to reach for the gelding's reins.

"Anatole," she cried. "What is it? What's happened? What about Will?"

He paused long enough to afford her a glimpse of his face. Her breath caught in her throat. Never had she seen so much despair reflected in a single pair of eyes.

"You . . . you didn't even ask Quimby what was wrong," she faltered.

"I already know," he said hoarsely.

Vaulting up in the saddle, he bent down and hauled her up after him.

Bringing the gelding around, Anatole clicked his tongue, urging the beast into a full gallop, allowing Madeline no more chance for questions.

She could do nothing but wrap her arms around his neck and hang on, shivering. Although the sun still glowed across the hillside, in a heartbeat, everything had changed, the warmth between her and Anatole quite fled.

Somehow the shadows had returned.

Chapter Seventeen

Most of the servants had gathered in the main hall, the footman Tim attempting to console Nancy, the kitchen lass, who was sobbing into her apron, while the burly cook whispered to old Rowley, the games keeper. Rough-visaged grooms from the stables rubbed shoulders with pretty housemaids, all of them exchanging low murmurs.

"Ah! So 'is lordship's dark power has been at work again, 'as it?"

"Aye, 'twas another of his terrible visions."

"But he warned the lad, now, didn't he? 'Stay away from the ax,' he said."

"Small good it would have done poor Will even if he had listened. Have ye ever known one of the master's predictions not to come true?"

But all whispering ceased as the master of Castle Leger himself stormed into the hall, stripping off his cloak and casting it aside, his bride trailing anxiously after him.

Anatole drew up short at the sight of his assembled household and cast a fierce glance around him. No one moved a muscle, but he could feel them shrinking away from him, all these good honest people Madeline insisted adored him so.

It wasn't love but fear that he saw reflected in their faces, none of them daring to meet his eyes, shuffling their boots, fidgeting with their apron strings, staring anywhere but at him. No, heaven forbid, for who knew when or where the master's dreaded power might strike next?

"Get out," Anatole snapped, "and be about your business. You can do Will no good hanging about here."

They hastened to obey him, only Bess Kennack bold enough to shoot him a hate-filled glance. One by one, they melted away until Anatole found himself standing alone as had happened so often before when one of his visions became stark reality.

Except he wasn't alone this time. His fingers clamped down around Madeline's hand. He suddenly realized he was clutching on to her like she was his last link to sanity.

Despite her own anxiety and bewilderment at the servants' behavior, she remained at his side, her calm stealing over him like a caress.

Aye, a tormenting voice in his head whispered, but would she continue to stand by him if she knew the truth? Or would she shrink away from him as the others had done?

And if she ever did that *now,* after the way they had loved beneath the standing stone, would he be able to bear it? Or would it be like a tearing away of his soul, leaving him dying inside?

He touched the curve of her cheek, and she smiled up at him, comfort shimmering in her warm, spring green eyes. He longed to lose himself in that comfort, sweep them both away from here, back to their hillside. But the afternoon he'd spent in her arms already seemed far away, heather and sunlight, loving and laughter, nothing more than a dream. He was a man who had been cruelly awakened back to his nightmare.

A nightmare he could not, *would not* share with her.

He released his hold on her hand. "You'd best go look after your maids," he said. "Nancy appears to be on the verge of hysteria. I will see to Will."

"But, Anatole, I would far rather come with you."

"No! My cousin Marius has been summoned. The lad will not have need of you."

"I wasn't thinking of Will, my lord. I was thinking that perhaps . . ." She raised wistful eyes to his face. "You might need me."

Need her? Oh, God! He needed her so badly he felt his chest constrict with the force of it. But his desire to shield her was stronger, protect her from the grim scene he knew lay ahead, the blood, the pain, Will's horrible screams. And most of all, protect her from the dark side of himself.

Turning his back on her, he forced himself to say harshly, "Just do as I tell you, madam."

He could feel her hurt as he stalked away, carried it like a heavy weight in his heart, adding it to the burden of guilt he already felt.

He followed the narrow passage that led toward the servant's wing of the house, and the door to the stillroom loomed up before Anatole. The chamber off the kitchens had been used to treat injury and illness since the days when the Lady Deidre had first brewed her mystic herbs. He could sense Will's presence behind that door, the boy's pain ebbing toward him like a crimson tide.

He had ridden like the damned to hurl himself back here, but now his step faltered. This was a journey he had taken too many times before, a desperate trek to prevent the unpreventable.

Flailing out into the cold sea in a vain effort to save those shipwrecked sailors he had known must drown. Galloping like a madman to the Kennack cottage, only to watch poor Marie's eyes close after her dying glimpse of her newborn babe. Tearing down the garden path at midnight, his heart burning in his chest as he'd tried to stop his own mother from—

And now there was Will.

God help him. He didn't know if he had the strength to go through this again. But it was not as if he had a choice. St. Legers looked after their own. It was perhaps the only lesson he'd ever absorbed from his gentle tutor Fitzleger. But there was one thing the old man had forgotten to mention, Anatole thought bitterly. How often he was going to fail.

Steeling his jaw, he reached for the knob and shoved the door open. Candles had been lit to hold back the gloom of twilight, their glow spilling over the grim scene; Will lay sprawled on an oak table, pillows propping up his head, shudders racking his slender frame. The fabric of his breeches had been cut away to reveal a gaping wound below the left knee, a mass of shattered bone and exposed sinew. Anatole froze on the threshold, although the sight was no different from what he'd expected. But that didn't make it any easier. It never did.

While Lucius Trigghorne hovered like a sentinel mounting guard, Marius St. Leger labored over the boy, the young doctor's gaunt features stamped with a strange dark beauty, like an angel of mercy or of death. Gentle, patient, reassuring, his sensitive mouth was pulled down with the look of one who'd felt more of the sufferings of his fellowmen than any mortal should be expected to bear.

Marius murmured soothing words as he tightened the heavy circular clamp fastened to Will's thigh. A terrible cry breached the boy's lips, and Trigg had to dive to restrain him.

Will tossed and moaned beneath the grizzled old man's hands, limp straws of hair tumbling over his pain-glazed eyes.

Eyes that had been so clear and trusting the night Anatole had first looked into them and pronounced this dreadful curse. And then . . . he'd simply forgotten the boy.

Aye, Anatole thought hollowly, he'd been consumed these past days and nights with his pursuit of Madeline, his every waking moment directed toward her.

But he should have spared one thought for Will. He should have done more to save him besides issue futile commands. He should have placed a constant guard on the lad, should have had every ax removed from the estate, should have maintained a more careful watch himself.

He should have . . . should have . . . The words pounded through Anatole's head like a hellish litany, all too familiar and futile. He sagged one shoulder against the door frame.

It was Marius who first noticed his arrival. Directing Trigg to keep sponging the wound, the doctor wiped his hands on his apron. He joined Anatole by the doorway, keeping his voice low, out of Will's earshot.

"Well, cousin, your young footman has done a proper job on himself, but he's not going to die."

"I know," Anatole said hoarsely.

"But his wound is far too deep. I have not the art to knit back flesh and sinew when it has been severed to such an extent. His leg . . . he will have to lose—"

"I know, damn you!"

Marius regarded him intently, his eyes flaring with a sudden understanding.

"I'm sorry," he said. "I didn't realize . . ."

Anatole's jaw tightened, finding Marius's compassion unbearable. "If you want to feel sorry for anyone, save it for the boy."

Brushing past his cousin, Anatole forced himself toward Will. The boy's head lolled toward him, the swaggering youth of these past days since Madeline's arrival quite vanished. He'd shrunk back into a frightened boy, his strained face already bearing the markings of the bitter, crippled man he was to become.

At the sight of Anatole Will's eyes widened with fear. "Oh, master," he choked out. "I'm s-sorry. I didn't mean it. I didn't want to disobey you. B-but I forgot your warning about the ax."

"It's all right, Will," Anatole said, the boy's broken apology making him feel as though an ax blade was being driven through his own chest.

"He was showing off for the lasses, Nancy and that Kennack girl," Trigg growled, concealing his own fierce emotions behind a heavy scowl.

"I—I was only trying to pr-prove how strong I was and—and the ax was too heavy, and it—it slipped. I'm sorry, master. So v-very, very—"

"Damn it! It's all right," Anatole said more harshly than he intended. He'd far rather Will had cursed him, spit in his face the way Bess Kennack had done when her mother had died.

Large tears tracked down Will's cheeks, and Anatole brushed back the boy's hair in a gruff, awkward gesture.

"I'm not angry with *you*, lad," he said in gentler tones.

"But—but I ruined my fine new livery. What shall I tell the m-mistress?"

"She'll understand, and she'll buy you another. Now, you just lie still, and everything will be . . ."

Fine. The lie stuck in Anatole's throat as he became aware of Marius busy out of Will's line of sight, reaching into his portable wooden medicine box, readying his instruments. The candlelight gleamed cold on the sharp teeth of the saw, the curved amputation knife, the needles.

Anatole's gut clenched. He seized his cousin by the arm, dragging him to the far corner of the room.

"For the love of God, Marius," he whispered in sheer desperation. "Are you certain this is the only recourse? Curse it all, man. You've studied in Edinburgh, read through all of Deidre's secret journals. You've defied all customs, learning to be both doctor and surgeon. No man living knows more of medicine than you. You must be able to . . . to . . ."

His words faltered and trailed away as Marius sadly shook his head.

"I am sorry, Anatole. But my capacity to feel someone else's pain too often exceeds my ability to cure it."

The answer was no different from what Anatole had expected, but he had experienced a flare of hope all the same. A hope that flickered and died away to nothing.

God, he was a fool! Releasing Marius's arm, he dragged his hand wearily down the line of his jaw.

"You'd best get about it, then," he said.

"Aye, but I think you should go. There is no need for you to stay here and—and—"

"And go through all this again?" Anatole gave a low bitter laugh. "It seems to be part of my peculiar St. Leger destiny, cousin. To experience every disaster in my life twice over."

"Then, I must beg you to gain some command over yourself. I am not certain I can feel both his pain and yours, and still do what must be done."

Marius's quiet words, the flash of agony in his eyes filled Anatole with a sense of shame. He tended to forget that he was not the only St. Leger who suffered from the dark side of their heritage.

But for Marius, there would never be any of the light. Not in this lifetime. Anatole at least had Madeline.

He had never been any good at offering comfort, any better than he was at receiving it. But he gave Marius's shoulder a bracing squeeze. For a moment their eyes locked in a communion of shared pain.

Then Marius turned back to his grim task, and Anatole tried to do as his cousin had requested. Tamp down his emotions, keep them locked up tight. He'd been better at it somehow before Madeline had swept into his life. Keeping all his fears, hurt, and sorrow buried deep. But his lady had taught him to feel again, perhaps too much.

It became even more difficult to contain himself as Will realized what was going to happen.

"No!" The boy shrieked, coming halfway up off the table.

Trigg struggled to ease him back down, but Will fought against him, all Marius's efforts to soothe lost in the boy's sobs of despair.

"No, n-not that. Oh, please, Gawd, just let me die."

Trigg pinned Will's shoulders back down, but Will twisted his head toward Anatole, his eyes wild with terror.

"Master . . . please, don't let them. I'm sorry. I'll never disobey you again. Pl-please. Help me!"

Anatole closed his eyes, turning away, the boy's cries tearing through him. As Marius hastened to the door to summon another of the servants to help restrain Will, Anatole could bear it no longer.

He came about and commanded fiercely, "Let him go!"

Trigg glanced up from his struggle with Will, astonished, hesitating. Marius shot Anatole a reproving frown.

"Keep the boy still, Mr. Trigghorne," he said. "My lord, I must insist that you—"

"Damn it, I won't have the lad held down by rough hands," Anatole said. "Trigg, release him. *Now!*"

Trigg's eyes roved between Anatole and Marius, but as ever it was his master he obeyed, removing his hands from Will, stepping back.

His thin chest shuddering with relief, Will worked his way up onto his elbows, casting Anatole a look of tear-streaked gratitude. A look that knifed through Anatole like a fire-hot blade, for he knew he was about to shatter the boy's forlorn hope.

He stared at Will intently, raising trembling fingers to his brow to help him concentrate, and he watched Will's face crumple, his eyes flooding with fresh terror as he realized what Anatole meant to do.

"Ah, master. No, please—please don't."

Steeling himself against Will's ragged pleas, Anatole focused his power into dark hands, gentle, but inexorable, pinning Will back to the table, holding him fast.

The throbbing commenced behind Anatole's brow, Will's resistance giving way before him like the helpless flutterings of a moth.

His vision blurred, and as from a great distance, he could hear Marius's voice, sharp with concern.

"Anatole, you can't—"

"Just get on with it, Marius," he rasped. "And quickly."

With those words Anatole's awareness of everything else in the room narrowed and fled, until there was only Will, his own black power, and the pain pounding in his head, thrusting at the thin barrier of his temples.

A pain that intensified as it mingled with the sound of Will's screams. . . .

Night settled over Castle Leger in a soothing silence. The sky was like painted velvet, melting with stars, moonlight shimmering over the distant inlet, the sea a mysterious moving shadow.

But Anatole saw nothing but the darkness as he stared out his study window, the memory of Will's terrible sobs continuing to haunt him long after he'd escaped from the stillroom. He could add that sound to the broken echoes of all the other voices of those he'd cursed with one of his predictions and failed to save.

His head continued to throb from the exertion of his power on Will, a futile effort to spare the boy at least some pain, and his heart swelled with the urge to do as he'd always done after one of these grim episodes. To run from his heritage, to flee from this house, lose himself out there on the cliff side, in the dark and the wind, like some savage beast gone to ground with his wounds. Where he could roar out his frustration and despair, and no one would hear but the night birds and the waves crashing against the rocks below.

But he was held back this time. By his pledge to Madeline that he would never run from her again. A promise he should never have given, any more than he should have made love to her on that hillside today, still concealing what he was.

Cursed as he was, he was no longer certain he had the right to love her at all . . .

He didn't know how he was ever going to tell her the truth. But he couldn't think about that now. Not with his head aching this way, exhaustion sinking into the very marrow of his bones. He leaned his arm against the casement and rested his head against it, wanting nothing more than to be left alone to recover himself.

Dulled as his senses were, he could already detect someone coming to intrude upon his solitude. One of the servants? He was amazed any of them would be brave enough to venture near their dread lord tonight.

Wearily Anatole raised his head, trying to concentrate. Something soft rustled through his exhausted mind, something warm and bright hovering on the jagged edges of his darkness.

Madeline.

He barely had time to straighten, assume some command of himself before the door inched open and Madeline peered inside.

"Anatole?" she called. "May I come in?"

"Yes." What else could he say? But he shrank deeper into the shadows by the window. He had avoided being alone with her ever since their return to Castle Leger, dreading what questions he might find lurking in her eyes, questions he was still too much of a coward to answer.

She slipped into the room, candle shine spilling over the gold of her dressing gown, the shimmering softness of her hair. Light haloed the faerylike beauty of her winsome features, the mere sight of her causing his throat to constrict with suppressed longing.

Maybe he didn't have the right to love her. But heaven help him, he did.

She drifted closer, and he could see that she, too, looked exhausted. While he'd been laboring over Will, she had worked to comfort hysterical housemaids, soothe jangled nerves, bring back some sense of order to the unsettled household. And she had succeeded.

Anatole could feel the house itself calming around her. But that is what his Madeline would always do, he thought with a rush of pride and tenderness, attempt to restore reason to the brink of hell itself.

Hell . . . Castle Leger. On nights like this they were one and the same.

She paused by the corner of the desk, brushing back a stray curl from her eyes. She even managed a wan smile as she said, "I believe everyone is finally settled for the night, and even Will seems to be resting easier."

"Good," Anatole murmured.

"However, Marius had to leave. He was summoned away to attend a crofter's sick child, but he left instructions. Mr. Trigghorne is to keep watch over Will, and if there is any sign of fever, Marius wishes to be sent for at once. He is a very kind man, your cousin."

"Aye."

"His last words to me were, 'Take care of him, Madeline.' "

"There was no need for Marius to tell you that. Surely he must have known you would do all you could for Will."

"He wasn't talking about Will." Madeline lifted her eyes to Anatole's face, her gaze too direct and earnest. "He was talking about you, my lord."

Anatole silently cursed Marius and his interfering concern. He turned back to the window, attempting to sound better than he felt.

"There is nothing the matter with me, my dear."

She rustled around the desk, positioning herself in between him and the night-darkened window. She stroked back his hair, drifting her fingers over his brow, the softness of her touch easing some of his pain.

"You look completely exhausted."

"I am."

"Then, come to bed," she whispered.

His heart went still. How long had he been waiting to hear those words, to have her look at him that way? He'd experienced a fierce triumph this afternoon, certain he roused her passions at last, but he hadn't been as sure about her heart until now.

But her eyes were shining softly, as though . . . as though she loved him. And he wanted to clutch her to him in sheer desperation, do anything in his power to keep her looking at him that way always.

Even continue to lie and deceive her.

Sighing, he put her hand away from him. "I'm sorry," he said. "I would be of little use to you in bed tonight."

A faint blush stole into her cheeks. "I don't want you to be of use. I only want you to rest beside me, let me hold you."

Her words sifted through him with sweet temptation. But he knew from bitter experience what he was going to be like tonight, restless, edgy, morose.

"I fear I wouldn't be fit company for you, even for that." Depositing a chaste kiss upon her brow, he said, "Go on to bed without me."

But she made no move to obey, regarding him with the most sorrowful expression in her eyes. "Please don't do this, my lord."

"Do what?"

"Break your promise. You swore you wouldn't run away from me again."

"And I have not. You see me standing here before you, do you not?"

"Aye." She touched her hand to his chest, resting her fingertips over the region of his heart. "But your heart and mind have drifted far away. To that dark and dreadful place where I can never find you."

"Nonsense. Madeline, you are imagining things."

"No, I am not. Please tell me what is wrong."

"Nothing!" Guilt lent a hint of impatience to his voice. "Only the small matter that I helped Marius saw a boy's leg off today."

"What happened to Will was horrible," she agreed sadly. "I know he was a great favorite of yours as he was with everyone. Such a sweet, gentle boy. But it was an accident, only an accident. Yet you are behaving as if somehow you are to blame. As if you failed him."

"Perhaps I did."

"No! You did everything you could for Will, rushed back here at once, had your own cousin attend him, even assisted with the surgery. I knew few lords in London who would have done as much for their own wives, let alone a mere footman."

"But it wasn't enough! I should have been able to protect him."

"You cannot protect the entire world, my lord."

"No, but I should at least be able to save those that I—" Anatole dragged his hand over the line of his mouth, checking himself barely in time.

But Madeline finished for him. "You mean those people whose eyes you've looked into and cursed with your *dark powers*?"

Her words cracked through Anatole with the force of a pistol shot. He could feel his face draining of all color.

"H-how did you . . ." he faltered. "Where did you—you—"

"Hear such a thing? From Bess Kennack. She has been whispering some strange things to the other servants."

"Such as?" Anatole asked, his veins icing with dread.

"That you are responsible for the death of her mother and what happened to Will. That you are some sort of sorcerer, gifted with demonic powers like all St. Legers are. All the most arrant kind of nonsense."

So Madeline had finally heard, but she still didn't believe. Anatole felt himself able to breathe again.

"I think Bess should be dismissed," she said.

"No," Anatole said. He couldn't do that, not simply because the girl had dared to speak the truth.

"But, Anatole, she is having a very unsettling effect on the other housemaids. Of course, no sensible person could believe such a thing, but—"

Madeline broke off suddenly, staring at him. Anatole had no idea what she saw in his face, what measure of shame or guilt, but something must have betrayed him, for her eyes flew wide.

"My God! Anatole, you . . . you believe it yourself."

He tried to turn away from her, but she caught his face between her hands, forcing him to look at her.

"Oh, Anatole. My dearest heart. I can learn to accept your Bride Finder legend. But this kind of superstition . . . it's evil, wicked, and wrong. And I will prove it to you.

"Look into my eyes," she coaxed. "Do you see any sort of terrible vision there?"

And she smiled tenderly up at him with that same innocence he'd seen in Will's eyes, Marie Kennack's, his own mother's.

"Oh, God!" he groaned, wrenching away from her, pure terror clawing through him at the mere possibility that one day he might look at Madeline and—

"Don't ever do that again! Don't even tempt me to—" He spun away from her, burying his face in his hands. "Madeline . . . will you just go? I am not up to this tonight. I am much troubled, but I will sort things out by myself, as I always do."

"But you don't have to." She clung to his arm, resting her head against his shoulder. "Anatole, please. How can you turn away from me? After all we shared together today . . . talk to me. Let me help you. Whatever this belief is that is tormenting you, we can reason it away."

He ground his fingertips against his throbbing brow, feeling harried, hunted by her very gentleness, her compassion.

"Some things cannot be reasoned. They simply must be endured."

"But, Anatole—"

"Damn it! Leave me alone," he roared, thrusting her away from him.

She staggered back a pace, regarding him with wounded eyes. An awful silence ensued, then her lashes swept down.

"Very well," she said, "if that is what you wish."

As she slipped from the room, he should have experienced relief at her departure, but it was like feeling the light ebb away from him, leaving him trembling in the darkness.

He cursed himself for a fool and a coward, but he clung to the thought that he had been right to make her leave. He was strained to the snapping point, not safe for her to be around tonight.

But then, he thought bleakly, when had he ever been?

He sank down in the chair behind his desk, her sad plea echoing through his mind.

How can you turn away from me . . . after all we shared today.

It was because of what they'd shared that he could not bring himself to tell her the truth. After enduring years of his own private hell, he'd finally touched heaven in her embrace. He couldn't risk losing that now, or her.

Tomorrow . . . he told himself, massaging his aching temples. Tomorrow when his head wasn't hurting like the devil, when he wasn't feeling quite so raw, he'd go to her and take her in his arms, sweep her back to that hillside and make things right again. And maybe she would forget about what she'd heard. Maybe they both could.

Tomorrow . . . But Anatole stiffened sharply, realizing that Madeline wasn't planning to wait that long. He could feel her coming back to him, each soft step filling him with dread. If she was returning to weep and plead, he didn't think he could endure it.

But when she appeared again in the doorway, her eyes were clear and calm. Yet there was a terrible stillness about her, her face so pale and determined, Anatole felt a stab of apprehension.

Especially when he saw what she clutched in her hands. The sheath containing the St. Leger sword.

"Madeline, what the devil are you doing with that?"

She marched across the room and laid the weapon on the desk before him, the hilt sparkling in the candlelight.

"I am returning this to you, my lord."

He gazed up at her, dumbfounded. "But it is yours. I gave it to you. According to the custom of my family."

"Yes, I know. You were to pledge the sword to me, along with your love forever." She shook her head sadly. "You almost made me believe in your legend today, Anatole. That we do belong together. But you'd rather keep your heart shrouded in darkness than surrender it to me.

"And without that, this is only a sword. It means nothing."

Her eyes misted over, and she rushed from the room, leaving Anatole staring after her, stunned.

He sat for a moment, fingering the hilt of the weapon, that hellish crystal glittering up at him. Sweet Jesus! No St. Leger bride had ever returned the sword to her husband before. Why didn't Madeline simply thrust the cursed blade through his heart and be done with it?

Could she not understand? He wasn't holding back the truth to hurt her, only to protect her. That is all he'd ever wanted, to shield her, to save her from the terror that had killed his mother, aye, and to save himself from losing her.

The cruelty of it was that he was losing her anyway, damning himself with his silence.

He resisted a moment longer, but he knew full well what he had to do. Struggling to his feet, he strapped the St. Leger sword to his side.

Madeline was almost to her bedchamber by the time he caught up to her. She tensed when she heard him call her name, but she came slowly around to face him.

"Yes, my lord?"

Her eyes were calm, but hauntingly sad, still softened with that affection for him he hadn't yet managed to extinguish. Anatole took one long last look so he would always remember . . .

"All right. You win, milady," he said, his shoulders bowing in defeat. "I will tell you everything. All that you believe you want to know. The truth about myself and my entire cursed family.

"And may God help us both."

Chapter Eighteen

Fiery light licked at the bare stone walls, casting a hellish glow over the taut planes of Anatole's face. The torch gripped in one hand, he crushed Madeline's wrist in the other, dragging her toward the old wing of the castle. She strained to keep pace with his lengthy strides, trying not to trip up against the St. Leger sword strapped to his side.

The heavy oak door loomed up before them, the painted sentinel above the arch maintaining guard over its forbidding secrets. In the flickering light the St. Leger dragon seemed to rise from its lamp of knowledge in a hiss of smoke. Knowledge Madeline was no longer sure she desired to possess.

Anatole's expression alarmed her, dark, wild, and desperate, like a man poised on the brink of destruction. Perhaps in her own misery, she had goaded him too far with her questions, almost cruelly so after all he had already suffered on Will's account.

He was afraid. Her fierce warrior, her dread lord was *afraid,* and that realization caused icy fingers to clutch at her own throat. What could possibly lie behind that door, what truth about the St. Legers could he be so terrified to share with her?

The memory of Bess Kennack's words returned to haunt her, whispers of sorcery, curses, demonic powers. Madeline's mind rebelled at such ignorant notions, but her heart . . . It thudded with unreasoning fears, nameless dreads caught up in the atmosphere of night and shadow.

Somewhere behind her, back in warmer, safer regions of the house, she could hear a clock striking midnight. The sound sent an inexplicable shiver through her. As Anatole slammed to a halt in front of the oak barrier, Madeline hung back.

"Anatole, please," she said. "Perhaps this could wait until morning."

"I may no longer have the courage then."

"But the door is locked, and you have forgotten the key."

He cast her a strange glance and then turned toward the door. The heavy oak shuddered and creaked slowly inward.

Madeline's breath snagged in her throat, unnerved by the sight. She had not even seen Anatole touch the door. But he must have done, she reasoned desperately. The only alternative would be . . . unthinkable.

There had to be some sort of a secret catch or a mechanism. Fear turned to fascination, but before she could question Anatole, he hauled her through the doorway.

She clutched at him, drawing comfort from the feel of his tensile strength as they plunged into yawning blackness. The torch he carried made no more impact on this cavernlike chamber than trying to light the night with a single candle. Madeline caught only glimpses of cold stone, ominous looking shapes.

"Wait here," Anatole commanded, peeling himself free of her. It was all she could do not to cling to his shirttails as he strode away from her.

She huddled near the doorway as he stormed into the darkness, using his torch to ignite other flambeaux mounted into iron sconces on the wall. Not igniting them so much as seeming to hurl flame and defiance, giving the impression he would as soon have burned the place to the ground if he could.

As illumination crept across the chamber, Madeline darted fearful glances around her, scarce knowing what horrors she expected to be revealed. The light leapt and flared, dancing macabre shadows over the rafters of what had once been a great hall, the heart and soul of a medieval castle.

It was a cold, lonely soul at this hour, the tapestries rustling out mournful whispers of a faraway time that was long gone. The glory of the St. Leger dragon woven into those silken threads was a little faded; the blackened hearth empty and devoid of any welcoming fire. Cobweb-festooned carved chairs and the dusty banqueting table appeared to wait in melancholy silence for redoubtable St. Leger knights, who would never return.

An eerie enough place to find oneself in the dead of night, but containing none of the terrors Madeline had once imagined. No moldering bones, no dead bodies, no madmen chained to the walls.

Daring to breathe again, she took a few cautious steps deeper into the chamber. Anatole jammed his own torch into an empty bracket and stalked back to her side.

"This is your secret room, my lord?" Madeline asked. "I see nothing so very dreadful that needs to be hidden."

She smiled up at him, wishing with all her heart he would smile back, seem more like the man who had wooed and loved her on the hillside, not this stranger with the hard-set mouth and despairing eyes.

"Why have you brought me here?" she asked.

"You wanted the truth, Madeline, and I'm going to give it to you. It is time you met the rest of the St. Legers."

"But I thought I already had."

"Only the ones still living."

Madeline gaped up at him incredulously. Surely he could not mean . . .

"Are—are you trying to tell me this castle is—is haunted?"

Anatole nodded grimly.

"But I don't believe—" She caught herself whispering almost as though she was afraid of disturbing the spirit of some long slumbering knight. Foolishness.

"I don't believe in ghosts," she said more firmly.

At that instant the door to the chamber slammed shut. Startled, Madeline leapt closer to Anatole. A low, silky laugh sounded close to her ear, raising the hairs along the back of her neck.

She glanced up at her husband, but never had Anatole looked less like laughing.

"Who—what was that?" she breathed.

"Him," Anatole ground out through clenched teeth. He gestured to the shadows behind them.

Madeline peered past Anatole's shoulder, but she saw nothing. It took another moment to realize that Anatole was pointing upward, to a larger-than-life portrait mounted above the massive fireplace. A medieval knight in full regalia.

Unease skittered up her spine, but she stubbornly shook her head.

"No, it had to be only the wind, howling through the windowpane. Portraits don't laugh."

"Neither does the wind, milady."

If he was trying to frighten her, he was doing a remarkably good job of it, Madeline thought. But the steel in Anatole's eyes softened with regret and deepest sorrow. He circled his arm protectively about her waist.

Frighten her? No, she sensed that if Anatole had his way, he would have swooped her up in his arms this minute and carried her far away from this disturbing place. He was tormented with fear himself of someone or something.

This strong, formidable male could have fiercely taken on any other foe, from hordes of villainous Mortmains to a sea of invading armies. But he was so vulnerable, so helpless against all these rampant legends, these terrors of the mind. They stalked him like the infernal St. Leger dragon, scorching him with myth and superstition.

If anyone was going to slay that dragon, Madeline realized, it had to be her. The realization fortified her courage as nothing else could.

Tenderly she stroked a wild snarl of hair back from Anatole's eyes. Humoring him, she said, "All right. Perhaps you had better introduce me to this ghostly ancestor of yours who seems to find me so amusing."

With great reluctance Anatole stepped aside, allowing her a fuller view of the portrait. Madeline could only marvel that she had failed to remark it sooner. The painting seemed to dominate the entire hall, the colors strangely vivid after so many centuries. As vibrant as the knight captured upon the canvas.

The midnight hair and beard, the swarthy skin, the hawk's nose, all stamped the man indelibly as a St. Leger. A scarlet cape falling off one shoulder, he conveyed an impression of restless energy, a boundless desire to be off on some fresh quest or adventure. One hand clasped a heavy book inscribed with foreign symbols of a language unfamiliar to Madeline, while the other rested impatiently on the hilt of a crystal-adorned sword—

A soft gasp of recognition escaped Madeline. "That sword. It's the same one that—that—"

"That you flung back in my teeth tonight?" Anatole said bitterly. "So it is, milady."

"I was considerably distressed, Anatole. I am sorry."

"Don't be. When I have finished telling you all, you may regret you didn't thrust it through my black St. Leger heart."

His words disturbed her, but Madeline could think of nothing to reassure him. She returned to studying the portrait instead.

The knight did not appear to have been as tall or as powerfully built as her own husband. But he had a presence that was undeniable. His power, she decided, rested in his eyes with their exotic slant, dark, enigmatic, mesmerizing.

"Who is . . . I mean who was he?" she asked.

"Lord Prospero St. Leger." Anatole spoke the name with obvious loathing.

Her admiration for the knightly figure was clearly the last thing her husband desired, but Madeline couldn't seem to help herself.

"He was magnificent," she sighed.

Anatole stepped behind her, clamping his hand possessively down on her shoulder.

"What he *was*, milady, is a goddamned sorcerer."

"Anatole . . ." she protested.

"It's true. Everything Bess Kennack told you. I *am* descended from a sorcerer, and yonder he stands. It's his cursed blood that flows through my veins and every other St. Leger."

"I am sure every family has its share of black sheep."

"Black sheep!" Anatole snarled. "That doesn't begin to describe Prospero. No one even knows where the devil he came from. *From* the devil most likely. According to the tales, he just appeared on the Cornish coast one stormy night, in a burst of lightning.

"Some say he was the bastard of a poor crusader who had the misfortune to fall prey to the seductive wiles of a witch on his travels. A Spanish harlot, a gypsy, or something even worse."

An icy draft knifed through the hall, chilling Madeline to the bone. The torchlight flickered, playing eerie tricks with the portrait, darkening Prospero's eyes to an ominous hue.

Madeline shuddered, cowering closer to Anatole. All her imagination, of course. She repeated to herself yet again that she didn't believe in supernatural manifestations. However, if she had, she would have cautioned Anatole that it might be less than wise to make this one angry.

But Anatole himself seemed to have second thoughts, for he moderated his tone. "In any event, no matter where Prospero came from, I can tell you where he ended. At the stake. Condemned for witchcraft."

"So were many innocent people."

"Prospero was not innocent! He was a master at all the black arts: alchemy, spell casting, especially love potions. No lady in all of England was safe from his seduction."

That at least was one thing Madeline had no difficulty believing. There was a truly wicked quirk to Prospero's lips, a come-hither expression, sensual and alluring.

"Some say he even bewitched the king into giving him Castle Leger, thus making the Mortmains our perpetual enemies," Anatole went on. "All of

Cornwall must have breathed a sigh of relief when Prospero was reduced to ashes."

"Did no one mourn for him?"

"No one. He died alone, leaving no family, no wife, no legitimate children."

An unexpected wave of sadness swept over Madeline. Beneath all of Prospero's flash and bravado, did she detect a trace of profound sorrow and loneliness in those unfathomable eyes?

She had to remind herself that she was looking at a portrait of a man long dead. Whatever Prospero's tragedy, Madeline's concern was more for his descendant.

Anatole. Her husband, who had stood too long in the shadow of Prospero's legend, until he had become tormented nigh to madness with the belief that he had inherited tainted blood, some strange cursed powers of his own.

Madeline rested her fingertips gently on the broad span of Anatole's chest, and tried to reason with him.

"My lord, these tales of Prospero are very . . . interesting. But only consider. If Prospero died as the legends say, alone, unloved, unwed, with no legal heirs, where did all the rest of you St. Legers come from? How was Castle Leger passed down through the generations? The story makes no sense."

Anatole issued an exasperated sigh. "Madeline, if you are going to try to make sense out of my family history, we are going to be here all bloody night. And we have a good many more of my ancestors yet to go."

"There are more? Like Prospero?"

By way of answer, Anatole whirled her about and propelled her toward the opposite wall. Like tombstones rising up from a moonlit graveyard were other portraits. Dozens of them, miniatures, ovals, gilt-framed rectangles. The subjects were attired in everything from the opulent brocades of the Tudors to the powdered wigs of the present day.

None of them appeared as overwhelming as Prospero, but were disturbing enough all the same. It was those eyes, those piercing St. Leger eyes.

"The family portraits," Madeline murmured, feeling a little daunted. "I often wondered why I never saw any likenesses hanging in the main house."

"These are not exactly the sort of ancestors a man flaunts with pride, my dear."

Madeline's gaze raked down the formidable row, alighting with relief on the oval of a surpassingly beautiful girl with masses of gypsy dark hair, her lithe figure dressed in the stiff silks of a farthingale.

"Now, *that* is a very sweet young lady," she said. "You cannot tell me anything dreadful about her."

"That is Deidre St. Leger. She's the one whose heart is buried beneath the church vestibule."

"Oh," Madeline said weakly.

"She was murdered by one of the treacherous Mortmains when she was but seventeen. If she had lived, she, too, would likely have been charged with witchcraft."

"Surely not, Anatole! How could the most ignorant fool in the world have accused such an innocent girl of such a thing?"

"Perhaps because among other strange talents, Deidre could make flowers grow."

"So can my cousin Harriet. But that does not make her a witch."

"Whatever Deidre planted, grew and bloomed *overnight*."

Impossible, Madeline started to protest, but Anatole hustled her along to the next painting.

"This is Deidre's older brother, Drake St. Leger."

"Which one?" Madeline asked. She saw two miniatures, side by side. One of a raven-haired cavalier, the other a stern-faced Puritan bearing Roman's blond looks and ice blue eyes.

"They are both Drake. He was a thief."

Madeline frowned in bewilderment. "You mean that he disguised himself? I had a great-uncle who was a thief, but not nearly so clever. He had a bad habit of pinching snuffboxes and occasionally someone's pocket watch."

"Drake stole another man's life."

Madeline groaned, but Anatole continued as though he had not heard. "When his own body became too badly disfigured during the war against Cromwell, Drake merely possessed himself of another one."

Merely? Madeline's mouth dropped open, only to weakly close again. How did one even begin to refute a notion as incredible as that? As Anatole moved relentlessly on to another painting, she pressed her fingertips to her brow, feeling the start of a raging headache.

She had hoped to reason with Anatole, argue him out of one superstition. Or two. But never in her wildest imaginings had she expected anything like this.

St. Legers. *Legions* of them. Conjurers, clairvoyants, mediums, exorcists, diviners, soothsayers, and the lord alone knew what else. Her husband related these bizarre histories with such deadly calm, such force of conviction that her mind whirled, her own reason began to feel battered and shaken.

The tales tumbled out of Anatole, more swiftly now, the truth he'd kept back, spilling out of him like a poison that had festered in his veins for far too long. He rushed through the years, generations of devil-spawned St. Legers, down to his father, the gentle Lyndon with his harmless talent for finding lost things, for knowing when letters would arrive before they did.

By the time he'd finished, he hardly dared glance at Madeline for fear of her reaction. She stood calmly enough, staring up at the portraits with frowning concentration. But so quiet. It was most unlike his inquisitive Madeline. He would have preferred bitter tears, recriminations, demands to know why he had deceived her regarding his dreadful family for so long. At least then he could have soothed, reassured, begged forgiveness.

But this heavy silence. It alarmed him as nothing else could. He would have given all he possessed at that moment for one fraction of Marius's power to delve into her heart. To know what she was feeling.

"Well? Have you nothing to say?"

The bark of his voice startled Madeline out of her trance. She offered him a wan smile. "What is there to say, my lord?"

"You usually have no difficulty finding something. No more arguments? No questions?" he asked, regarding her anxiously. "Not even the most obvious one?"

She knew full well what he meant. Her gaze darted from him to the portraits of his ancestors and back again. She shook her head.

But Anatole had gone too far to allow either of them to retreat now.

"Go on. Ask me, Madeline," he prodded. "You have to be wondering. If all these other St. Legers are so damned strange, what cursed powers does my own husband have?"

"I already know." She plucked nervously at a loose thread on her gown. "You—you think you can see visions of the future. And I suppose it's possible if you stared at a person hard enough, worrying about them, you might begin to imagine dreadful things, and if by chance, they come true—"

"Damn it, Madeline! I don't *imagine* anything."

She flinched at his angry tone, and he instantly regretted it. But the woman was beginning to make him a little crazed. After all he'd told her, she was still stubbornly groping for some rational explanation.

He attempted to be patient, find a way to make her understand. "I see flashes of the future, so horrible, so detailed, it is like—like stumbling into a nightmare in someone else's eyes, a nightmare I know will come true. And there's not a God-cursed thing I can do to prevent it."

Horror and pity shimmered in her soft green eyes. But not, he sensed, because she believed him. No, it was obvious, his lady was beginning to think him mad.

Anatole paced off several agitated steps. This was pure torture. He hardly knew what was worse. Having to tell Madeline all these damning things about himself, or having to compel her to believe him.

In sheer frustration he unsheathed the St. Leger sword, thrusting the crystal-embedded pommel before Madeline's dazed eyes.

"You see this weapon I gave you?"

She clearly did. She retreated a wary step.

"The sword itself is infused with magic, more of Prospero's infernal sorcery. The power of the crystal represents something different to each St. Leger heir that wields it. For me, if I stare into the crystal too long, I see visions of my own future."

"Visions?" Madeline quavered. "In—in the sword?"

"Aye. Last winter, I saw your coming, milady. A glimpse of your hair blowing in the wind, your shape lost in the mist. The crystal seemed to be warning me. Beware the woman of flame."

"Then, why did you marry me?" she asked in a small voice.

"Because I had no choice. I can't do anything to change my destiny, and in your case, I didn't want to. The only danger you presented was to my heart."

He regarded her with longing. Didn't she understand it was his heart that he was risking now? Laying all bare for her to see, the blackest parts of his soul. Like a man poised beneath an ax blade, waiting for her acceptance or her rejection.

She wasn't even looking at him, she was staring at the crystal, her eyes wide and fearful. What he had said about the sword seemed to have unnerved her as nothing else had done.

More than once during this hellish night, he'd felt a stab of irrational anger against her, for forcing him to share truths that could only hurt them both. But now she looked so pale and scared, like a child realizing for the first time there really might be hobgoblins lurking in the dark.

God forbid. He'd only wanted to convince her, not frighten her half to death. Anatole cast the sword aside, the weapon landing on the oak table with a heavy clang.

He gathered Madeline's hands into his, relieved that she did not shrink from him. Her fingers felt so cold. He attempted to chafe some warmth back into them.

"I'm sorry, Madeline," he said gently. "I know this all sounds so damn strange. Would to God, I didn't even have to tell you the rest of it."

"The rest?" Madeline raised her eyes to his in dismay. "There is more?"

"Aye . . ." He swallowed hard. "You yourself have often remarked that my hearing is extremely acute. It's not my hearing, Madeline. It's something else. I can sense just by concentrating if there is someone coming, who it is."

"Can you do this with me?"

"Not when you first came to me. Not until this afternoon beneath the standing stone when I finally understood how to love you. Now I can sense your presence wherever you are. There is no place in this world you could ever go to escape me."

He meant his words to sound tender, reassuring, his pledge that he would ever be there to watch out for her. But Madeline snatched her hands free of his grasp. Backing away, she locked her arms across her breast. Almost as though she would shut him out.

Such a simple gesture. How could it possibly hurt him so damned much?

"And is this all of it?" she demanded. "All that you can do?"

The temptation to lie to her was so great, he had to clench his jaw to fight it. This was the part of his confession he'd dreaded most of all.

"No," he said hoarsely. "I—I can also move objects without touching them. Just by using the power of my mind."

What color remained in Madeline's face drained away. Her gaze flicked toward the heavy oak door, obviously remembering, considering the possibility . . .

But her mouth firmed into an obstinate line.

"Show me!"

Her demand caused his heart to sink. "Madeline, you could not possibly want—"

"Yes, I do! If you truly possess such a power, let me see it."

Knowing Madeline, he should have expected that she would require proof. But how could he display the black talent that had most damned him in his mother's eyes? When Madeline was already on the verge of shrinking from him?

His fingers strayed instinctively toward his scar. He cast a helpless glance at Madeline, but she remained adamant. What choice did he have but to do as she asked? It was either have her think him a devil or think him mad. No choice at all.

He sighed. "What do you want me to move?"

Madeline bit down on her lip, her eyes questing about the room. "Can you lift Prospero's portrait off the wall?"

"Aye and sink the damned thing into the sea."

"Just shift it a little." Madeline stepped out of Anatole's path, clearly torn between disbelief and bracing herself in case.

His shoulders slumped with resignation, Anatole focused on the painting, peering upward into Prospero's mocking eyes. Loathing surged through Anatole, and he gave the portrait a vicious shove with his mind, pain flashing behind his eyes.

But nothing happened. The portrait didn't budge.

Anatole frowned. The painting was doubtless heavy enough with that unwieldy frame, but he had shifted far larger objects before. Perhaps he was weakened from his bout with Will. Narrowing his gaze, he thrust out harder, wincing at the throb of pain.

Still nothing. Not so much as a tremor. It was as though the damned thing was being held fast by . . . by an invisible pair of hands.

Prospero!

Anatole's skin tingled with awareness of the icy presence he should have noticed much sooner.

"Damn you!" he said. "Let go of the blasted painting."

"B-but, Anatole. I'm not touching it." Madeline's bewildered voice reached his ears.

"Not you. *Him.*"

Madeline glanced wildly about her and then back at Anatole, as if she were convinced he was losing his mind.

Gritting his teeth, Anatole shoved at the portrait again, but it was fixed in place by a grip of iron.

"Stop it," he snarled.

"You stop, boy," Prospero's voice hissed in his ear. *"Bad enough I have borne all your insults and disrespect this night. I'll be damned if you're going to perform any parlor tricks with my portrait."*

"You are damned. Go back to hell where you belong!"

"Anatole!" Madeline retreated a step, barricading herself behind a chair.

"I wasn't talking to you," Anatole said desperately. "It's Prospero. Can you not hear him?"

She shook her head, clutching at the back of the chair, her eyes wide circles framed by the pale rim of her face.

"Curse you!" Anatole bellowed up at the rafters. "What are you trying to do? Convince my wife I've gone mad? Can you not see you are terrifying her?"

"You're the one who is terrifying her, you young clod. I have behaved with admirable restraint, despite all the provocation you offered. If you want my advice—"

"I don't! Get the devil out of here, and leave me alone."

Madeline sidled, trembling toward the door.

"Not you, milady!" Anatole snapped.

"Anatole, please," she whispered. "Perhaps we should forget this and—"

"No! You wanted me to move the damned painting, and I'm going to do it. Smash the bloody thing to bits as I should have done years ago."

Anatole glared at the portrait in savage concentration, but it was like battering a wall of solid ice.

"Challenge me, will you, boy?" Prospero taunted. *"Heap curses upon my name? Very well. Let's see how you feel about this despised power of yours when you are unable to use it."*

Goaded beyond endurance, Anatole shoved harder, his lip curling in a snarl of anger and pain. From somewhere far away, he could hear Madeline's soft voice, begging him to stop. But he saw nothing beyond the red haze of his own fury.

A fury and frustration that had burned inside him for too many years, against Prospero, against the whole damned lot of the St. Legers, and most of all . . . against himself.

Crushing his fingers against his skull, he flung everything he had at the portrait. All his rage, all his despair, all his pain. . . . Pain like nothing he'd ever known.

His veins bulged and knotted with it, searing, twisting, burning until he tottered, sinking to his knees. And still he fought on, locked in a titantic battle of will with his infernal ancestor. Mind against mind, power against power.

Until Prospero yielded. Suddenly, almost playfully, the wily sorcerer let go. Anatole felt his mind crash forward, like hurtling through a door that had been abruptly released.

The portrait flew, dashing against the rafters, splintering its frame. With a mighty roar Anatole's unleashed power surged through the room, overturning the heavy table with a violent crash, hurling the St. Leger sword in a deadly arc. Chairs pitched and tossed. Tapestries ripped from the wall. Torches exploded in a flash of fire and smoke.

Horrified, Anatole fought to regain control. Half blinded by pain, he buried his face in his hands. Battling with the last of his strength, he wrested his power back where it belonged. Back . . . back into the dark cage of his mind.

The roaring slowly subsided, one last chair teetering over with a low thud. Collapsed onto his knees, Anatole struggled not to lose consciousness.

Dazed, he dragged in agony-filled breaths. By God, he had not lost control of himself this way since he was a boy. That time he'd shattered his mother's china figurines. All those fragile ladies—

Fragile . . . lady. The terrifying thought pierced his pain-numbed brain.

Madeline.

Oh, God! What had he done?

Anatole lifted his head, forcing his eyes open. The hall was plunged into near blackness, the only torch that remained lit burning on the stone floor about a yard away.

He crawled toward it, and seized it in his hand, using the overturned table for support to drag himself to his feet.

His legs trembled, threatening to buckle beneath him, only a mounting sense of panic lending him the strength to remain upright. He held the torch aloft in his shaking hand, the light flickering over the wreckage of the chamber.

If Madeline was the least bit harmed, he would never forgive himself. Desperately he scanned the room, trying to call her name, but his voice came out in a croak.

Summoning what remained of his shattered concentration, he reached out with his mind and found her—in the far corner, cowering behind an overturned chair.

As he tottered toward her, she stirred. Relief made him dizzy. She was moving. She seemed to be all right. She was getting to her feet, gently aided by . . . Prospero.

In a flash of courtly splendor, his ancestor hovered behind Madeline, the specter's hands at her waist to steady her. The torchlight fell over her face, ice white, her eyes dilated with terror.

"Get away from her!" Anatole's shout emerged as no more than a rasp, but Prospero was already fading, his brow arched disdainfully.

It didn't matter. Anatole realized that in her shocked state, Madeline hadn't even seen Prospero. It was Anatole she was looking at that way. A look he'd seen too often before in nightmares of shattered vases and broken flowers.

He held out his hand to her in mute appeal, knowing he must seem the very devil, his hair wild, eyes wilder still, face haggard. He tried to force the words past his raw throat, words to comfort her, beg her not to be afraid. Not of him.

He had his power back under control. He'd vow never to use it again, not even if his life depended upon it. He'd die himself before he'd ever hurt her. If only she would stop looking at him that way. . . .

He staggered closer, and she shrank back, snatching up something from the floor to hold him at bay. The St. Leger sword. She was fending him off with his own weapon.

"M-madeline," he managed her name in a broken whisper.

She only retreated farther. With one last terrified glance, she turned and fled toward the door. Running . . . running from him. Everything he'd ever feared, everything he dreaded coming true.

No! Denial choked him, and he tried to stagger after her. But by the time he gained the threshold, she had already vanished, and he swayed, overwhelmed by the sheer hopelessness of it. Even if he did catch her, what was he going to do? Force Madeline to stay with him even while she collapsed with terror? Compel her to understand, to accept him . . . to love him?

It was too late for that. Perhaps it always had been.

Weighted down by despair, he sank slowly to his knees, this time, the pain all in his heart. The torch fell from his hand and snuffed out, leaving him alone in the darkness.

He found his voice at last in an anguished roar.

"Madeline!"

Reverend Fitzleger slumped over his desk, the candle guttering low in its socket. His withered cheek pillowed against the pages of the sermon he'd been laboring over into the small hours of morning.

His troubled thoughts refused to allow him to concentrate, the same thoughts drifting him into tormented dreams: Of his peaceful little church choked with mist. Of Roman plighting his troth to some mysterious cloaked woman, her hands full of blackened roses from the Mortmain's grave. Of that painted Frenchman, dancing about like a marionette, leering at Fitzleger with his soulless doll-like eyes.

"What are you doing here, Monsieur Fitzleger? Your services are no longer required."

"But I am the Bride Finder," Fitzleger tried to protest.

"Not anymore, old man." Roman smirked. *"You've been replaced. Only see what a disaster you made of your last match."*

The mist parted, and Fitzleger glanced downward, realizing that he was tramping over names newly carved into the church floor.

Anatole and Madeline St. Leger.

He recoiled in horror as booming laughter filled the nave. Tyrus Mortmain rose up behind him, his hideous burn-scarred features looming closer as his bloated fingers reached for Fitzleger's throat.

"And all this time you thought the Mortmains were dead. . . ."

Fitzleger awoke with a start, heart thudding, his face bathed in a cold sweat. He felt disoriented, uncertain where he was, until his hand brushed up against the inkwell.

With trembling fingers he groped for his spectacles and straightened them back on his face. He'd fallen asleep, blotting his sermon. He could feel a smear of ink on his cheek, but thanked the Lord it wasn't worse. If he'd nodded any closer to that candle, he could have set himself on fire.

He should have taken himself up to bed hours ago, but he'd been unable to rest, his mind clouded with memories of that disastrous dinner party the other evening. He couldn't even write his sermon for Sunday, his head too full of St. Legers. Small wonder that he was even dreaming about them.

And, Lord bless him, what a strange and dreadful dream it had been. His heart was still pounding in his ears.

No. Fitzleger frowned. Not his heart. That was his own front door, someone hammering frantically for admittance. Not a sound calculated to soothe his already threadbare nerves.

Some poor soul come seeking spiritual comfort at this hour? Their need had to be desperate indeed, but he was exhausted, unequal to dealing with anything. He'd been feeling particularly old and useless of late.

But, with a soft groan, Fitzleger picked up his candle and shuffled through the recesses of the parlor toward the front door. The hammering continued at a frantic pace.

"Coming," Fitzleger called as loudly as he dared. His housekeeper slept like a brick, but his granddaughter, Effie . . . It was difficult enough to keep his naughty little angel from popping out of bed at all hours of the night.

Fumbling with the latches, he undid the door as quickly as he could. Though a trusting enough soul, he'd seen enough of the misery of human wickedness to be cautious.

He inched the door open a crack, only to forget all caution and fling it wide when he saw who it was.

Madeline. Her hair a flyaway tangle, her face white as death. No bonnet, no cloak, looking as though she'd run all the way from Castle Leger pursued by a pack of wolves.

"Mr. Fitz-fitzleger," she panted, her words barely distinguishable. "Need help . . . got to come at once."

Fitzleger's heart rolled over in fear. "My dearest child. Whatever is the matter?"

"It—it's Anatole." She moaned. "Either he has run mad. Or I have!"

She swayed forward, barely giving the startled Fitzleger a chance to catch her before she collapsed in his arms.

Chapter Nineteen

Dawn had not yet lightened the sky, darkness pressing against the small windows of the parsonage like some great black beast prowling the night. Madeline huddled deeper against the cushions on the settee while she told Mr. Fitzleger all that had happened back at Castle Leger. His tiny parlor seemed the only refuge left in a world that had run mad.

A cozy fire crackled on the hearth, the fragrant aroma of cinnamon wafting from the teapot as Mr. Fitzleger bustled about the room. Like a homespun angel with his snowy white hair and much mended dressing gown, Fitzleger tucked a downy coverlet more snugly about her and poured out tea.

The delicate cups and saucers warred for space on the piecrust table with a precarious stack of well-loved books and little Effie Fitzleger's forgotten china doll. The very normalcy of the parlor made what Madeline had just passed through seem even more like a nightmare.

She sipped the hot tea, not tasting it, wondering if there would ever be enough warmth to remove the chill that had settled deep into her bones. The flames crackled on the hearth, leapt and fell with her memories: of chaos and destruction. Of furniture tossed about like dollhouse toys. Of torches exploding in a shower of sparks. Of the great hall itself trembling as though the winds of hell had blasted through it. Of cowering in the darkness, reduced to the most primitive, terrified animal state.

And memories of Anatole, lurching toward her, bathed in the nightmarish red glow of the torch, the black fall of his hair half concealing his contorted face as he rasped her name.

She swallowed hard. "I fled from the house like the veriest coward, so terrified that Anatole was coming after me. When I reached the carriage drive, I thought I heard him behind me. But when I looked back, there was no one there. He—he doesn't also have the power to turn invisible, does he?"

"No, I believe the only St. Leger who could do that was Anatole's great-grandfather, Reeves."

Madeline choked on her tea. To be lying here, calmly discussing such things with the elderly vicar made her want to laugh, but if she did, she was afraid she might never be able to stop.

Clearing her throat, she went on, "I didn't even know where I was going. I only wanted to get as far away from Castle Leger as I could. I kept on running, stumbling, slashing out at every shadow like an idiot with that sword—"

The sword! Madeline sat bolt upright, splashing herself with tea, her heart giving a panicked lurch. "Oh, dear God, Mr. Fitzleger. Anatole's sword. I dragged it with me when I fled the house. But now I don't know what's happened to it. I've lost it. I—"

"Calm yourself, my dear." Fitzleger rescued the teacup from her trembling hand and set it back on the table. "You dropped the weapon on the garden path. I fetched it inside. The St. Leger sword is quite safe."

Madeline sank back down, releasing a long breath, not certain if she was entirely relieved. Was *safe* ever a word that could be applied to a weapon invested with the kind of power Anatole had described? With the ability to induce visions, such as she had seen for herself that night she had stared into the crystal and fantasized about Anatole making love to her. She had not been imagining anything. She had been peering into the future, not the black, tragic visions that tormented her husband, but a glimpse of what would be all the same. But how was such a thing possible? She was a St. Leger in name only.

As Fitzleger mopped up the spilled tea, Madeline gazed up at the vicar with a worried frown.

"Mr. Fitzleger. These powers of the St. Legers . . . Are they contagious?"

"Contagious?" the old man echoed in surprise.

"Aye, is it possible I could catch some of Anatole's strange power from him?"

For the first time since she had collapsed on his doorstep, Fitzleger smiled. "No, my dear. Though, mind you, the sword does have any number of odd legends attached to it. One being that the owner's special power is trapped in the crystal, often enabling his bride to use some of it."

As Madeline stiffened with alarm, Fitzleger made haste to disclaim, "But I have never seen evidence of such a thing in my lifetime. Part of the reason the sword has always been surrendered to the bride is to render it harmless. If you would but look at it, you could tell you have no need to fear—"

"No!" Madeline shuddered. "I never want to see the thing again."

He had turned away as though to fetch the sword to her, but he halted in midstep.

"And—and Anatole?" he quavered, as though fearing her answer.

Madeline ducked her head, knowing she must disappoint the old man as she had done the night of the dinner party. Perhaps even break his heart, but she could not seem to help it. She was a coward indeed.

"I honestly don't know, Mr. Fitzleger, if I will ever find the courage to go back to my husband."

The little vicar seemed to age before her very eyes, sinking weakly into the wing-back chair opposite. But he tried to rally, saying, "You've undoubtably had a dreadful shock, that is all. What happened tonight was most distressing. I cannot comprehend how Anatole could have so lost control. He has not done so since he was a young lad."

"It was my fault," Madeline said miserably. "I forced him to tell me the truth. I made him demonstrate his powers. He never wanted to."

Fitzleger looked aghast. "Why ever did you do such a thing?"

"Because I was going to prove to him none of these legends were true."

"But, my dear child, you cannot believe that Anatole meant to frighten you or—or God forbid—to hurt you?"

Had she thought that? Madeline closed her eyes reliving that dreadful moment when her husband had seemed to disappear, assuming the shape of some monstrous stranger.

Only monsters should never harbor such devastation in their deep dark eyes when one shrank away from them. Other memories intruded of the man who had watched over her with such fierce tenderness ever since her arrival at Castle Leger, protecting her, she now realized, even from himself.

"No, Mr. Fitzleger. Anatole would never hurt me. I believe the man would . . ." A sad smile curved her lips as she recalled Anatole's own words. "He *would stay the wind itself* for me if he could."

"Then, why did you run from him?"

"I don't know," Madeline said, wishing with all her heart she had a good answer to that question. Why had she turned into such a terrified, unreasoning being?

Perhaps because for the first time in her life *reason* had nothing to do with it. She had struck up against something that defied all her logic.

"I have always tried to be an enlightened woman. I take great pride in my reason. And tonight Anatole did more than wreak havoc with the great hall. It—it was like he brought the whole world crashing down around my ears."

She buried her face in her hands. "God help me, Mr. Fitzleger. Are you truly certain I am not going mad?"

Fitzleger pulled her hands down, tucking one gently into his own. "No, you are not mad, child. Neither is Anatole. I wanted him to tell you the truth sooner, but he was so afraid that you might react this way."

"Flee from him in panic? Not exactly the proper sort of behavior for a chosen bride. And I was the one who was going to slay the dragon!" Madeline gave a bitter laugh.

"But I failed, Mr. Fitzleger. At the first sign of a real dragon, I ran away. And I still find myself not wanting to believe that—that—"

"That *there are more things in heaven and earth than you've ever dreamed of in your philosophy?*" Fitzleger quoted softly.

"Shakespeare certainly had that right. Do you suppose he ever knew any St. Legers?"

"Very possible, my dear." The old man gave her a comforting smile.

Despite her distress, Madeline managed to smile back, warmed by the kindness and serenity that ever seemed to emanate from Septimus Fitzleger.

"I was like this even as a little girl, you know," she said ruefully. "When my brother Jeremy told us there were monsters hiding in the closet, my sisters hid under the bedclothes. But I always had to go look. I was so certain there would be nothing there.

"I'm too old to start being afraid of the dark now."

"There is no reason that you have to be. Just think of it as . . . as opening your mind to new possibilities."

"And if I do, the world suddenly becomes a black and terrifying place."

"Or one of wonder and magic."

"I don't believe Anatole finds it all that magical."

"No, poor lad, he doesn't." Fitzleger's eyes clouded with sadness. "But then, he has all too often been left to stumble alone through this strange world of his."

Alone . . . exactly as she had left him tonight. Madeline withdrew her hand from Fitzleger's grasp, a comfort she felt she did not deserve.

"But Anatole has the other St. Legers, does he not?" she asked, wondering what she was seeking most, solace for Anatole or for her own stricken conscience. "Are they not all like he is?"

"To some extent. The only one completely untouched by the family legacy is Roman. That happens every generation or so. The rest all possess some modest measure of the St. Leger talent: Caleb has an uncanny ability to communicate with horses, Paxton can divine precious metals, and our poor Marius can sense another's pain down to the depths of his soul."

Fitzleger regarded her gravely. "But, Madeline, you must have observed for yourself how estranged Anatole is, even from his own family."

She had. She recalled too well the disastrous supper party and how she had only made the situation worse.

"Yet they all must understand Anatole and accept him for what he is," she said. "Why has he always been so isolated, Mr. Fitzleger?"

The old man settled back in his chair with a mournful sigh. "Perhaps because he never had the acceptance of the two people in his life who mattered the most."

"His parents," Madeline murmured. "Anatole has told me so little. He does not like to speak of them."

"He would be too proud to do so. Or maybe it all still hurts too much." Fitzleger eyed her hesitantly. "My lord always commanded my silence on these matters, but I fear I may have done him more harm by obeying. Will you allow me to tell you the rest of the story now, Madeline? And then perhaps you will better understand the man you ran from tonight."

Madeline feared that nothing Fitzleger could say would help her to understand this madness, but she nodded. She longed to hear anything that would help her find her way back to Anatole, the man who had introduced her to the possibility of love beyond her wildest dreams . . . and a terror beyond her worst imaginings.

As Fitzleger steepled his fingers with a thoughtful frown, seeking for a place to begin, Madeline settled back to listen. Night winds rattled the windowpanes as though they meant to hold morning at bay until the old man finished his tale.

"Cecily Wendham was beautiful enough to enchant any man at first sight," Fitzleger said. "Petite, golden, and graceful. Possessed of such a passionate nature. Full of the most lively gaiety one moment, the next dissolved into heartbroken tears. She wore her emotions like a strand of pearls fragilely strung together. So easily snapped.

"It did not take a Bride Finder to see that she was the last sort of woman a St. Leger should marry. But Lyndon was determined to have her, and in the end there was nothing that any of us could do but wish him joy and . . . pray.

"All went well at first. The young couple traveled a great deal and Lyndon indulged his bride's every whim. But in time the death of Lyndon's father forced him to return to Cornwall and assume his place as the new lord."

Fitzleger grimaced. "Castle Leger is—is not precisely a home suited to someone of a nervous disposition."

"No, it isn't," Madeline agreed with a shiver. "Did Cecily know the truth about the St. Leger family?"

"Oh, yes, Lyndon had told her everything. But Cecily was very good at pretending away anything of a disturbing nature. Then Anatole was born, and she could pretend no longer."

Fitzleger paused to fortify himself with a sip of tea.

"Anatole was never a pretty child. Not like Roman. Always a little too large for his age, awkward. It took my lord a long time to grow into that formidable body and temper of his. Nor did he weep softly. Even as a babe, he possessed a rather lusty bellow."

"I know." Madeline's lips twitched in remembrance. "I have heard it myself on many occasions."

For a moment Fitzleger shared her smile, but his expression sobered as he went on with his tale.

"I believe Cecily was daunted by her son from the first. Matters only became worse when Anatole began to display some of his unique St. Leger talents.

"It first happened shortly after the lad's second birthday. One winter afternoon when Lyndon was unfortunately gone from home on estate business, Anatole sent his toy soldiers pelting around the nursery like a hailstorm. Cecily went into hysterics. She . . . she had the boy dragged away and locked up in the gatehouse."

"The gatehouse!" Madeline said, shocked. "In the winter? That place is nothing more than an old stone tower."

"So it was. Even then. When I found Anatole, he was huddled in the corner. It took a long time for me to persuade the child to even open his eyes. He thought if he did, he might make bad things start to happen again."

"He must have been terrified himself."

"He was, but there was no making Cecily understand that. She behaved as though Anatole were the devil himself. The boy was banished permanently to the gatehouse with only Lucius Trigghorne to attend him."

"And his father permitted this?" Madeline frowned. "Being a St. Leger himself, he must have known how bewildered and frightened Anatole would be."

"He did. Lyndon loved his son, but he loved his wife more. He hoped Cecily would learn to accept their child. But around this time Roman lost his own mother. Cecily would often have the boy at Castle Leger, spoiling him with a hundred indulgences that did Roman's character no good. I think she liked to pretend that some evil fairy had switched the two lads, that Roman was really her son."

Fitzleger's mouth thinned with a rare bitterness. "Lyndon did nothing to interfere with this nonsense. He was in many respects a weak man. His only solution was to summon me to the gatehouse, to tutor Anatole, teach him how to be a St. Leger."

"So you became Anatole's Merlin."

"A very poor one." Fitzleger shook his head sadly. "I am a Bride Finder. That is the limit of my extraordinary abilities. I did my best, but I was not suited to train the lad to cope with his powers.

"Bless the boy, somehow he learned on his own. He was so quick, so intelligent, and despite everything, he still adored his mother. When her carriage would pass, he would fly to the window for a glimpse of her, such yearning on his face, it nigh broke my heart to watch him."

Fitzleger's eyes gleamed with a suspicious brightness. He paused, groping for his hankerchief, blowing his nose gustily before he could go on.

"Anatole would escape from me at every opportunity, hide out in the garden just to steal a look at her. And it was fine when all he did was look, but one day . . ."

The old man stared into the fire, momentarily lost in his own unhappy reflections of the past. Madeline respected his silence for as long as she could, but she inched to the edge of her seat.

"What happened?" she prodded softly.

"Anatole tried to take some flowers to his mother. But she shrank from him, so—so he floated the blossoms to her across the room. She went wild in her terror and smashed a glass vase over the child's head."

"Dear God!" Madeline murmured. "His scar . . . his warrior's scar."

"Aye, gained in a war no boy should have to fight. A battle for his mother's love. Cecily nearly killed her own son that day.

"At that point the rest of the family sought to interfere. Hadrian demanded his brother surrender the boy to him, allow him to take Anatole away to sea. He and Lyndon nearly came to blows over it, but in the end Lyndon had his way. He could not bear to part with his son, and finally found the courage to insist Anatole be allowed to move from the gatehouse, back to his own room.

"Those were dark days indeed." Fitzleger sighed. "Anatole became like a shadow in his own home, creeping about the halls, fearful of terrifying his mother again. In spite of all his care, Cecily's bouts of depression and hysteria grew steadily worse until the end came that was inevitable to everyone but Lyndon. The lady perished."

"She died of fear and sorrow," Madeline said. "That is what Anatole told me. At the time, I did not understand. But now—"

"You still don't, my dear Madeline. Cecily St. Leger took her own life."

Madeline stared at Fitzleger in horror.

"She slipped from her bed one night, disappeared through the garden to the cliffs at the back of Castle Leger. And there she cast herself into the sea."

Madeline shuddered. She had seen for herself both the beauty and terrible power of those cold, foamy waves, the jagged outcroppings of rock that dotted the coast. But only from a distance.

Even sitting here in the warmth of the parlor, it was as though she could feel the wind in her hair, Anatole's strong arm about her, holding her back, fiercely forbidding her to ever get too close to those treacherous heights.

Only now did she understand why.

Fitzleger continued wearily, "The real tragedy is that Anatole foresaw his mother's death in one of his dreaded visions. The poor lad was tortured day and night with his fear for her, but he could not get his father to listen. Lyndon simply refused to believe it. He was convinced that Cecily loved him far too much to abandon him in such a fashion.

"After her death, Lyndon shut himself away from everyone. From Anatole most of all, cruelly blaming the boy for what had happened."

Fitzleger sagged back in his chair. But he did not need to go on, for Madeline knew the rest of the story too well. How Anatole had squared his young shoulders and assumed the responsibility of Castle Leger while his father slowly faded from life one day at a time. How the lonely boy vanished, gradually evolving into the lonely man.

Madeline knew that Fitzleger's story would linger in her mind for a long time, not the tale of Lyndon and Cecily and their destructive love for each other. But the son who had been sacrificed to that love.

Fitzleger had no need to tell her of the haunting sadness, the emptiness of Anatole's life. She had first seen it for herself, stroked into the face of the self-portrait he had done, seen it many times since in the melancholy darkness of his eyes. But she had never fully comprehended until now.

Rejection, being shrank from . . . it must have been Anatole's greatest fear. And Madeline realized with shame and horror that was exactly how she had behaved toward him tonight. Sweet God in heaven, what had she done to him? She was no better than the half-mad Cecily St. Leger.

Madeline flung the coverlet aside. "Mr. Fitzleger. I . . . I've got to go home."

The old man started, turning pale at her words. "Back to London. But, Madeline, after all I've told you, surely—"

"Not London. I have to go back to Castle Leger." Her heart thudded at the thought, but she pushed resolutely to her feet.

Her legs wobbled, and Fitzleger had to leap up to steady her.

"My dear, you cannot. You are not yet recovered enough, and it is still so dark outside."

"But I have to see Anatole!"

"I doubt you will be able to find him."

Madeline realized the old man was right. In past times of trouble Anatole had always fled to some hidden refuge. She had no idea where, but she had a sudden hunch that Mr. Fitzleger did. The little vicar was steadfastly avoiding her gaze.

"Where would Anatole go?" she asked softly. "I am certain you know, Mr. Fitzleger. Please tell me."

Fitzleger stepped back, releasing her. "I don't think that would be wise," he mumbled.

"But why? You said yourself he would never do me any harm. There is no need for you to try to protect me."

Fitzleger lifted his face to hers at last, his own stricken with regret and sorrow. "It is not you I am seeking to protect. My young master has endured more than enough hurt for one lifetime. Can you promise me that you could face him now without flinching again?"

Madeline started to swear that of course she could, but her vow faltered and died beneath the force of the old man's unwavering stare. Any doubts she had, she saw them mirrored back a thousandfold in Fitzleger's blue eyes.

Though he regarded her with as much gentle affection as ever, it was clear that the Bride Finder had lost his faith in her.

Madeline sank back down upon the settee.

Fitzleger dragged the coverlet over her lap. "Until you are more certain of yourself, Madeline, I think it best you remain here. I will go and look out for Anatole. I have done so many times in the past. You . . . you try to rest and please God; I will find a way to make all of this right again."

He brushed his lips across her brow and gave her shoulder an awkward pat. Shuffling away from her, he fumbled into his cloak, but as Fitzleger ambled out the door, there was a dejected bent to the old man's proud head, an air of hopelessness about his mien that afforded Madeline no comfort at all.

She tried to take his advice, stretching out on the settee. But rest eluded her. She stared instead at the parlor's tiny windowpanes, seeing the first streaks of dawn beginning to lighten the blackness beyond.

Where was Anatole? What was he thinking, feeling? Did he despise her now for her cowardice, hate her for running away?

No, he would never do that, she thought, a constriction tightening her throat. He would have feared her rejection, even despairingly expected it, but he would never blame her. Likely he was half out of his mind, worrying where she had gone.

But she realized that was not true, either. Even if Anatole were dying, he would have crawled after her until he made certain she was in no danger. St. Legers looked after their own.

And she was his. Had he not said he could feel each breath she took, could always feel her presence? Wherever he was, she knew that he was aware that she was safe.

When he had first told her of this ability, she had felt uneasy, violated, her very privacy threatened. But now the notion that Anatole could always sense her whereabouts was oddly comforting, like being sheltered in the warm folds of his cloak, redolent with his strong masculine scent. No matter what distance parted them, she would never have to feel alone again.

That only made it all the more unbearable to think of him out there somewhere, solitary, hurting. She loved him far too much . . . loved him.

The thought caused Madeline's heart to still. She had never whispered those words before, not to herself, not even to him when they had so passionately made love upon the hillside.

And yet it was like something that had always been a part of her, something she always should have known. In spite of all that he was, *nay, because of the man that he was,* she loved him. And if she had ever been able to turn away from her precious reason, and listen to her heart instead, she would have recognized that fact much sooner.

Madeline jerked upright, muttering, "You were not wrong, Mr. Fitzleger. I may be a great fool, but I am the woman destined to love Anatole St. Leger. And I am the one that he needs right now."

But what was she to do about that. How in the world could she find Anatole with Mr. Fitzleger already long gone? If only she had a bit of her husband's ability to reach out with her mind and feel his presence. If only she could share some of his power—

But she had already done so once before, a soft voice seemed to remind her.

The sword.

No. Madeline trembled at the very notion of testing the weapon's mysterious magic again. And yet . . . Had she not already played the coward enough for one night?

Forcing herself to her feet, she crept about the room, searching for the weapon. Not a difficult task in the tiny vicarage. Mr. Fitzleger had left the mighty sword propped up against the hall table bearing his discarded gloves and Effie's pink ruffled bonnet.

Madeline stared at the weapon for long moments, working up her courage. Finally she approached with all the trepidation King Arthur must have felt upon first stumbling across the legendary sword in the stone.

Wiping her damp palms in her skirt, she forced her trembling fingers around the hilt, half wincing, as though expecting the weapon to flash lightning. She was prepared to let go at any second should the crystal begin to do anything strange.

She carted the sword gingerly back to the fireside, holding it so the crystal-embedded pommel rested against the palm of her hand. Although she was quite alone in the parlor, she stole a self-conscious glance over her shoulder, feeling singularly foolish.

Now what? Did she need to chant some sort of magic incantation? No, she had not had to do anything like that the first time.

All she had done was peer into the crystal and concentrate.

"If you really do possess magic," she murmured, "then show me Anatole. Show me where to find him."

She stared until her eyes ached with the effort, the crystal reflecting back facets of firelight and a distorted image of her own pale face. Images that gradually shifted and blurred to become . . . mist.

The crystal was clouding with it, the fog parting enough to reveal the dark figure of a man kneeling.

Madeline's breath snagged in her throat. Anatole! Only he was not alone. A cloaked figure hovered near him, fiery red hair tangling in the wind. Surely herself . . . although Madeline could not clearly see her own face.

The sword was not showing her Anatole's present whereabouts, but affording her another glimpse of the future. A cold chill crept over Madeline's skin, but she forced herself to keep looking, willing her future self to reach out to Anatole.

The cloaked figure did indeed reach out. The mist swirled, there was a flash of steel. And then blood. Anatole's chest streaked crimson as he fell to the ground.

A horrified cry breached Madeline's lips. She dropped the sword. It clanged against the fire irons, then thudded to the carpet as she backed away trembling. For long moments she could not even bring herself to look at the weapon.

When she dared to do so, she saw only a sword, the crystal dulled and still in the dying firelight. But the dreadful vision remained, branded upon Madeline's mind.

Anatole. The mist. The blood.

She pressed a shaking hand to her lips. No, it couldn't possibly be. . . . But her mind was already racing, remembering. Hadn't Anatole said that he had seen something similar in the sword? A warning that he was to beware the woman of flame.

He'd smiled and said the danger was only to his heart, not his life. Yet Madeline had clearly seen herself lift the knife and—

"Dear God, no!" she whispered vehemently. "It won't happen. I would never . . . There is nothing that could possibly make me—"

Make her turn against her own husband? Had she not already done so once tonight? Backed away in panic, fending him off with his own sword.

What would she have done if he had raged closer? She clutched her hands to her stomach, suddenly feeling sick. She didn't know the answer, only that she never intended to find out.

This was one vision she would not allow to come true. She would find a way to prevent it. But how many times must Anatole have thought the same thing?

Once more she could hear his despairing voice. "It's like a nightmare I know will come true, and there's not a God-cursed thing I can do to prevent it."

"Oh, Anatole," she mourned. With all else he had been forced to endure, the loneliness, the rejection. To be afflicted with this sort of torment. She should have held him, comforted him, let him know for once in his life there was someone who understood, who loved him. But now it was all too late.

Her heart broke for him and for herself as well.

For she knew she must never go near her husband again.

CHAPTER TWENTY

All was not well at Castle Leger. The whispers scattered through the village like the crackling of dried leaves blown by a chilling wind. The dread lord's bride had fled from him, and was refusing to return. Master Roman was hell-bent on taking a wife of his own choosing and resurrecting Lost Land, the home of his mortal enemies.

Somehow Mr. Fitzleger, their venerable Bride Finder, had failed. Perhaps he had finally grown too old for his office, and there was no other to take his place. The dark days threatened to return all over again, that grim time when Cecily St. Leger had gone mad and the Lord Lyndon had shut himself away, abandoning his lands and his people.

Bess Kennack, recently dismissed from service at the castle, declared that this time it spelled the doom of all St. Legers. Soon every last one of them would be destroyed. But no one else in the village shared her malice-filled joy. The prosperity of the St. Legers had always meant *their* prosperity, and in the ensuing days cottagers all along the rocky coast turned anxious eyes toward the castle on the cliffs. . . .

Anatole wandered aimlessly through the front hall, servants whisking out of his sight. But he scarce noticed. They were no more than shadows hovering on the periphery of his senses as he made his solitary way through the house.

A house that continued to be haunted with *her* presence, Madeline's workaday bonnet and gloves still lying on the hall table, one of her books—

the woman seemed to scatter them everywhere—abandoned on the seat of a tapestry-covered chair.

Anatole picked up the volume, his gaze falling upon the title. *The Odyssey* of Homer. During that week when he'd been trying so awkwardly to woo Madeline, he recalled allowing her to read portions of the work aloud to him.

He had become surprisingly caught up in the tale of Odysseus, a lost warrior struggling to return home to his faithful wife, fighting his way through countless perils and adventures. Or had the magic of the story all lay in the soft lilt of Madeline's voice?

Strange, Anatole thought as he thumbed through the pages. It was Madeline who had fled, wandering from home, yet he was the one who felt lost. . . .

He dropped the book back on the chair with a dull thud. For days after her flight, he had insisted upon keeping everything just as she'd left it. Ordering the candles lit in the library, the furniture dusted, the vases kept filled with her favorite flowers. Holding himself in readiness in case by some miracle she discovered she could love the devil after all and decide to return to him.

And each morning as his prayers went unanswered, he allowed things to slip a little more. One less fire lit, one more curtain closed, the flowers left to wither and die. Until the house had become shrouded in gloom like himself, a hollow-eyed wreck, knowing more of nightmares than of sleep.

Hope, he was fast discovering, could be a killing thing, cutting a man down an inch at a time. More than once he'd thought of putting an end to this agony of suspense by saddling his horse, thundering into the village, where she sought refuge with Fitzleger, and forcing her back into his arms.

Something always restrained him. His pride, all the villagers thought. But Anatole knew better. It was fear. Fear of seeing that stricken look on her face, of feeling her shrink away from him.

It had driven him nigh to madness when she'd done it the first time. He could not endure it again. His only hope now was Fitzleger. If somehow the old man could persuade Madeline in time to forget what had happened that dreadful night, to forgive Anatole for being what he was, to learn to accept him.

Once more his fate rested in the hands of the Bride Finder.

"My lord?"

The quiet voice obtruded painfully upon Anatole's thoughts. After all these years, he finally understood what had induced his father to shut himself away from the world.

He turned reluctantly to face the slender figure who stood poised halfway down the stairs. Anatole's extraordinary senses had not been as keen of late. Perhaps being in constant pain began to dull the edges of a man's soul.

He wondered exactly how long Marius St. Leger had been lingering behind him, watching. If Anatole had had his way, he would have denied admittance to his cousin and those soul-prying eyes of his. But necessity had driven him to summon the doctor. Because of Will.

As Marius descended the rest of the stairs, Anatole asked, "Have you finished your examination of the boy? How does he fare?"

Marius's solemn face appeared graver than usual. "Will's surgery seems to be healing as it should. We have been fortunate. No sign of infection, no fever, but . . ." His frown deepened.

"But what?" Anatole demanded.

"The boy is still wasting away. Mr. Trigghorne tells me he can get Will to take little in the way of nourishment."

"Then, force him to eat! Can you not brew up some concoction that will stimulate the lad's appetite?"

"I have medicines for the body, not the mind, Anatole. Will won't even sit up in bed, let alone make use of the crutches you had fashioned for him. He feels he has no reason to go on trying, no reason even to live."

That was an emotion Anatole found all too acutely familiar.

"Then, there is nothing more you can do for the boy?"

"No," Marius said softly. "But you can."

"Me? I'm no God-cursed physician."

"But you are his master."

Anatole stared at Marius incredulously. What did his cousin expect him to do? Command Will to live? A rather ironic order that would be coming from a man who had little regard for his own life. A man so lacking in control that he had managed to terrify his wife half to death, drive her away from him.

"I don't feel much like anyone's master," he muttered.

Marius said nothing, his eyes laden with sadness and disappointment. Curse him! As though he had truly expected Anatole to perform some blasted miracle. Marius, of all people, should know better. And yet . . .

St. Legers looked after their own. Anatole could never escape that thought or another far more piercing one. What would Madeline say if he stood back with folded hands and simply allowed Will to die?

He clenched his jaw. He'd imagined himself nearly past feeling anything. But he discovered he was still capable of experiencing emotion. Anger and shame burned through him.

Muttering an oath, he thrust his way past Marius, storming up the stairs toward the small, front chamber where Will had been placed to recuperate.

Damn the boy! Anatole would cram food down his throat if he had to. If Madeline were here . . . she would have known what to say, how to coax Will out of his lethargy, how to reason, how to comfort him. His wife was remarkably good at that sort of thing.

If Madeline were here . . .

But she wasn't.

Remembrance of that drained away most of Anatole's anger by the time he reached Will's chamber. And what remained faded at the sight of the lad, small and shrunken beneath the coverlets. So apathetic he did not even shift his head to see who had entered the room.

Trigghorne had been attempting to cajole the boy into swallowing a few mouthfuls of soup, but as Anatole approached the bed, the grizzled old man stood respectfully aside.

Will stared listlessly up at the ceiling. His eyes, Anatole realized, were too much like his own. Empty wells of despair. He loomed over the boy, feeling goddamned helpless. He'd heard tell of a St. Leger, Deidre perhaps, who had the ability with a touch to take away pain, to grant the sufferer sweet oblivion.

Now, that would have been a gift worth the having. But he had only his own useless powers to employ.

Lightly touching the boy's cheek, he commanded, "Will, look at me. I want you to stare deep into my eyes."

Marius, who had trailed upstairs after him, froze on the threshold in alarm, and Trigghorne cried out, "Oh, Gawd, no, m'lord. Not another of them cursed vision things."

Only Will remained unmoved, surrendering his eyes to Anatole without fear. "I hope it's my death you see this time, master."

Ignoring him, Anatole focused, peering for long moments into those wide lakes of blue.

"It's worse than death," he pronounced grimly.

Some of Will's defiant bravado crumpled. "W-worse? You don't mean . . . not—not my other leg?"

"No. You are going to be married."

Will gaped at him, then issued a laugh, bitter and incredulous. "Who'd have me now for a husband? A useless cripple."

Anatole drew himself up to his full height, scowling. "Do you doubt my power, boy?"

Will shrank deeper into the mattress. "N-no, master, but—"

"I cannot see the face of the lass you will wed, only the outcome. You will sire twelve children."

"Gawd a'mercy," Trigg exclaimed.

Will's eyes widened, threatening to entirely swallow his pale face.

"So I strongly suggest you start to eat," Anatole said dryly. "It's clear you're going to need your strength."

Will nodded, a hint of color returning to his dazed face.

Anatole stalked from the room, retreating belowstairs to his study. He settled behind the desk, stretching back in his chair, preparing to sink into his own dark thoughts when Marius burst in without ceremony.

"Good Lord, Anatole. You should see the lad. Will is shoveling down food like he was expected to go out and sire those twelve children this very day." Marius gave a delighted laugh. "This is the first time you ever experienced a vision that did not portend some dire event. Do you realize what this means?"

"It means I am an infernally good liar."

Marius's grin wavered, became uncertain. "What are you saying?"

"I'm saying I made the entire thing up," Anatole snapped, both amazed and irritated by his cousin's naïveté. "Did you think that I'd suddenly turned into an angel of light?"

He waited, expecting that would finally wipe that foolish smile from Marius's face. But the admiration in his cousin's eyes only deepened.

"It doesn't matter. By the time Will figures out the prediction is false, he will have recovered enough, and who knows, it might even come true. A self-fulfilling prophecy. If you are a devil, my lord, you are a clever compassionate one."

Anatole didn't feel clever, merely drained.

"However did you think of such a thing?"

"Since my marriage to Madeline, I've become good at concocting fairy tales."

It was the first time he had mentioned her name since Marius's arrival. Marius became somber, his gaze flickering as he absorbed the details of the gloom-shadowed study, the drawn curtains, the ash-ridden fireplace, trying not to probe, clearly unable to help himself. He stepped farther inside the study, closing the door.

"Anatole, I've been wanting to tell you how sorry—"

"Don't," Anatole warned, shrinking from Marius's compassion, shrinking even more from the understanding he saw etched in his cousin's gaunt features. The understanding of a man who knew too well what it was like to face years of emptiness: dark, bleak, and alone. Something that Anatole neither wanted to know nor comprehend.

Marius heaved a deep sigh, but before he could say anything more, Anatole stiffened, sensing another presence invading his home.

Eamon was escorting someone toward the study. The footman's quick movements were interspersed with slow, weary, shuffling steps.

"Fitzleger!" Anatole muttered, jerking to his feet. He tried not to hope, but it rushed the barriers of his heart in a painful flood.

"Shall I leave you?" Marius asked diffidently.

Anatole waved his cousin aside, far beyond mustering the effort to conceal his anxiety from anyone. As the door opened to admit Fitzleger, Marius retreated quietly toward the cold hearth.

Anatole strode eagerly toward the vicar, only to recoil in shock. The old man had aged visibly during the past few days, the change in him even more marked this morning. Shoulders stooped, white wings of hair flattened to his scalp and his eyes. Eyes that had ever glowed with a strange combination of youthful innocence and timeless wisdom.

Now they looked merely old.

The answer to Anatole's question was writ large on the Bride Finder's haggard countenance. But he could still not refrain from asking it, despising the desperation in his voice.

"You . . . you have talked to Madeline? Will she return to me?"

The old man said nothing. With bowed head he trudged to the desk and laid down a long wrapped parcel. A gleaming hilt protruded from the canvas sacking.

The St. Leger sword.

The fragile hope that Anatole clutched so awkwardly in his hands splintered into a thousand shards.

"She refuses to even see me?" Anatole murmured, swallowing hard. "Did you tell her that I swear not to use any of my powers? That I will keep my distance? I won't even try to touch her."

"I'm sorry, my lord," Fitzleger said. "I have told her all that you instructed, and it makes no difference."

"Then . . . then she still desires to leave Cornwall?"

"Aye, she wishes to return to London at once."

Anatole told himself he had been expecting this, dreading it. Like a prisoner in the docks waiting to hear himself remanded for life. Then, why did the sentence still come as such a cruel shock?

He sank back down behind the desk. Madeline wanted to leave him. Not just for a week, a month, but forever. She feared him that much. Despair threatened to overtake him in one huge black wave, but he closed his eyes, fighting against it.

"Very well," he whispered.

Reaching numbly across the desk, he found his quill and dragged forth a sheet of vellum, his movements stiff and mechanical.

"I will instruct my solicitor to place whatever funds she needs at her disposal. I have already dispatched much of her clothing down to the rectory, but I'll arrange for the rest of her things to be sent on to London. She . . ." He faltered, his throat constricting. "She'll be wanting her books."

Marius had listened in silence all this while. But he burst past Fitzleger, leaning across Anatole's desk to exclaim in disbelief, "Good God, Anatole, what are you saying? You cannot possibly mean to let her go."

"What would you have me do, cousin?" Anatole demanded wearily. "Force Madeline to stay with me? Chain her to the walls?"

"No! You would not have to. Madeline does not fear you, my lord."

"You were not there that night. You did not see into her heart. But your powers would not have been necessary. Any fool would have known how terrified she was."

"I'd have been terrified too if you had flung half the castle at my head," Marius cried. "But I have examined your lady's heart before and seen only strength and courage there. And love for you."

Love? Anatole's mouth quirked into a tired, bitter smile. "Your powers must be weakening, Marius. It is impossible that any lady should love me. I have always known that. My only mistake was in forgetting it."

A choked sound escaped Fitzleger. Turning away from the desk, he paced off several steps, saying, "May God forgive me. This is all my fault."

"No, old friend, you are not to blame. You did your best. The fault rests entirely with me."

But rather than giving comfort, Anatole's words only seemed to increase Fitzleger's agitation. Bracing himself against the mantel, he buried his face against his sleeve, but not before Anatole saw a single tear slide down his withered cheek.

Fitzleger was . . . weeping.

Anatole cast a glance of horrified helplessness toward Marius, but for once his cousin's usual empathy was not in evidence. Marius stared at Fitzleger through narrowed eyes.

"He is concealing something from you, Anatole," Marius pronounced at last. "Something about Madeline."

Fitzleger concealing something? Marius's powers were indeed off, Anatole thought. The vicar was the most transparently honest man he'd ever known. The only time in his entire life he could ever recall Fitzleger being evasive was . . . when he had struggled to bring about the match between Anatole and Madeline.

Anatole tensed, coming slowly to his feet.

"Fitzleger?"

The old man seemed to shrink deeper inside of himself at the sound of his name. He groped for his handkerchief, mumbling to himself.

"I—I don't think I can bear this. Seeing him so hurt. Far worse than when his mother rejected . . . But I promised Madeline."

"Promised her what?" Anatole demanded.

"I think it has something to do with Madeline's reason for leaving you," Marius said.

Fitzleger blew his nose with a gusty snort, shooting Marius a look of mild reproach. "I can bare my own secrets, thank you, young man."

"Then, you'd best do so. At once." Anatole came around the desk and rested his hand heavily upon Fitzleger's shoulder.

The old man made a great show of refolding his handkerchief, still avoiding Anatole's eyes. "Madeline thought—and I agreed with her—that it would be better if you did not know the true reason she refuses to come back to Castle Leger."

"Which is?"

"Your lady is not leaving because of fear of you, my lord—"

"I knew it!" Marius interrupted triumphantly.

"But out of fear *for* you."

"Talk sense, Fitzleger," Anatole said, striving to remain gentle with the distraught old man, but feeling his patience strain to the snapping point.

"If Madeline stays with you, she fears she will kill you."

"She's killing me now!"

"No, I mean truly destroy you. She . . . she had a vision."

Was Fitzleger's distress starting to addle the old man's wits? Anatole wondered.

"You know that's impossible. Not unless you've recently discovered that Madeline is descended from another of Prospero's by-blows, and she has St. Leger blood."

"She used the sword. The power trapped in the crystal, your own power, my lord," Fitzleger insisted, his reddened eyes earnest and remarkably sane.

"It happened once before. The poor lady thought she was only imagining things, but the sword predicted to her the afternoon that you would take her riding to see the standing stones."

The old man's words filled Anatole with unease. He slipped his hand from Fitzleger's shoulder, scowling. "I cannot believe it."

"Why not?" Marius asked. "You're a St. Leger. You should be able to believe damn near anything. We've all heard the legends surrounding that sword."

"Our family spawns legends like the sea does shellfish," Anatole snapped.

"And most of them are true."

Anatole clenched his jaw, knowing Marius was right. His gaze shifted toward his desk where the St. Leger sword lay hidden beneath the canvas covering, like a serpent coiled to strike.

Aye, he vaguely recalled hearing some tales himself, of brides being able to share in their husband's powers through use of the sword. But most St. Leger women had tucked the formidable weapon away somewhere and never looked at it again.

It had never even occurred to him to warn Madeline that she should likewise do so. For what lady would be likely to toy with such a dangerous sword, examine it?

His own lady, that was who, with her ever bright, too inquisitive green eyes.

Oh, Madeline, Anatole thought with a groan. Flinging off the canvas, he snatched up the weapon, chilled by the mere possibility that his wife could have stumbled onto its dread power. He should have flung the infernal thing off the nearest cliff years ago.

There was only one way he could verify what Fitzleger had told him. Peer into the crystal himself, try to see what the old man claimed that Madeline had seen.

Gripping the hilt, Anatole held the sword aloft, staring hard at the glittering stone, allowing himself to be pulled deeper into those mysterious depths.

Mist . . . the same useless vision he had entertained all those months ago was what danced before his eyes.

He was lost in the mist with the ghostly figure of a woman, her bright-colored hair tangled about her shoulders. The same cold feeling of apprehension, the same vague warning.

Beware the woman of flame.

Gritting his teeth, he strained to force the mist to part before him, concentrating harder than he had ever done before. The crystal flashed, and suddenly the scene unfolded with blinding clarity.

And Anatole understood why he had never been able to bring the image into focus before. It took courage, even for a St. Leger, to look upon the face of his own death.

As the image faded, he laid the sword carefully back down upon the desk.

"Well?" Marius prodded when Anatole remained wrapped in his silence.

"Fitzleger was right. Madeline did see something," Anatole murmured. "I'm going to die."

Marius uttered a startled oath and turned pale. But Anatole was amazed by how remarkably calm he felt.

So Madeline was not leaving because he terrified her. If not for that vision, she would have found the courage to return to him. To have accepted him. To have loved him . . . A soft smile curved Anatole's lips, his entire soul lit with a quiet joy.

He had no hope of defeating the vision, of avoiding his death. But whatever time remained to him, he intended to find Madeline, love her enough to make up for a lifetime.

But this thought was crowded out by a more disturbing realization. If Madeline believed that she was going to be the cause of his death, then she had not seen the vision in the sword with full clarity, either. Fearing for him, she likely had no notion of her own danger.

It all began to form a rough sort of pattern in his mind. Fitzleger's sighting of the mysterious woman weeping over old Tyrus's grave, Roman's purchase of Lost Land, and the arrival of that so-called friend of his . . . Yves de Rochencoeur.

Small wonder Anatole was seeing visions of his own death, images that had nothing to do with Madeline.

She was not the woman of flame.

"I have to go find my wife," Anatole muttered, striding toward the door.

"No!" Fitzleger cried out. "That is exactly what you must not do, why Madeline did not want me to tell you any of this. Do you not understand, lad? She is trying to save you."

Anatole paused long enough to cast the old man a sad half smile. "She already has."

Before either Fitzleger or Marius could stop him, Anatole bolted from the study. He raced through the house toward the morning room, the door leading out into the gardens, and the path to the stable yard.

Flinging the door wide, he plunged out into . . . a morning choked with mist. A heavy fog seemed to hold all of Castle Leger captive, stretching toward Anatole with suffocating fingers of white.

His footsteps faltered. There had been a reason, then, that the vision had suddenly emerged so clear. A chill worked through him that had nothing to do with the damp mist or the raw spring air.

He had hoped to be granted a little more time, but it was obvious the prophecy's fulfillment was imminent. Today within the hour perhaps. He experienced a fleeting moment of fear, then shrugged it off.

Charging into the fog, he strode by instinct toward the stable yard, shouting for his stallion to be saddled. His hounds raised a fearsome racket, their baying echoing eerie and ghostlike through the mist. Ranger went nigh wild, refusing to heed any of Anatole's commands. It took the efforts of two stout stable boys to haul the hound away from his master's side, lock him with the rest in the kennels. Almost as if the old dog also knew. . . .

Anatole reached out with his mind, stretching his powers to the limit, trying to find Madeline through the fog, across the distance to the village. To Fitzleger's.

Groping and finding nothing. She was no longer there. Cursing, Anatole roared for his groom to make haste. As the black stallion was led out, Anatole started forward only to have a hand clamp down on his shoulder.

He was wrenched around to confront Marius's tense face, his slender cousin's grasp surprisingly strong.

"For the love of God, Anatole! Fitzleger is beside himself, on the verge of collapse. You must—"

Marius broke off, tensing, his eyes roving fearfully as though trying to pierce the mist that enveloped them. They were both too well attuned to the dark side of their heritage, he and this cousin of his, Anatole thought. He could tell that Marius was feeling it, too . . . the impending death of a St. Leger.

Marius's grip tightened. "Come back to the house."

"No, you must take care of Fitzleger for me. I have other matters to attend."

"Such as what? Rushing off to your death?"

"If that is my fate, I cannot avoid it."

"You can bloody well try."

Anatole wrenched himself free. "You don't understand, and I've no time to explain. Madeline may be in danger herself."

"Then, let me go to her instead," Marius said, desperately barring Anatole's path.

"Get out of my way, Marius," he growled.

"No, I'll be hanged before I just step aside and let you fling your life away in this foolhardy fashion."

"And what would you do, cousin? If you had the chance to hold your Anne one last time, make sure she was safe, would you do it? Even if it cost you your life?"

Marius didn't answer him. It was obvious from the agonized look in his eyes that he couldn't.

He stood numbly aside as Anatole brushed past him. Seizing the reins from the groom, he vaulted into the saddle. The stallion pranced beneath him, and Anatole struggled to bring the restive horse under control. As he did so, he stole one last look at Marius's tormented face, the cousin whose blood he so reluctantly shared, the St. Leger he had fought more than any other to keep at a distance all these years, the man who would have been his friend if he had ever allowed such a thing.

But it was too late now, even for regret.

"God keep you," Anatole said hoarsely. Wheeling the stallion about, he rode off into the heavy mist.

Guiding his horse along the treacherous path above the cliffs, he kept a wary eye on preventing them both from plunging to the rocks below.

He reached further ahead with his mind, searching for Madeline until he found her, a distant glimmer of light piercing his soul. She shimmered through him, slipping from his grasp like fragments of a rainbow.

But it was enough to tell him where she was, enough to fill him with dread.

She was already moving inexorably toward the one place she should not go, the destination that could seal both their fates.

Lost Land.

The mist billowed around Madeline, chilling her even through the thick folds of her cloak. She clutched the bandbox containing her few meager possessions tighter against her, picking her way carefully along the path.

Was it her imagination or was the fog heavier, colder here? Her logic would have told her it was because of the nearby sea, but during these past harrowing days, reason had been replaced by an older, more primitive instinct that she had not even realized she possessed.

It wasn't the fog or the haunting whisper of cold waves lapping the distant shore. It was the place that iced her blood. Lost Land. The villagers were so fearful of this isolated strip of coast, it had taken what coin she had left to bribe one of them to fetch her out here. The old fisherman had allowed greed to overcome his good sense, his terror of Lost Land, and his reluctance to incur the wrath of the dread lord by helping his bride escape from him.

Staring up at the twisted ruins and blackened battlements protruding through the mist, Madeline wondered what had become of her own good sense. Bleak, barren, and silent, it was as though spring itself had died stillborn in this disturbing place.

Once the home of the Mortmains, her husband's mortal enemies. Did their ghosts yet walk abroad, craving vengeance, the blood of another St. Leger? Anything was possible. Madeline shivered.

She'd once fancied herself a rather brave person, but it hadn't been courage at all, only a mind fortified with disbelief. Those fortifications had come crumbling down, and she was left trembling with fear.

It took all the bravado she possessed to force her unwilling feet forward. Or perhaps it was sheer desperation. How far did one have to go to outrun a prophecy? She had come to the conclusion that London might not be distant enough. She had to disappear abroad for a while, at least until she reasoned out what to do next. And there was only one man who could help her with that.

Yves de Rochencoeur. The Frenchman had once declared himself her friend, had said he would do anything for her, even aid her in escaping her husband.

Had it been idle words, a fleeting promise? When it came down to it, she knew very little of Yves, the man she had decided to entrust with both her future and Anatole's.

But what choice did she have? She could no longer depend upon Fitzleger. She worried that she had made a grave mistake by ever confiding in him what she'd seen in the crystal. He'd agreed with her that she must stay away from Anatole, but the old man's heart had clearly been torn in two, wanting to save his beloved young master, also wanting to spare him any more pain.

She realized now that Fitzleger had actually been delaying her departure, hoping for Madeline scarce knew what, a miracle, some magical spell that would help them undo the dire prediction trapped in the sword. She had indulged in such foolish hopes herself during the long lonely nights away from Anatole, only to end by weeping with despair.

When she had awakened to a world blanketed with mist, she had known she could bear this no longer. She could not spend every morning the fog rolled in from the sea choked with fear, dreading that this might be the day she would inadvertently destroy the man she loved.

She had insisted that Fitzleger tell Anatole she had to leave at once. The old man had departed to do so, shoulders bowed down with grief. She had watched him go, doubted that the good, honest vicar would be able to continue deceiving his lord. As long as Anatole believed she remained terrified of him, he would stay away.

But if he were to learn the truth . . . Nothing in heaven or hell would keep him from her side, not even the prospect of his own death.

It was then that Madeline realized she had to get away and at once. She'd thought of appealing to one of the other St. Legers, Hadrian, perhaps, with his fleet of ships. But she had no notion where to find the bluff captain, nor was she at all certain of receiving his help.

St. Legers had a grim way of accepting their fate, just as Marius had done. What if they thought it more important that Anatole hold fast to his chosen bride, keep the love that was destined to be his . . . more important even than his own life? Hadrian might well just escort her firmly back to Anatole.

Madeline could not take the risk. And as for her own family, they would think her quite mad if she attempted to tell them anything about legends, powers, visions. Even if they could be brought to believe her . . . Madeline was appalled to think it, but Mama and Papa might not see anything wrong with the prospect of her ending up a wealthy widow.

No, she realized she had only one hope left of cheating destiny . . . her friend Yves. Creeping past the fire-scarred remains of the Mortmain manor house, her eyes strained to part the fog and locate the cottage where Yves had told her he was staying.

She prayed she would find it, would find Yves at home. Casting a nervous glance over her shoulder, she feared she might have already delayed her flight too long.

These past few steps, she had become increasingly conscious of a presence. Nothing evil or sinister, but a warm loving one, like strong arms reaching through the mist to hold her fast.

Anatole . . . he had told her he could sense her wherever she was, wherever she would go. How far did his power truly extend? She had no notion, but she tried to quiet her own breathing, still her thudding heart from calling out to him.

A sharp sound cracked through the fog's deathly silence. Like the snap of a tree branch or—or— Pulse leaping, Madeline peered around her only to realize she was much closer to the cottage than she had supposed.

The stone walls and shuttered windows appeared comforting and solid in this nightmare-spun land lost in mist. With a glad cry Madeline rushed forward only to stumble to a halt.

A gray mare was tethered to the rickety gate, pawing nervously at the ground, the spirited mount not the sort of animal Yves would have chosen to ride.

Madeline believed she had seen both this mare and her rider galloping through the village one afternoon when she had chanced to look out the front window at the vicarage.

Roman's horse. Her heart sank in dismay at the thought of encountering Roman's mocking smile, his piercing gaze. It should have occurred to her that he might be here. He likely rode over often to consult with Yves about the progress for the new house.

What was she to do now? Madeline hesitated. She had intended to tell Yves that he had been right, that she needed to escape from Anatole because he was abusive and cruel to her. Roman had no love for his cousin, but he would never be brought to believe that.

The least he could do was delay her flight by demanding better explanations from her. And the worst, if he should somehow come at the truth in that uncanny way of his . . . Madeline had no doubt Roman would do his best to see the prophecy fulfilled.

She fretted her lip, wondering if she dared wait until Roman had gone. But while she attempted to decide, the cottage door suddenly swung open and Roman himself lurched out.

Madeline started to shrink back into the fog, when she realized something was terribly wrong. Roman staggered away from the cottage like a drunken man, grabbing at the gatepost for support.

He fumbled with his horse's reins only to let loose of them as soon as he'd freed the hitch from the gatepost. Swaying, he crashed down to his knees, and Madeline saw the dark crimson stain spreading across the front of his cloak.

Horrified, she forgot all else as she rushed to his aid. The horse shied back at her approach. Roman lifted his head to stare up at her, stunned, his eyes glazed with pain.

"Madeline! What the devil—"

She cried out as he fell forward. Dropping her band box, she tried to catch him, but she could not prevent Roman from sprawling face first in the dirt.

She struggled to roll him onto his back. His hand flashed out, using what remained of his strength to push her away.

"Get out of here!"

"But you are hurt," she said. "What happened?"

"No time for—for questions," he panted. "Get on my horse. Ride . . . fetch help."

She feared Roman would not last that long, blood spilling from the gaping wound in his chest at an alarming rate, leaving him white, drained. His eyes closed, and she was terrified that it was already too late.

With a toss of its head, the horse turned and bolted into the mist, spooked by the scent of blood or something else. . . . Madeline felt the presence at her back before she ever saw or heard him. He had crept down the path from the cottage as silently as the billowing fog.

"Ah, Madeline, what are you doing here, *cherie*?"

It was Yves's voice with that queer husky rasp.

When she dared to look around, she saw him, his elegant clothes torn and disheveled, his powdered wig pulled askew. His appearance shocked her, but not so much as the smoking pistol he clutched in one elegant hand.

Madeline slowly straightened, stepping in front of Roman's inert form.

"Yves?" she faltered, her mind reeling in confusion and disbelief.

"No, my dear." Yves smiled sadly and reached up to wrench away the wig that was slipping off his head.

"The name is Evelyn . . . *Evelyn Mortmain*."

But Madeline barely heard the echo of the dreaded name. She clutched the gatepost for support, feeling as though the entire world had just shifted beneath her feet into the realm of nightmare . . . or of a vision only partly seen and not clearly understood. Until now.

As if a veil of mist were being torn from her eyes, Madeline watched in horror as Evelyn Mortmain slowly shook out her hair. Wild hair as long and brilliantly red as her own.

"Dear God," Madeline whispered. "The woman of flame."

Chapter Twenty-One

She needed to run, escape from this place as fast as she could. A voice deep inside urged Madeline to do just that, but her limbs refused to obey. It was as though the mist itself had seeped into her mind, choking her with fear and confusion.

She could only stare at the person she had once thought of as Yves de Rochencoeur, unable to credit the transformation of the cultured Frenchman into this creature with her mass of flame-colored hair, her torn shirt revealing a hint of breasts cruelly flattened by a corset.

"Do not look at me as though I were a ghost," Evelyn Mortmain said, her throaty voice losing all trace of its French accent. "I am but a woman, the same as yourself, although not blessed with your charms. We Mortmains, alas, have never been noted for our beauty."

"But—but all of you Mortmains are supposed to be dead," Madeline faltered.

Evelyn regarded Madeline with amusement. "A wistful delusion on the part of the St. Legers, I am afraid."

As she came closer, Madeline shrank back, but Evelyn glided past her to stand with her pistol aimed at the man collapsed on the path.

Roman. In her shock Madeline had all but forgotten him. She needed to do something, try to help him, but she feared Roman was well beyond her aid or protection.

When Evelyn nudged him roughly with the toe of her boot, Roman did not stir. The Mortmain woman's mouth snaked back in a satisfied smile.

"Ah, well, that appears to be one less St. Leger I need worry about."

"You've killed him?" Madeline whispered.

"I had no choice." Evelyn shifted back in Madeline's direction. "He discovered my identity and attacked me in a most ungentlemanlike fashion."

She gave a raspy chuckle. "Strange, is it not? Ever since I came here, I have walked in dread of all the other St. Legers with their uncanny powers, fearing exposure. But that I should be unmasked by this one . . ."

She made a contemptuous gesture toward Roman. "A person as mundane as I am. That he should divine my secret by simply having me investigated . . . amusing, isn't it?"

Madeline shuddered. Evelyn was addressing her in the most blood-chilling conversational tone. As though they were back in Madeline's parlor, sipping tea, discussing Milton and Molière. But they were not.

They were locked together in this bad dream of suffocating fog, isolation, and death. Evelyn trained upon her the same pistol she had used to kill Roman, and yet Madeline felt oblivious to any sense of her own danger.

Her thoughts flew instead to Anatole.

How could she have misinterpreted so badly what she had seen in the crystal? Instead of saving Anatole by running away, her mistake in coming here might well cost him his life. The thought filled her with horror.

She endeavored to hide her fear from the Mortmain woman. There was no reason that Anatole should be seeking her out there, riding inexorably toward Madeline and his own destruction, no reason that he should even know where she was.

No reason at all, except that he was Anatole. And a St. Leger.

Madeline's stomach tightened on a wave of rising panic. She had to race back to Castle Leger, find Anatole first, and warn—No! that was exactly what she must not do. She had to keep Evelyn as far away from Anatole as possible, somehow deal with the woman herself.

But how? She tried to remain calm, to think, but it was difficult as Evelyn edged closer, her pistol aimed straight at Madeline's heart.

"And now, my dear," Evelyn said softly, "perhaps you will be so good as to tell me what you are doing here?"

"I—I ran away from my husband."

"I am already aware of that. Every dolt for miles around talks of nothing else but how the dread lord's bride fled from him and sought sanctuary at the vicarage. That still does not explain your presence at Lost Land."

"You said that if I ever wanted to leave Cornwall, you would help me."

"Yes, but as you can see—" Evelyn cast a wry glance at Roman. "You have chosen a most inconvenient time."

"Then, perhaps I should just go away."

Evelyn laughed.

"Or perhaps we should both go," Madeline continued desperately. "You will be wanting to escape yourself now that your identity is known. We—we could leave here at once, find a boat bound for France."

And as far away from Anatole as I can persuade you to go, Madeline thought, anxiously watching the woman.

After a nerve-stretching pause, Evelyn shook her head.

"I don't see the necessity for me to flee. Only two people know my secret, and one of them is already dead."

Evelyn stalked closer, the muzzle of the pistol all but brushing up against the fabric of Madeline's gown.

"I would not tell anyone." Fearing her face might betray her, Madeline ducked her head. "I detest St. Legers as much as you do. They—they are all so frightening and strange, my own husband the worst. We should both get away while we still can."

Evelyn's hand shot out and caught Madeline's chin, wrenching Madeline's head upward. The empty look in Evelyn's eyes was replaced with one far more shrewd.

Her voice was sad, almost tender as she said, "You are a very poor actress, my dear friend. Perhaps your husband is strange, even cruel. But like all the other poor little chosen brides who have gone before you, you have fallen in love with your wretched St. Leger."

Despite the threat of the pistol, Madeline jerked free of Evelyn's grasp, backing away. "Are you Mortmains also mind readers?"

"No, I obtained information the way our too clever Roman did. Through the use of a paid agent, one that I placed at Castle Leger myself."

"None of Anatole's servants would ever have—" Madeline began only to break off at the realization.

"Bess Kennack," she murmured. "You sent Bess to spy on us."

"Perceptive as always, my clever Madeline," Evelyn mocked. "Yes, I encouraged Bess to seek employment at Castle Leger, and find out anything she could that might help bring about the downfall of the St. Legers. It took very little coin to persuade the girl, considering the way she blames your husband for the death of her mother. Hate, as I have discovered for myself, can prove a very useful emotion."

An image flashed into Madeline's mind of the Kennack girl and her pale face, her quiet way of creeping about the corridors. Dear God, had the girl listened at keyholes, actually eavesdropping on Madeline's most intimate moments and conversations with Anatole? She sickened at the thought.

"But how could you possibly know about Bess?" she asked. "About her bitterness toward Anatole?"

Evelyn gave her a condescending smile. "After waiting over twenty years for this revenge, do you not suppose that I would try to learn all that I could about the St. Legers? I studied the entire family from a safe distance before I ever made myself known. That is how I came to seek Roman's acquaintance first. He was their weakest link: a selfish, greedy man. I lured him in easily, pretending to be his friend, advancing him the money to buy Lost Land, dangling out the prospect of marriage to a wealthy countess. He was completely taken in. Or so I thought."

Evelyn's mouth twisted into a moue of distaste. "But he was more clever and suspicious than I had ever supposed. I might have bribed him into helping me destroy the rest of the St. Legers, if he had not been so furious when he learned the truth. Perhaps he didn't like me playing him for a fool, or maybe he finally remembered his damnable St. Leger blood."

Evelyn shrugged. "Who knows?"

Her callous dismissal of Roman's death, the calm way she talked of destroying St. Legers, chilled Madeline to the core.

She scanned Evelyn's hard, painted features, seeking some trace of the gentleness she had known in Yves, some sign that the woman could be reasoned with.

There was none.

"You've spent twenty years of your life planning this revenge?" Madeline asked. "You must be mad!"

"No, merely patient. You see, that blackened shell of a house behind you was once my home, Madeline."

Evelyn's brittle calm cracked, affording Madeline a disturbing glimpse of the hatred seething beneath the whitened mask that was her face.

"I was only fourteen years old when I barely escaped from that fire. I had a voice then as lovely as yours, but I lost it that night, the heat and the smoke clawing at my throat, tearing at my lungs. I couldn't even scream as I cowered in the shadows, watching my entire family being burned alive by those damned St. Legers."

"But—but I was told your own father lit that fire."

"So he did. What else could he do? He had to save himself from being taken alive, dragged off like a dog in chains."

"Because he had murdered Wyatt St. Leger."

"It was not murder," Evelyn said through gritted teeth. "It was war. The war that has always existed between Mortmains and St. Legers, ever since the St. Legers stole our rightful land, using their cursed sorcery and witchcraft."

"No, Evelyn," Madeline tried to soothe. "I don't know what you remember from your childhood, what your father might have told you, but you don't understand—"

"Be quiet!" Evelyn flashed. She took a menacing step closer. "It's you who doesn't understand, Madeline. My father never told me anything. But I heard him often enough, lamenting he had no sons, only a weak daughter to carry on his fight against the St. Legers.

"And I was weak. I ran away that night, and hid the first place I could find."

"Surely that was not necessary. I cannot believe any of the St. Legers would have harmed you. They would have seen you were taken care of and—" But Madeline stopped cold at the black look Evelyn shot her.

"Do you think I would have accepted charity from those murderous bastards?" Evelyn demanded fiercely. "No, I had to get away. I stowed aboard a fishing vessel that carried me off to France. When the captain discovered me hiding below, he simply had me tossed ashore like a stray rat."

Evelyn came closer still, her eyes lit by a strange fire and boring into Madeline's.

"Do you know what it is like, my friend, to find yourself alone in the world, abandoned in a foreign country?"

Madeline swallowed, shaking her head.

"After the first time I was raped, I quickly learned the wisdom of disguising myself as a boy."

"Dear God!" Madeline breathed.

"I became rather good at disguising myself," Evelyn went on bitterly. "Good at many things. Acting, thieving, whoring. Whatever it took to survive, whatever it took to make my fortune and bring me back here one day to prove that my father was wrong. That he didn't need a son to avenge our family. He only needed me!"

She brandished her pistol, shoving her face only inches from Madeline's. For once Evelyn was not able to disguise the pain, the hatred, the degradations of a past that had bent and twisted her soul. Madeline stared at her with a mingling of pity and horror.

"I'm sorry," she said gently. The words seemed foolish, inadequate, but they had the effect of snapping Evelyn back to herself.

She retreated a step, muttering darkly, "Don't be sorry. Not for me. Save your pity for your husband."

The mention of Anatole caused Madeline's heart to miss a beat.

"You have no quarrel with Anatole," she struggled to reason with the woman. "He is not responsible for what happened to you or your family. He was not even born then."

"It doesn't matter. He's a St. Leger, and the head of his cursed line. He has to die. As all the others do."

"But you cannot possibly hope to kill them all. You will be caught, perhaps even killed yourself. Yves . . . Evelyn, please. You shot Roman in self-defense. You could plead that it was an accident, stop now, and leave all this behind you."

"I don't want to stop," Evelyn said with chilling softness. "And yes, I can destroy them all. One by one, slowly, carefully as I had always planned to do."

She showed no sign of raving madness, but that terrible calm had descended over her again, which Madeline found somehow worse. That dark emptiness that placed Evelyn beyond reason, beyond compassion, beyond any hope of persuasion. As inexorable as the vision in the sword.

Was it truly impossible to stop Evelyn, to defeat the prophecy? Madeline wondered in despair. Evelyn's eyes flicked over Madeline in a hard, assessing manner, but her voice held a note of regret as she said, "I am sorry you had to be caught up in all of this, Madeline. I liked you. I genuinely did."

Liked? Evelyn spoke of her as if she were already dead. Madeline's veins turned to ice.

"Unfortunately," she went on. "Now that you are here, I am compelled to make use of you."

"What—what do you mean?"

"No doubt your husband will come looking for you."

"No! No, he won't," Madeline said too quickly, betraying her fear. "I—I mean why would he? He has no idea of where I am."

"But he has his own special means of tracking you, does he not?"

"I don't know what you are talking—"

"Don't even think of trying to deny it, Madeline," Evelyn interrupted coldly. "I am fully aware of the extent of your husband's powers. Whatever information I was unable to wheedle out of Roman, Bess supplied.

"He presents a particular challenge, your Anatole. How does one destroy a man who can bat you away with one flick of his mind? One has to take him by surprise. And how can one do that when he is blessed with such an extraordinary sense of perception? But perhaps that perception doesn't work as well when he is distracted . . . say, with fear for the life of someone very close to him, hmmm?" Evelyn regarded Madeline with a mocking lift of her brows.

"No," Madeline choked. "I won't let you use me to lay a trap for Anatole."

Evelyn steadied her pistol. "You have no choice in the matter, my dear. You must help me or . . ."

"Or you'll shoot me as you did Roman? Go ahead," Madeline cried. "I'd rather be dead than lure Anatole to you."

"Don't be a fool."

Heart hammering, Madeline braced herself as the tense seconds ticked by, wondering why Evelyn didn't simply shoot. She'd had no compunction about just killing Roman.

Just killing Roman . . . the image flashed through Madeline's mind of Evelyn coming down the path behind her, the still-smoking pistol in her hand.

She stared at the woman incredulously. "You're bluffing. That pistol is empty."

Evelyn started then recovered with a smile. "Care to put that to a test?"

She cocked the pistol, but Madeline had seen the hesitant flicker in her eyes.

"You never had time to reload after you shot Roman!"

Evelyn's smile twisted into an ugly grimace. She let the hammer fall back into place with a dull click.

"Too clever by half, Madeline," she snarled.

Evelyn lunged at her. Madeline tried to dodge, but Evelyn's hand clamped on her arm. Madeline struggled wildly, but the Mortmain woman was possessed of a wiry strength. She dragged Madeline to her knees and swung the butt of the pistol at Madeline's head.

Madeline cried out, ducking to one side. The blow landed painfully upon her shoulder. Her fingers closed around a handful of earth. Before Evelyn could strike again, Madeline flung the dirt at her face.

Swearing, Evelyn released Madeline to claw at her own eyes. In that brief second Madeline scrambled to her feet. She ran blindly into the fog, with no idea of where she was going.

Away from Lost Land and its blackened ruins, away from Evelyn Mortmain's fury. She heard the woman bellowing her name, loading it with curses.

Madeline ran harder. The ground began to slope upward, making the going more difficult. She tripped, fell, and managed to get up again. Half running, half stumbling, she forced her way up the hill.

Her breath came in agonized pants, a painful stitch blooming in her side. She had no notion where she was, but she could not stop.

She believed she had put some distance between herself and Evelyn, but the woman would not be long in recovering. She would know this land so much better than Madeline did, even in a dense fog.

What am I going to do? Madeline wondered frantically, feeling her steps beginning to lag. Perhaps she should stop, find some sort of weapon. A rock. She could bring it crashing down on the Mortmain woman's head and—

But Madeline recoiled at the thought of such violence, the danger of getting that close to Evelyn again. No, she must go on, elude the woman somehow, find help, pray that Anatole did not find her first.

If only she could reach the cottage of some stout fishermen, enlist their aid. Evelyn could be caught, arrested. If she were locked away somewhere, then surely Anatole would be safe.

But first . . . Madeline staggered to a halt. She had to catch her breath, gain some sense of her bearings. Her hand pressed to her thudding chest, she listened intently for any sound of Evelyn's pursuit.

But she could hear nothing beyond the roaring in her ears. The sea . . . waves breaking against the shore . . . somewhere close. But where? The fog played such tricks with sound.

She spun around, taking a hesitant step back, trying to pierce the thick haze. She cried out the next instant as the ground gave way beneath her.

Her arms flailed as she fell, slipping down a sharp incline. Pebbles and rocks abraded her hands as she scrabbled for purchase. Her fingers struck up against a gnarled root, and she clung desperately, dangling until her feet found the support of a narrow ledge.

Her heart pounded, and she cursed her own stupidity as she realized what she'd done: backed right off a cliff. Luckily, not of such terrifying heights as the ones at Castle Leger. When she dared glance down, she caught glimpses through the mist of the sea, only yards below. Cold, angry waves lashing hard at the rocks, raking back with a savage undertow. Each time the water struck, it sent up a salt spray, dampening the hem of her gown like the slavering of some hungry beast.

Madeline turned her eyes upward, trying to gauge the distance she had fallen. Not as far as she would have supposed. The cliff's edge was a few feet above her, if she but had the strength to pull herself up, if the root would hold. She had to try.

She was testing it gingerly when she heard movement above her. Evelyn Mortmain's face appeared, staring gloatingly down at Madeline.

Evelyn muttered something too low for Madeline to hear, but she braced herself as Evelyn stretched a hand down to her. Uncertain if the woman meant to retake her hostage or send her crashing the rest of the way into the sea, Madeline shrank down as low as she could without losing her grip.

But the hand was withdrawn as quickly as it had been offered. Evelyn tensed. Her mouth pulling back in a strange smile, she vanished from the edge. Madeline peered upward, bewildered until she heard it, too.

The voice calling her name. Anatole.

"Oh, dear Lord, no," Madeline said, choking on a half sob as she realized in her blundering just what she had done.

She had helped Evelyn to lay her trap after all.

Only minutes earlier Anatole had ridden into Lost Land.

He slowed his stallion to a walk, both horse and man scenting danger ahead. As his mount shifted uneasily beneath him, Anatole attempted to penetrate the fog that hung like a shroud over the ruins.

His extraordinary perception was bombarded by too many sensations. From somewhere behind him, he felt Marius and Fitzleger attempting to follow. But ahead all was swallowed up by the aura of Lost Land itself, a feeling of evil, the hatred of an ancient enemy dormant for years . . . now awake, waiting for Anatole with a deadly patience.

She was out there somewhere, the woman of flame. Her presence raked dark fingers across Anatole's mind. He fought off the insidious sensation, groping for Madeline instead. Groping, but not finding her, the silence, the emptiness settling like a cold weight in the pit of his stomach.

He never saw the body sprawled in the path ahead until the stallion shied back with a frightened whinny. Muttering a startled oath, Anatole brought the horse back under control and stared down at the blood-soaked form.

Roman. The flattened grass, the black stains on the ground leading down the path from the cottage bore mute testimony to Roman's desperate efforts to crawl, to reach help. He'd clearly been left for dead, and Anatole had no doubt by whom. But despite Roman's deathlike stillness, Anatole could sense a faint threading of life, a soul hovering on the brink of slipping away from its earthly confines.

Anatole fought a strong urge to simply ride on, Roman's fate only adding to his fears for Madeline. This was the cousin he'd hated for so long, the cursed fool who'd introduced the Mortmain woman back into their midst. Let him die like a dog by the side of the road.

But somehow Anatole couldn't bring himself to do it. Swearing, he vaulted down from the saddle and rushed over to his cousin. Bending down, he turned Roman over.

"Roman!" Anatole called, loosening the wounded man's cravat. A useless gesture. He could feel Roman's life flicker like a candle left in the wind.

Roman stirred at his touch, his eyes fluttering open. The blue depths seemed clouded, already beyond recognizing anything in this mortal world.

But he murmured, "Anatole?"

"Aye, 'tis me," Anatole said. "What happened here?"

"B-bloody woman shot me," Roman groaned. "Played me for a fool. Never was any rich countess. Never a Frenchman. Only a—a cursed Mortmain."

"I know," Anatole said. "But what about Madeline? Was she here? Have you seen her?"

"She . . . tried to help me, but that creature came. I played dead. Did too good a job." Roman gave a weak laugh that sent him into a pain-racked cough.

"Where is Madeline now?" Anatole demanded.

"Don't know. That—that woman attacked her, but Madeline got away, ran . . . woman went after her. Both disappeared into—into the fog."

Roman's hoarse voice went through Anatole like the cold whisper of steel.

He swore hoarsely and started to wrench himself to his feet. But Roman clutched at his cloak.

"Wait! Don't go," Roman said.

"I have to," Anatole ground out. "I have to find Madeline before it's too late. Marius should be along soon. He will . . ."

Anatole trailed off, knowing there was nothing Marius would be able to do for Roman. Roman's time was nearly spent. But then, so was his own.

He tried to rise again, but Roman clung to him with the last of his strength.

"No. Must—must tell you something before—" The effort cost Roman another spasm of pain, a thick trickle of blood issuing from the corner of his mouth. But he persisted, pressing an object into Anatole's hand.

Anatole's fingers closed over the cold circle of his father's watch, stained wet with Roman's blood.

"Yours . . . always was supposed to be," Roman said. "On his deathbed, Uncle Lyndon said to make sure you—tell you how much he loved—ask for your forgiveness.

"Only I never did. Because you already had everything, the power, Castle Leger."

"Damn it, Roman," Anatole said fiercely. "None of this matters to me anymore. I have no time—"

"It—it matters to me," Roman whispered. "Can't die without telling you how I—I took watch, how I lied."

"And what do you want from me? Absolution?" With a ruthlessness born of desperation, Anatole wrenched himself free.

"No, too late for that. Was too late from moment I cut you with the knife." Roman's mouth twisted in a semblance of his mocking smile. "Brought down by the old family curse. Damned strange, isn't it? Dying, and yet for first time in my life, I feel like a St. Leger. . . ."

His eyes closed, his hand falling limp to his side.

Anatole experienced an unexpected pain, sharp, swift, a snapping sensation as though a branch had been torn from a towering oak.

Roman was gone.

Tucking the watch in his pocket, Anatole straightened, gazing down at his cousin. He never would have expected to feel anything at Roman's death, except a savage sense of satisfaction. This odd emotion of something akin to regret surprised him, but he had no time to explore it further.

Without Roman's tormented spirit to cloud his mind, Anatole's perceptions quickened once more to the whispers of danger. His own. Madeline's.

Anatole stalked toward his horse. The stallion, too well trained to bolt, was on the verge of doing so. Ears flattened, it had backed away from the scent of blood, the smell of death on Roman.

The wind had picked up, shifting the mist, beginning to clear patches of it. Anatole tensed, probing. Madeline was out there and at the mercy of a Mortmain. He could feel traces of his wife's gentle spirit and the chilling presence of the other, closing in.

A surge of pure panic shot through him, and he fought to quell it. Fear for Madeline could only blind him, and he needed the clarity of his mind's eye more than he ever had before.

He trained it outward, pressing his fingers to his brow. Which way had she gone? Toward the ruins? No, away from them, toward the headlands rising upward, ringing Lost Land's bleak and dangerous cove.

Anatole grabbed for his horse's reins only to reject the notion. That slope of land was far too treacherous, too unfamiliar, the fog still too heavy for him to go charging in on horseback like a reckless fool, alerting the enemy to his arrival.

Tethering the stallion, he set out on foot, resisting the urge to run. He strode up the hill, every muscle tensed, every fiber of his being alert to the possibility of sudden attack. He could feel her more strongly now, the strange woman who had disguised herself, hidden her very soul in the trappings of an insipid Frenchman no one would perceive as a threat. She'd even managed to fool Marius.

And now she awaited Anatole, hating him, wanting him dead for no other reason than he was a St. Leger and she was a Mortmain, woven into his destiny perhaps from the day he was born.

A destiny he could not avoid. He only prayed to do so long enough to find Madeline, see her safely away from this cursed place.

He felt as vulnerable as a man pacing out those last steps across a dueling field as he strode up that hill. He could sense his enemy, nearer now, obscured by the veil of mist. Just like in the vision.

Her hatred seemed to crush down on him like a giant fist. But beneath that suffocating darkness, he could also feel Madeline, drawing him to her like a beacon of light.

When he heard her frightened cry, he forgot all else. Racing forward, he roared out her name.

"Madeline!"

Damn it. Why didn't she answer him? She was very close. He could sense that as though he cradled her racing heart in his hands. He bellowed her name again, clutching his forehead, honing in. There. She was over there. But as the mist parted before him, he saw nothing but the drop-off to the sea.

His own heart thundering, he stumbled forward, dropping to his knees to peer over the side. His gut clenched. Madeline dangled just out of his reach, scrambling so frantically to scale upward, she was in imminent danger of losing her precarious footing.

She froze when she saw him, no relief in her agonized features, only sheer horror.

"No!" she screamed. "Get away from here. Run!"

He scarce registered her words. Leaning down, blotting out all else, he focused his power, tightening it around her hands like a thick rope. Pain flashed behind his eyes as he hauled her upward until she was within his grasp.

Closing his hands over her upper arms, he dragged her to the edge. She sprawled forward, legs still dangling. One more tug and—

"Anatole," Madeline cried, lifting her head. "Watch out!"

Like a fluttering of dark wings, he felt the Mortmain woman close in for the attack, but had no time to spin around. She brought her pistol crashing down on his head. He felt Madeline slip from his grasp. Pain exploded inside his skull, and he fell back, stunned.

Through a haze, he saw the creature hover over him, her witchlike hair tangling in the wind, her grotesquely painted features contorted into a grimace. Something flashed in her hands.

Anatole fought to concentrate his power, defend himself. But it was of no use. His head throbbed. His vision blurred. Evelyn Mortmain raised her knife.

Madeline clawed wildly at tufts of grass, her nails digging into the dark earth. She struggled to pull herself the rest of the way over the ledge. To fling herself at Evelyn. To stop her.

But she was too late. The knife arced downward. Like in a bad dream. Like in a crystal-wrought vision seen through a wall of mist. But Anatole's agonized cry was all too real as Evelyn drove the knife deep into his chest.

"No!" Madeline shrieked, fear replaced by a rush of fury like nothing she'd ever known. She hurled herself forward, catching Evelyn's wrist before the woman could strike Anatole again.

They locked in a deadly struggle for the knife, a tangle of fire-colored hair and fierce emotion, swaying dangerously close to the edge of the cliff. Evelyn's teeth were bared and her eyes glowed with crazed intensity, but Madeline was possessed of an instinct equally as feral, the need to protect her mate.

Evelyn bore down, forcing the blade toward Madeline's neck. Madeline's arms ached, shuddered with the effort of holding the weapon at bay. The knifepoint inched closer to her throat.

With a strength born of desperation, she twisted Evelyn's arm to one side. Dropping her shoulder, she drove into the woman's chest, shoving hard.

The force of it sent them both off balance. Evelyn teetered back to the edge, fury giving way to panic as the ground crumbled beneath her. She made a wild grab for Madeline as she fell. Madeline's heart lurched as she felt herself being pulled over the cliff.

The world flashed before her, dipping in a blur of rock, sea, and sky, Evelyn's savage, distorted features. Then strong arms locked about Madeline's waist, holding her fast.

Her hand slipped from Evelyn's frantic grasp. Evelyn hurtled down the embankment, her guttural cry lost in the roaring of the sea. She struck hard against the rocks, the cold gray waves crashing over her.

Madeline felt herself being pulled back to safety. Her legs shook as she settled once more on solid ground. Dazed, she peered downward through the haze, but there was no sign of Evelyn. Only the unyielding rocks, the relentless sea.

Shuddering, Madeline turned away, instinctively seeking comfort from the arms that had saved her. Anatole . . . Somehow she expected to find him standing behind her, indomitable as ever, miraculously restored.

But he wasn't there. The sensation of being wrapped warm, safe in his arms faded, and she found him collapsed at her feet, exactly where Evelyn had first struck him down.

He'd managed to drag himself up onto his elbow, one hand pressed to his brow, and Madeline realized what he'd done. Used the last of his strength, what remained of his power to save her.

A muffled sob escaped her as Anatole's hand fell away from his face, and he sank back down. Dropping to her knees, Madeline bent over him. She pressed her hands to his chest in a desperate effort to stop the flow of blood from his wound, but it was as if she could feel his life slipping through her fingers.

Tears coursed down her cheeks, and she groped within herself, seeking out the calm, practical Madeline who had always been equal to dealing with any emergency. But she could not seem to find her.

She wept, trembling with helpless anger, shocked to hear herself swearing as though she'd discovered a second language. Cursing Evelyn Mortmain, herself, Anatole.

"Damn you! Why? Why did you have to come here?"

She hardly expected him to answer. She feared he'd already lapsed into unconsciousness. But his lashes fluttered, and he peered through their thickness.

"Had to. Fitzleger told me . . . and I saw the vision myself."

"Then, you should have stayed away!"

"Needed to make sure you were safe. See you . . . one last time."

His words sent a sob racking through her, and she was furious with herself. Wailing like an idiot when she needed to be doing something sensible, something to save him.

Drawing in a deep breath, she wiped her bloodstained fingers on her cloak. Hiking up the hem of her gown, she began tearing ruthlessly at her petticoats, attempting to form a makeshift bandage until help arrived.

It came far sooner than she dared hope. From a great distance she could hear something stirring down the hill, the sound of an approaching horse, someone anxiously calling out to her through the mist.

Marius.

A strangled cry escaped her. Somehow she managed to clear her throat, answer him. "Marius! We're over here!"

She turned joyfully to Anatole, "Oh, hold on, my dearest lord. It will be all right. Marius is coming."

But Anatole shook his head. "No hope of defeating the vision, my love."

His eyes clouded, and she knew that she was losing him. The look of resignation on his face frightened Madeline more than his growing pallor.

Her eyes blazed with fierce tears. "We will defeat it, do you hear me, Anatole? You are not going to die because of—of some stupid prophecy from a piece of glass. I won't let you. I love you too much."

"Forever and ever?" he whispered.

"Yes," she choked.

"That will be just about . . . long enough."

Despite his pain, Anatole St. Leger smiled, his eyes drifting closed as he surrendered himself to the welcoming darkness.

Epilogue

The funeral took place a week later, only Madeline and Fitzleger in attendance. Sunlight spilled through the trees, bringing a sense of warmth and peace to the shaded grave site. More than Evelyn Mortmain had known in her entire troubled life, Madeline thought.

As Madeline watched Evelyn being laid to rest amidst her ancestors, she reflected that perhaps she should not even be here attending services for someone who had attempted to murder her husband. She should feel nothing but hatred. If Evelyn had succeeded . . .

But she had not. And Madeline could mourn, not for the bitter woman who had thrown her life away in a quest for revenge, but for the girl Evelyn had once been, alone, frightened, orphaned by her own father's mad obsession for destroying the St. Legers.

Evelyn had been found washed ashore but yesterday morning, her face battered beyond recognition, identifiable only by her shock of flame-colored hair. Little trace of her existence remained, her possessions kept at the cottage found to be meager. Some powdered wigs, the elegant trappings of her disguise, a small cache of coin. Nothing of real value except for the miniature of a dark curly-haired child. A little boy somewhere in France waiting for a mother who would never return.

Madeline cradled the miniature in her hand as she and Fitzleger turned from the grave site, making their way slowly back through the churchyard. As the vicar closed up his prayer book, Madeline was able to ask him the question that had been on the tip of her tongue all morning.

"Were you able to talk to Bess Kennack?"

"Aye, I did." Fitzleger's troubled expression warned Madeline the interview had not gone well.

"Bess was not able to tell me much more about the Mortmain woman than we already know. The girl was very stubborn about answering my questions, but she finally confessed to the part she played in these events. In the end I think Bess had grown a little frightened herself of Evelyn Mortmain, what she had helped to set in motion.

"I have arranged for Bess to leave this place, find a fresh start by taking service with a family in the north. She seems glad to go."

"I am relieved to hear it," Madeline said, but she was also disappointed Bess had been unable to provide any further information. The agent of inquiry's report, discovered among Roman's things, had been very sketchy, providing the barest details of Evelyn's life in Paris. Nothing had been said of a child.

Madeline displayed the miniature to Fitzleger. "The night of the supper party, Evelyn showed me this and told me the boy's name was Raphael and he was away at school."

Fitzleger squinted at the portrait. "A handsome little lad. But, my dear, are you sure he even exists? Perhaps this tale of a son was only one more part of the woman's elaborate disguise."

"No, Mr. Fitzleger," Madeline said, remembering too well the spark of pride, the genuine emotion in Evelyn's eyes when she had spoken of her son. "I am sure the child is real, and I am dreadfully afraid he has been left all alone. He must be found!"

"It will be difficult. And you must consider, if you do find him, he has likely already been poisoned with hatred for the St. Legers. The feud between Anatole's family and the Mortmains is of long standing."

"Then, it must end. If this hatred is, as you say, a poison, then perhaps love and kindness can be its cure. Anatole and I are determined to try."

"Then, I wish both of you Godspeed, and I will do my best to help."

"Thank you, Mr. Fitzleger," Madeline murmured gratefully, tucking the portrait away. "I was certain you would."

He linked his arm companionably through hers, giving her hand a gentle pat as he walked her to the gate.

"And how is my young master faring today?" he asked.

"Oh, Anatole is doing very well. Marius is astonished at the speed of his recovery."

"And relieved." Fitzleger chuckled. "I daresay my lord has not been the most docile of patients."

"You are quite wrong, Mr. Fitzleger. Anatole acquiesced to every one of Marius's orders for his convalescence."

Fitzleger's bushy white brows shot up in wonderment. Madeline did not blame him. There had been a stillness about Anatole these past days that both surprised and worried her a little.

Of course, she had always done most of the chattering, but Anatole was unusually quiet. When she hovered over him, fussing, as he once would have growled, he said very little, merely following her every movement with his eyes. But the man had nearly died, she reminded herself. Small wonder he should be somewhat subdued. She was certain Anatole would be more himself when he had fully recovered and now that all of their guests were gone.

Roman's death had brought the entire St. Leger family descending upon them. Uncles, wives, cousins. Given Anatole's condition, it had been left to Madeline to move among them offering explanations and consolation.

Roman's death had not produced a profound sorrow among the St. Legers, but a great deal of regret. He had, in the end, proved himself one of their own. Madeline had helped arrange for his wake, assisted Hadrian in settling Roman's estate, wrote letters canceling the orders of materials for the house at Lost Land that would now never be rebuilt.

By the end of each day, Madeline had frequently felt exhausted. But somehow during that time, she reflected with a soft smile, she had finally become a St. Leger herself. And in more than name only.

Still, she had been relieved to see the last of her new family depart, even Marius returning to his own home early that morning. Madeline looked forward to being alone with her husband.

She was anxious to return to Anatole as Mr. Fitzleger handed her into the waiting carriage. But she paused long enough to squeeze the old man's hand and reassure him.

"You need not worry about Anatole anymore. I promise to take very good care of him."

"I am sure that you will." Fitzleger beamed. "You are exactly the right lady for that most difficult task."

Madeline pulled a wry face. "Thank you, although I am sure I gave you much cause to doubt that was so."

"My dear Madeline, it was never really you I doubted so much as myself. I feared I had finally lost my talent for choosing St. Leger wives."

"You did not. You remain as ever, our best and wisest of Bride Finders." Leaning down, she brushed a kiss against the old man's withered cheek.

Fitzleger blushed to the white wings of his hair. He stepped back as the groom clucked to the horse and set the gig into motion. The vicar remained at the gate, waving until Madeline was out of sight.

But the memory of her smiling face lingered pleasantly in Fitzleger's mind long after she had gone. He had laid to rest two troubled souls within the past week, Roman St. Leger and the unfortunate Mortmain woman. He should be feeling that somberness he always experienced upon attending any of his parishioner's deaths.

And yet his soul was flooded with light, a serenity such as he had not known since he had made the match between Madeline and Anatole St. Leger.

That brooding darkness, that unsettled sensation that had troubled the entire village was gone, blown away with the mist that day Madeline had defied destiny itself to save her husband's life.

Matters had resolved themselves far more happily than he had ever expected, and Fitzleger had gone down on his knees and humbly thanked God. After all his fears and doubts, Madeline had indeed proved to be the one fated to bring good to Anatole St. Leger, ease the longings of his lonely heart. Fitzleger's bride-finding instincts had not failed him after all.

But, Lord, another match as difficult as this one would prove the death of him, Fitzleger thought wryly. The best and wisest of Bride Finders was more than ready to surrender the reins of his office as soon as a likely candidate presented himself.

That is, if one ever did.

Heaving a deep sigh, Fitzleger made his way up the stone pathway leading to the vicarage. Before he reached the stoop, the front door flung open and his little granddaughter marched out.

Her brassy blonde curls bobbing indignantly, Elfreda wagged one small finger at him. "You are late for tea, Grandpapa."

"Am I indeed? A thousand pardons, milady." Fitzleger proffered the little girl a solemn bow, fighting hard to suppress his smile.

The child was a comical sight in her feathered bonnet. An India muslin shawl that was far too large for such a small girl draped around her slender shoulders and trailed the ground. But Miss Effie did adore her finery.

She had been overindulged in this regard by her doting parents. Quite spoiled by them, in fact, and Fitzleger feared that he was no better.

He held out his arms to the child and was agreeably surprised when she ran into them. Effie was usually inclined to complain that hugs wrinkled her frocks and crushed her bonnets.

But as Fitzleger lifted her up, she wrapped her small arms tightly about his neck and planted a smacking kiss on his cheek.

"Bless me! What's all this?" Fitzleger cried in delight.

The child drew back to peer solemnly at him with her great brown eyes. "I thought you needed a kiss, Grandpapa. You were so very sad."

"Well, I did indeed. But I am not sad, child."

"You made a sad sound when you were coming up the walk. I heard you from the window." Effie's small shoulders heaved as she gave an imitation of Fitzleger's own deep sigh.

"Ah, that was a sound of relief," he said, lowering the little girl back to her feet. "Something that I had been concerned about has turned out much better than I hoped."

"And what is that?" Effie demanded.

Fitzleger started to put her off with one of those vague explanations usually offered to children regarding adult matters, but something in the girl's earnest gaze stopped him. Effie seldom evinced interest in anything beyond the pert tip of her own small nose.

So Fitzleger tucked her small hand in his and explained, "I was worried about some young friends of mine. You remember, Madeline, the beautiful lady who stayed with us here at the vicarage for a short while."

"She's the lady who belongs to the dark man who lives in the castle." Effie sniffed, adding with disapproval, "The one who forgets to comb his hair."

"That is correct." Fitzleger bit back a smile. "I suppose Mrs. Beamus told you that Madeline is Lord Anatole's lady."

"No one told me," Effie replied haughtily. "I already knew when I saw the lady riding with the dark lord on his great horse. Looking at them made me feel all spingly."

"Spingly?" Fitzleger echoed in confusion.

"Yes, you know, Grandpapa. *Spingly.* When you get that funny feeling right here." Effie thumped her fist over the region of her heart.

Before Fitzleger could question the child further, Effie tugged her hand free and wandered off. Like the distractible butterfly she was, she pursued the kitten she had recently acquired. The gray tabby eluded her grasp and dodged beneath the rosebushes.

Fitzleger stared after his granddaughter, stunned. Dear Lord. Could it truly be possible? That the next Bride Finder had been before his eyes all along, and he had never guessed it?

The office had always been filled by a male descendant of the Fitzleger line. And yet . . . there was no reason that it had to be, none that Fitzleger had ever heard of.

Effie had just described the same sensations that he himself experienced when he knew that a match was right. Only he had never had a word for it before.

Spingly. It fit perfectly.

Trembling with excitement, Fitzleger bent down beside Effie, where she peered into the rosebushes, imperiously demanding, "Miss Gray Paws, come out of there at once. It is time for tea."

Fitzleger gathered both the child's hands into his own. "Oh, my dear little Effie," he murmured.

She frowned at him, clearly annoyed at having her pursuit of the kitten interrupted. "Why, whatever is the matter, Grandpapa? Why do you look at me so?"

His heart flooded with joy at his discovery, Fitzleger was almost too overcome to speak.

"My dear child," he said thickly. "I have just realized you have a remarkable destiny before you. You are going to be the next Bride Finder."

"What's that?"

"You are the one who will find brides and husbands for all of the St. Leger family. Like Grandpapa does now."

Effie crinkled her nose, clearly unimpressed. Her bonnet feathers waved as she shook her head. "No, I won't. I shall be far too busy finding a husband for *me*."

Fitzleger was momentarily daunted by Effie's response to his great tidings. But he smiled fondly, remembering the girl was full young. There was plenty of time to teach her the importance of the special gift she had inherited.

Helping retrieve Miss Gray Paws from the bushes, he handed the kitten to Effie and allowed the child to lead him inside for tea.

When Madeline returned to Castle Leger, Anatole was nowhere to be found in the house. But she was able to guess where he had gone.

Slipping through the dining room, she plunged out into the enchanted tangle that was Deidre's garden. She followed the worn path that led through the fragrant burst of color and soft petals, picking her way carefully as the trail began to slope downward, leading to the cliffs at the back of the house.

When she'd cleared the last of the rhododendron trees, she spotted Anatole in the distance. He stood where the land ended so dramatically, his face angled toward a flock of gulls wheeling their way back to the sea. His black hair and broad shoulders etched against the brilliant blue sky, he made a stark figure, as strong and solitary as his rugged sweep of land.

Madeline staggered to an abrupt halt, hesitating. This was Anatole's place, where he had often vanished before. To escape from the house, from bitter memories, even from her. She suddenly felt like an intruder. Perhaps it would be better if she returned to the house and—

But it was already too late for that. Anatole had stiffened, sensing her, though he took great pains not to make it obvious. He came about slowly, beckoning her toward him. Lifting up her skirts, she made her way down the hill.

As she approached, Anatole smiled, holding out his hand to her. She slipped her fingers into the strength of his. She knew she had to stop treating the man like an invalid, but she could not refrain from an anxious scan of his features.

He was still a trifle pale, his face thinner than it had been, deep lines etched by his eyes, but she was not certain they stemmed from any physical pain.

"My lord," she said. "Are—are you sure you should be pushing your recovery this way, walking about so soon?"

"I cannot stay in bed forever, Madeline. At least not alone."

She blushed. They had been through so much together during their short marriage. It almost felt like a lifetime. And yet the man could still fluster her with but a word, a look.

She glanced away from him, drinking in the vista that spilled out before her, the sea so far below lapping against the shore, the sun casting diamonds of light upon the restless waves.

"So this is your special place," she murmured. "It's beautiful here."

"I've always thought so. So did my mother. Perhaps that is why she chose to come here the night . . . This is where she died."

"Oh." The beauty dimmed somewhat for Madeline. She became more conscious of the staggering height of the cliff, the jagged rocks below. It was easy to forget that Castle Leger could be a cruel and unforgiving place to those who did not belong here.

She understood now why Anatole had never wanted her to come down here. Even now his hand tightened on hers, drawing her back a pace from the cliff's edge. She studied his face for any sign of the pain he always experienced when mentioning his mother, but his eyes were more pensive than sad.

"I've always come here to be alone, to think," he said. "And I've been doing a great deal of thinking while I've been laid up."

"About what?" she asked softly.

"Many things. About my mother, my father. Even Roman. Myself . . . wondering why I am still alive."

"Oh, please don't, Anatole," Madeline cried, shivering. That was something she did not even want to consider, why the terrible vision had not come true. It was absurd, she knew. But she felt as though questioning the miracle might undo it, somehow result in the dread prophecy yet reaching out to snatch Anatole away from her.

Appearing aware of her distress, Anatole abandoned the subject. Wrapping his arm about her waist, he drew her close to his side and spoke of Roman's death instead.

"It was a strange experience, after so many years of hating the man, to feel a connection to him. Stranger still to feel it with that Mortmain woman."

"With Evelyn?" Madeline asked, astonished.

"Yes, I know this is going to sound odd, but . . ." Anatole frowned, as though groping for the words to explain. "I realized that in many respects Roman, Evelyn Mortmain, and I were not so different. We'd all been distorted, embittered, even held prisoner in some way by the mistakes of the past."

"But the mistakes were not yours."

"Perhaps not all of them. But I cannot help wondering. If I had tried to be more careful with my mother. If I had not been so frightening . . ." He paused, brushing back one of Madeline's stray curls. "I have never even asked your pardon for the way I terrified you that night in the old keep."

"Oh, Anatole! I'm the one who should be asking your forgiveness. I should never have run away from you."

"There is nothing to forgive. I nearly brought an entire castle down on your head. Hell, I terrified my mother, and all I ever did to her was attempt to send her flowers."

He tried to speak lightly, disguising his feelings behind a rueful smile. But as he guided Madeline back up the path, she saw it in his eyes, the flickering of the old pain, the old fears.

He towered above her, this powerful husband of hers with his formidable stature and fierce stare that could set any enemy atrembling. But she saw him at his most vulnerable and was filled with a rush of emotion. A fierce sense of protectiveness she knew she would feel toward Anatole St. Leger to the end of her days.

She realized now what he had been doing these past days, the reason for the quiet, the stillness. He was trying to suppress his powers around her, trying to be so careful. She had told the man she loved him, would do so forever, and yet he was still afraid of losing her.

"Send the flowers to me," she said softly.

"What?" He cast her a confused glance.

"Send the flowers to me," she repeated more firmly.

She felt him stiffen when he realized what she wanted him to do. He gave a shaky laugh. "Madeline, if you want flowers, I can march up the hill and gather you as much as you want without resorting to any devil's gift."

"It was that devil's gift that saved my life," she reminded him. "There are some particularly fine blossoms at the very top of that tree. Please, Anatole, send them down to me."

Anatole stared at her, feeling his gut clench. He'd finally come to terms with the fact that Madeline had to know what he was. But to continue flaunting it before her . . .

She thought his life being spared was too fragile a gift to be questioned. But it was her love he feared risking. He longed with all his cowardly soul to refuse, to put her off.

But she was waiting, looking at him with such a wistful expression.

"Please," she repeated, offering him a nod of encouragement.

He was not proof against the plea in those warm, spring green eyes.

"A-all right," he said hoarsely. He turned toward the pink flowers blossoming on the rhododendron trees a few yards up the path. His hand shook as he raised his fingers to his brow.

At the first sign, the first hint of fear in her, he was prepared to shut himself down as though an ax had fallen. Staring hard at one of the branches until it quivered, he snapped a blossom from its delicate stem.

Pain stabbed behind his eyes. The power itself seemed to tremble with his fear and reluctance. He floated the flower, somewhat unsteadily toward Madeline.

She stretched out one hand and caught it. He held his breath as he looked at her face. Her lips parted, her eyes round, not with fear, but pure awe.

Glancing back to the tree, he moistened his dry lips and focused and tugged free another rhododendron, his mental grasp stronger this time. Stronger still with the next. He wafted the flowers toward Madeline, though they were born aloft by a gentle breeze.

A trill of delighted laughter escaped her as she caught the next one and the next. Anatole found himself forgetting even the pain that throbbed behind his brow as he filled her hands with flowers.

Burying her nose in the fragrant blossoms, she peered at him over the bouquet of lush pink flowers, her voice breathless with fascination. "How—how does it work? How are you able to do such an amazing thing?"

Amazing? Anatole reflected wryly that he had never quite seen his power in that light before.

"I don't know," he said gruffly, feeling strangely embarrassed. "I just focus. There is this burst of pain in my head as I think of what I want to happen. And then it does."

"Pain?" Madeline's smile dimmed. "It hurts you?"

"A bit." He grimaced a little, rubbing his brow.

Madeline reached out. Brushing his fingers aside, she caressed his forehead herself with her warm soft fingers, her eyes alight with concern.

"Oh," she said. "Then, you must not do it anymore."

The statement was so simple, so practical, so completely Madeline that he wanted to laugh. But his throat was strangely constricted, and he found he could not even speak.

His arms closed around her instead, crushing her hard against him. Blossoms tumbled unheeded to the ground as she returned his embrace, wrapping her arms around his neck.

For a long time he just held her. It was as though in these last few moments, with those few simple words, she had undone years of pain, fear, and self-loathing. He could almost feel the fetters of the past falling away from him, setting him . . . free.

Straining her close, he kissed her feverishly, her soft yielding mouth, her delicate brow, her silky soft hair. He paused only long enough to brush the tears from her cheek, astonished to realize that some of them were his.

"Madeline," he said huskily. "I know you don't want me to speak of this, but I have to. The vision in the sword . . . the only reason it was defeated, the reason I did not die is because of you."

Tears glittering in her eyes, she started to shake her head, but he caught her face gently between his hands, preventing her denial.

"I have never had the power to change the future, but you do, my dearest heart. You have already altered my destiny forever. The real miracle is not that I am still alive, but that you are still here, loving me."

"As I always will be," she whispered.

He gazed into the mists of her eyes, his own heart swelling with such love for his small, but indomitable wife, he ached. But he managed to smile.

"Forever is a long time to spend with an ogre in his haunted castle by the sea."

Her soft mouth wobbled in a smile. "I believe I will manage, my lord."

But when he moved to kiss her again, she ducked her head. "Er, Anatole . . . about the haunted castle. I—I have something to confess to you." She toyed nervously with one of the buttons on his shirt. "Something I did while you were laid up in bed this past week."

She looked so adorably guilt-stricken, his smile widened with tenderness.

"And what have you been up to, milady?" he demanded with mock fierceness.

"I—I went to the old castle keep to visit Prospero."

"You what!" Anatole's smile fled, his blood freezing at the mere thought. His Madeline, braving that God-cursed sorcerer all alone. "Whatever possessed you to do such a thing? Woman, this curiosity of yours will prove the death of me."

"It wasn't mere curiosity," she protested. "I had something important to discuss with him."

"Something to discuss? What in heaven's name could you have to say to that devil?"

Madeline squirmed, but she continued resolutely, "I—I told him that I respected his role as founder of this family. But that I was not going to have him haunting or teasing you anymore. And then I—" Madeline tensed herself as though bracing for Anatole's anger. "I—I asked him to go away and leave us in peace."

"Damnation! Did he let loose a lightning bolt or did he simply laugh in your face?"

"No, he was very charming. He agreed."

Anatole eased her away from him, peering into her down-turned face, certain he could not have heard her right. "W-what?"

"He promised that he would stay away as long as I kept you out of trouble and Castle Leger continues to prosper."

Anatole gaped at her, absolutely thunderstruck. He'd wanted free of Prospero's interference and plaguey tricks for as long as he could remember. He'd even once tried to persuade his cousin Zane, the exorcist, to get rid of the ghost. But Zane had refused to practice his arts on a member of the family.

In truth, Anatole had thought Zane afraid to challenge Prospero's power. Well, hellfire . . . when it came down to it, all the St. Legers were.

That Madeline should be the one to do so, his delicate slip of a wife, conquering her fear to confront the ghost . . . It positively staggered Anatole. The more so as he realized she'd done it for him.

Crooking his fingers beneath her chin, he forced her to look up. She fretted her lip anxiously. "Are—are you angry with me?"

"Angry?" he breathed. He caressed her face, his touch fraught with wonder. "My brave . . . beautiful Madeline. There surely has never been another St. Leger bride to equal you, my lady. Whatever is a wretch like me to do with such a remarkable woman?"

A mischievous dimple quivered in her cheek, but her eyes were soft and shining as she replied, "Simply love me."

That night the bedchamber glowed with an array of candles, for Anatole St. Leger was no longer a man with anything to hide.

He felt like a battered knight who battled his way through a hard and perilous quest to reach this moment when he approached his lady to offer up his sword one last time.

"Madeline," he said, his voice low but strong. "I gave this sword to you once before in a ceremony that had no meaning. Because I did not understand then what it meant to surrender my heart to a woman, as I now do."

He knelt before her, her fire gold hair shining about her shoulders, her slender form draped in the soft white nightgown, almost luminescent in the candle's glow.

He raised up the sword. "Will it please you, lady, to accept it now? My heart, my soul, yours, forever?"

"Aye," Madeline whispered, thinking there was so much she had not understood herself on that long-ago day. Her fingers closed reverently over the golden hilt of the weapon, this time fully aware of the power, the great trust that had been placed in her hands.

She said solemnly, "I promise to keep both your heart and the sword safe in my keeping."

An anxious look flickered briefly across Anatole's face. "You—you won't ever attempt to use it again?"

"No, my lord. All I ever want to know of the future, I see shining in your eyes. I'll tuck the sword away until hopefully one day we will have a son of our own."

Bending down, she sealed her pledge by brushing her mouth across Anatole's in a tender kiss. He rose to his feet, and she put the sword aside to move into his arms. But he held her at bay for a moment.

He was all too aware of one secret he had yet to tell. He had thought it more fitting that she find out herself in the natural way of these things. But this woman had become too much a part of him. He could no longer hold anything back.

"Madeline," he said slowly. "You—you are already carrying my sons."

"Sons?" she faltered. "You—you mean—"

"Aye, twin boys."

Her eyes flew to his, stunned, her hand moving almost reflexively to the region of her womb.

"I believe they were conceived that day beneath the standing stone."

"But—but how could you possibly— Never mind." She gave a shaky laugh. "What a foolish question."

She caressed her midriff with both hands, surprise giving way to a look of intense joy suffusing her features. Anatole shared that joy in equal measure, but he felt obliged to warn her.

"Madeline, you have to understand. The life growing inside you has not yet even seen a month's duration. I could not feel our sons' presence so strongly if they were not true St. Legers in every sense of the word. What will you do if they prove to have powers such as mine?"

She smiled, her mind clearly already spinning soft dreams of what was to be. Her answer came without hesitation.

"Love them as I do you. Help them learn to read, be great scholars. Guide them the way Mr. Fitzleger did you. Teach them that while one may float a ball in the garden, it is not proper to levitate forks at the supper table."

Her words banished whatever apprehension may have lingered in Anatole's heart. He surprised himself by letting loose a great shout of laughter. It had never been his nature before for joy to flow so freely into mirth.

But then, he had never known what it was to be this happy.

The laughter stilled quickly into emotion more deep, far more intense. Madeline felt it, too, her eyes locking steadily with his as he lifted her into his arms and carried her to the bed.

There he laid her down to tenderly undress her. To kiss, to caress, to love her. To take her again and again to that height of passion where bodies united, hearts touched, and souls became one.

And somewhere in the night, another legend was born.